STEPHANIE ROWE

LEOPARD'S *Kiss*

For further information, please contact:
Stephanie@stephanierowe.com

Dedication

For Malinda Davis-Diehl, for being a great friend, and for inspiring women everywhere to love themselves unconditionally. The world needs more people like you, Malinda!

Acknowledgements

Special thanks to my beta readers and the Rockstars. You guys are the best! There are so many to thank by name, more than I could count, but here are those who I want to called out specially for all they did to help this book come to life: Malinda Davis Diehl, Leslie Barnes, Kayla Bartley, Alencia Bates Salters, Alyssa Bird, Donna Bossert, Jean Bowden, Shell Bryce, Kelley Daley Curry, Ashley Cuesta, Denise Fluhr, Valerie Glass, Heidi Hoffman, Jeanne Stone, Dottie Jones, Janet Juengling-Snell, Deb Julienne, Bridget Koan, Felicia Low, Phyllis Marshall, Suzanne Mayer, Jodi Moore, Ashlee Murphy, Elizabeth Neal, Judi Pflughoeft, Carol Pretorius, Kasey Richardson, Caryn Santee, Amber Ellison Shriver, Summer Steelman, Regina Thomas, and Linda Watson. Special thanks to my family, who I love with every fiber of my heart and soul. And to AER, who is my world. Love you so much, baby girl!

LEOPARD'S Kiss

Chapter One

THE NIGHT SMELLED of a damp spring rain.

It would soon smell of nothing but death.

Like all of his nights.

Slade Cross moved silently down the darkened sidewalk. Each streetlight went dark as he strode beneath it, falling into veiled shadows that cast the upscale Boston residential neighborhood into an ominous haven of doom. He didn't need to turn his head to know that the residents were instinctively closing their windows as he passed by their brownstone townhouses. They didn't understand their sudden impulse to protect themselves from what lurked outside their windows, a threat so subtle they couldn't even grasp it consciously. Slade, however, was aware of every nuance of life near him. He could feel their withdrawal, and he could hear the sudden hiss of fear in their breath. He could taste their quickened pulse, and the sudden shift of oxygen into their arms and legs, subconsciously preparing to fight to the death.

But tonight they would be spared.

Tonight, they were not the target.

After Slade passed by, he could hear the windows being

opened again, the occupants having no understanding of their body's reaction to a threat that they were too civilized to comprehend. In another block and a half, he'd be at his destination. His quarry was there. He knew she was. He could feel her presence, which was growing stronger by the moment. He'd locked onto her essence seven thousand miles away, through the scrap of fabric given to him. It had been easy to track her once he'd locked onto her.

Always easy.

They never had a chance to escape him.

Never.

She would be dead within minutes of his arrival, and another chunk of change would flood into his bank account. Money for death. Death for money. He was the best, and he made sure to keep it that way.

A low growl caught his attention, and he glanced to his right. Back in the shadows of the alley was a black dog. It was tall and rangy, with pointed ears and a shaggy coat that suggested it was part wolf, a hybrid that skirted the edge of civilization, unseen by oblivious humans. It raised its lips, baring them in a snarl. Slade stopped to face the dog. For a moment, the two hunters studied each other.

He went down on one knee and held out his hand.

The dog didn't move, its lips curled back to reveal sharp, pointed teeth.

Slade didn't move either.

He simply waited.

After a moment, the dog's ears flattened against his head, and he lowered his head and his tail, abandoning his aggressive posture. He darted across the filthy garbage, stepping over the trash littered across the alley, heading right for Slade's extended hand.

The moment he reached Slade, he shoved his head against Slade's palm. His fur was coarse and slick, like porcupine quills that had been worn down by overuse. Slade rubbed his hand over the dog's head, scratching it behind the ears. The hybrid moved forward, and pressed his head into Slade's stomach, somehow sensing that Slade was not an ordinary human that he had to avoid.

"I know," Slade said softly. The animal was warm beneath Slade's hand, a living creature that offered no judgment and asked for nothing.

It was but a sliver of a moment in time, a whisper that would be gone in the next breath. Slade drank it in, his fingers sinking into the thick fur, offering comfort and taking solace in the connection. The dog stayed utterly still, as if it, too, wanted to live in this one moment, before reclaiming its solitary existence.

He couldn't take the dog with him, but he knew the dog wouldn't go with him even if invited. The animal's solitary, shadowed existence was woven into the fabric of his soul, and Slade sensed his need for freedom. "We're the same," he said softly. "You and I. Except that you kill for food, and I kill for money. You win the battle of ethics tonight, my friend."

Not just tonight. Every night.

Something moved in the shadows, and the dog stiffened, jerking his head up to look into the darkness. His body tensed for flight, and Slade shoved his hand into the pocket of his leather trench coat. He found what he was looking for, and pulled out two large dog biscuits. "It's not much, but it's all I've got left. Left a bunch with a mama a few blocks back."

The dog snatched the biscuits out of his hand and took off down the street, his paws moving with silent efficiency on the cobblestones. Slade continued to crouch, pausing to admire the animal. The hybrid moved with the confident elegance of a predator navigating familiar territory, using shadows to escape notice. Slade smiled slightly. "We're the same," he repeated softly. So much the same.

Running swiftly, the dog disappeared almost instantly into the shadowy night, no doubt taking his food to a safe place before stopping to eat it. Slade rose to his feet. Was there such a thing as a truly safe place? Or simply one where you *thought* you could let your guard down? Those were the places he invaded, the safe rooms, an illusionary oasis in hell where his quarry forgot to pay attention for one fateful moment.

He flipped his collar up against his neck and turned to resume his hunt when he felt a wave of terror...the kind of terror that made a soul scream with anguish. Chills raced down his spine and he spun back toward the alley, searching the darkness.

There was no whisper of movement. No brush of breathing. Just silence. Too much silence. He glanced over his shoulder at the street. He had to keep going. The timing on this job had to be precise. He began to turn away, and then caught another wave of terror. Guilt. Regret.

Swearing, he spun back toward the alley, striding quickly toward the back of it. He had no time for this. But the guilt, regret, and fear could not be ignored. Very few living souls deserved to feel that kind of pain.

He'd walked another ten feet when he saw them, pressed into a darkened, dank alcove deep in the alley.

It was a woman in a short black skirt, a skimpy leather top that didn't hide her nipples, and seven-inch heels. Her bleached hair was tangled around her shoulders, and her painted face was designed to lure men into opening their wallets in exchange for a few moments of feeling like they mattered. A man had her pressed against the wall, his forearm across her throat, his hand on her breast. He blended into the shadows, his existence almost more of a suggestion than an actual presence.

He turned his head slightly, his gaze slanting toward Slade. "I paid for this, so back the hell off."

Slade ignored him and looked at the woman. She was staring past both men, looking at a blank spot on the opposite wall of the alley. Her expression was stoic and resigned, accepting what she'd taken money for. She made it clear she wasn't asking to be rescued.

It wasn't Slade's problem, and neither one of them wanted his interference.

Then he felt her emotions again. Anguish. Guilt. Regret. Fear.

Shit. He couldn't ignore that. *You want help?* He sent the question into her mind.

She jerked her gaze off the wall and looked at him in shock, clearly startled to hear his voice inside her head, but instantly grasping that was what had just happened. Silently, she shook her head.

But it was too late. He'd seen her face. He knew she was young. Probably not even eighteen yet.

Shit. He couldn't be late. His quarry couldn't be allowed to have her meeting. It was scheduled to start in five minutes. His instructions were exact: *wait until the meeting starts, then kill her before information can be exchanged. Make an example of her.* The timing had to be precise, and he couldn't be late.

But neither could he leave her here. "Leave her alone," he said. One warning was all he would give. He didn't have time to negotiate...plus he didn't like negotiation. It bored him. Make a decision, then move on. Don't waste time looking back.

The man turned his head to look at Slade. "Back off, asshole." Red light gleamed in his eyes, and Slade swore under his breath. It wasn't a man. It was a *demon*, one that

Slade couldn't afford to cross. He wasn't capable of killing a demon, but if he left it alive, the creature would hunt him down...and anyone who mattered to him. *Hell.*

His fingers closed into fists. One of his iron rules that had kept him alive for so long was to never acquire an enemy who was stronger than he was. Not many fell into that category, so it had been an easy rule to implement. Full demons met that standard, and he'd made sure to never, ever be noticed by one, let alone acquire one as an enemy.

He couldn't interfere. He *couldn't.* But she was a *child.* Gritting his jaw, he asked the question anyway. "You going to kill her?"

The woman's terror jacked up at his question, and her eyes widened.

The demon's eyes glowed brighter, a blood-red glow of death and pain. "You would be wise to walk away, scum. I want female flesh now, not male. You have a chance..." He drew out the "sss," like a snake preparing to strike.

"Listen, you can have your money back," she said quickly, reaching for her hot pink purse. "I don't think—"

The demon slammed his arm into her neck, cutting off her air. Ignoring her as she clawed at his arm struggling to get free, it sniffed the air. "You smell familiar," it said to Slade. "Do I know you?"

Hell. He couldn't afford to be identified. His face was a mystery, his existence a legend. Anyone who met him soon forgot, but he couldn't wipe a demon's memory. His identity would be compromised if he made a move. He kept his gaze on the demon's face. "Pick another. This is not the place. Not tonight." He pushed with his voice, trying to command obedience from a creature that followed no rules.

"It is the place. It is tonight. This is the one." The demon smiled, its lips stretching into a grotesque grin. "You want to watch? Is that what you want?" It dismissed Slade and turned back to the girl, who was struggling frantically, her efforts useless against the beast. "Watch how it is done," it whispered to Slade. "It's nothing like you've ever seen." It opened its mouth, a gaping cavern of fangs and poison.

Slade struck fast, with lightning speed. His fingers sank into the demon's hide, his skin burning from the acid as he ripped the demon off her. He threw it into the brick wall, shattering the brick as the woman raced down the alley, screaming for help.

The demon didn't move. It lay on the ground, black blood oozing from a cut on its head as it stared at Slade. "No one moves that quickly," it said thoughtfully, its eyes gleaming with interest. "No one."

Slade didn't answer. He just waited, using himself as a shield while he listened to the woman's fading footsteps. *Find a cab,* he ordered her. *Get away.* He had less than three minutes to kill his quarry. He had to leave. *Get a cab now.*

"The Black Swan," the demon said softly, its gaze boring into Slade. "He is real. The legend walks on two feet and smells like a man."

Double hell. He'd just been identified. He latched onto the demon's mind, hurtling past its shield, plunging deep into its psyche. It screamed in pain as he twisted its memories, scraping its consciousness into a tangled mess, smearing all thoughts of the Black Swan into a muddy hell. It wasn't complete. It wouldn't last. But it would give him time.

He heard a taxi door slam. The woman was safe. The demon's thoughts had been lacerated into fragments. It was time to go. Slade spun around and sprinted down the alley, vanishing into the night and leaving no trail.

For now.

How long would it take before he became the prey of this opponent who was more powerful than he? A day? A week? A month? A century? How long until the demon discovered the one thing that made Slade vulnerable? He thought of his brother, and the world seemed to close down on him.

He'd made a mistake.

A massive, horrific mistake that could cost the life of the only person in the world who mattered.

* * *

Shoving the demon out of his mind, Slade focused on his prey as he sprinted down the street. No longer was there time for strolling. He had never failed to complete an assassination, and he wouldn't now. A broken neon light hung across the doorway of the bar he was headed toward, flashing vomit-colored letters that had once said "The Dungeon," but now claimed "h D g on."

He laughed softly at the idea that there were people in the world who wanted to go to a place with that name. People who liked to play with danger and hell were people who had no idea what it was really like.

Slade vaulted to the door, glaring at the bouncer before the heavily muscled human could even react. Wisely, the bald-headed glutton turned his head, pretending he hadn't seen Slade at all. Of course he reacted that way. Everyone did. No one wanted to see him, as if the danger he posed would just go away if they pretended he didn't exist.

Shadows were real, even if you didn't see them.

Slade shoved open the door and stepped into the bar. It was crowded and dark, with the kind of lighting designed for people who didn't want to be seen clearly. He scanned quickly, ignoring the laughter, the low hum of conversation, and the camaraderie filling the boisterous Friday night atmosphere.

He located his target almost immediately. She was in the back right corner, hidden behind several groups of people. He could sense her, but he couldn't see her yet.

He didn't know her name. He never knew names. Names were messy. Names were things that people had, and his targets could never be allowed to present as people. He identified his targets by touching something they'd owned, something that had mattered to them, something that they'd connected with. To him, his targets were an essence, a scent, an energy signature, a job.

Ducking a bride trying to do shots off a tattered veil while her girlfriends screamed with laughter, Slade began to weave around people, his internal clock calculating exactly how much time he had until he had to strike. Two minutes and thirty-seven seconds.

He hadn't asked why it was so certain that the meeting would start at that exact time. He didn't care. His job was just to kill her.

As he neared the corner, he began to discern the shape of a person tucked in the shadows. His focus sharpened, and he began to reach out with his mind—

"You'll have a choice." A woman stepped in front of him, staring at him.

Slade stopped, startled by her appearance. He wasn't used to anyone addressing him directly. He was accustomed to eyes sliding past him, not seeing him, not wanting to see him. He couldn't remember the last time a random woman had stepped in front of him and demanded his attention.

It wasn't normal.

So, he said nothing, studying her carefully. Her auburn hair cascaded almost down to her waist, and her deep blue eyes were haunted and stark. Her black leather pants and sequined pink top showed off a body worth admiring, but he didn't bother. He never bothered.

"You get to choose, Slade," she said.

She knew his name? He narrowed his eyes. "Choose what?" He didn't believe in coincidence or accidents, including obscure statements by apparent strangers who knew the name that no one knew. He'd seen too much in his lifetime to disregard anything. He still had over two minutes to take care of his target. He had time to engage her.

"Immortality in hell, or one mission in exchange for your life." The redhead raised her hand, as if to brush a speck of dirt off Slade's shoulder.

He stepped aside, out of reach, as he always did. No one got to initiate physical contact with him. Ever. "Clarify that statement." There was something about her he couldn't place. An etherealness to her eyes. A grace to her movements. She was more than she seemed.

"Death is coming for you. *You will get to choose your fate.*" Her fingers drifted toward his face, as if to stroke his cheek, and he caught her wrist, blocking her.

"No."

She smiled at him. "The Black Swan gets to choose. So much potential. So much evil. *So much evil in you.*"

Shit. She knew both his name *and* his alter ego. There wasn't a person alive besides himself who knew that Slade Cross and the Black Swan were the same person. There was no way she could know that. And yet...she did. His interest in her sharpened. "Who are you?"

But before she could answer, Slade sensed agitation from his target, and his gaze shot past the redhead to the corner. He could still see his quarry's outline at the table. She hadn't moved. Still there.

He looked back at the redhead...but she was gone. His fingers were still curved from when he'd grasped her wrist, but she had vanished. He dropped his hand and looked sharply around the bar, scanning with lightning speed, but the redhead was gone.

He ground his jaw against the compulsion to hunt her down for more information on how the hell she knew who he was, but he had to get in position. The time to kill was almost upon him.

He would track her later.

Drawing his energy inward to focus on his target, he strode toward the back of the bar, his gaze searching the darkness for her. He got closer, and closer, until he could finally see her clearly. She was sitting at a high table at the bar, facing the wall.

Who sat with their back toward a room? People who weren't worried about being killed. The people he was sent to kill rarely sat like that. They knew better. Something pulsed at the back of his mind, a faint hint of discomfort that she might not deserve what he had in store for her...but he quickly suppressed it.

His job wasn't to judge.

His job was to execute, and he never failed.

But as he moved closer, he couldn't help but study her more carefully. Her hair was long, tumbling over her shoulders as if the wind had unleashed it from its bindings and left it loose and wild. Her shoulders were bare, and black straps crisscrossed over her toned back. Jeans hugged her hips, and her feet were bare in low-heeled sandals. Her ankles were sexy as all hell, dainty enough to be all woman, but strong enough to shove her heel into a man's throat if she needed to. She was sexy and badass, but she was also demure, the most alluring combination a woman could use to trap a man.

He moved up closer behind her, until he caught her scent. It was faint and delicate, and it made his gut wrench with sudden lust. Swearing, he stopped dead. What the hell? *Lust?* Because he liked her ankles? But before he could recover, she turned her head to scan the bar, giving him a profile view of her. She was in her mid-twenties, but there was an innocence to her face that made his gut twist. He killed very few innocents, and he wouldn't have taken this assignment if he'd seen her picture. Yes, he'd done those jobs a few times when it had been necessary, but there was something about *her* that made him recoil from the idea of extinguishing her light.

But he'd taken money, and when he took money, he always followed through.

There was a small scar underneath her jawbone, and her face was tense as she scanned, no doubt searching for the person she was supposed to meet. A waitress walked up to the table. "You have to order if you're going to take a table," she snapped. "You need to get up or order."

The woman barely glanced at the waitress. "Tequila shot."

Jesus. Slade's cock got hard as her voice rolled over him. It was soft and sultry. Throaty. Rough. But incredibly feminine at the same time. There was nothing innocent about the way she spoke. She was pure sin, pure sex, and pure danger...and he wanted her.

Completely shitty luck that the first woman he'd wanted to seduce in years was one he had to kill.

There were less than thirty seconds left until he was supposed to kill her, but her meeting hadn't appeared yet. If the meeting hadn't started by the time he was scheduled to kill her, should he kill her anyway, or wait for the meeting? He'd asked the question, and he'd been assured that the meeting would happen on time. What if it didn't? What was more important? The absolute timing of her death, or the timing of it relative to the meeting? Rapidly, he replayed every detail of the situation he knew, processing every fact to determine when to move.

Making her an example was more important than the time of death, he concluded.

He would wait.

Chapter Two

ANYA DIAZ FELT as if invisible fingers were sliding down her spine in a sensual, dangerous caress. Uncertainty rippled through her, and for a brief second, she wondered whether meeting this unknown contact was worth the risk. She couldn't afford a single mistake, and she really couldn't afford to die.

She swallowed, wishing she'd ordered water instead of a tequila shot that she'd never drink. She'd wanted to appear tougher than she felt, but who cared if she looked like a badass who downed tequila? If her mouth was so dry she couldn't even manage to ask the questions she so badly needed answered, she'd look like an idiot, not a formidable opponent.

Dammit. She needed to do better than this.

She stiffened as she felt that same invisible caress sliding along her back. What was going on? Striving to appear calmer than she felt, Anya slanted a sideways glance behind her, trying to ascertain the cause of the sensation along her spine. Her breath caught when she saw a man, well over six feet, standing several yards behind her, *staring right at her*.

His dark hair was short, his blue eyes so intense it was

as if they were a tropical ocean on a blazing sunny day. Even through his black leather trench coat, she could tell he was heavily muscled, a predator more than a man. He was unshaven, his dark whiskers making shadows fall across his angular cheeks. He looked like he roamed the untamed wilds beyond the reaches of civilization, a man who lived by his own rules, not the ones society tried to impress upon him. He was pure sex, deadly sin, and unmitigated danger...and his gaze was fixated on *her*.

Her heart rate began to escalate as his attention dropped to her mouth, his eyes darkening as if he were imagining what she tasted like, or what she would feel like against him. Desire pooled in her belly, and she stiffened at the unfamiliar sensation. She'd learned her lesson long ago about letting her need for a man rule her, and she never allowed herself to notice men anymore...but it was impossible for her to drag her gaze off him.

She felt as though his hands were gliding over her skin, touching every inch of her body as he assessed her. Was it his invisible touch she was feeling, or was she just imagining things because she was so strung out? She shivered, trying to shake off the yearning pulsing low in her belly. How was a complete stranger stoking such need in her? And more importantly, why was he focusing on *her*?

He wasn't the person she'd come there to meet. He was all wrong. An unwelcome distraction and an unsettling attraction...but she couldn't stop her response to him.

He sauntered toward her, moving with the lithe grace of a predator. As he got closer, a cold chill seemed to wrap around her, an ominous cloak of death and danger. She went still, sliding her hand along her lower back for the dagger she'd hidden beneath her shirt. It was small, but she was very good with it. She'd known how to defend herself since she was three, but as he neared, doubt flickered through her. He radiated raw power, the kind that could devastate his prey without him so much as blinking.

He was a man who delivered death, she was sure of it. Her heart rate sped up as he neared, and a cold sweat broke out between her shoulder blades. She didn't know if she could defeat him, and she didn't have time to try. *Keep walking*, she urged him silently. *Just keep walking.*

One dark eyebrow quirked at her, and for a split second, she thought he'd heard her silent command. Then his gaze dropped to her mouth again, sending searing heat cascading through her. She caught her breath, as he raised his gaze to hers again. His expression didn't change, and his stride didn't falter as he strode past her toward the bar.

She let her breath out as he moved past her, her hands shaking with relief as she wiped her wrist across her damp brow. Spared. The intensity of her response to him was shocking, and she had no time to waste trying to cope with it.

He took over a stool at the bar, swiveling the seat so he could face her. Her moment of relief fled as his gaze settled upon her once again. Tension began to rise hard and fast. He wasn't even trying to hide the way he was watching her. His attention was locked on her, assessing her every move. The way he'd eased onto the edge of the bar stool, relaxed yet primed to react in a split second, made him look like a wild panther, a predator so agile and lethal that he could take her out in a single leap. He was too dangerous to be handsome, and too elusive to be appealing, and yet, there was something about him that was drawing her in. Something compelling. Something...

Yes. You want me.

A deep, darkly seductive male voice rolled through her mind, making her belly clench with desire. Had he just spoken in her *mind*? His voice was sensual, rough, erotic, with a faint cultured accent that made her think of black tie dinners and foreign royalty instead of the dangerous predator sitting so still on his perch.

Don't hold back. His voice slid through her mind again, a tantalizing, deliberate caress that made her breath catch. *Think about kissing me. Think about my hands sliding over your naked skin—*

Whoa. She swallowed as the image popped into her head exactly as he'd suggested it. The satisfied gleam in his eyes told her that she'd been correct in assuming it was his voice in her head, and he knew that his decadent suggestion had worked. What the hell? She glared fiercely at him. "Stop it," she snapped. "I didn't invite you into my head. Get out."

He didn't smile, and he didn't back off. *What's your darkest fantasy? Handcuffs? A threesome? A little pain...* as he spoke, images of each scenario flashed through her mind. Her naked, silken ties around her wrists—

Heat rose off her skin. "No." She jerked her gaze away from him, breaking their connection. She fisted her hands, quickly weaving safeguards in her mind, invisible walls that encased every last thought, every feeling, every bit of herself that wasn't physical. Within a millisecond, he was out of her mind.

Her lungs expanded in sudden relief as the sensual sensation of being caressed along her spine vanished. Had it really been *his* touch she'd been feeling on her back? Some metaphysical extension of his mind that felt like actual physical contact? What kind of power did he carry? And why was he directing it at her?

His expression didn't change once she'd booted him from her mind, but he seemed to become even more still.

She met his gaze, daring him to try again.

He did.

She felt him testing her protections, feeling his way through her mind, searching for the one gap she'd missed. Anya smiled, allowing the same satisfied gleam in her eyes that he'd had in his. "I'm good," she said. "Don't bother."

He didn't answer, his gaze flicking behind her.

At the same instant, she sensed someone approaching behind her. She froze in sudden anticipation, realizing that the woman she'd come to meet had arrived. Anya's heart began to hammer, and she had to fight not to whirl around to look behind her. Her instructions had been not to turn around, and not to look at the person she was meeting, or the deal would be off.

All she could do was wait.

One second passed.

Then another.

Anya dug her fingernails into her palms to make herself stay still, terrified she would do something wrong and her contact would vanish without telling Anya what she so desperately needed to know.

Another second passed... then, finally, mercifully, someone leaned up against her seat, and a warm breath brushed over her neck.

Anya's heart was racing so fast the beats were like a relentless crescendo hammering in her ears. This was it. Her chance. "Is Julia still alive?" she asked, her breath frozen in her chest as she waited for news of her best friend, her only friend, the only person still alive who mattered to her.

Fingers drifted through her hair, and lips feathered over the back of her neck. A seduction, for anyone in the bar who was bothering to watch. A charade to protect them both. "For now." It was a woman's voice, breathy and sensual.

Tears of relief burned in Anya's eyes. Alive. Her best friend was *alive*. "How do I find her?" She slid her gaze toward the mirror behind the bar, taking a forbidden look at the woman she'd spent the last three weeks hunting down. Raven black, ultra-straight hair reached just past her shoulders, and her eyes were hidden behind dark glasses. Her lips were pale, her skin the color of a latte, and her simple outfit of a tight black tee shirt and fitted jeans made her look sexy, but unmemorable, blending easily into the atmosphere of the bar.

Who was she? How did she know what had happened to Julia? How was she involved? Anya had found the woman's email address in Julia's belongings, the only clue she had as to what had happened to her friend. It had taken weeks to track this woman down, and even longer to convince her to meet…assuming the woman standing behind her was the same person who had answered her emails.

The man at the bar leaned forward, drawing Anya's attention off the mirror and back to him. He was staring at her even more intensely, his gaze boring into hers as if it were a dagger that could cut out her heart. She could feel him testing her psychic defenses, trying to get back in her mind.

She jerked her gaze off him, refusing to let him distract her. She closed her eyes to cut him off, so she could focus on the woman behind her. She couldn't afford to miss a word. "Where is Julia?"

The woman's breath tickled her neck. "You must go to the warehouse on the corner of Hartford and—"

Fingers closed around her wrist. Anya's eyes snapped open as the man at the bar jerked her off her stool and across the floor. She slammed into his hard body, and his arms locked around her. No longer were his eyes blue. They had shifted into dark, bottomless pits of death…and something else. Something more dangerous. Something more personal.

"I love you," he said, his whisper rolling through her, making sudden tears fill her eyes as longing swept over her. To be loved, to be held like she mattered, to be—

He kissed her.

Not just a kiss.

A kiss so tender, so beautiful, so seductive that it made her heart cry for more. Never had she been kissed like that. *Ever.* His lips were decadently soft. His tongue seduced with a sensual dance of promise and tenderness. His hands framed her hips, as if he were her shield against the world. He was pure male, offering himself to her as her protector, her lover, the man who would never let her be alone again.

Her soul cried out for his kiss and his declarations with an intensity so strong that it made her heart ache with longing. The pain in her heart jerked her back into her own mind just enough for her to realize that something was wrong, terribly wrong. He was in her mind again, reeling her in, offering her the words and emotions that she burned for, as if he knew exactly what triggers would ensnare her. He was manipulating her, drawing her into his kiss…

Dear God. His kiss was his weapon, wielded with the skillful, ruthless finesse of a well-practiced assassin. Why had he come for her? Sudden conviction pulsed through her, and she knew it had to be because of Julia. Was he simply trying to keep her from talking to the woman? Or was he there to kill her?

Her gut knew the answer instantly. She was in extreme danger from him. She had to break his hold on her. She had to talk to the woman. She had to find Julia. She shoved at his chest, trying to raise her mental shields and sever the grip he had on her mind—

He deepened the kiss, a searing hot kiss that seemed to ignite her very soul. His lips were hot and sensual, his kiss deep and intoxicating, sending desire sparking through every part of her body. Yearning filled her, a desperate need for him, for his kiss, for his touch, for everything he could offer her.

In the deep recesses of her mind, she knew it was wrong. She knew what she felt was unnatural, but the realization was faint, fading, too weak for her to grasp. He tunneled his hands through her hair, angling her head as he deepened the kiss, drawing her away from her mission and into his spell.

She couldn't stop herself from responding to his seduction. Her soul was crying out for him, despite the threat he was weaving around her so tightly. She was called to the emptiness of his soul, even as she knew that his whispers of love were lies he didn't mean. But it didn't matter. Something about him touched her heart, something far deeper and more real than the illusionary seduction he was weaving in her mind.

She needed to stab him.

She needed to save him.

She needed to run.

But she couldn't do any of it.

She simply wanted *him,* this moment, and his kiss.

Chapter Three

SLADE KNEW HE'D broken his rule.

When he administered his kiss of death, it was always impersonal. Yes, he made sure they died in peace, but *he* never felt anything. It was important that he felt nothing. No joy. No remorse. No guilt. And no sexual attraction. It had to be simply a job.

But the moment his lips had touched hers, something inside him rebelled, refusing to allow him to feel nothing. He noticed how soft her lips were. He was aware of her breasts against his chest. He was entranced by the taste of her mouth, a sweet, decadent hint of white chocolate she must have just eaten. He took a moment, a brief moment, to *feel* her. He couldn't help it.

She melted against him, even as he felt her mind struggling to break the hold he had on it. He could sense the attention of the woman she'd been speaking with, watching warily, but not retreating yet. She was uncertain—

Now was the time he had to strike.

I love you. He said the words again, because he could sense that those were the words that would give his victim the most peace, the ones she wanted to hear more than any others. He gave her the same gift he gave every one of his victims—true peace, before he took their lives.

Then he turned the kiss into what he was paid to do. He held tight to her mind, projecting images of being loved and seduced into it while he began to suck the life from her body. She stiffened, somehow sensing what he was doing, and he swore. Not a single one of his targets ever knew they were being killed. He would never allow them to suffer that kind of fear. *Ever.*

Unwilling to allow her to experience the terror of imminent death, he backed off with his kill, and focused on the kiss itself. He deepened it, pouring more words of love and images of seduction into her mind while he slid his hand over her ass in the most sensual caress he could muster. He didn't seduce. He didn't caress. He never had to work hard to make a woman fall under his spell, but this time was different. She was struggling to surface, somehow sensing what he was doing, forcing him to go to a place he didn't ever go. He had to slow the kiss. He had to taste her lips. In order to convince her, he had to commit himself.

The moment he did, raw lust poured through him. Desire. Need. He swore under his breath, trying to hold his concentration as her essence as a woman filled him. Her scent drifted through him. Her body was warm and soft against his, and her mouth... *Hell.* Her mouth tasted amazing. Like sin and purity, entangled into a dangerous knot that he wanted to unravel bit by bit, until he'd revealed every last one of her secrets, until there was nothing left between them but nakedness and heat.

Shit. He was losing control, not of her, but of himself. She was the one seducing him, not the other way around.

With a low growl, he fisted her hair and angled his head, kissing her even more deeply, pouring every last bit of his need and lust into the kiss. He had to overwhelm her, or he was the one who was going to be lost. He couldn't hold his focus under the assault she was waging on his senses. Her mouth... hell...it was like the ultimate promise of decadence, sex, and innocence. He struggled to make himself reach for her mind again, to mingle his consciousness with hers so he could direct her thoughts. Sweat trickled down his temple, as he fought against the need rushing through him. He needed her, right now, in every way. A lifetime of holding himself under lockdown and refusing to acknowledge his humanity was losing the battle fast.

He drew upon decades of practice, thrusting his mind into hers, dragging her into the delusion of seduction and fantasy, into a world where she thought she was being kissed by whoever represented her greatest fantasy. That was the gift he gave his victims, to be loved by the one they needed the most before they died. Not by him, by *the one.*

He felt the moment she lost the battle. She sagged against him, pressing her body against his, fully succumbing to the illusion of seduction he had built in her mind. Her nipples were hard against his chest. Her body was warm and pliable against his, as she surrendered herself to him for safekeeping, even while he prepared to drain the life from her body.

A flash of guilt shot through him, and he swore, shoving it aside ruthlessly. He had no room for that shit. He had to focus. Tightening his grip on her hips, he shifted the kiss from being one that gave into one that took. Her life began to drain from her body again. She surrendered willingly, thinking she was giving herself to whatever man was in her fantasies...not to him. She was so deep in his illusion that she didn't even know she was kissing the Black Swan...and for the first time in his life, he felt like he was the one who was losing. She was tightly bespelled, blissfully unaware of what was happening. She had no idea he even existed, and she would die in that state, taking no memory of his kiss to the afterlife. For a split second, a deep longing rushed through him, a burning need to be acknowledged by her, to be noticed, to have her know, even for a fleeting moment, that he existed, that he was the one who she was kissing so desperately.

Pain suddenly shot through his chest, violent, incinerating pain. He stumbled back, his hands falling away from her as he looked down. Stunned, he saw a barbed tip was protruding from the upper left side of his chest. Smoke poured off the hook, black and purple smoke that smelled of sulfur and rot.

Gasping, he slid off the stool, his hands sliding down her hips as he fell. She grabbed his hand, her eyes widening as she saw the blood pouring from his heart. "Oh, God," she gasped. "What happened?" He knew she was reclaiming her senses, but he couldn't hold onto her mind any longer.

He couldn't breathe. He couldn't use his legs. He couldn't hold himself up...

He looked up, and in the mirror behind the bar, he saw the demon that he'd mind-scrambled only moments before. It met his gaze in the glass, its eyes blazing. It was the demon's arm that was plunged through Slade's chest. "The Black Swan does not live up to his reputation," it snarled. It jerked its arm back, severing Slade's heart from his body. "He is pathetic. Distracted by a woman. He is no more."

Slade fell to the floor, the wood hard and cold against his face. The bar erupted in screams, and he could only lie there...dying...hell. He was dying. How had that happened?

His vision began to darken, and his thoughts began to scramble. Swearing, he fought to hold onto his mind, fought to stay conscious. He had to think. There had to be something he could do—

Suddenly, the redheaded woman's voice rang through his mind. *You have a choice.*

A choice. What kind of a choice? Between death or something else? Her face appeared before his eyes, swimming in and out of focus. He knew his eyes weren't open anymore. He could barely feel his body. He was already drifting. Red eyes gleamed at him, and he could smell the burning fires of hell awaiting him.

We need you to be a guardian, she said. *One assignment. If you fail, you go to hell. If you succeed, you get your life back. We need you, Slade Cross. You get a second chance because we need you more than hell does.*

A guardian? Was she kidding?

She began to fade from his sight, and somehow, he knew that once she was gone, his moment of choice was over. What kind of guardian? A protector of some sort? He was an assassin. He cared about money and death, not saving people.

She wanted him to *save* someone? No chance. How could he go there? How could he walk a path that made him think of mercy? He'd never be able to live with who he was if he went there.

Choose, Slade Cross. Choose now. There is no second chance. She fluttered and faded, until only her eyes remained, boring into him.

And yet, he said nothing. He didn't want the choice she offered him. There was no room in his soul for a mission of mercy. It would open the gates to the personal hell that he kept locked away. He'd never survive the onslaught of who he was if he stepped out of the path he'd carved out for himself.

Disappointment filled her eyes as she realized he wasn't going to take her up on her offer.

Her disappointment bore into him, unleashing a roar of denial within him. He wasn't a failure. She was wrong. He realized suddenly that if he died now, he would leave his contract on this woman undone. He *would* die a failure.

Screw that. His reliability was the only thing he had to be proud of. He could do this guardian thing, and then take his life back. He'd take her assignment, come back to life, finish the assignment he'd come to this bar to complete, and then do that guardian thing for a day or two, until the red-head was satisfied. Easy. Done. Simple. *I'm in. What's my assignment?*

A ray of hope flashed in her eyes, and her relief washed over him, a fierce burst of emotion. *You will know.* She met his gaze. *May strength guide you on your journey, and wisdom be your light.*

Then she was gone.

* * *

Slade bolted awake, gasping as air rushed back into his lungs. The bar was filled with screams, and the acrid smell of sulfur filled the air. Slade scrambled to his feet, slipping in his own blood as he tried to stand. His body was trembling violently, his legs so weak he could barely stand. Swearing, he leaned on the bar, frantically searching the chaos for the woman he'd been kissing. Where was she? He had to kill her before he did the guardian thing. He couldn't screw up his assignment. *He couldn't.*

He saw her then, across the bar, racing out the door...being followed by the demon. Shit! He leapt after her, then stumbled, crashing into one of the tables. Beer and wine glasses flew everywhere, the glass shattering as they fell. He scrambled back to his feet, grabbing people he passed to stay on his feet. The redhead had given him his life back, but that was about it. His body was wasted.

The demon leapt through the glass-plate front window

of the bar, tackling the woman. She screamed as he dragged her to her feet. Slade fell, his legs giving out as the demon yanked her close to him. His eyes were glowing red, and his mouth opened wide, baring fangs.

Shit. It was going to kill her. Not just kill her. It was going to brutalize her. "No!" he bellowed his denial.

The woman slammed her knee into the demon's crotch, but it didn't even react. Slade went down on his knees, too weak to stand. The demon slammed his mouth down over the woman's, and Slade attacked its mind, lacerating through the demon's strongholds and attacking it psychically, just like he had before. The demon screamed and dropped the woman, gripping its head as it went down under the fresh assault on its barely-healed mind.

It wouldn't last long. Slade had to act. Had to get her. Take her away. Kill her.

She scrambled to her feet, and looked over at Slade, as if she'd somehow known that he was the one who'd helped her. Their eyes met, and instantly, the rest of the world vanished in a white light. The only thing in color was her, a radiant, glistening beacon of life and energy in a world that had been frozen for a split second.

Shock spliced through him. Son of a bitch. It was *her*. She was his guardian assignment. *She* was the one he had to keep alive. What the hell? If he kept her alive, after he'd taken a contract to kill her, everything that mattered to him would be destroyed. He couldn't do that. *He couldn't do that.*

The world flooded with color again, and she spun away to run down the street. As she turned, he saw the flash of a knife blade to his right, cutting through the air right for her. "No!" Sudden strength rushed through him, and he leapt to his feet, sprinting through the ravaged bar with lightning speed. He tackled her just as the knife hit, and the blade thudded deep into his shoulder.

They hit the ground hard, sprawling across the cobblestones with an embarrassing lack of grace. He groaned as he hit, his recently dead body utterly drained of resources. Swearing, he summoned strength he didn't have and lurched to his feet.

She was already standing, her clothes smeared with his blood, her eyes horrified as they took in the knife in his shoulder. "What happened?"

He yanked it out. "They're coming for you. We have to go." He reached for her, but she leaped back, holding her hands up defensively, as if she could actually block him.

"You tried to kill me! You messed with my mind!"

"Yeah, I did. Now I'm your only chance to live. Coming?" Something made him hold out his hand, instead of grabbing her and forcing her to leave. He gave her the chance to make the right choice.

She looked at his hand, and then at his face, then past his shoulder. Her eyes widened, and she paled. "Oh, no."

He spun around to see what she'd seen, scanning the screaming crowd rapidly, searching for the threat she'd noticed. The demon was still down, and he didn't feel anyone's focus was on her. What had she seen?

He turned back to her...only to discover she was gone.

Son of a bitch. She'd distracted him and then taken off. She'd played the Black Swan, and beat him like he was an infant.

And now he'd lost her, making him a double failure. Failure to fulfill his contract to kill, and failure to fulfill his promise to save.

He had to find her. *Now.*

* * *

Anya sprinted through the screaming crowds, ducking around people as she raced down the street, frantically scanning the crowds for the woman from the bar. Black tee shirt. Blue jeans. Black hair. It seemed like every woman was dressed like that, but none were the one person she needed to find. Her heart was hammering desperately, and tears were burning in her eyes. This was her chance to find Julia. She couldn't miss it!

Ahead of her, she saw a flash of movement slip around the corner of a building. "Wait!" She shouted over the roar of the crowd, sucking in air as she pushed herself to run faster than her body felt like it could go. She skidded around the corner, tripped on something, and her ankle gave out. She crashed hard to the cement, pain flooding her left ankle and leg. She ignored the pain and stumbled to her feet, frantically scanning the quiet street of luxury boutique storefronts that were closed for the evening.

The street was empty.

Where had she gone? Where was she?

Something soft brushed against her leg, and she jerked her gaze down. A tangled black nest was piled up on the sidewalk. She recognized the glistening black fibers immediately. They were the same satiny tresses she'd seen on the woman. Elation exploded through her. The woman had come this way! Anya grabbed it off the ground, her fingers clenching the polyester fibers as she ran forward. "Hello?" she called out. "Where are you? Please help me!"

The street was empty and isolated, the perfect place for them to meet in privacy. "Hello? Talk to me!" Tears burned in her eyes as she raced along, looking into every doorway, peering down every alley, but there was no other sign of the woman she'd worked so hard to track down.

Finally, agonizingly, she stopped. Her legs were trembling from running so hard. Her breath was heaving in her lungs. She couldn't lie to herself anymore. The woman was gone. "Julia!" she screamed her friend's name, even though she knew it was useless. "Where are you? I—"

Chills suddenly prickled down her spine, and she whirled around, her heart freezing when she saw the man who had kissed her at the bar standing directly behind her, his dark eyes boring into her. His trench coat flapped around his calves, and a hole gaped open in his shirt, right over his heart. His chest was bloody, but it looked intact, despite the fact she'd seen the demon's hand sticking out of it. He was tall, with broad shoulders, and his legs were powerful beneath his jeans. His dark eyes were relentless, and she could still remember what his lips had felt like when he'd kissed her. A silken seduction of desire and dangers...

Oh, *God.* It was happening again! She leapt backward, clutching the wig to her chest. "Get away from me." She immediately wove the mental safeguards in her mind as she backed away from him, looking around frantically for someone, anyone, she could ask for help.

"Who wants you dead?" His deep voice rolled through her, powerful and ruthless, but again, with that same underlay of culture and refinement that made her envision him sitting at a white-linen tea with scones served on elegant china, discussing polo strategies and the status of his vineyard.

"You, apparently." She slid her hand into her back pocket, and wrapped her fingers around her phone, trying to get her thumbprint aligned properly to unlock it. If she could dial 9-1-1, then they could track her phone, hopefully before he killed her. "Why do you want me killed? I know you went there for me. Why?" She pressed her thumb on the divot, hoping that she'd aligned it correctly. She continued to edge away from him, toward the middle of the street, hoping that a car would drive by and have to stop to keep from running over her.

"I don't *care* if you die," he clarified, making a distinction that didn't feel all that important to her at the moment. "I was paid to kill you. Someone else cares."

She froze then, staring at him as his words sank in. "Someone *paid* you? And you took the money? What kind of value system is that?"

His gaze didn't waver. "And then someone had a back-up assassin with the knife blade, and I'm thinking that the demon was sent for you as well. No one *ever* double-books one of my kills, and yet you were triple-booked." He studied her thoughtfully, as if she were a great science experiment he was curious to investigate "Why is that? Is it that you're so difficult to kill? Or is it *that* important that you die?"

She stopped edging away from him as his question sank in. Three assassins had been sent to kill her? A chill raced down her spine, and this time, it had nothing to do with sexual awareness of him, and everything to do with a deep foreboding. Warily, she glanced up, scanning the rooftops. Where there were three, there could be more. "Why are you talking now, instead of killing me?" She pressed her phone screen where the emergency call button would be if she'd managed to get it right.

"I missed my window to kill you," he said softly, still watching her. "The rush is over. Late by one minute is no different from late by ten minutes. I'm already late."

"Why do you care why they're after me?" She pressed her screen again, her heart pounding, as she scanned the area again. Suddenly, every shadow seemed to be undulating. Every piece of trash blowing made her jump. And every roof seemed the perfect spot to launch an attack. What had Julia been into? What had she inadvertently walked into by hunting for her? *Three* assassins? What was going on?

"Because I have a decision to make about whether to

kill you." He was watching her inch away, not making a move to follow her. His muscled body rippled with confidence and capability, and she had no doubt that he'd be able to grab her in a split second, just like he'd done at the bar. She hadn't even seen him coming, but then his hand had been around her wrist and she'd been against his chest, without her even knowing how it had happened. Kinda like how he'd snuck up behind her on this street. It was as if he were made of shadows and death, and everything that was most definitely not nice.

"You should decide not to kill me," she said. "That's a good decision. Go feed the homeless instead of taking money to kill people. It probably won't save your soul, but at least you can feel better about yourself." She decided finally that she had to take advantage of the fact he wasn't in the mood to kill her right then. He could change his mind at any second.

Quickly, she spun around and began to walk down the street, away from him, back toward the melee from the bar.

He fell in beside her, shortening his stride to keep pace. He was so tall, looming over her, like a cloud of doom. "They'll be looking for you if you go back there," he offered conversationally.

She stopped, staring at the crowds racing around at the end of the street. "The assassins?"

"I hunted you down easily after you left the bar. Granted, I'm talented that way, but so are they, if they're any good at their job." His voice was soft, hesitant, as if he were trying to decide the best way to converse with her. Was he testing out different intonations on her, to see which one would get her to fall into his arms again?

A voice crackled behind her, and she spun around. The street was empty.

He stared at her, his face like stone. "It's the speaker on

your phone. You dialed 9-1-1 and the operator is asking you questions."

She jerked her phone out of her pocket, and saw that he was right. She raised the phone to her ear, surprised he wasn't trying to stop her.

"If I choose to kill you, help will never come in time," he said casually. "I don't need to stop you from talking to them. The police are no threat to me, or to the others who are looking for you."

A chill gripped her at his matter-of-fact tone. She could easily see how he was a man who dealt in death. The way he spoke of killing her was so emotionless it was chilling. "My name is Anya Diaz," she said into the phone. "I'm in front of Angela's Cafe in the Back Bay. Someone is trying to kill me. Please hurry." The operator started asking questions, but Anya's words died in her throat when she saw him looking past her, his eyes narrowed.

Slowly, she turned. Striding toward her was the demon, its eyes glowing red, its handsome, human face contorted in rage.

"Twice," it snapped. "Twice you messed with my mind, Black Swan. For that, you die before I kill her."

"Oh, God." She froze, her heart pounding real fear. It was closing fast, its fingernails lengthening into claws.

"It seems we both have a decision to make," the trench coat man, apparently called Black Swan, said to her, keeping an eye on the demon. "I have to decide whether to save you again, and you have to decide whether to trust me."

"Trust you?" She glanced at him. "Why would I trust you?"

"Because I recently accepted an offer to become your guardian for a brief time. I'm beginning to understand why you need one, though I don't know yet why you are so vitally important to so many powerful beings." His gaze swept over her. "Kill you or save you. A complicated question of many levels and implications, and I don't have as much information as I need to make an informed decision. I never make decisions without full information, so, for the moment, your best chance of staying alive is me."

The demon was getting closer, less than twenty yards away. She knew she didn't have time to run from either of them. All she knew was that she had to stay alive, or Julia would never be found. She had no one else to look for her. She couldn't outrun them. She couldn't outfight them. Her only chance was help. "Be my guardian," she suggested to him. "I'm worth it. You can always kill me later if you decide that's the best choice." It wasn't much of an offer, but she had a feeling that her guardian/assassin wouldn't make a long-term commitment to her well-being.

He glanced at her. "Excellent point. I will reserve the right to kill you later, should I deem it appropriate." He held out his hand. "Shall we go? I prefer not to fight unless I'm getting paid to do it."

Again, with the cultured tones that were the antithesis of the dangerous predator in leather and denim that had hunted her down. Was she really going to put her safety in his hands? He'd tried to kill her—

A flash of light whipped past her, and she yelped, jumping backward as her potential guardian snatched a knife out of the air, a split second before it plunged into her heart. She stared at the knife in his hand. He'd tried to kill her once, but saved her three times. She was going to have to go with the odds. "Okay." She put her hand in his. "What now?"

"We disappear." He yanked her over to him, swept her up in his arms so she was anchored against his chest. "Hang on. I've never done this with a passenger."

She didn't have time to ask what. She had time only to

lock her arms around his neck, and then he took off like a streak of lightning, moving so fast that the world became a blur, and all she could do was hang on for dear life.

Chapter Four

SHE SMELLED INCREDIBLE.

She felt right in his arms.

She made him want.

She made him crave a lot of things. Her. Sex. An endless night of bare skin and long kisses. All of it. Now.

What he did, however, was dump her on the couch in one of his safe houses and back up until he was standing on the other side of the room. Slade folded his arms over his chest and stood with his weight even on both feet, ready, watching her, curious.

He hadn't conversed extensively with a woman in a long time. He didn't know how they thought. He wanted to know why she affected him like she did. He needed to know why she was so important. And he was burning with the need to know what it would be like to kiss her again, without the goal of killing her. He wanted to kiss her just to see what it would be like.

She righted herself on the couch, her dark hair tumbling over her shoulders. Her shirt was stained with his blood, as was her left hand, where she'd reached for him when he fell. He considered that. He'd been in the process of killing her, and yet she'd reached for him when he'd been attacked.

It was unwise, indicating a lack of attention to her well-being and personal safety.

But at the same time, he found it immensely interesting. "Why did you reach for me?"

She glanced around the room, rapidly assessing their surroundings, which were no more than a single room, furnished only with a couch and a blanket. "What are you talking about?"

"When the demon took my heart, and I fell. You reached for me even though I'd been about to kill you. Why?"

She looked at him, her brows knit as she considered his question. "I don't know. Instinct. You'd been hurt terribly. What was I going to do, drop you?"

"Yes. I was trying to kill you. When you get a chance, you run. Do you understand?"

She stared at him, and then a slow smile spread across her face. For a split second, he was too shocked to do anything but stare. Her smile was absolutely riveting. Her smile was genuine, directed at him, of her own free will, without guile or manipulation.

He'd never had anyone smile at him like that before. Women smiled because they wanted to coax him into their beds. Men smiled to try to defuse his aggressiveness or win his favor. His prey smiled because he projected their fantasies into their head. No one had simply *smiled* at him before.

He liked it. It felt good. It felt like she'd poured sunshine into his body.

So he frowned. "Why are you smiling?"

"Because the fact you're instructing me on how to save myself indicates that you've decided to go with the guardian option. I'm really glad to hear that."

His frown deepened. Was she right? He hadn't intentionally made a decision. The cost of keeping her alive when he'd taken a great deal of money to kill her was high. It violated his honor and his reputation, and that was beyond unacceptable. And yet, the cost of letting her die was to forfeit his life, which was equally unpalatable. Was it better to die with honor than to live without it? He'd never considered that before. He'd always intended to live with honor and hadn't entertained any other possibilities. "Maybe I should kill you."

"My name is Anya Diaz," she interrupted.

He narrowed his eyes. "I don't do names."

"Too bad." She stood up, walking across the floor toward him. "I'm not a nameless, faceless victim," she said, coming to a stop in front of him, less than a foot away. She was much shorter than he was, but the fact she had to crane her neck to look him in the eye didn't seem to deter her. "I'm a real person," she informed him, "and you don't get to pretend I'm not."

He studied the play of emotions in her eyes. Passion, energy, fire. He was wildly intrigued by her. Was she unusual, or was it simply that he'd never taken the time to notice anyone in the way his no-win-decision was forcing him to. "I know you're real," he said.

She raised her brows and set her hands on her hips, lifting her chin defiantly. "No, I meant, I'm *real*, as in I care, I love, I hate, and I deserve to be alive and to be valued for who I am. I'm not simply a physical object that you can kill and dismiss. That's what I mean by real. "

He blinked. "Oh." He didn't really have an answer prepared for that statement.

She met his gaze with steely resolve. "My mother was murdered six months ago."

He felt the depth of her grief, a soul-shattering horror that had brought her to her knees.

Shit. He didn't want to know this. He didn't want to feel it. And he didn't want her to feel it, either. No one should feel pain. Not him. Not her. Not anyone who didn't deserve it.

He immediately reached out to her mind, trying to shut down her grief, but she was ready for him, her mental barriers locking him out, keeping him from taking away her memories. "No," she snapped, shoving her palm into his chest, careful, he noticed, to avoid the place where the demon had clawed him. "You don't get to control me anymore, and you don't get to hide from the truth of what you do. I'm someone's daughter. I'm someone's best friend. I matter, and you don't get to pretend I don't. If you kill me, you will be killing *me*, not a nameless, faceless victim. Do you understand?"

Swearing, he stepped away from her, striding across the room. "I'm not in the business of details. I don't care." It was his mantra, but even as he said it, he felt a tug, a need to learn more about her, a rabid desire to let her become the living, breathing, woman she was trying to show him.

Shit. He couldn't live like this. He couldn't survive in that world.

"Well, I do care!" She spun toward him. "My mother's best friend was a woman named Marjorie. They were..." she paused, and he looked sharply at her, sensing a shift in her. "They were being hunted their whole lives," she amended, clearly having changed her mind about what she'd been about to reveal, which made him want to know what she'd decided not to tell him. "Marjorie's daughter, Julia, was my only friend, my best friend. The four of us lived on the run, moving from place to place, making a home wherever we were at that moment."

"What were they hiding from?" He watched her now, wanting to know what she'd chosen not to tell him. He probed her mind ruthlessly, but she still had him locked out.

"Stop it!" She glared at him. "I'm excellent at protecting my mind, and you're not getting in there again, even if you try to win me over with kisses designed to melt my brain."

Heat rushed to his cock instantly at the thought of kissing her again, and he swore, disgusted by his lack of self-control. "My kisses are designed to soothe the psyche," he said. "I don't melt brains."

"They don't soothe the psyche. They ignite more passion than any woman should be subjected to," she snapped, apparently extremely irritated by that fact. Personally, he found it deeply satisfying that she'd been as turned on by the kiss as he had, even if she'd been envisioning someone else during the kiss. "My mother and Marjorie were killed six months ago. Julia and I escaped. We went into hiding, just as we'd been taught. But then, two weeks ago, Julia disappeared. No one else knows she's gone. Only me. If I don't find her, no one will. She's all I..." Her voice broke, and tears swam in her eyes for a split second, before she cleared her throat and lifted her chin. "She's all I have left. I have to find her."

Her tears got to him. He wasn't used to tears. He always went straight for the death kiss, flooding his victims with peace, serenity, and lust. Negative emotions weren't his thing, and he had no defenses against them. He felt wildly unsettled, thrown off his foundation by this bold woman who should have already been dead. Instead, she was in *his* safe house, challenging him at every turn, refusing to stand down to the legend that bred such fear into so many.

She was making him feel off-kilter, and he didn't like it. He did, however, find that there was something about her that compelled him deeply, which meant that her tears felt real to him. For the first time in his life, he wanted to acknowledge someone else's pain. He wanted to help her. Offer comfort. Ease her anguish. But how? He cleared his throat, searching his mind for the appropriate words. "I'm sorry." Yes, that was it. That was what people said.

She eyed him. "You didn't even attempt to make it sound like you meant that. Don't patronize me. I like it better when you're honest. I have no energy for platitudes." She took a deep breath, then walked back over to the couch and sank down on it. The weariness in her body was evident in the slump of her shoulders, and the shadowy weight of her aura. She closed her eyes and pressed her face to her hands, silently coping with her own trauma.

Slade grimaced and ran his hand through his hair, watching her fight to regain her composure. She was so fragile compared to him. Vulnerable. And yet, she held herself with the courage of the boldest soldier, fighting for honor and love.

He killed for money.

She fought for love.

He believed in honor. She was the one who lived it. The way she lived made him into a lie. *Shit.*

He turned away and braced his palms on the steel wall, trying to reestablish his equilibrium. There were no windows in this safe house. Just a single door, which was invisible to anyone unless he was in their mind, making them see it. He hadn't been to this hideaway in a long time, because it was old and cramped, barely furnished, a throwback to his early days, when money had been scarce and all he'd wanted was a place to sleep deeply without having to watch his back.

He'd been ten years old the first time he'd slept here.

Ten. A child who hadn't yet killed anyone, a kid who

had been so consumed with the need for revenge that nothing else had mattered.

And now he was back, with a woman he was supposed to play guardian to. What did that even mean? Was the fact he'd saved her life enough? Or was there more? How long did the assignment last? He didn't even know. "What does the word guardian mean to you?" he asked aloud.

She didn't answer.

He turned and looked over his shoulder at her. She was still sitting on the couch, hugging her knees to her chest, staring blankly at the opposite wall. When he looked more closely, however, he could see that her stare was anything but blank. She was thinking intently, her mind flying through options, sorting out her next steps...exactly as he was doing.

He watched her, fascinated, as emotions raced across her face while she considered and dismissed options. She was utterly unaware of his scrutiny, too focused on her own problem-solving to watch him.

Irritation rippled through him. He'd already tried to kill her once, and he'd openly admitted he hadn't decided whether to abort the mission. Yet, she'd dismissed him as a threat and was taking no precautions against another attack? Did she have no sense of self-preservation whatsoever? He scowled. "Anya."

She didn't even look at him, her lips moving silently while she talked to herself.

"Anya." He repeated her name, and still she didn't notice him.

"Anya!" He leapt across the room, grasped her arms, and lifted her against the wall, pinning her there with his body.

Her eyes widened, and she froze. "How do you move so quickly?"

He blinked. "What?"

"That was so fast. What are you? Part cheetah? Are you a shifter?"

"Hell, woman. Are you thick?" He pressed his body more tightly against hers, and slid his hand through her hair, tangling his fingers in her tresses so he had a good grip. "Don't you understand the situation you're in?" He bent his head, trying not to think about how good it felt to be pressed up against her. "I'm an assassin assigned to kill you, and you're not paying any attention to me." His mouth hovered over hers, a fraction of an inch from her lips. "I could kill you in a heartbeat, and I still might. One kiss and you're mine. You need to be protecting yourself, not asking me about my feline heritage."

She sighed, her breath warm against his mouth. "I'm not an idiot. If I sat on that couch ready for you to attack me, it would make no difference. I have *no chance* against you if you decide to kill me, but by being so tense and ready, I would quickly drain myself of what little reserves I have left. So, why worry about it? If you decide to help me, then I need a plan. If you ditch me here, I need a plan. And if you do change your mind and decide to kill me in the future, I'd better have figured something out by then. But right here, right now? I can't stop you."

He narrowed his eyes, trying desperately to wrap his mind around her logic. "Why aren't you trying to plead your case? Change my mind. Beg for my mercy."

She smiled then, that same honest smile that made his body tighten. "Because you're a merciless assassin. You've trained yourself not to process that kind of thing. I'm sure people beg for their lives the moment you walk in the door, and you don't even notice it. The only thing that will reach you is if you see the real me, if you feel me in your heart. That's all that will stop you, so the best thing I can do is just be me." She searched his face, making no attempt to squirm free or pry his fingers from their threatening hold on her hair. "You already see me differently," she said softly. "I can see it in your eyes. They aren't as cold. They're less black when you look at me now. They're softer. Not much, but a little."

He swore under his breath, making her smile widen. "See?" she said. "You're already struggling with the idea of killing me. I can see the conflict on your face."

"No." He met her gaze. "I'm not struggling with that decision. I've tabled it for now. What I'm struggling with is the fact that you awaken a burning lust inside me that makes me want to throw you on that couch, rip your clothes off, and bury myself inside you a thousand times until my need for you is sated. That's what I'm struggling with."

She blinked, and heat suddenly ignited between them.

Shit. He hadn't meant to say that. What the hell was she doing to him? He was an icon of discipline and focus. He didn't get uncontrollable hard-ons for women, and he didn't lust after the females he was supposed to kill.

Her eyes widened, and her body tensed against his. "You mean that."

"Of course I do. I have no time for games." He didn't bother to recant. He'd said it. He meant it. It was what it was. He bent his head, angling his face near the crook of her neck. He closed his eyes and inhaled deeply. "Flowers," he whispered, as a sudden image flashed through his mind, an image from so long ago that it felt rusted and faded as it struggled to surface. "You smell of the flowers that my mother used to grow in front of our cabin in the spring when I was a little kid. They were pale pink, dozens of petals, thorns—" He realized suddenly he'd revealed personal details about himself, and he froze.

Anya said nothing, but he felt her fingers slip into the

hair at the nape of his neck, a light, tender caress. He closed his eyes, shocked at the sensation. He stayed utterly still, tracking every move of her fingers over his skin, memorizing the sensation so he could recall it at will in the future.

"You were once a child," she said softly, "just like everyone else in this world. Once, there was a time when you'd never killed anyone." Her voice was soft, drifting over his flesh like a warm breeze. "That's why you can see me," she said, "because that part of you isn't dead. The part that cares."

He ground his jaw and pulled back, glaring at her. "I don't care."

"It makes sense why you're so closed off." She nodded, ignoring his statement. "How else could you do your job? Of course you can't let yourself feel anything. But why do you kill people for money? What took the boy who noticed his mom's flowers and turned him into someone who defiles the most beautiful thing in the world and uses it to kill people?"

He stared at her, searching her face. "You think I defile the kiss?" *Defile?* That was such a brutal word. To defile was to take the beauty out of something that deserved to blossom and thrive. It was a word of judgement and emotion and disdain, and he hated it.

She was still tracing her fingers along the back of his neck, her fingers moving almost absently, as if she wasn't even doing it consciously. "Yes."

"I don't defile the kiss." Outrage poured through him, a need to defend the truth of who he was. "I use the kiss to make death beautiful. People spend every minute of their lives afraid of death and suffering, wondering if they will waste away in a horrific ending to their lives, or die too early from some shitty accident. I turn that hell into peace. I give them the great joy, their most glorious fantasies into their reality. I make death beautiful. If you think that's de-filing a kiss, then that's your problem, not mine."

Her fingers stilled on the base of his neck. "You *kill* with a kiss. How is that not defiling it?" She searched his face as she asked, as if she truly wanted to understand.

"I bring peace with a kiss." He was pissed, so pissed right now. He had such a well-ordered, precise world. It had to be that way. Every emotion, every observation, every thought carefully processed or denied.

She raised her brows. "The fact you give people peace with your kiss doesn't atone for what comes one second later. It doesn't work like that."

"No?" He tightened his grip on her neck. "You don't think so?" He was too furious to think clearly, too angry to hold back. He hated that this woman had the audacity to condemn him, to try to strip away the foundation of what held him together. "You think this doesn't make it all worth it?"

She frowned at him, "This what? What are you talking about?"

"This kiss." He trapped her head with his grip on her hair and then kissed her. Not his death kiss. His pre-death kiss, the one where he poured everything that was good and worthy into the kiss, everything that made life worth living.

He kissed her like there was nothing else that mattered except his lips on hers, and the connection between them.

Chapter Five

THE BLACK SWAN'S kiss was like pouring boiling hot lava into her body, turning Anya into a cauldron of lust and desire so intense that she wanted to crawl up his body and lose herself in him forever. His mouth was hot and demanding, his lips like wildfire, his tongue a penetrating assault of skill and seduction.

He wasn't in her mind this time. Her response was entirely her own, falling wildly into the seductive spell he wove through her with only his kiss. She held on tight, her hand tangled in his hair as she leaned into him, kissing him back frantically. He pressed tighter against her, pinning her to the wall, angling his head to kiss her even deeper.

She needed more of him. She needed to get closer.

As if he'd heard her thoughts, he palmed her hips, and then slid his hands down her thighs. He grasped her knees, then lifted her legs so they were around his hips, still holding her upper body against the wall with his weight.

Yes. She locked her legs around his hips, shocked by the feeling of his erection pressed against the juncture of her thighs. It had been so long since she'd been in a man's arms, so long since she'd lost herself to a rush of desire and need, so long since she'd felt safe enough to feel so intense-ly that she couldn't think of anything else.

He was an assassin, but he was also so much more. He was potentially her guardian, and he was a deadly threat to anyone who tried to attack her. He'd saved her multiple times, and she knew that if someone broke into the safe house, the intruder would be dead before they could come close to her. In this moment, in his arms, she was safer than she'd ever been in her whole life.

He slipped his hand under the hem of her shirt, the heat from his palm searing hot against her side. *Hell, Anya.* His voice brushed through her mind, not intrusively, but rather as an intimate caress, a private secret just for her. *I want to fuck you.*

She jerked back, breaking the kiss. "Fuck me? Is that what you just said? You want to *fuck* me?"

His eyes were dark with lust, his hand spanning her ribs. "Yes."

She would have laughed at his unabashed confession if she weren't so offended by it. "I don't want to be fucked. Didn't you hear me before? Fucking me puts me in the same nameless, faceless category of a victim you kill."

He cupped her breast, making her squirm with need. "What's the right word? What do you want to hear? Tell me, and I'll say it."

"So, you can give me platitudes like you did when you said you were sorry my mother was murdered?" She pushed at his chest, trying to get him off her, but he didn't move. "That's not how it works. Words mean nothing. It's the intention behind the words that matter. You could have said absolutely nothing when I told you my mother had died, but if you'd silently brushed your finger across my cheek, offering me comfort in the only way you knew how, it would have meant something. Spewing out words you don't mean is like killing someone with a kiss. It's a lie, and it's meaningless. Now get off me!"

"You want me to care? Is that it?" He still didn't back off, and he slipped his finger beneath her bra, his thumb brushing over her nipple, sending shards of desire through her.

"Stop it!" She slapped at his wrist, and his hand stilled. "I'm not a machine, you dumb oaf! My mother is dead, Marjorie is dead, and Julia is missing. I'm barely holding it together, and I don't need you trying to feel me up because you need to get off. So stop preying on my emotional state and get off me!" Tears trickled from her eyes, streaming down her cheeks, but she couldn't stop them. "See what you did? You made me fall apart! I don't have time to cry! Damn you! Just damn you!" She slammed her fists into his chest, but he *still* didn't move away. "What do I have to do to get you away from me?" She let her head fall back against the wall in frustration. "What do I need to do?" she whispered, staring at the ceiling.

He said nothing.

For a long time, neither of them moved. She was still pinned against the wall by his body, his hands resting on her hips, her legs still around his waist, not because she wanted them there, but because she had nowhere else to put them. Finally, she looked at him. He was staring at her, his eyes dark and intense. "What?" she asked. "What are you waiting for?"

"The words."

She closed her eyes, too tired to think. "What words? What are you talking about?"

"I'm trying to figure out what words to use that won't offend you."

"It's not the words," she said, not bothering to open her eyes. "Didn't you hear me? It's the emotion that matters. It doesn't matter what you say now. The mood for sex is long gone. God, no wonder you can be an assassin." She opened her eyes, studying him through barely-open lids. "Is there *anything* left of the boy who noticed flowers? Is there not a shred of humanity inside you? Was I that wrong about you?"

He still didn't look away, his gaze boring into her so intensely. "I have never been driven by my physical need for a woman in my life." His words were slow and clipped, almost awkward, as if he were trying each one out before he said it. "My kisses are entirely one-sided, for the pleasure of the one who receives them. I feel nothing when I do them, other than a sense of responsibility to make death appropriate."

"You feel nothing?" she repeated, the implications of his words dawning on her. The intense physical response he'd evoked in her had been one-sided? He'd felt *nothing?* Embarrassment flooded her cheeks. How could she have been such an idiot? She gritted her teeth and glared at him. "Get. Off. Me."

He didn't even acknowledge her request, and his body was an immovable weight that she could never dislodge on her own. "When I gave you the kiss of death, I was unable to keep myself from feeling. I noticed how your lips tasted. I noticed you smelled like flowers. I noticed the feel of your body against mine. I was aware of your breasts against my chest. And I was not pleased that you were trapped by my mind control and were not in that kiss with me. I wanted you to be kissing *me*, not the illusionary fantasy man that you were seeing in your mind."

Heat rushed over her body at his words, and she stared at him, searching his face. "Really?"

"Who were you thinking of when I was kissing you?" His fingers tightened on her hips almost imperceptibly.

"Who was your fantasy?"

She shook her head. "I knew I was kissing you. There was no one else in my mind."

He frowned. "What do you mean?"

"I was kissing you. I knew I was."

Shock rippled over his handsome face. "But that's impossible. I had control of your mind. I gave you the man you dreamed of kissing, the one who would make you die in peace knowing you were in his arms."

She shrugged. "There's no one like that in my life. I guess a hot, irritating assassin was the closest thing I could come up with."

His gaze searched hers, and then he released one hip long enough to brush his finger over her cheeks. "My parents were murdered," he said softly. "When you told me about your mother, I felt your grief. I know that pain, because I lived it. I said I was sorry because I thought that was the appropriate thing to say. You want to know what I felt?" His voice turned icy. "If you wanted my truth, what I would have done is ordered you to tell me the name of the bastards responsible. I would have hunted every one of them down and killed them in the same way they killed your mother, every last one of them. It would have been the only deaths I've done for free in my life, with the exception of those who killed my parents. I would have killed every last one of them, and walked away without a shred of remorse, guilt, or empathy, and I would have sent you their blackened hearts to burn in your mother's honor."

His words were clipped and cold, his face like steel, but his fingers had tightened on her hips, as if even his supreme self-discipline couldn't completely mask his emotions. Tears trickled down her cheeks, both for his own pain, and for his offer. "I didn't know," she said. "And thank you for that." She knew he meant every word, and as horrible as his offer was on some levels, it was also beautiful. To offer to carry the burden of murder on his soul so she could avenge her mother's death was such a powerful statement of who he was.

"I *will* hunt them down," he said. "For you. For her. For me."

She nodded, fighting back the sobs threatening to take her. "I don't know who did it."

"I'll find out." His hand slid around to the back of her neck, and his fingers tightened in her hair. "And I wanted to fuck you because you make me feel things I don't want to feel, things I don't have control over, things that threaten my entire existence. I wanted to fuck you because I don't do anything halfway, and every last bit of my soul is screaming at me to bury myself in you until all that's left are two bodies so depleted that there's no more space for the pain that's trying to come back and take me down. So, yeah, I want to fuck you. I want to sink my cock into the one woman alive who actually knows I exist, who sees me, who kissed *me,* who has been through the same shit I live with every day, who is strong, bold, unstoppable, and ridiculously, obliviously outmatched for what life has thrown at her."

He cut himself off then, his words echoing in the tiny room, bouncing off the steel walls. She felt breathless, overheated, and utterly lost in the intensity of his words. With that one little speech, he'd reignited a raging physical need in her. She was intensely aware of him not only as a man, but as someone who'd suffered, who'd become a machine of steel in response. Except he wasn't steel. He was more.

She realized he was waiting, watching her, his dark eyes inscrutable. She met his gaze. "That was better," she said honestly. "I still think it's a little crass to say you want to fuck me, but—"

He kissed her then, hard, fast, deep, utterly without mercy, utterly without restraint.

His desperate need for her plunged straight to her heart, awakening all the emotions she'd tried so hard to control for so long. She felt utterly raw and exposed with him, barely able to hang onto her emotional control. She didn't want to feel like that, and she didn't want him to tear her apart so ruthlessly, but at the same time... she needed his kiss even more desperately than he needed hers. It was as if he gave her somewhere safe to pour her emotions out. He gave her something safe to feel. With his arms around her and his steel-hard body shielding her against the wall, she was utterly protected and safe.

Anya. His voice was a raw, rough caress in her mind, a desperate call of isolation and need that filled the emptiness of her soul. With a low moan of capitulation, she wrapped her arms around his neck and pulled him close, turning herself over to him.

She had no time to think about what she was doing, or to wonder if it was right. The moment she surrendered to him, the situation took on a power of its own. He consumed her with his need. The kiss was boiling hot, spinning out of control. This man was deadly, incredibly lethal, with her life in his sights, and yet she was completely sucked into the sheer fierceness of what was between them.

He dragged her shirt up and took her breast into his mouth, teasing her nipple. Anya grasped his shoulders, her head back against the wall as he gripped her hips, holding her so tightly that she knew there was no chance she'd fall. Desire raced through her, heat so excruciating she felt like she was going to burn up. The lust was intoxicating, because it left no room for the ache in her heart and the constant terror she had for Julia's safety. With the way he was kissing her, there was no space left for anything but him.

He slipped his hand between them, unfastening her jeans with deft ease, his fingers brushing over the bare skin of her belly, even as he continued his assault with his mouth. He grabbed her around the hips, pulled back just enough to get her jeans off, then hoisted her up higher against the wall, locking her legs over his massive shoulders.

His mouth closed on her swollen nub, and she gasped, twisting as he invaded her body with his tongue, his lips, and his fingers. His assault was electric, overwhelming, more than she could handle. She twisted in his grasp, unable to dislodge his iron grip on her as he held her where he wanted her, sweeping across her folds with exact precision, knowing exactly where she wanted to be touched, knowing when to stay, and when to switch.

She flattened her palms on the ceiling, trying to ground herself as he continued his assault. The orgasm began to build, gaining strength, ready to tear her apart—

Tell me who you're with right now. His voice was a ruthless command. *Who are you with, Anya?*

She looked down to see him staring up at her, his dark eyes turbulent with desire and something else. Vulnerability. Her heart tightened, and she touched his head. "I'm with you. I'm not thinking of anyone else. I know it's you."

His jaw flexed, and he nodded once. Then he pressed a kiss to her belly, just below her navel, a kiss that wasn't about sex. It was a kiss of tenderness and intimacy that went way beyond a raw physical connection. She bit her lip, and then gasped as he kissed her again, this time lower, sweeping her damp folds into a kiss that shook her all the way to her core. His assault was relentless, endless, and demanding, mercilessly dragging her over that precipice.

The orgasm erupted through her, and she screamed, her

hips bucking as he continued his relentless assault, drawing the orgasm on and on, until she thought her body was going to shatter. It wasn't until she was about to collapse that he finally let up, catching her as she fell down into his arms, exhausted and spent, her muscles still shaking.

He stared down at her, his face an impenetrable mask as he held her. She was too exhausted to hold herself up, and she sagged against him, trying to catch her breath.

"Good?" he asked.

"Good?" She almost laughed, until she saw the furrow to his brow, making her realize that he was genuinely asking. "Yes. Incredible. Best ever."

It was only then that he smiled, a brief flash of humanity in his stoic face as he scooped her up, his hand tunneling through her hair as he cradled her against his chest. He kissed her again, not a kiss intended to start her up again. More of a claiming kiss, one designed to take the credit for her exhausted state.

She rested her head against his shoulder, unable to hold it up on her own. She'd never been stripped so bare in her life, but she was too drained to care. She slid out of his arms as he set her on the couch, barely holding herself up long enough to collapse on the cushion.

He crouched beside her, watching her as she rolled onto her side to face him. His forehead was etched with concern. "It was too much for you," he said.

"At the time I had no complaints." She was trembling now, unable to stay warm. Her skin felt too cold, and her muscles were too shaky to hold herself up. She closed her eyes. "I don't feel well now, though."

"I drained you." He swore under his breath, and immediately shed his trench coat. He draped it over her, tucking it around her. It was warm from his body heat, and it smelled of him, a faint scent of woods and man, and something darker and more dangerous. "I've never kissed for pleasure," he said. "Not like that. I should have realized that this could happen. My kisses are meant to take life, not give it."

She managed to open her eyes at the edge in his voice. His face was grim, and the self-recrimination was etched in the lines on his face. "You've never kissed for pleasure? Ever?"

He shook his head. "I've kissed to kill. I've fucked to satisfy the base urges of being a male. But I've never kissed simply for pleasure."

"How was it?"

He shook his head, refusing to accept pleasure for himself in the wake of her state. "I hurt you. Unacceptable."

She hugged the coat closer to her. "You're an assassin. How can it bother you that your kiss took a lot out of me?"

"I kill only those I intend to kill. No one else gets hurt. Ever." His jaw flexed. He stood up and strode across the barren room, then walked back and crouched beside her. "I'm deeply sorry, Anya. I let myself get caught up in giving you pleasure, and it was a mistake. It won't happen again, I promise."

"Stop being like that," she interrupted, feeling starkly exposed. "I just turned myself over to you on every level of my soul. I made myself vulnerable, and I need to hear something from you other than your damned martyrdom. Was that just about giving me pleasure? Did you feel *anything*? Did you even get an erection?" She felt so humiliated, lying on the couch, unable to move, while he crouched there, talking like the orgasm had been some sort of failed clinical offering of comfort.

His eyes flashed and he leaned forward. "You demand much from me, Anya."

"I don't really care." She struggled to sit up, brushing

off his hand when he tried to steady her. "I need to know where things stand between us. When you kissed me, did it matter to you? Did you even want to make love to me? Did you feel *anything?*" She felt stupid asking, but she had no choice. She had to matter. She had to keep reminding herself to feel and breathe and love. If she didn't, she would shut down, and she didn't want to go there. She had to fight to be acknowledged, because if she wasn't, then she was nothing.

His jaw flexed. "I have never lost control of myself in my life," he said, his voice clipped. "I lost control of myself when I was kissing you. That has never happened before."

She looked right at him. "And did you like it? I know you don't like the fact you drained me, but at the time, while you were kissing me, did you like it?"

For a long while, he said nothing. Then he nodded once. "Yes."

She smiled, her heart filling with relief. He hadn't been immune during that kiss. "Okay, then." She closed her eyes and snuggled under his coat.

"That's it?"

"It was enough. I need to sleep. You drained me." She could already feel sleep taking her, the oblivion she hadn't succumbed to in weeks, because she hadn't felt safe enough to cease her vigilance. Maybe it hadn't been his kiss that had drained her. Maybe it had simply been that his protection made her feel safe enough to stop fighting. "Keep me safe while I sleep," she mumbled. "I need you."

Again, there was no answer, but then she felt his fingers brush over her hair in a tender, protective gesture.

She was safe...for now.

Chapter Six

$\mathscr{S}$LADE SAT AGAINST the far wall, watching Anya sleep. She looked innocent and vulnerable, almost completely hidden by his coat. He studied every feature on her face, taking advantage of the opportunity to look at her. Her lashes were long and thick, so different from his own. Her skin was fair, again, different from his own darker tones. And her hair, so soft it was unreal. She was pure woman, delicate and vulnerable, despite the strength emanating so intensely through her. He was a cold-blooded killer with no remorse or empathy, but she made him feel. He wanted to protect her. He wanted to help her. He wanted to burn her mother's killers in hell.

He'd taken money to kill Anya. He'd staked his reputation on it. And yet...he knew he could not do it now.

She was right. She'd forced him to see her as a human being, and that had screwed everything up for him. He hadn't intended to admit what he'd do to her mother's killer, but she'd dragged his confession out of him with embarrassing ease. When he'd seen the expression on her face after his admission, everything had changed for him in that moment. What he'd said had mattered to her. He'd seen it. She'd looked at him as if he were her savior, someone good, someone who could shatter the grip that death, fear, and evil had on her life.

No one had ever looked at him like that, but when she had, it had profoundly affected him. He'd lived his life as a shadow, wiping the memories of all who'd sighted him, living his life in complete isolation. But being seen, truly *seen*, by Anya had been surreal.

He wanted her to wake up, to look at him, and see him *again*.

He wanted to kiss her again.

He wanted to drive his cock into her until...

Shit. He stood up, pacing away from her. He couldn't do that. How badly would he hurt her if he fucked her the way he wanted to? His kiss had nearly killed her. How deadly was he? He didn't know. He'd been so careful and precise his entire life. What was he capable of if he lost control? Could he kiss her again without losing his ironclad grip on his powers?

He turned back to look at her. *I will protect you from me, Anya.* And from anyone else after her. He looked around the empty, barren room, and spoke aloud. "I accept my role as guardian," he said. "Tell me what I need to do for her."

There was no answer. The red-haired woman didn't appear, either in his mind or in person. Just the empty, silent room that protected them both.

Swearing, he ran his hands through his hair. Once they stepped outside, they would both be hunted. With the demon on his tail and the broken contract on Anya's assassination, he was a target. Until he was able to remedy his breach of contract somehow, he was now one of the hunted...and so was Anya. Three assassins had been sent to keep her from having that conversation. Her mother had been murdered. Her mother's friend murdered. And her friend missing. She was a woman who came with a hell of a lot of baggage, and he had to acknowledge that it intrigued him.

He'd be bored if she were some pristine, flawless angel. The fact she came to him with death, assassins, and grief made her compelling to him. Her emotions and conviction were so strong that she'd broken through his shields, and *he liked that.*

Slade walked back across the room and crouched beside the couch, studying her more closely. "What have you gotten involved in, Anya? Why are you so important that you need to be killed? And why are you so important that you warrant a guardian?"

There was no answer from the sleeping woman, and Slade knew he'd have to wait until she awoke to get what information she had, which he suspected wouldn't be nearly enough, given the fact that she was so important that three assassins had been sent after her.

As he stood up to pace the room, anger began to smolder inside him, the same anger that had ignited when he'd watched his parents be murdered, the kind of anger that had almost destroyed him once. Who dared hunt her? Who dared to kill her only family? And who the hell had the power to snatch him from hell's doorstep and return him to the mortal world in exchange for his help? What the hell was going on?

And what chance was there that he had the power to take on whatever they were dealing with? He was a badass, yeah, but he had his limits. Stealing people from hell's front porch was beyond anything he could comprehend...and yet it had happened. Who had she stirred up? Why her? Why him? Where were the damn answers?

He knew he needed to find out before all hell rained down upon them.

* * *

Her mother was screaming. The flames were consuming her. Anya lunged for her, shouting for her mother, trying to get to her, but the flames were too high. "Mom!" She screamed, oblivious to the burns on her arms as she tried to get through them to reach her mom—

"Anya." Strong hands shook her gently, and she bolted upright, sucking in her breath as she looked around wildly.

There were no flames. No fire. Her mother was nowhere in sight. She looked around frantically, searching the barren room. "Mom?"

A male voice spoke gently. "Anya, you're with me. In my safe house. Look at me. Now."

She jerked her gaze off the far wall, staring blankly into a dangerously handsome face. For a split second, she had no idea who he was, her mind still caught up in her dreams, and then everything came flooding back to her. The Black Swan. "It's you."

"Yeah." His brow was furrowed. "You were dreaming."

"A dream." She took a deep breath and closed her eyes. "I was reliving my mom's death."

"I figured." He was still holding her shoulders, his dark eyes searching hers. "Tell me what happened."

She shook his grip off and stood up, her legs wobbling precariously as she tried to find her balance. He steadied her, but she pretended not to notice, too shaken up by her dream, and the memory of what she'd let him do to her body. "I don't want to talk about it." She noticed her jeans and underwear folded on the arm of the couch, and embarrassment flooded her. She grabbed them and pulled them on, so past the point of wanting to be naked in front of him. What had she been thinking?

"You have to talk about it," he said.

"Why?" Her pants back on, she spun toward him, anger rushing through her. Anger at him for making her feel vulnerable. Anger at the world for what had happened to her. Anger that she felt weak and exhausted when she needed to feel strong. "Why do I need to tell you anything? Why can't you just leave me alone?"

His eyes darkened, but he remained seated on the couch. "My name is Slade Cross. I'm known as the Black Swan. I have a perfect assassination record. I am the ultimate, perfect killer. I kill. It's what I do. I am among the most lethal, dangerous creatures who currently walk this earth."

She swallowed at the intensity of his gaze as he spoke. "I believe you."

He didn't even acknowledge her comment. "When the demon took my heart, I died. But when I was on the threshold of hell, a woman came to me and said she would give me another chance at life if I complete one mission, to be your guardian."

Anya stared at him in shock. "What? Someone pulled you back from *death*? How is that possible?"

"I don't know how it's possible, but you saw me. The demon ripped out my heart. I'm pretty difficult to kill, but that's beyond my capacity to heal on my own. But I'm here." He pulled his shirt down, revealing a massive scar on his chest from the demon's fist. She flinched, remembering the sight of that clawed hand protruding from his chest. So much blood...

"I died, and now I'm sitting nice and pretty, alive because you matter, and apparently, I'm the one who has been handpicked to keep you safe." He rested his forearms on his muscular quads, watching her closely. "Of all the people she could have chosen to save you, she chose a man who only kills, never saves, never protects. Why me?"

Anya shrugged, shifting her weight restlessly. "Because you're the best. You just said you were."

He shook his head. "I'm the best *assassin*. As you saw earlier when I kissed you, I'm not the best at protecting life, and I have no interest in developing that new skill." He scowled. "Or I didn't, until you got to me."

Her heart flipped. "I did?"

He shot her a baleful look. "Yeah, and you know you did. You did it on purpose."

She couldn't help but smile. "I did. This is true. I'm glad it worked."

He ran his hands through his hair, leaving it messy and askew, which somehow gave him more humanity. He looked more like a man named Slade, than a famous, deadly assassin named the Black Swan. "The point is, I'm not the best one she could have chosen, and yet she selected me. She used some kind of miracle to bring me back to life, and it couldn't have come without a price. But she did it, she chose me, and she chose you. Why? What's so important about either one of us?"

Wordlessly, Anya shook her head. She had no answers.

"We need to find out. I need to learn every single thing there is to know about you, and I need to figure out why she chose me. And we need to do it fast." His gaze bore into hers. "You have powerful enemies, and powerful allies, neither of which can be trusted. We're both on someone's radar, someone important, someone powerful, and they're hunting you. If I fail to keep you safe, we're both dead." His voice gentled, as if to take away the sting of his words. "So, I don't care if you don't want to relive your mother's death, Anya. You're going to do it anyway, because it's our best lead to understand what is going on."

Anya bit her lip, unable to stop the swell of grief that

filled her. The pain was still so raw, eating away at her. When she'd been focused on tracking down Julia, she'd been able to keep the pain at bay, using Julia's disappearance to consume her every thought, whether awake or asleep. She'd never slowed down long enough to face the horror of her mother's death, and she didn't want to do it now. She understood Slade's point, but...she shook her head, her chest aching with the raw grief that she'd fought off so hard. "I don't know if I can relive it," she said honestly. "I don't want to, and I don't know if I can let myself go back there."

The stoic expression on his face softened, and he held out his hand. "I've been there," he said quietly. "I'll help you. We'll do it together."

She stared at his outstretched hand, somehow knowing that if she took it, she was committing herself to him, surrendering herself into his protection, and thrusting herself deeper into the situation. Her mother had always told her that if someone came after them, that she had to run. Her mother had always said that fighting would wind up with them all dead. *Run, Anya.* The words had been engrained in Anya's mind over and over and over through her life. The four of them had spent their lives on the run, moving every couple months, never making connections, living as shadows that no one noticed. *If someone kills me, run as fast and as far as you can. It's your only chance. Promise me you'll run, Anya. Promise me.*

She could still see her mother's amber-brown eyes beseeching her for that promise. *Yes, Mom, I've told you a million times. I'll run if something happens to you, but nothing's going to happen. We'll be fine. We know how to disappear.*

And her mother's response. *Just promise me you'll run. Nothing matters to me more than your survival. You must run, Anya. You* must *run.*

She'd promised to run, and that's what she and Julia had been doing when Julia had gone into a grocery store and never come out.

"Anya. Come." Slade lifted his hand higher, beckoning to her. "We don't have time to waste. I need to know it all. Now."

If she took Slade's hand, they weren't going to run. He was going to make them stand and fight until it was over. She would be breaking the promise she'd made to her mother. Her throat tightened, and guilt twisted her gut, but the truth was, she couldn't save her mother anymore. But was Julia still alive out there, somewhere, needing help? What kind of choice was that? Break her promise, or abandon the one person still alive in this world who mattered to her?

Her mother had said run.

But running hadn't saved any of them.

Maybe it was time for something new.

She looked at Slade, with his taut muscles, his deadly visage, and the steely glint in his eyes. This was her protector now. Her guardian. Her key. Now was the time to fight. She could always run later, if she needed to. She took a deep breath. "Okay." She put her hand in his, and when his fingers closed around hers, she knew she'd sealed the deal with the devil himself.

A devil, who just might save her...as long as he didn't kiss her again, of course.

But as he drew her beside him on the couch, his powerful body coiled with deadly energy, there was no way for her not to notice the hunger in his eyes or the way her body responded to him.

Chapter Seven

ANYA PERCHED ON the edge of the couch, too restless to sit still. Slade was watching her intensely, too intensely, as if he were trying to bleed out every memory she had of her mother. "I don't know who killed her," she said. "Julia and I were at the post office, mailing bread, and when we came back—"

"Wait." He held up his hand. "Mailing *bread*? What does that mean?"

She stared at him in surprise. "You don't know what bread is?"

He scowled. "I know what bread is. I just haven't heard of anyone mailing it at a post office."

"We bake bread. I mean, we baked bread. I mean, I baked bread. God. It's just me now. I forgot. I hate it when I forget." She stood up, pacing away from him. "It's my comfort thing. I make bread. I have a small online business, and I ship anywhere in the world."

He frowned. "How do you have an online business if you've lived on the run?"

"Believe it or not, there are kitchens in most houses." She rubbed her hands together, her stomach rumbling at the mention of food. "Baking grounds me. Not that it matters, right?" She turned toward him. "I don't know who my mom and Marjorie were running from my whole life. They wouldn't talk about it. I have no idea."

"What about your dad?"

She bit her lip. "I don't know anything about him. I wasn't allowed to ask about him."

He raised his brows. "Didn't you find that unusual?"

It was difficult not to gape at him. "Do you think I'm a complete idiot? Of course I knew it was unusual. What was I going to do about it? She wouldn't talk about him, and I learned not to ask." She ran her hand through her hair, trying to smooth it. "Listen, we were in a warehouse in New York City. We'd been there two days. Nothing was different. But when Julia and I came back, it was burning up. We saw the fire from three blocks away, and we knew it was our place."

"The warehouse was on fire?"

"No, just the part where we were living." She paced away from him, hugging herself. "Fire trucks were on their way, but we beat them there. When we got inside, the place was a disaster. It looked like there had been a fight. Everything was tossed, and my mom and Marjorie—" She swallowed at the image that flashed through her mind, the one she'd tried so hard not to think of since that night.

He leaned forward. "They were what?"

She looked at him. "They were dead. They…" She hesitated, not sure whether she should tell him.

He raised his brows. "They what?"

Oh, hell, what did it matter if he thought she was crazy? Or if he figured out the secret they all shared? It wasn't as if he could hurt her mom or Marjorie now. "It looked like they'd been attacked by a wild animal, like they'd fought for their lives, and lost." Teeth marks. Throat torn. Eviscerated.

Torn to shreds while she and Julia had been out *shopping*.

He didn't even react. He just nodded, as if he encountered that every day. "Did you stay around to see what you could find out?"

His ease with her description made her relax slightly. She shook her head. "The sirens were close," she whispered, hugging herself. "We knew we couldn't stay. We couldn't be found. So, we grabbed what we could reach, and then ran." She looked at him. "We left them there, Slade, alone. We didn't even give them a proper burial. We just lost everything in that one second." Grief ached deep in her heart, the agonizing pain of a past that could never be changed, no matter how much she wished it.

"She didn't want a burial," he said gently. "She wanted you safe."

"I know." She wiped the back of her hand across her eyes and took a deep breath, trying to settle. "I know that, but I still think of how she looked, laying on that concrete floor, so alone—"

"Not alone. She had you, even in death." Slade took her hand, squeezing gently. "What happened after that? Did anyone contact you? Did you get any more information on what had happened?"

"No. The papers didn't even report anything. It was like someone buried it." She looked at her hand in his, almost unable to comprehend the fact he was offering kindness to her. "We stayed off the radar for six weeks. I didn't even bake bread. Then, one day, Julia left our hideaway to get food. She never came back. I followed her path, and her scent ended at the grocery store. She just disappeared."

"Her scent stopped?" At her nod, he narrowed his eyes. "No other trace at all?"

She shook her head. "Nothing." She managed a smile. "But if they'd killed her, then they would have left traces, right? So, I think she's okay."

Slade studied her for a long minute, and she could almost see his mind working through the information. "Are you sure she didn't leave on her own? Why do you think someone took her?"

She frowned. "She's like my sister. She wouldn't have left me."

"How can you be so sure?"

"How can you even ask me that? Don't you have anyone in your life who would never walk out on you? Or someone who you would never walk out on? A bond that would stand through anything, no matter what?"

Something flashed in his eyes, a pain so sharp she felt it in her own heart, but it was gone almost instantly. "No," he said evenly. "I do not. That would not fit in my lifestyle, and it would be a liability. I don't do liabilities."

He was lying. He had someone. Her heart sank. "Who is it? A woman?"

His face became a cold visage of impenetrable steel. "There is no one," he said again, an edge to his voice, that made her wonder whether she'd been wrong. She'd been so certain that he had someone he cared about. "I don't like people enough to want to get that close. If you're correct that Julia was taken," he said, refocusing the conversation, "why did they take her alive instead of killing her like your mom and Marjorie?"

"Because they fought back? Maybe whoever it was tried to take them, too, but they chose to fight to the death instead of surrendering." A chill rippled over her at the idea. She knew her mom would have chosen death over succumbing to whatever horror had been hunting them for so long. "But Julia was taught to fight as well."

"Maybe they were ready for her. Maybe they underestimated your mom and Marjorie, and had upped their game when they went after Julia."

Her stomach dropped. "Julia was taught to fight. We both were. If they took her without a fight—"

"They had a plan." He sat back, clasping his hands behind his head. "What's so important about your little clan, Anya? Your mom and Marjorie were on the run your entire life. What were they hiding from?" He leaned forward suddenly, a gleam in his eyes. "Unless it was you and Julia they were hiding, not themselves. Maybe you and Julia were the targets originally. Did anyone else try to get to you over the years?"

"You think we're the targets?" Fear leapt through her, and she turned away quickly, pacing away from him to hide her face. "It wasn't us that my mom and Marjorie were hiding. We aren't the targets." But even as she denied it, she couldn't keep her voice from trembling.

"It is you," he said softly, apparently being a master at reading body language. Bastard. "You're the one they were hiding. You and Julia. Why?"

There was no way she was giving him the answer that would betray her. Besides, she didn't even know if it were true, at least for her. And if it was, even Slade couldn't be trusted with the truth. No one could. "I don't know if it was us," she said evasively, "and I don't know why. How would they have found us, anyway?" She turned to face him suddenly. "How did *you* find me? Who hired you?" She couldn't believe she hadn't asked that before.

"I scented you, and I don't know the name of the man who hired me. I never ask. They have no idea who I am, and I don't know who they are."

"You scented me? What does that mean?" How could he go around killing people without doing research on who he was hunting? She didn't understand how he could live like that. She knew it didn't really matter what drove him, but she needed a distraction from the line of questions he'd latched onto.

He didn't take his gaze off her, as if he knew exactly what she was doing, and was plotting a strategy to get the information he wanted anyway. "I was sent a piece of fabric of something that belonged to you. Once I locked onto your essence through it, I could track you no matter how far away you were."

She frowned. "What fabric? Can I see it?"

"I burned it, but it was a small piece of denim about two inches wide." He narrowed his eyes. "Do you remember losing a pair of jeans?"

"I left everything behind at the fire," she said. "Including jeans."

He drummed his finger on his knee. "So, we start with the warehouse."

"Start what?"

"The hunt for who is after you. I need to figure out what this guardian assignment means, and I'm guessing it starts there. I suspect Julia was taken by the same people who went after your mom and Marjorie."

"No, the warehouse was months ago." She shook her head. "We need to find Julia. This woman I was supposed to meet had information—" She stared at him suddenly. "You can track people through fabric? What about a wig?" She ran to the couch, grabbed her jacket, and pulled the wig out of the pocket. "This was what she was wearing. Can you track her?"

Slade's eyebrows went up, and he took the wig from her. He held it in his hands and closed his eyes, and went still, so still that she couldn't even tell if he was breathing. He didn't move for almost five minutes, but he finally opened his eyes. "Got her."

Her heart leapt. "Really? Is she near? Let's go!"

"Hang on." He balled the wig up in his hands, folding his hand over it until it was completely covered.

"What are you doing?" Smoke suddenly burst from between his fingers, and flames glowed. She lunged toward him and tried to pry his hands apart. "You're burning it? I need that! What if we can't find her your way?"

His arms were immovable. "My essence is on there now. It has to be destroyed. I can't leave any evidence of my existence behind."

"Damn you, Slade!" Frantically, she slammed her foot into his shin, but he didn't even flinch. "Stop it! That was my only connection to her!" The scent of burning polyester filled the air, and she coughed, pulling her shirt over her mouth as the smoke burned her eyes. "You're such an arrogant bastard!" Oblivious to the flames burning her palms, she pried desperately at his hands, but it was like trying to claw through steel with her bare fingers.

"Stop." His voice was soft. "I will find her. I never fail."

She sat back on her heels, tears in her eyes as she stared at him, feeling utterly lost. "How could you?" she asked. "How could you be such a bastard? You're so concerned with protecting yourself that you don't even care about how your choices affect anyone else?"

He met her gaze. "I never fail."

"And what if another demon rips out your heart? What if you *die*? Then what do I do? Pry your brain out of your dead body and use it like a GPS? You *bastard*. Open your hands!"

He did as she instructed, but they were empty. He'd literally incinerated it into dust so fine it had dissolved into the atmosphere. No ashes. Not a single shred left of the one tie she had to Julia. Anger burned through her, a feeling of helplessness. She lunged to her feet and shoved at his chest. "I don't care if you've lived in isolation since you were a baby," she snapped. "This is no longer about only you. It's *my* life, and I'm the one you're supposed to be protecting. You don't get to make unilateral choices like that just to protect your precious reputation. Damn you, Slade! This is my best friend who's in danger!"

He stared at her for a long moment, and said nothing. *Nothing.* Like he was some arrogant prima donna who didn't have to explain himself.

She paced away from him, struggling for control. She couldn't walk out on him now. He was her only link to the woman who knew where Julia was. "Was that why you did it? So you could control me?"

"No." He braced his forearms on his thighs, watching her. His eyes were tracking her every movement, and she suddenly felt like prey being hunted again. "I did it because survival matters. I'm going to be with you. If I can be tracked, then you can too. How long do you think until the assassins find you again? My guess is that there are several of them pacing the street outside, trying to figure out why our trail ends so abruptly."

She snapped her gaze to the walls. "They're outside?"

"I assume so. They can't see the entrance unless I am in their minds, but I have no doubt that they're close. We've been here a long time, long enough for them to track you."

Her heart began to pound, and her palms became clammy. Assassins hunting her? She was in so over her head. "Crap."

A small smile twitched at the corner of his mouth. "I am very, very good at what I do. I never fail. I want my life back, and the only way to do it is to see this guardian assignment through, so that is what's going to happen. Trust me."

"Trust you? So you can get back to your life of assassinating people, including me?" She shook her head, keeping her voice low, suddenly afraid that the demon could be on the other side of the wall, listening, planning, knowing exactly where she was. "I don't trust anyone, Slade. It's stupid to trust people, especially assassins!"

He cocked his head, studying her. "Yes, this is true."

She leaned her head back against the wall, suddenly too overwhelmed to think. "I can't do this," she whispered. "I can't defeat assassins. Three of them? I bake *bread*, for God's sake. What am I going to do? Shoot yeast in their eyes and blind them?"

"You're going to trust me. You have no other choice."

She gave him a skeptical look. "Would you trust yourself if you were me?"

"If I gave my word, yes. My word is my bond. I never go back on it. Everyone knows my reputation."

"Really?" She pushed off the wall and walked over to him. "You haven't made any actual promises to me, Slade. What is there to trust?"

He ground his jaw, and she could tell she'd caught him. She already knew him well enough to know that he was a loner, and the last thing he would *ever* want to do was bind himself to the well-being of another, or to owe anyone anything. If his word was truly binding to him, then to give it to her would be more than he would be able to do.

Finally, he said. "I accepted the position as your guardian."

"That's a deal you made with someone else, not a promise to me. Neither of us even know exactly what being my guardian means, except that it probably doesn't mean killing me." She gave him a challenging look. "Make me a promise, Slade. Promise me that you won't stop until Julia is saved. Promise me that you'll keep me alive. Promise me that you'll take on my hunt for Julia as your own. Then I'll trust you."

For a long moment, he said nothing. Then he shook his head. "I don't know what I can promise you at this time," he said. "I don't know enough about the situation."

Damn him. She turned away, pacing across the room. "Can you at least promise me you're not going to kill me? Ever?"

He ground his jaw. "No. I can't. I don't have any immediate plans to kill you, and at the moment, my intention is to be your guardian, whatever that entails, but I can't promise that it won't change in a week, or a day, or in the next thirty seconds."

Her stomach dropped at his honesty, and fear rippled down her spine. She'd been feeling safe with him, and his answer was a terrifying reminder of what she was facing. "Then how can you ask me to trust you? Trust you to do what?"

He finally shrugged. "I don't know. I guess nothing." He stood up. "Don't trust me. You're right." He held out his hand. "You ready?"

She stared at him. "You want me to go with you after you just said not to trust you?"

"You might not trust me, but you still have to make a choice. I have a lock on the woman who wore the wig. I'm going after her. You can come, or I can drop you off somewhere. But it's time to leave, because there's a demon outside that's getting too close."

Her heart stuttered, and she looked at the steel walls. He was her only link to finding Julia, now that he'd burned the wig. There was no decision to be made. "I'll go with you."

He nodded, giving no outward sign of whether he liked her decision. "Your choice," he said. "What method would you prefer for ensuring you can't reveal this location to anyone? I can blind you temporarily as we leave so you don't see where this safe house is, or I can wipe your memory of this location and everything about it. I always wipe memories, but for you..." Something shifted in his voice, a hitch that was barely noticeable. "I'll give you the choice to remember."

She suddenly recalled how he'd looked at her while they were kissing, making sure she knew he was the one kissing her, and her heart softened. This was a man who lived in absolute isolation, wiping the memories of everyone who knew he existed. He was invisible...except, he was willing to let her keep the memories. Allowing her to remember every detail about him was against every code he lived by, and yet he was making that offer. She realized that, despite his isolation and his life choices, there was a part of him that still burned for that human connection, just as she did. He wanted to be remembered. He wanted there to be someone in the world who remembered...and he'd chosen her.

The tension fled her body, and she knew then that although he was a man who didn't trust, he'd trusted her with the most important thing he had to offer...his existence. Suddenly, she knew what he didn't even know, that he would never, *ever* be able to kill her, no matter what.

She realized suddenly that she had no memory of arriving at the building. The last thing she remembered was agreeing to go with him, and then sitting on the couch. "Did you wipe my memory when we got here?"

He nodded. "Your shields go down when you sleep."

"Did you wipe it of anything else? Other than getting here?"

"Just the trip here." He glanced at the wall. "We need to go."

"Blind me." She said it without hesitation. She didn't want to lose a moment of memory. Being blind would make her completely dependent on him until she could see again, but she knew now that she would be safe with him, no matter what he thought.

He nodded. "Let me into your mind."

She felt his mental push immediately. Her instinct was to block him, but she forced her mind to stay relaxed, allowing him to enter. His presence was heavily masculine, strong, and deadly. She expected to hate it, but the intimacy of the connection with him felt good, safe, grounding...which was irony at its best.

"Lights out," he said softly.

The moment he said it, the room went black. She sucked in her breath, losing her balance at the sudden loss of visual reference. He was beside her instantly, scooping her up into his arms. She wrapped her arms around his neck and locked her legs around his hips, holding tight. His arm was solid against her back, holding her securely against him. "Stay quiet," he instructed.

She nodded, tucking her face into the crook of his neck to stabilize herself.

His muscles tensed, and suddenly, she felt him explode forward, moving so fast that her hair whipped against her face like razor blades. She recalled the times she'd seen him move quickly, and thought once again of her question earlier.

Was he part cat? Or something else? Something even more dangerous?

Chapter Eight

 *J*UST LIKE BEFORE, having Anya in his arms made him want her.

Slade swore as he eased to a stop in a dark alley several miles from the bar where he'd been murdered. The moment they were still, he released his hold on Anya's mind, but didn't release his grip on her waist. "We're here."

She lifted her head, blinking as she looked around. "That's so weird how you can turn my vision on and off."

"One of my many talents."

She let go of him and slid down, her body sliding across his in a decadent temptation that made his cock harden. He swore, grinding his teeth as he fought for control. He was going to have to stop touching her until he pulled his shit together. He had no time for being distracted by a woman, and he didn't have protocol in place for dealing with it, since he had always preempted it.

It was a completely different situation once he was already in it.

He dropped his hands from her, but she kept her hand on his side as she looked around. "Where are we?"

"A shitty area of Boston," he said. He scanned the area

around them for mental imprints that would suggest some-one or something was nearby, but the only thing he was picking up was the bouncer at the door of the bar.

"The kind of place where you do your business?"

He glanced at her. "You think people only get murdered in alleys?" He moved away from the wall, heading down the alley. "People get killed at black tie fundraisers. They die at State House dinners. They die at five star restaurants in the men's room. They die in their boxed seats at the op-era. That's where most people die."

She stopped. "I knew it."

He looked back at her. "Knew what?"

"That you're cultured. Refined." She gestured to his leather trench coat and jeans. "You don't walk around like that much, do you? You live some fancy, high class life, where no one would *ever* suspect you're an assassin."

He was surprised she'd bothered to notice. Most people didn't. "I'm going to have to wipe your mind if you keep being observant."

She grinned. "I forgot already." But as she walked up beside him, there was a definite gleam in her eyes, as if they shared some sort of bond. "Why do you do it? If you have all that money, why do you still go around killing people?"

"I like it."

As he expected, she stopped dead in her tracks, her eyes widening. "You *like* it?"

"I don't need the money. I don't know the people I kill, and I don't care if they're saints or sinners. I'm not saving the world or trying to rule it. So why else would I do it?"

"You *like* it? What, like you're a serial killer? Some sort of psychopath?" She looked faintly ill, and for the first time in his life, it bothered him to have someone look at him that way.

"Forget it." Gritting his jaw, he headed out into the main street, heading straight toward the basement door that was barely visible from the sidewalk. "Come on."

He didn't even bother to look over his shoulder to see if she followed him. He didn't need to. He was viscerally aware of every move she made. He could smell her shampoo, and her fear. He could hear the steady rhythm of her breathing. He could still taste her from that kiss. What the hell? He needed to focus.

Swearing, he opened his mind to the woman he'd tracked. She was inside, downstairs. He vaulted over the railing to the stairs that went below street level, then paused to wait for Anya to walk down them. Shit. He wasn't used to waiting for anyone. It took him off his game. "Wait out here," he said.

She put her hands on her hips. "No."

He swore. "I can't watch out for you. I need to be focused."

She raised her eyebrows. "If I stay out here and demon-boy finds me, but you're inside, what then? How does that satisfy your guardian thing? If I die, and you fail, does that mean you forfeit your second chance at life and go right back to hell?"

He narrowed his eyes. "You're a pain in the ass."

"And I'm right."

He let out his breath. Damn. He didn't like anything about this. He didn't like being bound to that red-haired woman he'd made the deal with. He didn't like having Anya with him. He didn't like having to make choices that were about anything other than what he wanted to do. How did his brother do it?

Shit. Now wasn't the time to think about his brother. He had to focus. "Then stay close, but don't bother me. This is what I do."

Anya paused. "What you do? Are you going to kill her?"

He didn't answer. He didn't kill unless someone paid him, but just about every other rule he lived by had been violated in the last twelve hours, so he wasn't going to make any promises. Instead, he pulled open the door and stepped inside.

It was dark, smoky, crowded, and filled with the scent of sex.

* * *

What kind of place was this?

Anya was shocked when she saw people half-naked, up against the wall, apparently having sex, or almost. There were people dancing, couples that were so tightly entwined that the beat of the music seemed to have merged them together. The music was low and sultry, and the mood of the place was sex, seduction, and illicitness.

There were several threesomes on the dance floor, so many hands and body parts that it was difficult to tell what belonged to who. One of the men in the nearest trio caught her staring, and he held out his hand to her, inviting her to join them.

She managed to shake her head coolly, trying to act like she belonged...but good God, she'd never been in this situation before. *Ever.* Aside from a few men she'd dated when she was younger, before she understood how dangerous it was to expose herself, she had stayed tight and low profile with her mismatched family, and this kind of world had not been hers.

Slade was staring at the corner, and she followed his gaze to shadows that obscured a door. He started to walk right toward it, but she caught his wrist. "Stop," she hissed.

He looked sharply at her. "What?"

"You'll scare her. You can't just barge in there."

"I'll catch her if she runs." He raised his brows. "Why? You want to dance first?"

Heat flared in her cheeks, and she dropped his wrist like it had burned her. "What? No."

He didn't turn away, however. He simply stared at her like he was devouring her with the heat of his stare. *I want to dance with you, Anya.*

She swallowed at the sudden rush of desire that burned through her. She glanced at the dance floor, at the couples moving to the music as if they were in the throes of passion right there in front of everyone. To dance with Slade like that? Good God. It was so sensual, so bold, so public. So not her. But it was also so tempting, calling to a part of her that she'd never acknowledged. God, no. What was she thinking? She didn't have time for that! "We have to find the woman with the wig."

"She's not going anywhere right now. She's in the bathroom. We have time. One minute. Two." Slade caught her wrist and drew her close to him, his touch like heated silk around her wrist. "I want this."

She swallowed, her heart hammering. She already knew what he could do to her sexually. She didn't need to come apart in his arms in public. Or in private, for that matter. He made her weak and vulnerable, and she hated that feeling. For heaven's sake, he'd made her pass out just from kissing her. Literally. She had to feel strong, not weakened. As badly as her body yearned to accept his invitation, she couldn't risk it.

"You know you want to," Slade said softly, his voice sliding beneath her skin like a tantalizing seduction.

"Yes, but I have the willpower to resist." Barely. She ducked under his arm, and scooted past him. "I suddenly have to go to the bathroom. Guard the door, okay?" She didn't wait for an answer as she wound her way across the dance floor, as desperate to get away from his temptation as she was to meet with the woman who might have information about Julia.

The man on the right had his hand on a woman's breast, and seemed to be trying to suck her soul out of her body through her mouth, the kiss was so deep. It was sensual, but also disturbing, like there was something predatory about it.

Suddenly nervous, she looked back over her shoulder. Slade was right behind her, less than six inches away. She flashed him a brief smile, then resumed her trek toward the bathroom, so very glad he was with her. This kind of place wasn't her world. Assassins weren't her thing. Her mom had taught her how to run and hide, to fight if necessary, but it had all been theoretical. She'd lived her life on the outskirts of society, protected by her mom and Marjorie, and she had no experience to draw upon to handle this.

I got it covered. Slade's voice brushed through her mind. *This is my world.*

She couldn't help the rush of relief. *Stay out of my head. You're broadcasting. You need to work on that.*

You're an ass.

Is that bad?

She reached the bathroom and pushed on the door. Slade was standing right beside her. "It depends on what you want to be," she said. "Now don't come in unless I'm in trouble. Women's bathroom and all, right?"

His gaze narrowed, and she had a sudden suspicion that he had never, ever, let something as simple as a gender restriction keep him from going where he wanted to go. "We need her to talk, Slade, not be killed. You know how to kill. I know how to talk. So let me do this. You can easily catch her if she runs, right?"

He pressed his jaw together, then looked past her, as if he were scanning the occupants of the restroom. Then he inclined his head. "You have three minutes." He moved in front of the door, facing the bar, his arms folded across his chest, looking like an ancient, immovable, deadly gladiator.

God, he was daunting. She wasn't going to lie. She was really happy he was on her team right now, but the more she got to know him, the more aware she was of the fact that if he ever changed his mind about being her guardian versus assassin, she was so dead, so fast.

She let out her breath. Right now, he was on her side, so she was going to have to take advantage while she could. "Be right back." She dragged her gaze off him and focused on the bathroom. Inside there was the woman who claimed to know where Julia was.

Had it been a lie designed to trap her? Or was there really a chance? There had to be a chance. She had no other connections to Julia.

She took a deep breath, then shoved the door open and stepped inside.

The bathroom was small and dimly lit. Paint was peeling off the walls. It stank of urine and alcohol, the kind of stench that would never go away no matter how many times it was scrubbed. Both stall doors were open, but there was a woman bent over the sink, splashing water over her face. Her hair was light brown, in a messy ponytail, but she was wearing the same jeans and black shirt that she'd been wearing in the bar. Her jeans were splattered with Slade's blood, a dark rusty brown that stood out on the blue denim.

"The warehouse on the corner of Hartford, and what?"

The woman whipped around, her blue eyes wide with shock. Water streamed down her face, and her complete lack of makeup made her look vulnerable and young, so different than the black-haired seductress who'd kissed her neck at the bar. "How did you find me?"

"Where is she?"

The woman spun around, and went back to scrubbing her face, frantic now. "Don't you get it? They know I was going to tell you. They won't let it happen." She shut off the water, and yanked her shirt off, revealing her naked torso. She wasn't wearing a bra, and her body was fit and strong, the complete opposite of how vulnerable and scared she appeared.

Anya cleared her throat, but didn't look away. She wasn't going to take a chance of losing her just because she wanted to give the woman privacy. "Who are 'they?' Who has her?"

"No." The woman grabbed a hooded gray sweatshirt from beside the sink and pulled it over her head. "It's not worth it."

"It is worth it! It's my friend's life!" Anya leapt across the bathroom and grabbed the woman's shoulders. "Please help me. I won't tell anyone, I swear."

"Don't you get it? They already know I met with you!"

"If they already know, then what's the harm in telling me?"

The woman pulled away, and yanked off her bloody jeans. "Because your friend isn't worth it to me."

"We can protect you. The Black Swan is with me. He will protect you."

The woman grabbed another pair of jeans and pulled them on. They were too loose, sagging in the butt. Her baggy outfit hid her slim body, and her messy hair and lack of makeup made her impossible to link to the woman in the bar. "The Black Swan is no match for them. No one is." She yanked her sneakers on and turned to face Anya. "Do yourself a favor. Forget about your friend and walk away."

Anya's fingers balled into fists. "Is she still alive?" If Julia was dead...tears threatened, but she held them back. If Julia was dead, she would honor her mother's wish and go into deep hiding. She would free Slade to live the life of the avenger. She was the only one left alive, and she had to stay that way. But if Julia was still alive, there was no chance she was going to abandon her. "Just tell me that much. Is she still alive?"

The woman paused, then inclined her chin ever so slightly in affirmation.

Oh, *God.* Julia really was okay. Anya's legs almost collapsed under her with relief. "Where are you going? To hide?"

"I'm going to disappear." The woman pulled a baseball cap on her head. "I lost everything by being seen talking to you. I'm not risking any more."

"If you lost everything, then what else is there to lose? Why won't you help?"

The woman walked over to the window, balled her first, and then slammed her hand through the glass. Anya jumped back as glass exploded from the force of the blow, raining down over the tile floor "Walk away, Anya."

I'm coming in. Slade's voice brushed over her mind.

No! Give me one more minute! She grabbed the woman's arm as she was about to climb out. "My mother was murdered, and Julia is all I have left. I can't leave her alone out there. I won't stop until I find her. If you were Julia, wouldn't you want someone to care? Wouldn't you want someone to find you?"

The woman looked at her, then back at the window. "They will *kill* you, Anya. Don't you understand? You need to disappear."

"I can't. Not as long as Julia is alive." She jutted her jaw out. "Everyone I love has been murdered or kidnapped. I don't have a lot left to lose. I'm going to find her."

The woman paused, searching Anya's face intently, as if she were trying to see the truth behind the words. Finally, she nodded. "Okay, then. My name is Beckett Harper," she said finally. "If they get to me, you and the Black Swan have to find me, the way you're looking for Julia. That's the deal. You find me if they find me first."

Anya realized suddenly that she'd touched a chord. Beckett was as alone as she was. She wanted someone to care if she went missing. Anya knew what that was like. No wonder Beckett was afraid. It was hard to go it alone. "I promise," she said. "Where is she?"

Beckett leaned forward and lowered her voice to a barely audible whisper. "There's a warehouse on the corner of Hartford Boulevard and Parker Street in West Bucknell, Connecticut. Go there after midnight tonight. Don't be early. That's all I can tell you." She grabbed the window frame, apparently oblivious to the shards of broken glass, and hoisted herself up.

"Wait! If you're going to disappear, how will I know if they're the ones that got you?"

Beckett paused, her blue eyes wide. "If they take me, they'll want others to know. They'll want me to be an example, just like you were supposed to be. You'll hear about it." Her eyes glittered. "You break your promise, and I will make sure they hunt you down. Do you understand?"

"I swear. I'll be there if you need me."

Beckett nodded, then hesitated. "Just so you know, I didn't know who I was working for. I didn't know what I was doing, and who I was hurting." Her voice broke, and her eyes were suddenly shiny with tears. "I'm sorry. Please know that."

Anya frowned. "Sorry for what? What did you do?"

But Beckett didn't answer. She just slipped out the window. There was the sound of her feet hitting the ground outside, and then she was gone.

* * *

Slade walked into the woman's bathroom just as Beckett dropped out of sight through the broken window. He listened to her footsteps scurry down the alley, and he tracked her as she fled down the street, moving quickly, with an innate grace that was beyond human.

He suspected he knew what she was.

Anya was gathering up Beckett's abandoned clothing. "Don't burn these," she instructed with a glare.

He almost grinned at the fierceness of her scowl. No one ever dared to order him around, and he kind of liked the fact that she treated him like there was a chance he was a decent human being instead of a relentless killing machine. She made him feel almost normal, and he wasn't sure he'd ever felt like that before.

"I won't burn them, but it's because I don't need to," he clarified. He appreciated her, but at the same time, she needed to understand that self-preservation came first, every time. If he had needed to infuse them with his psychic energy to track Beckett, he would have destroyed them. It was how it was. "I can always find her now." He kept part of his attention on Beckett as she got into a car that was soon moving quickly out of the area. Her energy was calm, and for the moment, she was safe. He let her go, turning instead to study Anya. "Why did you make a deal? I could have read her mind, or forced her to talk to us."

Anya paused, and frowned at him. "First of all, you can't read *my* mind. Maybe you can't read hers. Clearly, there are some people in this world who have the capability of blocking you."

"Not if I don't care if I hurt them. I could get in your head if I didn't care about the damage I would cause."

Her eyes widened. "You have this high and mighty moral code when it comes to killing, but not when it comes to frying people's brains?"

He narrowed his eyes, watching her. "I wasn't planning to fry your brain, but yes, death is different. Sometimes I need information. If the stakes are high enough, I'll do whatever is necessary to get it."

"Well, I don't believe in hurting others. There's enough pain in this world." She rolled the clothes up into a ball. "We need to go to Connecticut after midnight tonight. Can you get us there that fast?"

"Yes, of course." Her attitude grated at him, treating him like he was some kind of deviant for being willing to push boundaries to get the job done. "You'd never hurt anyone to help yourself?"

"No—"

"What if it would have saved your mother?"

She snapped a sharp glare at him. "Don't be an ass. That's not fair."

"No? Maybe that's my standard. Did that occur to you? That maybe I inflict pain on others only when it really matters. And where do you draw the line on what matters, Anya? Are your hands so clean?" He didn't know why he cared. He never cared what anyone thought. Ever. Damn. Why was he even getting into it with her? "Never mind. Let's go."

She didn't move, though, studying him. "I don't understand you," she said softly.

"Good. An assassin can't be predictable. You coming, or what?" He was feeling pissed off right now, and he didn't know why.

No, he knew why. Listening to the exchange between the women had made him think. It had made him remember. It had made him want to have that conversation with the one person in his life who mattered to him, who didn't even know he existed. He never thought about having an actual relationship with his brother, about what he had given up for his life, but listening to Beckett and Anya had made it impossible for him to ignore it, and he didn't like thinking about it.

He didn't like anything that Anya had brought into his life, in fact. He was royally screwed for blowing the contract he'd accepted for her death, even though he'd wired the money back into his client's account while Anya had been sleeping. He didn't like *at all* how much he wanted her physically. And it could serve no useful purpose that she was making him think and feel shit that an assassin couldn't afford.

Plus, he had to be a *guardian*. What the hell?

Then she smiled at him, a radiant, genuine smile that made his heart thunder to a stop. "Did you hear her?" she asked, her eyes glistening with excitement. "Julia is still alive, and she told us where to go. It's my first real lead. We have a chance!"

Shit. Shit. *Shit.* She was absolutely beautiful when she was happy. He wanted to yank her into his arms, pin her against the wall again, and lose himself until there was nothing left of who he was, and all that remained was her.

But he wouldn't. He'd learned that from his father. The more he wanted her, the less he could take.

Her smile faded. "What's wrong with you?"

"I want to fuck you." He knew it was crass, but he wanted to piss her off. He wanted her to hate him, so she would stop smiling at him like that.

Her smile faded, and she studied him speculatively. Unfortunately, she didn't look pissed. She looked thoughtful.

After a moment, she walked over to him. He stiffened as she neared, and shoved his hands into his pockets to keep from grabbing her. He glowered at her. "You're playing with fire," he warned her.

"Will you please do me a favor?" she asked, so politely

that he felt like he should be wearing white gloves and a top hat.

"Probably not."

"Go down on your knees."

He stood taller. "What the hell kind of request is that?"

"I want to be able to look in your eyes, and you're too tall for me to do that."

A part of him was curious. Another part of him was like, no way. He didn't get down on his knees for *anyone.* So, he compromised, and simply said. "Sorry. Not in my repertoire."

She sighed, and then looked around the restroom. He was actually somewhat fascinated watching her. She clearly had something in mind, and he was damned curious as to what it was. He wasn't used to dealing with people, or seeing them as living beings who had personalities and souls. They were either his targets, or he used them as a means to an end, whatever end that might be at that time, though every single thing he did was for two purposes: to protect his brother and to avenge his parents' murders.

Well…that had been his modus operandi until he'd met Anya, at which point he'd been forced to add protecting her to his list of life purposes. He wasn't going to lie, however. Anya was absolutely fascinating to him, and he kind of liked the fact that he had no choice but to hang out with her. Spending time with her didn't violate his two life goals, because he couldn't accomplish a damned thing if he were dead. So, he didn't have to cut her out. He had to stay with her for now. She was his mission, so he could indulge his curiosity about her without breaking his rules.

Her face lit up when she saw a small, plastic trashcan. She grabbed it, upended it in front of him, then stepped up on it, bringing her damn near exactly at eye level to him. He studied her, noticing the gold flecks in her eyes, and the extraordinary length of her lashes. They were dark, unnaturally so, and he suspected that she had put makeup on them to darken them. He wanted to see them without makeup, as they really were.

"You're trying to piss me off," she said.

He barely heard her, so fascinated by the way her lips moved when she spoke. Her lips were a soft red, no lipstick, just purely natural, and he liked it. He knew how they tasted, and he wanted to taste them again.

"Slade!"

"What?" Her hair was tumbling down around her face, a little tangled and disheveled, and sexy as hell. He took a lock of hair between his thumb and forefinger and rubbed it. The strands were smooth, like silk "Would you consider this soft?"

She blinked. "What?"

"Soft. If someone described something as soft, would this qualify?" He frowned. "I've never really considered that word before, but your hair makes me think of it."

A small smile played at the corner of her mouth. "There are different kinds of soft," she said. "There's soft, as in the sensation of the surface as your fingers brush over it, and there's also soft, as in really cushioned, like it would squish if you pushed on it."

"Like your breasts?"

Her cheeks turned red, and he swore. Shit. He hadn't meant to say that. He dropped his hand and glared at her. "What do you want?"

She smiled again, a half-smile that made his heart turn over. "I want to show you that soft is a good thing. Not just hair, but in every way. Close your eyes."

He shoved his fists deeper into his pockets. "No."

"Close them, Slade. Seriously. It's not like you need to see anything in order to know what's going on, right? Your mental tentacles are everywhere."

He scowled. "You're trying to mess with me."

"Oh, for heaven's sake, Slade. You're impossible." She shoved the bundle of clothes into his chest and he instinctively grabbed them. Then, she placed her hands on either side of his face. "If you want to be a better assassin, you have to truly understand people. Close your damn eyes."

He stared at her for a long minute. He knew she was trying to manipulate him, but a part of him was absolutely riveted by her. She was so far from what he was accustomed to. He knew that he was in no danger from anything or anyone if he closed his eyes, so finally, he shrugged. "You get five seconds."

She grinned, that same grin that made him want to lose himself in her, and he shut his eyes, cutting himself off from her. For a split second, he felt a sense of deep relief to be freed from her influence, and then he felt the warmth of her breath against his mouth.

He went utterly still, frozen in place, as she pressed a light kiss to the corner of his mouth. It was like a butterfly had brushed against his face, it was so delicate. Then, she did the same to the other corner of his mouth, her lips a whisper against his skin. *Hell*. He'd never felt anything like that before in his life.

He waited, taut with anticipation, for the next one.

No kiss came, but her fingers stroked along his jaw, her touch so light it was like a feather along his skin...except it wasn't a feather. It was Anya, her skin warm and sensual against his. He felt his whiskers rough beneath her touch, and the contrast of his whiskers against her skin was entrancing.

"Feels good, doesn't it?" The question was a whisper every bit as soft as her touch on his jaw.

He didn't answer, unwilling to break the spell she was

weaving.

He felt her smile, and then she kissed him again, this time, a real kiss, a kiss of lips barely parted, a kiss of tenderness and intimacy, a kiss of slow, sensual teasing, a barely-there kiss that promised a night of sin and seduction...and intimacy.

Blood raced to his cock, and lust boiled through him—

No. She whispered the command in his mind. *Don't. Let me.*

He went still, forcing himself to stay relaxed as she kissed her way along his lower lip, mixing in a light nibble, and the brush of her tongue. Her touch was so light, he could barely feel it, but his blood was thundering through him, searing every cell in his body.

She slid her lips along his jaw, and then down the side of his neck, kisses so light he would have missed them if he wasn't so intently focused on her. She brushed a kiss over his collarbone, and his entire body trembled in response.

Her hands settled lightly on his shoulders, as if to settle him, while she pressed a kiss to the center of his neck, into the hollow of his throat.

Jesus, Anya.

She pulled back then, and he opened his eyes. He knew that his need for her was stark on his face, but he couldn't do a damn thing about it. She made him transparent, and he hated that, but at the same time, there was something hot as hell about it.

She smiled, a triumphant, satisfied grin that was so arrogant that he wanted her even more. "That, my dear assassin, is why *fucking* someone is not always the way to go. Sometimes soft, slow kisses are so much better. Get it?"

"I got it." Yeah, he got it. "Do it again."

She laughed then, a light-hearted, engaging laugh that made him smile. "Maybe someday, if you're a good boy, but right now, we need to go to Connecticut. I assume we're going the same way as before?"

He wasn't sure that having her wrapped around him was the best idea right now. "We have time. We'll drive."

"Drive? You have a car?"

He raised his brows. "Of course I have a car. I have fifty-seven of them."

Her eyes widened. "Why on earth do you need fifty-seven cars?"

"Because I never know where I'll be when I need one. Come on." He took her elbow and turned her toward the door. Hell. He was going to have to walk her past all those gyrating people again? When he was this turned on? Shit. He'd always thought he had impenetrable discipline, but he was no longer so sure, at least when it came to Anya.

She didn't lose a beat in her questioning. "What does that mean? You have them stashed in assorted places around the globe?"

"Yep." He opened the bathroom door, and the scent of sex and lust hit him. His cock got even harder, and he swore as he urged her out into the room.

"Exactly how rich are you, Slade?"

"Richer than sin." He made it halfway past the dance floor, and he thought he was safe, when someone bumped into Anya, knocking her against him. His arm brushed against her breast, and heat poured into him.

She stared up at him, and time seemed to freeze for an instant. Then, suddenly, he wanted to be the one in control, the one who knew how it was really supposed to be. He tunneled his hand through her hair, a slow, sensual caress a thousand times more intimate than what she'd done to him in the bathroom. "It doesn't always have to be about fucking," he murmured. "And it doesn't always have to be like a butterfly's kiss. Sometimes, it can be pure sensuality."

Her eyes widened, and her hands went to his forearms. "We need to go, Slade."

"Yes, we do, but not for another minute or two." He shoved the bundle of clothes back into her arms, slid his other hand into her hair, and then kissed her.

Not just a kiss.

It was the kind of kiss that existed only in his fantasies...until now.

Chapter Nine

*A*NYA KNEW THE moment Slade kissed her that it was going to be different. At his safe house, the kiss had been bruising and intense, exploding through her so fiercely that she thought she would shatter.

This time, as he slid his arm around her waist and pulled her against him, she knew it was going to be a thousand times more dangerous.

And it was.

His kiss was pure sensuality. His tongue slid across her lower lip in a decadent invitation that made her belly tighten with longing that seemed to come from deep within her, from places in her soul she didn't even know existed.

He wasn't fucking her this time. He was ridiculing her attempt to show him what else there was besides fucking. Her kiss seemed like a five-year-old's innocent exploration compared to the pure sin he was pouring into her.

She wanted to lose herself to him, to surrender completely to his strength and his seduction, but she knew she couldn't. She had to stay focused, strong, and grounded, and there was no way that was going to happen if she kept kissing him. Somewhat desperately, she shoved against his chest. "Don't. We need to go—"

"We have time." He pulled her more tightly against him, his hands roaming her body as he moved to the music, dragging her into its seductive rhythm with relentless, unending kisses, and the slow, sensual undulation of his hips against hers. His powerful thigh slid between hers, pressing up against the junction of her thighs as he slid closer against her, moving like a wild predator closing in on his prey.

God, it felt good to be touched like that. To be held like she mattered. To be kissed like there was nothing in the world that existed besides this moment. She knew she didn't have time to enjoy his kiss, and she knew she didn't have the luxury of trusting him, but for one minute, one tiny minute, she wanted to forget about her life and who she was. For one minute, she wanted to simply breathe in the sensation of his strong body against hers, to feel his muscles flexing beneath her fingers, to taste his mouth, and to feel the heat from his body pouring into hers, easing the tension that had become such a part of her that she'd forgotten what it felt like not to be afraid.

You're dangerous. His voice was a private seduction drifting through her mind. *You make me want to forget about everything that matters to me.*

God. He felt the same way? His confession stripped away the last bit of her resistance, and she lost the battle to fight. All she wanted was *him.* Still cradling Beckett's abandoned clothes in one arm, Anya slid her other hand around Slade's neck and let herself melt against him. Her nipples ached where they pressed against his chest. Her entire being burned for his kisses and craved his touch, an aching need even more powerful than what he'd unfurled inside her at his safe house.

He groaned. *You're projecting.* He angled his head and deepened the kiss, teasing her with his tongue and lips, dragging her mercilessly into his sensuality. Fire licked through her, and when his hand slid to her ass, she couldn't stop the low groan that slipped from her lips.

He grasped her hair and pulled her head to the side as he kissed her collarbone, then her throat, and then the swell of her breasts—

Someone bumped them, and she opened her eyes to see a couple grinning at them. The man was tall and dark, almost as muscled as Slade, and the woman had straight brown hair and glasses, like a scholarly nerd who was being a bad girl by playing at the club. They both grinned at them, and the woman held out her hand to Anya in silent invitation.

"Oh..." Anya's fingers dug into Slade's shoulders. "No, thank you..."

"I don't share," Slade locked his arm tighter around Anya and spun her away. His eyes were dark and moody as he studied her. "You are too much of a temptation," he observed. "Everyone here wants to get you naked, both the men and the women. I thought I was special." There was an edge to his voice as his arm tightened around her.

Her belly tightened at the possessiveness in his eyes. "You are special," she said, her voice more breathless than she had intended. "You're the only one who gets to kiss me, right?"

He eyed her. "There is that." He locked his arm around her more tightly. "What the hell is it about you that is so irresistible? Tell me."

She shook her head, almost unnerved by the intensity of his stare. "Nothing. I'm just me." She became aware of others watching them, of the raw lust on the faces of strangers. Discomfort rattled through her, and she pushed at his chest, suddenly wanting space. She wasn't accustomed to being with men, certainly not one who was so intense, so sensual, and so overwhelming. Her life was with the three women who mattered to her, a foursome who relied on each other for survival, a foursome that had been shattered ruthlessly, leaving her vulnerable and scattered. "Let's just go."

She pulled away from him, and he let her go, an act which both relieved her and disappointed her. As much as she needed her independence, her yearning for intimacy with him was almost insurmountable. Forcing herself to walk away, she led the way out of the bar, but he stayed close, only a few inches behind her. The one time she glanced back, she caught him glowering at the other patrons, his "don't-fuck-with-me" stare clearly staking his claim on her.

"You don't own me," she hissed at him, embarrassed by his caveman persona...but at the same time, there was a part of her that was thrilled by it. She was so used to skulking about, trying to stay unnoticed, that it felt good to have someone so powerful on her side, making it safe for her to be noticed.

"No, I don't," he agreed as they reached the exit. "But I accepted responsibility for your safety, and I'll do whatever it takes to make sure people know that if they approach you for any reason, it's me that they'll have to deal with." He held the door open. "I don't own you, but I own your safety, so you're going to have to deal with it. I'm not going anywhere."

Her heart skipped a beat, but she gave him a steady gaze. "You're not going anywhere...until it suits your purposes. And then you will."

He met her gaze for a long minute, so long that a flicker of hope rushed through her. Maybe he wouldn't leave... Then, to her dismay, he nodded once. "Until then."

"You still might kill me?"

His gaze flicked away from her for a brief second, scanning the streets outside, then he nodded for her to leave. "I don't make promises unless I know I can keep them, Anya."

"I know." Feeling strangely deflated, she moved ahead of him to walk down the empty street. It didn't matter how amazing his kisses were, or how powerful he made her feel by protecting her. She could never forget that he was on her side only because someone had trapped him into protecting her. If he found a way out, she was dead, and he was gone.

She couldn't forget that.

Ever.

* * *

Slade shifted gears in his Lamborghini, pissed off as hell.

Usually, the chance to drive this baby gave him a sense of peace. He liked the luxury of it, a vast change from sleeping in alleys and jungles like he did on missions. He was damn proud of it, and he liked the way he could feel every single bump in the asphalt, a machine of raw power and pure luxury. It made him feel civilized, like there was a chance that he wasn't only a monster. It was his moment of humanity.

This time, however, he couldn't concentrate on the car. His entire focus was on the woman sleeping in the passenger seat next to him. He could hear every breath she took. Her scent seemed to wrap around him, overwhelming the fine leather smell of his seats. She was small and fragile, vulnerable even, and his entire body vibrated with awareness. He didn't let anyone into his personal space, but for some damn reason, he'd invited her into his car. What the hell? He could have rented a car. He could have used one of his throwaways. But he'd selected *this* one and offered her a ride, which went against every rule he had.

No one *ever* got to see anything about him that was real. It was critical to his survival. So, why the hell was she there? Sleeping, like she was supposed to be there.

She mumbled something in her sleep, and he looked over at her. Her brow was furrowed, and she was shifting restlessly. Instantly, his irritation vanished. He brushed one hand over her forehead, soothing her energy. She relaxed under his touch, falling into a deeper sleep again. Satisfaction pulsed through him. He'd given her peace, not just peace before a death kiss, but actual peace.

It felt good. Really good. He wasn't used to doing shit like that. He hadn't done it on purpose. It had been instinct, something she'd drawn out of him, even though he hadn't even known it was a part of him.

Frowning, he glanced at her again, inspecting her more carefully, trying to figure out his reaction to her. He liked having her beside him, sleeping. Last time, when she'd slept in his safe house, he'd felt like shit, because his kiss had drained her to the point of exhaustion. She'd slept because he'd hurt her.

This time, she'd slept simply because she was tired, and because she felt safe enough with him to sleep. He, the shadow whose only purpose was to kill, had provided her with enough security to allow her to sleep. He knew it, because he'd picked it up from her as she was falling asleep. She was shielding her thoughts less and less from him, and her emotions when she'd gotten in his car had been evident.

The moment she'd sank into the soft leather, she hadn't been thinking about how nice his car was. She'd been thinking about how good it felt to sit down. She'd been thinking about how tired she was. And she'd been thinking about how she had to remember not to trust him, even though she'd never felt this safe in her life.

She'd never felt this safe in her life.

It was strange that she felt that way about him. It irritated him, because he wanted her to be smarter and more careful than that, but at the same time, it made him feel like he was worth something more than delivering death.

She'd fallen asleep five minutes after they'd gotten on the highway, and he liked it. He loved looking over at her and seeing her beside him. It was probably wrong in a thousand ways that he felt that way, but he did. Hell, she could drool all over his fine leather seat, and he wouldn't even care.

Which was why he'd been in such a bad mood. He lived by a careful, rigid set of rules, and she was making him break them one after another. It made him vulnerable, and he couldn't afford that...but at the same time...he didn't regret any of it.

Which was even more disturbing.

He hit the gas, inching the needle up even higher, muttering a litany of swears that usually made him feel better. They didn't work tonight, because he was beginning to realize why he'd invited her into his car, and why he liked having her sleeping next to him.

Her irreverence, her determination to make him see her as a person, her loyalty to her friend, and her vulnerability had gotten under his skin.

He liked her. He likcd her as a person. As a human being. *As a woman.* Which was a major problem.

Since the day he and his dad had found his mom and sister murdered, he'd learned how important it was not to let anyone matter to him. Not just because it hurt like hell when something happened to them, but because if they mattered to him, it made them a target. His dad had made a lot of enemies in his work, and it was those enemies who had decided to make him pay by taking away something he loved.

The instant that Anya had given him that first stare in the bar, the one where she'd looked right into his soul, he'd noticed her as a woman. In that instant, she had become a weapon that his enemies could use against him. She had become a target. And now, after he'd tasted her? Talked to her? Listened to her stories? Every minute he spent with her upped the ante.

Shit. Letting her get into his car had put a bulls-eye on her forehead. Her scent would be in his car, and it would never leave. He'd smell it every time he got in his car, and so would anyone else who came near it, anyone in his line of business, that was.

What the hell? What personal code was he going to violate next? Was he going to start visiting his brother for a beer on Fridays? Might as well paint a target on his head as well.

The thought of his brother becoming linked to him made a cold sweat break out on his forehead. For a brief moment, he couldn't focus. All he could think of was a bullet finding his brother between the eyes, or a claw plunging into his heart, all because someone had found out he was related to the Black Swan. Swearing, Slade fought to bring his mind back under control, shoving aside the fear that haunted him every second of his life, that somehow, some way, he'd screwed up and his enemies would realize he had a brother who had been raised with humans, had no preternatural powers, and no defenses against anyone wanting to cause him harm.

His brother was a heart surgeon, a genius who spent all his time in people's chests saving them with his skill, as opposed to Slade, who spent his time in people's heads, killing them with his thoughts and his kiss. Even if being related to Slade wouldn't make his brother a target, it didn't matter. Slade would still never let his brother know that the anonymous funds that had supported him all his life was blood money from a brother he wouldn't want to know.

Slade tightened his grip on the steering wheel, swearing as he tried to get his thoughts under control, to get back to the equilibrium that enabled him to live his life. He took a deep breath, steadying the balance of oxygen in his body as he forced himself to analyze the situation.

There was no doubt that Anya had knocked him off his game. The only logical solution was to cut her loose. Easy. Clean. Simple.

He couldn't walk away from her, because then he'd die, and he'd leave shit undone that couldn't be left undone. Plus, he didn't want to hurt her. He didn't want to kill her, let anyone else hurt her, or even let her go.

Oh, hell. This was bad. Really bad. He couldn't let her go, but every second with her was making him want her more. He liked the attitude she gave him. He liked how she didn't hide the fact she cared. He liked touching her, kissing her, and testing her.

He hadn't been lying when he'd said he wanted to fuck her. The urge had gotten stronger with each passing minute. Yeah, the soft kisses she'd given him had blown his mind. So, maybe not fuck her. Maybe a long, slow night of seduction, sin, and nakedness. Yeah, that sounded good.

Too good.

Shit.

He glanced over at her as he shifted lanes, blowing past the other cars as if they were parked on the highway. Maybe he *should* fuck her. Maybe ten minutes of hard-core, sweaty, no-feelings-involved fucking would clear his head and get her out of his system.

She'd tucked her hands beneath her chin, her face relaxed in her sleep. She looked younger, almost innocent, so different than the life he led. Scowling, he reached over and brushed a lock of hair away from her face, tucking it behind her ear.

Shit. Her skin was soft. Her hair was silky smooth. She was fragile and vulnerable.

All words that weren't a part of his life.

Scowling, he wrapped both hands around the wheel and flexed his shoulders, staring grimly at the highway in front of him. He had to focus. He couldn't be derailed. He couldn't—

The sign for his brother's exit loomed ahead.

Instinctively, he flicked his blinker on and began to shift lanes to get off the highway. He always stopped by to check on his brother when he was in the area. It would take an extra five minutes to drive by and check his energy. Three times Slade had actually spoken to him, but he'd wiped his mind afterwards. All the other times, he'd simply observed from a safe, strategic distance, making sure his brother was still okay, living a normal life devoid of murdered parents and an assassin brother. It had been too long since he'd checked on him. It was time.

He took his foot off the gas, and the car slowed down to take the exit, but as he did so, Anya's eyes opened. She looked at him blankly for a second, and then yawned. "We're here already?" Her voice was sleepy, making her sound even more vulnerable.

He gritted his teeth, and hit the gas again, flying past the exit. Now was not the time to check on his brother, not even for a moment. He was too far off his game. It wasn't worth the risk. "Not yet. You can sleep more. Another half hour."

He already had Anya to deal with. Now wasn't the time to stop by and visit his brother. He wasn't sharp right now, and he didn't need the assassins on Anya's tail to track them to the house of a guy who The Black Swan had absolutely no professional reason to visit.

Anya went back to sleep immediately, showing just how exhausted she was. She'd been on the run her entire life, alone for two weeks since Julia had disappeared. How much had she slept? Eaten? Done anything except look over her shoulder for the danger hunting her?

Did she have any skills at all? Was it pure luck that she was still alive?

And why the hell was she so important that the red-haired woman had pulled him back from death so he could protect her?

He still hadn't answered that question, and it was bothering him. It was important. If he understood why the two of them had been chosen, he would know how to keep her safe.

He had to find out more, before it was too late.

Chapter Ten

WAKE UP. SLADE'S low voice brushed through Anya's mind with an urgency that had her alert instantly. *But don't move.*

Her eyes snapped open. She'd slumped down in the seat while she was sleeping, and had her head on his right thigh. Awareness leapt through her as she felt his thigh muscle flex beneath her cheek. Oh, God, really? Her face was almost at his crotch? Horrified, she started to get up. He pressed his hand to her shoulder, his fingers digging hard in a silent message not to move.

She tensed. *What's going on?*

Something has been following us for the last six miles. Stay down. I'm going to try to shake it. His quad tensed beneath her cheek again, and the car sprang forward, throwing her back against him. The back of her head hit his stomach, and she looked up to see him glance in his rearview mirror. His face was taut, his eyes dark and focused. He looked like a predator, primed for assault, not like the man who'd kissed her senseless such a short time ago.

She swallowed, watching his face as he searched the

night, searching for some indication of how much danger they were in. *What is it?*

I can't get a read. I don't know.

Anya's heart began to pound, and she had to fight her instincts not to sit up and look behind them. She forced herself to lie still, so conscious of his hand on her shoulder, his grip steady and secure, even though she had no intention of moving. *What can I do?*

I was going to ask you that, he replied. *What can you do?* The car swerved to the left, and then to the right, as he navigated the highway. *Do you have any combat skills?*

She almost laughed at his question. *I can bake bread. Will that help?*

No paranormal skills at all?

She bit her lip as a thought crossed her mind, but she shook it off. *No. None. I told you.*

He didn't answer, and she risked a glance at him. His jaw was set, his gaze intense as he scanned the highway. *Don't lie to me, Anya. You're more than a run-of-the-mill human being. You have to be or you wouldn't have gotten me for your guardian. I can't help you if you don't talk to me.*

She tried to block him from her mind. *I'm not lying—*

Come on, Anya. I'm still alive because I can see through lies and illusions. What the hell is going on? I— He cut off their connection suddenly, and she felt his mind shift in another direction. *It's the demon.*

Sudden pain exploded in her mind, and she gripped her head as he unleashed some sort of psychic energy outward. He threw up a shield between them almost instantly, but the damage had already been done. She gasped, holding her head, fighting nausea and dizziness.

"Shit. Sorry." Slade laid his hand over her forehead, and just as suddenly, she felt waves of healing energy flooding her mind. "I'm not used to being connected with anyone. I didn't protect you before I hit him. You okay?"

"Yes. Just give me a second." Whatever he was doing with his hand was incredible, and she closed her eyes, letting his energy heal the fragmented parts of her mind. "How are you doing that?

"It's how I heal myself."

She didn't ask how they could be that connected, and he didn't offer it. After a moment of silence, she spoke up. "Is it gone? Can I sit up?"

"Yeah." He released her, and she scooted back to her side of the car. The guardrail was flying past so quickly it was a blur, and she peeked at the speedometer. "Oh, God. Really?"

"Speed is my thing," he said, knowing what she was talking about without her even saying it. "It's okay. I almost never crash."

"Almost never?" Then she saw the curve of his mouth, and realized he was teasing her. "You choose *now* to get a sense of humor? You almost gave me a heart attack." But her tension eased, and she closed her eyes and leaned back in the seat, trying to calm herself. "How did the demon find us?"

"It tracked us from my safe house. You're easier to track than I am. We're going to have to work on that."

"How?"

"I don't know yet." He sounded irritated, and she looked over at him.

He was gripping the steering wheel tightly, and his jaw was flexed. He looked tense and irritable, nothing like the man who had kissed her so sensually at the bar. He also didn't look like the smooth, cold, killing machine of a few moments ago. He looked like a man who was human enough to let something annoy him.

She turned sideways in the seat, studying him. "You're changing," she said. "It's harder for you now, being cold. You feel more. Does that endanger you?"

His jaw tightened. "I'm fine."

She sighed. "Liar," she said softly.

He ignored her.

The miles clicked past silently for a few minutes, then he spoke. "You know things you aren't telling me," he said. "You have suspicions about why you and your family are being hunted. I need to know."

She checked her mental barriers to make sure he wasn't sniffing around her mind. "I don't know—"

"Give it up, Anya." His voice was hard as he gunned the engine. "You need to tell me what you know. Now."

She bit her lip, looking out the window. She'd been taught not to trust anyone, especially men. Her mother had drilled that into her head, and experience had reinforced it. "I have never told anyone," she said quietly.

He didn't say anything for a moment. Then, finally, "It's that dangerous to you if someone finds out?"

She glanced at him, surprised by his astute understanding of the situation. "Yes."

He let out his breath and shifted gears, the car's engine whining as he pushed it. "You're right not to trust me," he finally said. "No one is worth trusting with something that important."

She was surprised by his comment. "You're not worth trusting?"

"No. I'm not. I have no idea what choices I'm going to have to make in the future, so no, I'm not." He looked over at her. "Doesn't mean I'm going to stop demanding you tell me what I need to know, but you're right not to tell me. But I do need to know."

She raised her eyebrows at his dichotomous remark.

"Seriously with that circular logic?"

"Yeah." He changed lanes, moving closer to the breakdown lane. "I'm running blind right now. I have no idea what the hell to do with you, or how to protect you. I'm used to being in complete control of the situation and the information. I'm not now, and that makes me ineffective and puts us both at risk."

She leaned back against the seat, wishing she could tell him. She was exhausted from a lifetime of carrying a secret that could destroy her. She wondered what it would be like to turn her problems over to someone else for help...then she shuddered. The mere thought of exposing herself like that was terrifying.

"We're here." He interrupted her thoughts by pointing to her right.

She sat up and looked out the window. There was a six story, gray cement warehouse looming up beside the highway. It looked old and abandoned, with broken windows on the top floors, and debris scattered in the empty parking lot. Her heart sank when she saw it. If Julia was trapped there, it couldn't be good. "Do we just go in?"

"We'll see." He eased off the gas as he sped down the ramp, circling under the highway and emerging by an entrance to the parking lot. He idled the car at the edge of the parking lot, and they both leaned forward, inspecting the tall, desolate building.

"I don't sense anyone there," he said, after a moment.

She glanced over at him. "You can sense people?"

"Yes. I can track their mental energy. There's nothing in there that's alive."

Anya's heart sank, and sudden tears threatened. "We're going in anyway," she said. "Beckett said Julia was here."

"She told you to come here. There's a difference." Slade eased the car into the parking lot, the engine humming as he drove up next to a massive garage door. He parked the car and turned off the engine. He draped his arms across the steering wheel, scanning the building. Anya could feel his energy drifting across her skin, and she knew he was scanning with his mind again.

"Anything?"

"No." He looked over at her, his face stoic and grim, the face of a predator about to go into battle. He looked every bit the assassin, a lethal force of nature. "Ready?"

She nodded, suddenly very glad he was on her side right now. "Ready."

* * *

Slade's skin prickled as he eased open the door to the warehouse, the lock hanging in shattered bits after he'd taken it apart. He'd had to take down an extensive alarm system, which made him wary. Someone was hiding something significant, but he couldn't pick up a live presence. There was something about the place that was setting off his internal radar, but he couldn't place it.

Maybe it was just that it had been a long time since he'd walked into an unknown situation. He was always on a mission, always on a plan, but this time, he was going in blind.

Maybe it was the fact that Anya was right behind him, vulnerable. He didn't like that she was here, but there was no way in hell he was leaving her alone, without his protection. Everything about this situation was wrong, but it was their only lead, and he had to find out what the hell was going on.

His mind constantly scanning for psychic energy, he stepped inside the dingy warehouse. It was dark and dusty, with just the tiniest sliver of light beading through the cracks in the upper windows from the highway streetlights.

"What's that smell?"

The moment Anya asked it, he caught the scent too. It was very faint, but once he noticed it, he could smell it clearly. The deep, rich scent of musk, mixed with something more human. He froze, his entire body slamming into alertness. Son of a bitch. He knew that scent. He knew that scent much too well.

Memories assaulted him, ugly memories, and he shut them out, shifting into assassin mode. *Stay close.* He moved silently across the floor, tracking the scent from the far side of the warehouse.

Anya was right behind him, moving as silently as he was. He couldn't hear so much as her breath, and actually glanced over his shoulder once to make sure she was there.

She was.

On the other side of the warehouse, there was a steel door. He headed right for it, and when he reached it, the scent was stronger. There was blood mixed in with it now. Sweat. Fear. Pain. *Shit.*

He knew what he was going to find behind that door. *Stay here when I go in. Guard the door.*

Anya shook her head. *No way. I'm going with you.*

He swore, even as he put his hand over the electronic alarm panel. *You don't want to go in there, Anya.* He reached out with his mind, using his psychic energy to connect to the electronic impulses in the alarm system.

She paled. *Is Julia in there? Do you sense her?*

No one is alive in there. The alarm cleared, and he put his hand on the doorknob, using his mind to manipulate the electronic key pad.

Is someone dead *in there?*

He shrugged, and turned the doorknob. *Stay here.* But as he moved through the door, she followed him, keeping so close he could feel the heat from her body. He found sixteen infrared cameras, and he disarmed them carefully with psychic pulses.

It was pitch black inside, and he pulled out a micro flashlight. He flicked it on, and the thin beam of light illuminated a long corridor of cells with steel bars, and impenetrable glass, a sight he'd seen before, one that he knew all too well. Son of a bitch. That's why he'd been tapped for this assignment.

Beside him, Anya sucked in her breath. She let out a yelp of distress, and tried to run past him to check the cells. He caught her wrist and yanked her back behind him. *No.*

She went still as he eased forward, constantly scanning the surrounding area for mental signatures of someone approaching, but it was still clear. They reached the first cell, and he directed the thin beam of light inside.

There was a mattress, a toilet, and a set of shackles.

Anya pressed up against his back, looking past him. *Oh, my God,* she whispered. *What is this place?*

It's a staging area. He moved down the corridor, faster now, checking each cell. Every one was empty, but most were soiled. Blood. Urine. Semen. *Hell.* It was just like before, as if he'd never left it behind.

He felt Anya tense. *A staging area? For what?*

They reached the end of the corridor and ran out of cells to check. All of them were empty, but they'd had occupants recently. He turned to face her, studying her face closely. "Shifters, Anya. It's a staging area for shifters. The black market trading of shifters. Panthers. Cougars. Wolves. You name it. Captured for experimentation, sexual use, breeding."

Her face drained of color. "Oh my God."

"Julia's a shifter, isn't she? Your mom? Marjorie?" He paused. "You?"

She stared at him, her eyes wide with fear, and then he knew. He knew what she hadn't told him. She wasn't simply a shifter. "You're a white leopard, aren't you? All of you. White leopards." The holy grail of the shifter black market. Worth billions of dollars to the merciless elite who wanted to use them as breeders, for their pelts, as sex toys to be hidden in the dungeons of the depraved. Almost extinct, now, wiped out by hunters. No wonder she hadn't told him. No wonder he'd been selected. Son of a bitch.

She shook her head silently, but her terror was stark on her face. "White leopards don't exist," she whispered.

"Oh, yes they do. And I know that, because my mother was one."

Her eyes widened. "She was?"

"Yeah." He looked grimly down the empty corridor. "I know all about this shit," he said softly. "Every last detail." He met her gaze. "My mother was murdered because of it. So was my dad, and my younger sister. This trade is the reason I am what I am, and it's the reason I kill."

Chapter Eleven

ANYA FELT LIKE her world was closing in on her. She hadn't wanted it to be about this. Her mother had told her, but she'd never imagined *this*. She could still taste the fear of each occupant, and she could smell the blood and the pain they'd endured. And Slade...the icy cold steel in his eyes made her shiver. He was no longer the man who'd kissed her. He was an assassin, pure and simple, and in that moment, she knew he would kill anyone who stood in the way of what he wanted to accomplish.

"You're a white leopard, aren't you?" He asked it again, his voice low and cold, warning her against lying.

So, she didn't. She gave him the truth: "I don't know for sure."

His eyes narrowed. "How do you not know?"

She looked past him, down the hall. "Can we talk later? Can we look for any signs of where they went first, and then get out of here?" The place made her skin crawl. Was this where her mom and Marjorie had been held when they'd escaped so long ago? Or worse? And Julia, dear, sweet Julia.

Slade swore under his breath, and muttered something about being distracted by her as he turned away. "Five minutes," he said. "We're out of here in five minutes." He strode over to the nearest cell, and put his hand on the lock.

"Can you pick up something?"

"I'll be able to track anyone who has been here recently." He handed her his flashlight. "Look for Julia. I don't know her scent. If you find it, tell me. I'll do the rest."

Her heart pounding, Anya raced toward the nearest cell. She hesitated at the threshold, suddenly terrified. She felt as if she stepped across that line, the door could slam shut behind her, just as her mother had warned so many times. She'd heard her mother's cries in her sleep, nightmares from the days she never talked about...in a place like this.

She looked back at Slade, who was still at the doorway, moving his hands rapidly along the steel and glass. Energy was humming off him as he scanned for residue. "Slade?"

He glanced at her, then paused when he saw her looking at him. "What's wrong?"

"You never make promises unless you know you can keep them, right?"

"Yes."

"Will you promise me that you won't let me be locked in here? That you'll get me out, no matter what?"

His eyes slid to the steel doorframe above her head, and then back to her face. Something shifted in his eyes, something she couldn't decipher. "I promise I will not let you get trapped here," he said quietly, his voice like steel.

Relief rushed through her, and suddenly she felt like she could breathe again. "Okay. Thanks." She flashed him a smile, then stepped into the cell. She glanced back as she moved inside. Slade was standing in the doorway, watching her. With the flick of his finger, he could slam the door shut and lock her in.

For a split second, terror ripped through her. What if she were wrong to trust him? What if she'd just made a fatal error? What if—

My mother was in a place like this, Anya. I would never let you stay. His voice was clipped and tight in her mind, but she felt the wave of pain deep in his soul, buried so deeply that she could sense only the faintest hint of it, but it was the kind of pain that burned all the time, every minute of every day. He was a man of steel, but she saw more. She saw what he didn't even let himself see.

He wouldn't leave her there. She was certain of it. For the first time in her life, she was safe. Yes, she was in the most dangerous setting she'd ever been in, but she had no doubt the Black Swan would unleash his greatest wrath to keep his promise.

"Thank you."

He nodded. "Four minutes left. Make it count."

"I will." She took a deep breath, and turned toward the cot. Trusting him to keep her safe, she turned all her focus on her search. She raced over to the bed, and ran her hands over it. The mattress was filthy, tainted with fear and blood, but not Julia's presence.

Sweat beading between her shoulder blades, she raced out of the cell and into the next one, running to the cot. Again, she was assaulted with the scent of the person who'd been there last. It had been a woman. Terrified. Desperate. Not Julia. Tears filled Anya's eyes as she tore herself away, sobs seizing in her chest as she ran to the next cell, and then the next. So many women had been here, dozens of different scents, so much pain, so much fear. God, it was so much worse than she'd ever understood. With her hands on their beds, she could sense the emotions of those who had been there before. So much suffering, so much pain.

The fifth cell she was in had housed a woman, but there

was also the scent of a male twisted through it. A partner? Or an assailant? Or another prisoner? Tears blurred her eyes as she stumbled for the door, barely able to focus through the assault of psychic energy.

Slade caught her arms as she tripped on the threshold, his grip firm and strong. "Anya." His voice was low and steady. "Look at me."

She obeyed, barely able to focus on his face through the tears streaming down her cheeks. "It's so awful," she whispered.

"You need to focus on Julia," he said firmly. "Just Julia. Don't get overwhelmed by everything else. You have a mission right now. I'm assimilating everyone else. You need to find Julia. Focus only on her, and dismiss everything else. Got it?"

She took a deep breath, and pressed her trembling hands to her forehead. "Okay, yeah, I'm all right. Keep going. I'll be fine."

He gave her a skeptical look, but released her.

She took a moment, pushing her hair out of her face while she tried to focus. He was right. They were here for Julia. She bit her lip, and strode into the next cell. She sifted through the scents, and quickly dismissed them, somehow managing to keep her focus.

"Thirty seconds," Slade called out. "We can't risk staying longer."

Urgency pulsed through her, and Anya sprinted into the next cell. Then the next. Then there was only one left. She raced into it, and dropped to her knees by the cot. For a moment, she could smell only the scent of bear shifter, a male, and then, beneath it, she caught a faint scent she recognized. *Julia.* "She was here, Slade! Here!"

He appeared in the doorway almost instantly, then strode across the floor to crouch beside her. He placed his hands on the mattress, and closed his eyes. She felt his energy circulate around her, prickly and powerful, as he breathed in Julia's scent. "Can you track her? Do you have a strong enough lead?"

He swore under his breath. "Almost." He slowed his breathing, and she felt the surge of energy that he summoned as he poured it into the mattress, trying to create that bond with Julia.

The seconds ticked by, and the back of her neck began to prickle. She instinctively looked out into the hall, fear creeping down her spine, a signal she had long ago learned not to ignore. *Slade. Someone's coming.*

He didn't answer, but he poured more energy into the air around them, until it began to crackle audibly.

Fear continued to build inside her, and Anya rose to her feet. *Slade.* Her heart began to thud, and she edged toward the door. Danger was getting close. She couldn't pinpoint what she was sensing, but she had no doubt. *We need to get out of here—*

She hadn't even finished it when the door clicked and began to slide shut. She lunged for it, but she knew she'd never make it in time. Terror ripped through her, and then suddenly Slade grabbed her and bolted for the door, slipping them through the opening a split second before it slammed shut.

He swept her up in his arms and raced down the hall, toward the steel door that led to the rest of the warehouse...a door that was now closed. *Slade—*

Psychic energy pulsed through the air, and the lock clicked. Slade ripped the door open and sprinted through the opening, bursting into the open area of the warehouse. He stopped sharply, keeping her close as he scanned the area. "No one's here. Let's go." He took off with her toward the car. Moments later, they were on the highway, moving so fast they were nothing more than a blur.

Anya's heart was pounding, and she felt like she was going to be sick. She couldn't clear her mind of the sight of that cell door closing on her, that terror that she was going to be trapped. She bent over, trying to regain her breath while Slade drove. "Are they following us?"

"Not right now, but I expect they'll be closing in on the place any minute. It was some sort of security system that picked us up. The doors closing was an automatic response, but I'm sure people were alerted." He hit his hand on the steering wheel. "I never make a mistake with a security system. It must have been something I've never encountered. Shit. They're good, Anya. Very good."

Anya leaned back in the seat, her hands shaking violently. "Did you get a fix on Julia?" she asked. "Tell me you can find her." The thought of Julia being chained up in that cell was debilitating. What were they doing to her? Had she already been sold to some psychopath, already chained in his basement to be his plaything, impossible to ever track?

"I'll find her." His voice was grim, edged with enough tension that she looked over at him.

"You weren't able to get enough of a lead on her, were you?"

"I got some. I can work with it."

"Oh, God." Anya leaned her head back against the seat, unable to stop her hands from shaking. "My mother told me about places like that," she whispered. "That's why we ran. She and Marjorie escaped when they were pregnant with Julia and me. No wonder they were so scared of being found." She closed her eyes, trying to breathe. She needed to focus now, not freak out. "We need to go back. We need to find the people who did it." Even as she said it, she felt sick.

"I'll go back. Not you." The engine revved as they hurtled down the highway. "You can't be near there. They'll know what you are in an instant. If they realize what you are, they will stop at nothing to acquire you." He looked over at her. "No one knows about you, do they? That's why only Julia was taken."

"I don't even know if I am one." She sat up, alarmed as she suddenly realized the implication of his plan "You're going to leave me alone while you go back?" Even as she asked it, she felt like a fool. Since when was she afraid to be on her own? Since she'd acquired a demon assassin and experienced the depravity of the world that had been hunting her for so long.

"There's one place you'll be safe." He didn't look at her, and didn't slow down. "It's not far."

Anya leaned back against the seat, and took a deep breath. Her hands were still shaking from being in the warehouse. She looked out the window at the guardrail hurtling past, trying to process what she'd seen, to correlate it with everything she'd learned from her mother over the years.

Slade said nothing, but his face was intense and focused, and she knew he was doing the same thing she was.

Finally, she broke the silence. "You've been there before?"

"Not to that one. To others." He exited the highway, the wheels screeching on the ramp as he sped off it, racing through streets that were almost empty at this late hour. "There's a black market for shifters, Anya. It's powerful and ruthless, and involves a lot of high rollers. Money. Lots of it."

"And how do you know about it?"

He sped down a ramp toward a closed garage door. Anya flinched, gripping the door handle as they got closer and closer to the closed door, still moving quickly. "Slade—"

The door opened at the last second, admitting them just before they crashed into it. He didn't slow down, hurtling straight toward another closed garage door. She grimaced, tensing as they sped toward it, but that also opened at the last moment, averting a head-on collision that would have killed her.

"Oh, God." She took a deep breath, trying to relax. "Is it possible for you to be a little less terrifying when you drive?"

He glanced over at her, his dark eyebrows going up in surprise. "What are you talking about?"

It figured. The man was so entwined with speed that he couldn't even comprehend that hurtling top speed toward a solid wall could be daunting. "Never mind." She twisted around, watching the door close behind them just as fast. As she turned forward, yet another garage door appeared.

This time, even though she knew that it was going to open, she still couldn't keep from grimacing or pulling back as the car hurtled toward the garage door. It opened again just long enough for them to speed through, but this time, as it closed, she felt Slade watching her.

"It's timed to precision," he said. "I can't slow down or we'll crash. Just close your eyes."

She glanced over at him, surprised that he'd actually taken time to register her fear. "You're not as insensitive as you want to be, you know." She decided to watch him instead of the next door they were approaching. How many damned doors were there anyway?

His jaw tightened. "I'm extremely insensitive. I'm an expert at it."

She almost laughed at his tension. "It's okay to notice the emotions of others, Slade. It's a good thing."

He glanced over at her as his car shot through another garage door. "No, it's not. It's the most dangerous thing I could ever do. Don't try to make it happen. Understand?"

There was a desperation in his voice that made her heart turn over, making her wonder, once again, how he had gone from a boy who noticed his mom's flowers to the man who took lives without hesitation. She nodded. "I understand," she said softly, sighing to herself when she saw his shoulders relax slightly.

A man who couldn't afford to feel. She'd never met anyone who didn't want to feel. She couldn't imagine how empty his life was...but at the same time, a part of her envied him. Wouldn't it be great not to live in terror? Not to awaken in the middle of the night having a panic attack that she'd never find Julia? To never have to worry that if she stopped running, that the weight of her grief would crush her so severely she'd never be able to stand up again?

She sighed, leaning back in her seat as she watched their progress through the tunnel. She counted ten doors that they sped through, each of them taking them deeper and deeper underground. Eerie green lights marked their way, casting them in a sea-green glow as he drove deeper.

Finally, Slade eased the car to a stop in front of a cement wall. The garage door slid shut behind them, and then the platform the car was on began to rise, moving quickly and silently upward, like an elevator. He unfastened his seat belt and opened his door as the platform continued to rise. "Let's go."

"Where are we?" Anya hurriedly unfastened her seat belt, and stepped out of the car just as the platform stopped beside a set of massive steel double doors.

Ignoring her question, Slade walked over to them, looking up at a flashing light above the door. She felt that same mental push from him, and then the doors slid open, as if he'd opened the doors with his mind, which he probably had. "Come on in." He stepped through the doors without looking back, and without waiting for her. His shoulders were tense, and his voice was clipped. "Welcome to my home."

Chapter Twelve

$\mathscr{S}$LADE DIDN'T WANT Anya in his home.

He wanted to toss her back into his car and pretend he'd never made this choice.

But he didn't.

He just stepped back, letting her walk past him into the foyer of his sanctuary, the safe house he most considered home, the one that was so well-hidden that no one could ever find it, unless he showed it to them. It was his private oasis, the place where he could relax completely, where his solitude was unbroken.

No one had ever touched the inside of the place. He'd built it himself, unwilling to allow a single person to know it existed. It was pure and complete isolation, and yet he'd just let Anya into it.

What the hell was he thinking?

His pulse hammering out of control, he folded his arms across his chest and watched her as she walked into the entryway, her eyes wide as she scanned it. "It's beautiful," she whispered.

Some of the tension eased from him, and he shrugged. "It's okay."

"No, it's not okay. It's beautiful." She walked over to the Picasso that he'd hung by the door, leaning forward to study it. "It's an original, isn't it?"

"Yeah." He shifted, uncomfortable. "Let's go in. Come on." He walked to the French doors that separated the foyer from the rest of the place, and pulled them open. But when he turned to allow her to precede him, he found her standing in front of the Van Gogh that he'd added just last year.

His heart skipped when he saw her expression. She was completely riveted by the drawing, her lips parted in silent awe as she studied it. Her expression was completely unguarded, enchanted by the drawing that he'd coveted for so long before he'd finally acquired it. He knew instantly that she saw the same beauty in it that he did. It was a long-forgotten sketch, one that only a handful of people even knew existed. It wasn't famous, it wasn't prestigious, but it was raw and powerful in its beauty and expression.

He walked over and stood beside her, studying the sketch again. He hadn't been here in months, despite the fact it was his favorite place to be. It simply didn't fit his life to stay in the same place for long, but that meant he didn't get to see the things he'd acquired that mattered to him.

Like the sketch. It had taken him years to convince its owner to sell it to him, yet he'd studied it only a few times since he'd acquired it. The isolation of the landscape was bitter, and the silence of the peasant farmer was raw as he fought the arid earth to forge a survival in a world that meant nothing. Slade had felt a connection to it the moment he'd seen it on one of his missions, recognizing the author of the unsigned work instantly.

"It's the same kind of loneliness that surrounds you," Anya said quietly as she lifted her finger to trace the shape of the man. "It breathes the anguish of a parched earth and shattered soul, trying desperately to find one drop of water or ray of sunshine to sustain life."

Slade's throat tightened as her words raked over him, articulating exactly what he'd felt when he'd first seen it. "It's just a drawing."

"Liar." Her voice was soft, non-judgmental. "It's how you feel every day, isn't it? You're that peasant farmer, even though you're surrounded by luxury, money, and have the freedom to do anything you want."

"I'm not a peasant farmer." He stepped back and scowled at her. "Come on. Let's go in."

She turned to face him, her hands on her hips. "This life you live is going to break you," she said, watching him. "It already is. No one can live completely alone, without any kind of connection to anyone."

Emotions warred within, trying to be heard and felt, emotions he wanted no part of. "I'm not alone," he said.

Her eyebrows went up. "No?"

"I have you, don't I? Irritating me, invading my privacy, and forcing me to save instead of kill."

She studied him, and then a small smile curved her mouth, a smile that made his heart skip a beat. She was just so damned enchanting, so dismissive of the darkness of the life he worked so hard to lead.

"Hell," he whispered, moving closer to her. "I don't need this from you."

She lifted her chin so she was looking up at him, una-fraid, unabashed, and unrepentant even though he was crowding her. "I think you do, Slade. Maybe I'm the one who was sent to be your guardian, and not the other way around."

He fisted a lock of her hair, tugging on it. "I don't need to be saved."

"We all need to be saved," she said, not pulling away.

"From different things, yes, but we all need to be saved." She put her hand on his chest, over his heart. His muscles twitched beneath her palm. "You need to fill that horrible emptiness inside you before it eats away at you completely."

He didn't need this kind of psychotherapy. He really didn't. He knew that he should just turn his back and cut her off, not even acknowledging her. But he couldn't. There was just something about her that compelled him, something that made him want to drop to his knees and beg her...for what, he didn't know, but there was something she had that he needed desperately. Something he wanted. Something he burned for so deeply that it hurt. "And you? What do you need?" He slid his hand around to the back of her neck and drew her closer, so close that he could feel her breath against his mouth.

"To save Julia," she whispered.

"No." He grasped her jaw, his finger sliding along her skin. "What's broken inside you so badly that you can't breathe anymore? What shadow follows you everywhere you go, every second of your life? What's your secret, my white leopard?"

Tears swam in her eyes, but she tightened her jaw. "I'm not broken."

"Then neither am I. We're both a couple of winners." Then, before he could change his mind, and before she could pull away, he kissed her.

* * *

Slade's mouth was decadent temptation. His kiss was pure power, sliding through her like a predator taking control of his prey. It was his death kiss...only it wasn't. She could feel the heat pouring from him into her, as if he were offering part of his soul instead of taking hers.

She knew she shouldn't kiss him again. But just like before, the feel of his mouth on hers was impossible to resist. Her entire body craved his, her soul ached for connection, and her skin tingled with the need for his touch.

He was broken, an empty wasteland where his soul had once been, but she knew there was something else inside him, something fighting to stay alive in the arid desert that consumed him.

Anya. His voice caressed her mind, slipping into her consciousness with silky ease as he slid his fingers through her hair. His touch, his kiss, and his voice were so gentle, touching her heart in a way that his rough, against-the-wall seduction hadn't been able to.

She leaned into him, fisting the front of his jacket as she kissed him back, unable to tear herself away from him. His body was sheer muscle, shrouded in darkness and strength. He was a mystery, a shadow, a man who didn't exist...and yet he was solid and strong beneath her palms. He was real, at least for her, a killer who stole life more easily than he gave it...and yet, his kiss seemed to ignite something inside her. Something fierce. Something brave. Something that fit her more than spending a life running away did.

He pulled her closer against him, deepening the kiss. With a sigh, she capitulated, allowing herself to melt into him. She wrapped her arms around his neck, her nipples aching at the feel of his hard chest against her breasts. Heat flushed her body—

"Shit." He pulled back suddenly, jerking his hands back from her. "Sorry."

She blinked, trying to regain her equilibrium. "It's okay."

"No, it's not." He ran his hand through his hair, looking unsettled, an emotion she doubted he felt very often. "I almost killed you in my safe house, and I wasn't even trying. I can't risk it. I have no control when it comes to you." He glared at her, as if it were her fault, and then he spun around, jerked open the French doors, and strode into the main part of his home.

Anya stared after him, startled by his display of emotion. Then, the faintest ray of hope began to blossom inside her. The Black Swan was coming to life, for her. Because of her. She was beginning to matter to him. Her chest tightened, and she had to swallow back the sudden lump in her throat. She couldn't believe how incredible it felt to matter, to have someone who cared, despite his best efforts not to. She'd lived in fear her whole life, on the run, and now, suddenly, she had someone in her corner who believed in standing strong and fighting back, who was willing to help her do it.

Strength seemed to pour through her, and she pulled her shoulders back. She might be weakening him by making him more human, but he was giving her self-confidence and courage she'd never had before. The horrible shifter holding center that she'd had nightmares about her entire life had finally become a reality, and yet, for the first time she could recall, she didn't feel scared.

She felt strong, and she owed it to Slade.

Chapter Thirteen

*S*LADE DIDN'T TURN around when he heard Anya's soft footsteps enter the kitchen. He never allowed anyone to approach him from behind, but with her, he didn't need to turn around. He trusted her completely. Already, he knew the sound of her walk intimately, and knew exactly where she was, how fast she was moving, and what her mood was. He could envision the sway of her hips as she walked. He knew the way her hair was curling over her shoulder. He could already see the way her mouth was pressed tight, as if she were trying to hold back what she wanted to say.

She strode into the kitchen and took a seat at one of the black leather bar stools by the center island. "Why do you have four stools if you've never let anyone in here before?"

He took a dish of chicken stir-fry casserole out of the freezer. He didn't bother to ask how she knew he'd never let anyone in there before. He just liked that she'd figured it out. He wanted her to know that the fact she was in his house was a statement of exactly how deeply he trusted her. Not that he *trusted* her, because he never trusted anyone, but yeah, she was here, and that was big. "Because I like it that way." He flipped on the oven and tossed the pan into it.

"You want something to drink?"

She raised her brows at his answer. "Water would be great."

He thought of what she'd ordered in the bar. "No tequila this time?" He glanced over at her, and for a split second, all thoughts fled from his mind. Her elbows were on the counter, her chin propped up in her hands, her eyes at half-mast as she watched him. In his kitchen, on his stool, taking up space he'd never allowed anyone to occupy. The scene was so intimate and domestic that he froze, emotions warring between raw terror and a fierce longing.

Her eyes widened at his expression, and her breath caught. "You're afraid of me? Why?"

He grabbed a beer out of the fridge and took a long swig. He braced his hands on the counter, trying to pull himself together. "Chicken okay with you? It's all I've got in the freezer. I haven't made anything new in a while."

Her gaze flicked to the oven. "You bake casseroles and freeze them?"

"I like to minimize the number of times I leave here when I'm in town. I make a supply so I don't need to go out and get food." He turned away and grabbed a glass from his cabinet. All his glasses were pristine and unused, covered with a light coating of dust. He grabbed one and shoved it under the faucet to rinse it off. The finest crystal available, and no one had ever used them before. "No big deal."

She said nothing, and the silence stretched for so long that he finally looked over at her. She was watching him, apparently waiting, because the moment they locked gazes, she repeated her question. "Why are you afraid of me?"

He scowled at her as he set her glass of water in front of her, making sure to add crushed ice and filtered water from the fridge. He never cared about that, but for some reason, he wanted to do it for her. "I'm not afraid."

She grabbed his wrist as he started to pull away. "Slade," she said softly. "We're facing something huge that we don't understand. It probably has to do with my background and yours, but we don't have answers. If we screw up, we're both dead, and so is Julia. We need to communicate and trust each other if we're going to survive this."

He stared down at her fingers locked around his wrist. He could flick her aside so easily, but he didn't. He had no interest in making her release him. There was something about her delicate fingers encircling his wrist that made everything inside him settle, as if he could take a deep breath for the first time in his life.

He dragged his gaze from her fingers and looked at her. He never gave anyone answers to anything they asked him, unless it served his purposes, but for some reason, he wanted to tell her. Not a lot. Just a little. Just enough that she would know something about him other than the fact he killed. She was so embracing and emotional, he felt like an empty wasteland in comparison. Something inside him needed *her* to see he was more. "My mother and my sister were murdered because of my father's work." He shrugged, keeping his tone casual, even though the words he spoke literally defined his entire existence. "Their deaths taught me that when you care about someone, it makes that person a target."

Her face softened. "I'm sorry you had to learn that lesson."

"I'm not." He flipped his hand over and took her hand in his. He began tracing circles over her palm. He was trying to distance himself from her emotionally, but it wasn't working. He needed to touch her, to feel her, to hold her. Somehow, he needed to reassure himself that she was real, not a ghost or a shadow like he'd always been. "It's a critical lesson to grasp. Only a selfish bastard would let anyone into his life."

She cocked her head. "Or a man who understood that sometimes love is worth the risk."

"Love?" His fingers tightened instinctively around hers. He hadn't thought of the word *love* in a long time, not since the day he saw his father crumble in grief at the death of the woman he loved. "Love makes a man weak. It makes him vulnerable. It makes him do stupid shit."

She raised her brows. "Like what?"

He flattened his palm against hers, measuring her fingers against his. So small, so dainty, so fragile. "Like going on a rampage to kill your wife's murderers and getting yourself killed in the process, leaving behind a nine-year-old kid who knows about nothing except loss and revenge." His stupid father. After a lifetime of honing his skills to perfection, he'd lost his shit and gotten himself killed just because the woman he loved had died. When the old man had been murdered, Slade had also committed himself to revenge, but he'd learned from his father's mistakes, and he'd been strategic and smart. He'd wiped out the bastards, gotten rich as sin in the process, and had established a career that made sure no one ever messed with him again.

Anya tightened her fingers around his. "I'm so sorry, Slade," she said softly.

He stiffened, realizing he'd said more than he intended, and realizing he wanted to say even more. He wanted to grab his beer, sit down next to her, and tell her every sordid detail of his life...which was stupid and weak. She was too damned tempting. "It's fine," he said coolly, releasing her hand. "It's long over." He turned away to grab some plates from the cabinet for them to use for dinner.

She watched him, her eyes seeing more than he wanted her to see. "So, by having me stay here, you're making me a target?"

"Yeah." That much he wanted her to know.

She raised her brows. "You do realize that I'm already a target, right? Three assassins were hired to kill me before you added to my burden with your treacherous, relentless enemies."

He grinned, unable to hide his amusement at her word choice. "I know. That's the only reason I brought you here. You attract the bad sort, and this is the only place I really trust."

She snorted. "I attract 'the bad sort?' Back at ya, big guy, right?"

"Yes, true." He set the plates on the counter, then braced his palms on the granite, studying her. "But even so, my life is different," he said, unable to keep the urgency out of his voice. He had to make her understand. "You're a target for something having to do with shifters. We don't know what. But I have enemies in a thousand different places. People want to hurt me, and they want me to do things for them. Not a single one would hesitate to use you if they thought it would hurt me, or control me. There isn't a chance in hell I *ever* would have brought you into my life or my house if I'd had a choice, both for your sake and mine. But you have to stay alive, and this is the only place I truly trust." But even as he said it, cold seeped through his gut as the enormity of what he'd done settled on him, as he recalled the shock of finding his bloodied mother and sister. "I shouldn't have done it," he said suddenly. "I shouldn't have brought you here." If she were killed by one of *his* enemies, he would have no one to blame but himself.

Swearing, he turned away, lacing his hands on his head. Why the hell had he made this choice? Why? She was screwing with his mind, his perfectly ordered world, and everything that had kept him alive and sane for so long. What the hell? He couldn't—

Her hands slid over his shoulders, and he froze. "Don't touch me."

"Turn around."

"Get away from me."

"Slade. Turn around."

Slowly, gritting his jaw, he obeyed her. She'd apparently crawled across the island, and she was now sitting on the granite, her feet dangling, her face at eye level with his. She set her hands on his shoulders, studying him intently. "Listen to me, Slade. My whole life has been spent in fear of being hunted down. We had no home, no money, and no security, but it was okay, because we had each other. We had complete trust in each other, and that made us stronger. We never would have survived that long if we hadn't had such a tight bond."

He could feel the warmth of her words, the love entwined around each word she spoke about her makeshift family. For a split second, envy rushed through him, the cold, lonely green of jealousy. He could barely remember his childhood before all hell had broken loose, but he had vague flashes of feeling safe and loved, especially by his mother. The way Anya spoke of her family made him want to see what he'd forgotten, to remember what he'd lost, to be able to hold it the way she did. "Tell me about your mom," he said. "Tell me something."

She smiled softly, her eyes distant as she revisited a place in the past. "When I turned sixteen, I really wanted a sweet sixteen party with tons of friends. I hated the fact that I had no one except the three of them. So, my mom spent three days cutting out massive pieces of cardboard and decorating them to look like the teen celebrities I idolized. Julia took me out shopping for dinner, while Marjorie and my mom decorated the cabin with more balloons, streamers, and candy than I'd ever seen in my life." She smiled.

"They had a disco ball, speakers blaring music, and every celebrity I'd ever idolized was there, in full-scale size, for my party. It was amazing. She had so little, and was able to create exactly the party I'd dreamed of."

Slade grinned, watching her eyes sparkle as she told the story. He'd never cared about celebrities, unless he'd had to kill one, and he'd never bothered with friends, but at the same time, the warmth and love in her eyes as she told the story touched him. "I've never created anything good," he admitted. "I wouldn't know how to. Your mom sounds like she was an incredible woman."

Anya grinned at him. "She was the best," she agreed. "But that's not the point." She held out her hand to him. "The point is that we'll be stronger if we connect with each other. It might make me vulnerable to your enemies, but if I don't find Julia, I have nothing to live for anyway, so it doesn't matter to me." She smiled. "Besides, I think you need to matter, Slade. You need to realize that someone cares whether you get home at night."

To his surprise, something tightened in his throat, and he turned away for a moment to regain his focus. When he turned back, Anya was still holding out her hand. "Don't keep pushing me away, Slade. Let me in. I need this, and so do you."

He stared at her hand for a long moment. A part of him desperately wanted to accept her offer, to believe that he would be stronger if he were teamed up with her. Maybe he would, but that wasn't enough of a reason to endanger her. "I won't risk you like that."

She searched his face. "Don't you understand that if we fail, then I die? What does it matter if your enemies target me, if I'm already dead? Or if I'm locked up in that cell so I can be sold to some bastard who wants to knock me up and give him a shifter baby?"

He went cold, absolutely ice cold, and grabbed her shoulders. "Don't say that."

"It's the truth! I don't want to end up like that just because you're too afraid to let me in! Don't you understand? We don't even know who is pulling the strings, why we both got chosen for this plucked-from-death miracle, or what's coming next! We have no one to trust except each other. You can't do this one alone, Slade, so just stop it, focus, and let's make this work!"

"Dammit, Anya! Why are you so ready to make yourself vulnerable? You should be scared of me, of my life, of these bastards, of it all, not sitting here telling me that I need to get cozy with you!"

"I am scared!" she shouted at him. "I'm terrified! I have only three people in my life that matter. Two of them are dead, and the third is being held by horrible monsters. I live in a constant state of panic that I'm not running away like I'm supposed to, and absolutely terrified that all my mother's sacrifices to keep me safe are going to be for naught because I'm still going to end up in the hands of the bastards that nearly broke her the first time! So I could use a little support from you, instead of you pushing me away like that!"

He stared at her, shocked by her outburst. She seemed to have her shit together so completely all the time. He'd had no idea of the depth of her fear. She was trembling now, tears of fury glittering in her eyes. "Shit. I'm sorry." He didn't know how to fix it, how to make it right.

She shook her head. "It's fine, Slade. I just..." She looked at him. "I'm just stressed and tired. I know how dangerous everything is, but it doesn't do any good to dwell on it. I'm not used to being on my own, and I need to be able to count on you. Please, be on my team. Don't push me away."

He ground his jaw. His instincts demanded he keep his distance from her, but she kept dragging him back in. He'd managed separate himself from his brother all these years, no matter how strong his urge to connect, but for some reason, Anya was different. Maybe it was because she was so relentless, pushing at him to let her in. Maybe it was because she'd lived in darkness her whole life. She was no stranger to death, to fear, to hardship, but somehow, she'd kept her heart alive, and she'd managed to retain a view of life that had long since left him. He wanted to be a part of her world. He wanted to see and live through her eyes...and he couldn't afford that.

But at the same time, he couldn't let her go.

He'd made a promise to keep her safe, and both their lives depended on it. Silently, he took her hand in his and pressed a kiss to her palm. He didn't know what, exactly, he was promising her. He knew it wasn't to bond over love and connection, but at the same time, he was offering her something more than what he understood, trying to cross that chasm into her world.

Her face softened and she smiled, a smile so tender that part of the gritty steel around his heart seemed to crack. "I accept," she said. "Thank you."

He nodded, relieved that she understood without forcing him to articulate that which he couldn't explain. He leaned on the counter, his hands flanking her hips, somehow needing to be close to her, close enough to breathe her scent and absorb her energy, to reassure himself that he was right to trust her. He caught the same delicate scent as before...but this time, he noticed another scent underlying it. Something earthier. Something he recognized.

He met her gaze, not pulling back. "Tell me about the white leopards."

She paled. "Slade—"

"I'm here, Anya. I'm sticking with you. I brought you into my place. My fate is entwined with yours. It's time to let me in."

She lifted her chin. "You said you never make a promise you can't keep. You wouldn't promise not to kill me before."

He narrowed his eyes. "What do you want me to promise?"

"That if I tell you the truth, that you will never repeat it to anyone, that you will never betray me, and that you will never let anyone read the knowledge in your mind. You will do whatever it takes to make sure no one ever knows what I tell you. *Ever.* No matter what the cost to you."

Ever? No matter what the cost? "That's a tremendous promise," he said, after a moment. "I have no idea what the future will bring. I can't trap myself."

"I know." She didn't back down. "But I can't accept less."

He stepped back, grabbed his beer, and paced the kitchen. The only thing that kept him alive was the ability to do whatever it took to survive no matter what the moment brought him. He had no loyalty to anyone, except his brother, and that made him agile. If he carried her secret, protecting it would be a burden that he'd have to shoulder his entire life. Hell, he didn't even know what he was promising, since he didn't even know her secret.

He took a long drink of his beer, aware of her watching him, and waiting.

"Is it so bad to have something to live for besides killing people?" she asked softly. "You have enough money. Maybe it's time to let something else matter."

"I already have something that matters," he snapped.

Her eyes widened, and he swore. He hadn't meant to reveal that.

"What is it?" She leaned forward, her fingers wrapped around her glass. "Who matters to you, Slade? I know there's someone."

He turned toward her, frustration roaring through him. "What if I have to choose? What if I have to make a choice between him and your secret? What then?"

She stared at him, not even reacting to his veiled admission that there was someone else in his life. "You find a way to do both," she said simply.

"What if there's not? What then?"

"You find a way to protect both." She leaned forward. "Don't you understand, Slade? There's always room for more goodness in your life. It just makes you stronger."

"It makes you vulnerable," he snapped.

She sighed. "You just don't understand, do you?"

"I understand fine. I—"

"When I was born, my mother had tattoos put on the bottom of my feet. They're an ancient rune designed to keep shifters from shifting," she said. "I've had them my whole life. I've never shifted, but I don't know if it's because of the runes, or because I'm not a shifter."

He swore, realizing she was telling him her secret. He wasn't ready to commit to her yet. "Don't tell me—"

She stood up. "My mother was a white leopard. So was Marjorie. So is Julia. Am I one? I don't know for sure, but if I had to say, I think I am. I think that if I took the tattoos off my feet, I would shift." She walked over to him. "I'm a white leopard, Slade. The most prized, most endangered, and most hunted shifter alive. That's my secret. You might not have given me your promise with your words, but I know I have it. I trust you."

Slade stared down into her vibrant blue eyes, fear tearing through him at the enormity of what she'd shared with him. Not just that her family were white leopards, but how to expose hers. Her secret would make her a target of all the worst scum he'd ever met, collectors who had the money, power, and ruthlessness to get whatever they wanted. "Why did you tell me?"

"Because you need to know, and because you need to realize that you can make that promise to protect me." She met his gaze. "And because I trust you."

Something shifted inside him, something warm and real, something he'd never felt before. His heart thudded, once, then twice, as if it were beating for the first time in years. How could she have offered him this? Her secret, her identity, her truth was all she had. Her mother had died because of it. And she'd given it to *him*?

"Was I wrong?" she asked. "To tell you?"

Yes. He wanted to roar his denial, to berate her for being so naïve, to tear the knowledge out of his brain. He wasn't in the business of protecting secrets, of preserving confidences, of making choices to benefit someone else. He didn't even know how to do that. "All I know is how to live by myself," he said. "I only know how to protect myself."

"What about 'him?' The one you mentioned earlier. Don't you protect him?"

"Yes, but—"

"Slade." She clasped his hands, her fingers warm and delicate in his roughened ones. "You're so much more than you realize. You never would have been chosen as my guardian if you weren't worthy. Accept it. Accept what I gave you. Let it make you stronger."

He gripped her fingers, something surging inside him, something desperate, something that wanted to step into the role he'd been given. What if he *was* more? What if he could do something greater than what he'd accepted as his life and his fate? What if he could do something as simple and tremendous as preserving the spirit of this incredible woman standing before him? He touched her hair, running his fingers along the tangled strands that fell across her shoulders. But how could he make a promise like that?

But even as he asked it, he knew it was too late. The moment she'd shared her truth with him, he'd accepted responsibility for protecting it. It didn't matter whether he officially promised her or not. He'd made it the moment she'd told him the truth.

She smiled, triumph gleaming in her eyes. "You don't need to say it. I can read it in your eyes."

He glared at her, sliding his fingers to the nape of her neck. He was pissed, but at the same time, there was a part of him that was deeply relieved, even excited. He never would have made that promise, but now that it had become a part of him, it felt right. It felt good. It felt powerful. "You manipulated me," he said, scowling at her.

She nodded, unrepentant. "It appears to be the best way to manage you."

"I don't like it." His fingers tightened along the back of her neck.

"I know."

"But I admire it."

Her face softened, and he felt the tension ease from her body. He realized then that despite her bravado, she'd been worried. "Thank you."

"I don't admire many people." Her skin was unbelievably soft, so silky that he almost felt like he'd soil her simply by touching her with his tainted hands. "No one, actually." Except his brother.

She smiled, raising her hand to rest it on his chest. "I don't trust very many, so I guess we both must be incredibly fantastic to win each other over."

"Fantastic?" He leaned forward, just close enough to catch a whiff of her scent. "Fantastic is a superficial, vapid, stupid word." She smelled incredible. He wanted to taste her again. Not drain her. Just a whisper of a touch. "You're not fantastic." He lightly brushed his lips along her jaw. *God, yes.* "You're courageous. Loyal. Smart as hell." He kissed the curve of her neck, his gut tightening when she sucked in her breath. "You're irritating and manipulative."

"Which you admire." Her hands went to his shoulders and she closed her eyes, going utterly still.

"Which I admire," he agreed softly as he traced intimate circles along the back of her neck. "You're the most alive, vibrant, warm, engaging, demanding person I've ever met." He lightly, so lightly, caught her earlobe between his teeth.

She made a small noise of pleasure, her fingers tightening on his shoulders. "I'm the only person you've ever actually noticed," she said. "You have nothing to compare me to."

He pulled back, searching her face. She opened her eyes, meeting his gaze. "You're right," he said softly. "It's only you. You're my only frame of reference, but you're all I need." Son of a bitch. He wanted to kiss her. He wanted to taste her mouth again, to draw her against him, to feel her body flush against his. He literally burned for her, on every level of his being.

Her eyes widened, and her gaze flicked to his mouth, then back to his eyes. "I've never let anyone in either," she whispered. "Not the way I've trusted you. I wanted you to know my secret. If I die, I want to die knowing that there's someone left in this world who knows who I really am."

Anger surged through him, and he tightened his grip on the back of her neck. "You don't get to die," he snarled. "I just found you." Desperate fear ripped through him, a stark, gaping terror of reverting to the absolute isolation he'd existed in for so long, if she died. "Do you understand? *You don't get to die!*"

Confusion flickered across her face at his vehemence. "I'm not planning to but—"

He couldn't stand it anymore. He couldn't hold off. He just couldn't do it. He needed what she gave him too badly. "Mine," he whispered, just before he dragged her against him and claimed her as his own.

Chapter Fourteen

NYA WAS COMPLETELY unprepared for the emotional depth of Slade's kiss. In the safe house, it had been rough-edged attraction. Pure sex. Unbridled lust. In the hallway, it had been something else. Something gentler. But this one was raw emotion, exactly what she'd craved from him initially, only a thousand times more than she would ever have expected from this cold, ruthless loner.

His fingers were tight in her hair, his grip desperate, as if he were afraid she would slip away. His other arm was locked around her back, trapping her against him. She could feel the muscles in his arm flexing, straining against his instinct to grip her so tightly that he would hurt her. His kiss was deep, penetrating, and demanding, thrusting his need into her, flooding her with emotions so raw, so dark, so fierce that she could barely breathe.

He was overwhelming her, almost suffocating her with the depth of his need, but at the same time, it was hauntingly beautiful, mimicking the emotions she kept wrapped so tightly inside her.

She slipped her arms around his neck, and instantly, he

grabbed her hips and lifted her against him, taking what little she could offer him and turning it into more. He locked her legs around his waist, angling his head as he kissed her more deeply, scrambling her mind with kisses so desperate and intimate that she could barely even think.

He carried her across the floor, not breaking the kiss long enough for her to see where he was taking her. His kiss...God, his kisses were extraordinary, igniting feelings and emotions in her that she'd never felt before. She wanted to crawl inside him and connect with him forever, be in his arms every moment for the rest of her life, and turn herself over to him for protection and safekeeping.

But at the same time, she wanted to protect him. She wanted to safeguard the emotions he was pouring into her. She was desperate to preserve the raw, emotional side of him that he was sharing with her. She knew it was a gift, something he'd never do on purpose, something he would probably take back as soon as he regained control, shrinking into the cold, lifeless killer he worked so hard to be.

He leaned forward, and she felt herself sink into a decadently soft fabric. She broke the kiss to look around, and she froze when she realized they were in a bedroom. His bedroom. A massive bed of the most beautiful wood she'd ever seen. Custom silk curtains. Crown molding. Gorgeous antiques. More original paintings by legends. Pure sophistication and class, a haven so beautiful and elegant that she knew he'd designed every inch of it with precision and care to make it his. And he'd shared it with her.

She propped herself up on her elbows, as he pulled back, standing beside the bed, staring down at her with an expression of such unguarded longing that her heart ached. This was the man who claimed he needed no one? How had he possibly survived a lifetime with no human connection of any kind?

She sat up and held out her arms to him. "Come," she said gently.

He shook his head, his hands flexing by his side. "I'm afraid I'll hurt you," he said, his voice hoarse. "I...I don't know what to do... My kiss kills..."

The agony in his voice almost broke her heart. "You don't kill with your kiss," she said softly, understanding finally dawning. "You kill with your mouth. I was wrong when I said you defile the kiss. When you kill, it's not a kiss. It's just a weapon. When you kissed me just then, that was a *kiss*." She got up on her knees so she was level with him and she buried her fingers in his shirt. "Kiss me," she said. "Feel the difference."

Stark longing flashed across his face, but he didn't reach for her. "What if you're wrong, Anya? What if I lose control and realize, too late, what I've done?" He went down on his knees, looking up at her, balling his fists in the comforter. "I lose who I am when I kiss you. I become someone different, someone who's no longer in control."

"No, you don't lose who you are." She sat on the edge of the bed, her knees on either side of his hips. "You find your true self when you kiss me." She framed his face with her hands and leaned forward to kiss him.

He went utterly still when her lips touched his. Tension vibrated through him, fear entrenched so deeply in him he couldn't shake it. His entire frame was taut, his muscles strung so tightly she knew he was ready to spring away from her...but he didn't.

He remained utterly still, frozen in place, as she kissed him. Tender kisses, but not holding back. She leaned into him, letting her body mesh with his. The heat from his skin melted into her, sending warmth catapulting through her.

Still he didn't move, his hands fisted in the comforter. His breathing was tight, his muscles flexed, as if he were waging a tremendous battle. "I can't do this," he said, his voice raw.

"Do what?" She pulled back to look at him.

"Care. Touch. Kiss." His face was desperate. "I can't survive coming alive for you. Do you understand the life I've led? If I saw it through your eyes...I couldn't survive it. I have to stay the way I am."

Anya dropped her hands and sat back. His torment was evident, tearing him apart, and guilt ratcheted through her. He'd chosen this life because of the murder of his family, a boy thrust into a world he was too young to understand. He'd done what he had to do to survive and try to make his life one that he could endure. What right did she have to destroy the foundation of his life just because she craved intimacy with him so much? Her life had been ruined by others. Why did she think making him seduce her was better for him?

She sighed and let go of him. "I'm sorry." She swallowed. "I just...I've just been lost for so long, and when I'm with you, I feel like I can breathe again. You make me feel safe. You make me care again." She flopped back on the bed and folded her hands behind her head. "We don't have time for sex anyway. We just—"

He sprang from the floor and landed on top of her in a single, effortless move. He was on his knees and elbows, holding himself above her, not touching, but somehow, it was more sensual and more intense than if he had been. "I want you," he whispered, his dark gaze boring into hers. "When you let me go just then, I didn't like it."

She swallowed, heat searing though her body. "What do you want from me, Slade?"

"I want you to disappear from my life." But as he said it, he moved his knees, allowing his hips to ease down on top of hers. "I want you to vanish from my mind and my memories, so I never remember what it felt like to kiss you." He threaded his fingers through her hair, his eyes darkening. "I want to never feel again like I felt when I realized I hurt you with my kiss."

Her belly started to tremble. His voice was hoarse and raw, as if he were struggling to say the words. "I wish my mother and Marjorie hadn't been murdered," she whispered. "But we can't make the past go away. I'm sorry I've caused you pain, but I never want to forget you. I don't want you to take away my memories of you. I want to always remember what it's like to be kissed by you, to feel your hands on my body, to see the way you look at me, like I'm your greatest hell, and your most powerful salvation. I'm not afraid of you, Slade. You're the one thing in my whole life that I'm not afraid of."

"Anya." Her name was a reverent whisper on his lips, and his fingers tightened in her hair. "Make me stop, because I can't do it myself."

"No. I won't stop you." Tears filled her eyes. "You make me feel alive, Slade. You make me feel brave, cherished, and protected."

He swore under his breath, even as he lowered his head, pausing with his mouth a breath from hers. "You make me weak," he whispered. "You make me feel."

She placed her hands on his chest, and then slid them around to the back of his neck. "Feeling makes you stronger," she whispered. "It hurts, I know, but it's pain that empowers."

"I'm not afraid of that kind of pain." His fingers tightened in her hair. "But I'm fucking terrified of what it could make me do." And then he kissed her, a deep, ravenous, burning kiss that stripped her of everything but her need for him.

She pulled him closer and kissed him back, groaning as

he lowered himself the rest of the way onto her, his body pinning her to the luxurious bedding. The kiss was desperate and haunting, as if it were pulling the darkness from both of them and using it to bind them together, using tears, loss, and loneliness to break down the walls keeping them apart.

She clung to him as he kissed her, terrified of losing this moment, this man, this chance to feel again. He was dangerous and isolated, but she knew she'd reached him. She mattered to him, this man who let nothing get close to him. She wanted to help him, to somehow get him away from this life that was trying to destroy him...but at the same time, she needed him. He gave her hope, he gave her courage, and he made her feel like she truly existed.

They were the same in some ways, two people who had lived in shadows their whole lives, unable to connect with anyone, unable to even exist as someone's memory. Until now. Until they'd found each other. Until they'd come to life in each other's arms.

"Anya." He whispered her name as he palmed her belly, sliding his hand beneath her shirt. His touch was searing, burning over her skin, igniting the same desire that he'd awakened so easily in the safe house.

It was different this time, though, because this time, she knew him. It wasn't raw lust or attraction. It was deeper, different, and real. With a deft move of his fingers, he unfastened her bra and cupped her breast, thumbing her nipple in a tantalizing rhythm.

She twisted beneath him, her body aching for more, every nerve on fire for his touch. She tugged at his shirt, and he immediately sat up and ripped it over his head. His body was heavily muscled, with scars crisscrossing his flesh, a co-mingling of strength and vulnerability. She spread her palms on his chest, catching her breath at the feel of so much skin. In the safe house, he'd kept his clothes on the whole time, so this was her first moment of seeing him, of touching him, of stripping away his shields that protected him.

"The expression on your face..." He touched her cheek, and she looked at him. His face was unguarded and vulnerable, almost wondering as he watched her. "I'm not used to anyone really seeing me," he said quietly. "You see me, don't you?"

She smiled, understanding what he meant. She'd lived in shadows as well. "I do," she said, meeting his gaze. "I see *you*, Slade, not some shadowy assassin. I see a real man, one who bleeds, breaks, and rebuilds."

He lifted her hand to his mouth and pressed a kiss to her knuckle. "I kill. It's all I do. It's all I am. Don't delude yourself that I'm more than that just because I have to play the role of guardian with you. Never forget that I'm the Black Swan."

She tilted her head, studying him, no fear in her eyes. "Why are you called the Black Swan? Swans aren't predators."

"Because my mom's favorite bird was the swan. There was a family of swans that lived on a lake near our house. The day she was killed, they flew past the house. The setting sun made them look black, as if they were mourning her death and honoring her." He shrugged. "So, I became the Black Swan in her memory, so I would never forget why I killed, and why I became an assassin."

Anya's face softened. "You named yourself out of love," she said, her voice filled with awe. "You're so caring and gentle, Slade. How could you possibly delude yourself that you could survive in isolation when you care so deeply?"

The way she looked at him made something twist inside

him, as if she would never believe he was the monster he knew he was, no matter how many times he tried to make sure she understood. It pissed him off, but at the same time, it awakened something fierce and primal inside him, something that wanted to trap her, protect her, and ensure that nothing ever happened that could strip of her of the way she saw the world. He leaned forward, bracing his weight on his palms on either side of her head. "I want to tear off every piece of your clothing. I want to bury myself inside you until I own you on every level of your soul. I want to rip away every wall you've built up, until there's nothing left but the real you."

Desire swelled through her, an intense, aching need that cried out for his pain, for hers, for the way they could save each other. "Kiss me," she whispered. "Just kiss me and see what happens."

He tunneled his fingers through her hair, sinking his hips deeper against hers. "I'm afraid of my kiss." He thumbed her breast, teasing her nipple until her body ached from the torment he was twisting inside of her. "I've never given a shit about anyone I've killed, until you." He palmed her chest, spreading his hand over her heart. "But if my kiss kills you, it would break me."

Tears filled her eyes at the rawness of his words, at the pain he was allowing her to see. "I'll stop you."

"You won't know. They never know." He ran his hands over her hips again, and then slipped his hand beneath the waistband of her jeans. "No kissing," he whispered. "Just touching."

She gasped as his fingers slipped into her folds. "I want to kiss you. I need it." Kissing was different than touching or sex. It was about intimacy, and it made it personal.

"I can't." With one deft move, he unfastened her jeans, then rolled to the side to pull them off. His eyes were burning with heat as he slid them off her, his hands stoking fires along her thighs. She sat up to pull her shirt off, but he was there first, disrobing her with reverence and a sensual intimacy that made her heart tighten.

"You, too." She reached for his jeans, but he stood up and shed them himself, giving her a full view of his gloriously male body. His muscles were cut, his thighs tremendous and powerful, his cock hard and ready. Her belly clenched, not just for how powerful he was, but for the fact that he was standing before her, allowing her to see him, after he'd lived his entire existence as a shadow that no one was allowed to remember.

She held out her hand to him, and he came, easing onto the bed beside her. He didn't try to kiss her or ravage her. He simply propped himself up on his elbow and traced his fingers along her side, over her hips, and down the outside of her thigh. His expression was pure reverence, almost awe, as he watched his hand move along her body. "So beautiful," he whispered. "Your skin is so soft. I've never felt anything like it."

Her heart ached for the depth of emotion in his voice. "Have you ever done this? Just touched a woman like this?"

"No." He looked up, searching her face as his fingers traced lightly over her breast, making chills pop up on her skin. "This isn't how I live," he said softly. "It's all about isolation, being invisible, and staying in control. It's critical, but with you, I want to slow down. I want to be present. I want to experience it all."

This was the man who'd been able to say nothing more than "I want to fuck you" when she'd first met him? She suddenly understood that it was the same man, and his crass words had said exactly what he was saying now, but he hadn't had the vocabulary to say it this way before. His soul had always been deep and beautiful. He just hadn't known how to access it. Her heart tightened, and she reached out with her own hand, spreading it across his chest.

He went still, his muscles quivering beneath her palms.

"Is this okay?" she asked.

He nodded. "Don't stop."

She smiled at the hoarseness in his voice. "Has anyone ever touched you like this?" She trailed her fingers down his toned torso, watching as each muscle tensed beneath the skin.

"Of course not. I'd never allow it."

Her throat tightened at the words he didn't add. He was allowing it now, for her. "Touching is so important," she said softly, as she ran her hand over his hip. His skin was taut, with hardly any fat to cover his muscles.

He closed his eyes and breathed deeply, even as he continued to run his hand over her body, not just her breasts, but her shoulder, her arm, her elbow, her jaw. Everywhere, like a man starved for touch. "It's incredible," he said softly.

"I know." She bit her lip, and then brushed her fingers across the velvet soft skin of his erection.

He moved instantly, rolling on top of her and pinning her to the bed. His eyes were dark, and heat was burning in them. "Don't do that," he growled.

She caught her breath at the roughness to his voice. "Why not?"

He shoved his knee between hers, spreading them apart. "Because it'll shatter my control, and that's very dangerous."

Heat pooled between her legs, and she swallowed. "I'm not afraid of you."

"You should be." He pressed his erection against her entrance, and he swore when he felt how slick she already was. "Hell, Anya. I have no resistance to you." His gaze went to her mouth. "I want to kiss you so badly right now."

Anya's pulse was thrumming through her, and her blood felt as though it was on fire. "Kiss me, Slade." She tangled her fingers in his hair, her own body starting to tremble with need. She'd never felt drawn to anyone the way Slade called to her. She wasn't afraid of him on any level. His torment, his past, his deadliness...none of it scared her. It defined him, this dangerous, lethal assassin, and that was the man she wanted, the one she burned for. "*Kiss me.*"

"No." His gaze was boring into her as he shifted his hips, pressing his cock harder against her entrance. "I need this. I need you. I..." His eyes darkened. "I need to fuck you, Anya. I've needed to bury myself inside you since the first second I saw you in that bar. I can't hold out anymore." His entire body was shaking with the effort of holding back. "My entire soul burns for you. I can't hold back anymore." Sweat was beading on his brow. "I need you."

The same need was raging through her, and she framed his face with her hands. "Kiss me," she whispered.

Yearning flashed across his face, a stark, raw ache that made her heart turn over. "No." He buried his face in her neck and thrust with his hips, sinking himself deep inside her.

She gasped, gripping his shoulders at the sudden invasion. She hadn't been ready, but at the same time, she had. He slid inside easily, her body welcoming him.

Slade went still, deep inside her, his face still pressed in the curve of her neck. Anya wrapped her arms around his head, holding him close as her body adjusted to him. He was heavy, but not crushing her. She felt safe and shielded beneath his bulk, cherished even.

He pulled back suddenly, easing out of her body and raising his head so he could look at her. His eyes were dark, turbulent with emotion. He braced himself on his elbows and threaded his fingers through hers, trapping them together as he sank deep inside her again. He didn't take his gaze off hers, almost overwhelming her with its intensity.

She shifted restlessly, desire racing through her as he withdrew again, teasing her, stoking the fires burning within her. It was amazing, but it wasn't enough. She needed all of him. *She needed his kiss.* She turned her head and pressed a kiss to the inside of his forearm.

He went still, buried deep inside her, watching her as she kissed his arm. "That feels incredible."

She pulled her hands free of his, and lightly framed his face with her fingers, his whiskers rough beneath her hands. "You don't need to kiss me," she whispered, "but let me kiss you. I need it."

His eyes darkened. "Not on my mouth."

She almost laughed. "You sound like a prostitute," she teased.

"No." He grabbed her wrist, his grip tight. "Don't belittle this even with a joke. Do you not understand this moment? This moment…it's…" He struggled to articulate it. "Anya. This is everything."

Her amusement faded at the intensity of his words. She nodded, her heart aching at his words. "I know." She lightly brought his face down to hers, and she kissed his cheek. He went still as she trailed kisses along his jaw, lightly nipping as she went.

He groaned, his fingers tightening in her hair as she took his earlobe between her teeth and bit gently. Slade swore, and he began moving his hips again, slowly, back and forth, making heat blossom through her. He moved his hand from her hair and cupped her breast, his thumb tracing circles over her nipple.

She gasped, her back instinctively arching toward him,

her hips shifting in response to his movements.

He swore, and began to drive deeper and faster, bracing himself on his arms to keep from crushing her. She gripped his shoulders, her gaze riveted to his as he moved inside her. The depth of emotion in his gaze was riveting, but at the same time, it wasn't enough. Her heart cried out for the kiss she knew he couldn't give her. She didn't know why a kiss mattered so much to her. The intimacy of it, maybe? Having sex could be impersonal, two bodies connecting in the absence of emotions. But a kiss was different. With a kiss, the truth came out.

The truth that he could kill her.

Chapter Fifteen

$\mathscr{S}$LADE WENT STILL, forcing his hips to a stop. He could feel Anya withdrawing, and it cut him right to the core. The need and lust that had been burning through him hovered in suspended abeyance as he fought to regain control. "What's wrong?"

She searched his face, and he found himself falling into those vibrant eyes, just as he did every time she looked at him. "It's okay, Slade."

He narrowed his eyes. "It's not okay. What's going on?"

Her lips parted to answer him, and then she pressed them together, silencing herself. She shook her head. "Nothing."

But as she said it, her gaze slipped to his mouth. That one look sent heat and desire exploding through him. He swore as his entire being responded to that silent invitation. The need to claim her with his kiss was almost overwhelming. Only a lifetime of discipline kept him from capitulating to his need and making her his. He understood then what she wanted: a kiss. "I can't."

"No?" She met his gaze. "I think you're afraid."

"Shit, yeah, I'm afraid. I almost killed you before." A

cold chill crept down his back at the memory of how she'd collapsed after he'd kissed her so thoroughly.

"You didn't, though." She met his gaze, her eyes blazing. "I'm not a machine, Slade. I can't make love like a robot. I know I matter to you, but you have to let me feel it. I need that from you."

Swearing, he withdrew, gritting his teeth as he pulled out of her body. He rolled away from her and stretched out on his back, draping his arm across his eyes as he fought for control. His cock was so hard it hurt, and his body was screaming for the completion he'd denied it.

But there was no way he was going to use her for his own pleasure and leave her empty.

He was okay with being empty inside. He worked hard to attain it. But this brief time with Anya had shown him what it could be like not to live in a void. The sensation of being seen, of having someone look at him like he mattered, being touched, being heard, and having demands made of him...it was insane how powerful it was. It made his existence before her seem like an arid wasteland, one that was sucking him dry.

One drop of rain had made the desert unbearable for him.

She, on the other hand, had grown up in that world of love and affection, and if he dragged her into his world, and thrust the empty chasm of his existence on her, he'd never forgive himself. He would not do that to her by making her feel like a fuck bunny when she was everything to him.

She rolled onto her side to face him. "Don't hide from me," she said softly.

He swore and rolled onto his side so they were face to face. Her hair was tousled, her eyes were sultry with desire, and her skin was glistening with a faint sheen of perspiration. She was more tempting than anything he'd ever seen, and it took all his self-control not to reach for her. Instead, he said simply, "I can't do this."

"Do what?"

"This." He gestured to her body, to the deep brown of her nipples, and the curve of her hips. "Make you feel empty." He swore under his breath. He felt like he had when he'd first met her, uncertain about what to say or how to say it. For a while, he'd become comfortable with her, falling into an easy pattern as her guardian. But now, this arena of sex and intimacy was throwing him off balance. He had no experience with it, other than a mindless rout in the shadows to satisfy some primal need or to get information he needed.

He wasn't going to be stupid enough to say he wanted to fuck her again, but he didn't have other words. "I won't make you feel like shit," he said finally. His gaze settled on a lock of her hair that had fallen forward over her breast. He wanted to move it, to feel its softness, to relish the pure femininity of her.

"You don't." She sighed. "I just...I'm very expressive and physically affectionate. I need that in return." She met his gaze. "I know you use your kiss to kill. I understand that, but I also don't believe you're so weak that you'd hurt me."

"I already did."

"You wouldn't now."

He swore. "Anya, you have no concept of what it feels like to kiss someone and drain their soul. It's instinct for me—"

"You didn't do it when you kissed me at the bar. You didn't do it when you kissed me in the foyer. And you didn't actually kill me in the safe house."

"Because I was in control! Don't you get it? If I make love to you and kiss you, I'm going to be lost to you. I don't have a single shred of discipline when it comes to you." He swore at her surprised expression. "Don't you get it?" He moved closer, heat raging through him. "When I taste your lips, the rest of the world ceases to exist. All that matters is the feel of your mouth against mine. I want to invade your mouth, claim it, and make it mine." Fire began to pulse inside him, licking its way through his veins. "I want to taste every inch of your body. Your nipples, your stomach, your collarbone. I want to kiss my way down your body, lower and lower, until I taste the part of you that you share with no one."

Anya's cheeks flushed, and he caught the scent of her desire, wild, raw, and untamed.

An ancient need hummed through him, and he swore, gritting his jaw with the effort of holding himself back. "I don't know how to be a good guy," he said. "I've made sure it's not a part of who I am."

"Really?" She moved closer, and he stiffened, sucking in his breath when she draped her leg over his hip. "I don't believe you. There's someone you love who you protect with every fiber of your soul. If you were cold, you wouldn't do that. You wouldn't care enough to ensure his safety."

He swallowed as she moved even closer, until her face was almost touching his. Her mouth was hovering over his, her lips so close that he could taste them. He'd never wanted anything as much as he wanted her right now. To taste her again. To claim her. To lose himself in her. To feel alive again, as only she made him feel.

"See me, Slade," she whispered, her blue eyes searching his. "My name is Anya Diaz. I'm a daughter. I'm a best friend. I'm real, Slade, and you know it. Let yourself feel who I am, because I know you treasure life far too much to ever take it, once you let yourself see that it's real."

He closed his eyes, cutting himself off from her, his breath coming in tight gasps as he fought for control.

"Do you know I'm real, Slade? Do you?" She wouldn't let him go, hammering at him with words meant to break through his shields. "Do you know that I breathe? That I cry? That I feel pain? That I feel love?" Her hand went to his chest, and he sucked in his breath as her fingers brushed over his skin so gently it was almost surreal. "Do you know that you're real, too? That you breathe? That you once loved someone, and maybe still do? That you can't hide behind a wall of isolation anymore? You can't go back, Slade. It's too late."

"No!" He opened his eyes and rolled on top of her, rage exploding through him. "It's not too late," he growled desperately. "It's not too late! I can go back. I'm going back!"

She didn't retreat. She just met his gaze. "But do you really want to?" she asked. "Truly?"

"Yes," he whispered, suddenly drained. "I want to wipe my memory of all of this and just return to the life I've carved out for myself. I have to."

She locked her hands behind his head. He could break her grasp easily, but he couldn't make himself do it. He just *couldn't* make himself pull back. "One kiss, Slade. One real kiss where you let yourself truly feel how beautiful your kiss really is."

"I can't." But he couldn't take his gaze off her mouth. Tremors shook his body with the need to lose himself in her. Not just fucking. More than that. He wanted to kiss her. He wanted to taste her. He wanted to taste every inch of her body, and then bury himself inside her until all the darkness fled from his soul.

She was so ruthless and relentless in her assault on his isolation. It pissed him off, but at the same time, he felt like she was throwing him an anchor in the middle of a raging storm, and it was up to him to grab it or to let the winds tear him apart.

"Slade." She framed his face with her hands, her fingers so soft he almost couldn't grasp it. "I'll protect you from yourself."

Her statement was so ludicrous that he almost laughed...except something inside him shouted that she was right. That *she* was the one who could save him...even though he didn't want saving. He didn't need saving. He just needed to go back to who he was...except he couldn't. He'd been thrust into a new role, a role that had him grasping for a handhold he couldn't find, making choices he didn't understand, like bringing her back to his home, his greatest sanctuary.

He felt like his mind was spinning and fragmenting, splitting apart, and he couldn't figure out how to put the pieces back together again. Nothing fit. Nothing made sense. Nothing except her. He looked at her, really looked at her. He let himself see the loneliness in her eyes. He traced his finger over the circles under her eyes and the lines of stress around her mouth. He rested his hand over her heart, feeling the steady thump. He saw the faint freckles dotting her cheeks, and the smudges of makeup beneath her eyes, giving her a luminous, haunted beauty.

She was imperfect and flawed, emotional and open...and real, just as she'd hammered at him to see.

Something inside him turned over, and he slid his fingers into her hair. "I see you," he said softly, unable to keep the awe out of his voice. She was real, she was beautiful, and she was life.

She smiled then, a heart-wrenchingly beautiful smile. "And I see you, Slade. You're real, too, no matter how hard you try not to exist." She traced her index finger along his jaw. "We both need to be seen," she said softly. "I need you. I need what you give me. And you need the same thing from me." She took his hand and set it over her heart again. "Look at me, Slade. Do you really believe you could kill me, even by accident?"

He did as she requested, and he looked at her. He let himself see her. He allowed her blue eyes to entrance him. He revisited the pain she'd shared with him when her mother had died. He let himself feel the soft warmth of her breast beneath his palm. He allowed himself to take a deep breath, to inhale the emotions she poured into him. He envisioned the kiss in the bar again, the moment he'd switched his kiss from pleasure to killing. Instantly, revulsion roiled through him, a dark, angry hate for what he'd almost done. Shock rolled through him. "I don't think I could," he said slowly, shocked by the truth of his words.

He couldn't kill her any more than he could kill his own brother.

Victory surged through him, laced with a disbelieving awe. Was it really possible that she was right? That he could kiss her and not fear? Hot, raging desire rushed through him, and silently, he fisted her hair, angling his head until his lips were almost touching hers. "I want you," he whispered, his voice raw and hoarse.

She laced her hands behind his neck again. "There is nothing more important to me than staying alive long enough to find Julia," she said. "I would never put myself in a position where I thought I would not survive it, but I believe in you, Slade. I trust you."

I trust you. No one had ever trusted him for anything decent in his life. The words reverberated through him, like a bass drum thundering through his soul. He wanted to be that man, the one worthy of those three simple words. He *had* to be that man.

He bent his head, moving slowly, giving her the chance

to stop him.

She didn't.

His lips touched hers, a shocking assault to his senses. To protect her, he'd opened himself to her on every level, forcing himself to embrace every essence of her being. His heightened awareness changed the kiss from sensuality and sex to something so much more potent and overwhelming. Desire ripped through him, plunging right to his gut, ignited by the simple sensation of her lips against his, by the taste of her mouth.

He angled his head, deepening the kiss, sliding his tongue between her teeth. Her response was passionate and unhesitating, kissing him back as if all of her barriers had been torn down as well. Lightning seemed to flood the room with white flashes and searing fire. With a low growl, he dragged her against him, unable to contain the need pouring through him. Her kiss was like the oxygen he'd lived without for so long, flooding him with strength and light, everything he needed in order to live.

Her curves meshed with the hard lines of his body as he folded her against him, devouring her with kisses that were so much more than he'd ever delivered before. It was mutual, a sharing of pleasure unlike he'd ever experienced before. His kisses had always been one-sided, an offering of peace to the souls he was about to claim. Even when he'd kissed her before, he'd held back, accustomed to remaining impassive during the most intense passion.

But she'd wrested his control from him. At the same time, she'd given him permission to experience the kiss for his own pleasure, to bask in her response, to appreciate the joy he could give her. It became about mutual satisfaction and exploration, about expression and appreciation.

He broke the kiss and trailed his mouth over her breasts, his hands greedily spanning her hips, and tracing over her thighs and ass. Every inch of her was pure sensation, unbridled perfection, and flawed humanity. He loved the saltiness of her skin, evidence of the sweat she'd shed fighting for her life. It made her real.

Greedily, he swept his mouth across her body, tasting every inch of her while his hands framed her hips, holding her still, keeping her close. He'd never experienced his own kiss before, not like this. He'd always held back, observing his kiss, evaluating the response of his victim, carefully monitoring what he was doing.

But now, he let himself become swept up in the mesmerizing experience of the kiss. He closed his eyes, focusing all his senses on the feel of her skin beneath his lips. The taste of her flesh. He could feel the quivers of her muscles beneath his kiss as he moved across her belly, lower and lower.

She twisted beneath him, the intoxicating scent of her desire tantalizing him even more. He parted her legs and kissed her damp folds, the same way he'd done before, only this time, he let himself experience it. It was a rush to be so attuned to her body and her responses. She tasted of honey and sweetness, and a darker twist of something that called to him, summoning him. He growled low in his chest and kissed his way back up her body, parting her legs with his knee.

He caught her mouth in a fierce, uncontained kiss that swept through him like a forest burning out of control. She locked her arms around his neck, kissing him back so fiercely that he knew he had no chance of holding back. She'd stripped him of his control and discipline, leaving him completely at the mercy of his emotions and his instincts.

She locked her legs around his hips, inviting him in. He sheathed himself inside her, a seamless connection that shook him deeply. He moved inside her, his senses howling at the feel of her body clamped around him. He gripped her hair, unable to break the kiss, devouring her mouth at the same time he bound them with each thrust. The sensations were overwhelming, twisting around him like invisible chains that would never release him, chains he never wanted to escape from.

He thrust deeper and harder, until the world became nothing more than Anya. He clung to her, his soul howling in response to the heat she'd awoken in him, driving deeper and deeper with his hips, at the same time their kisses careened out of control. He was so connected with her that he knew the moment the orgasm took hold of her, dragging her ruthlessly into a place where sensation and explosion would consume her. He went with her, turning himself over to her and the connection that bound them. The climax rocked him violently, wresting every last bit of self-discipline from him, thrusting him into a miasma of flashing lights and intoxicating connection where only he and Anya existed.

Chapter Sixteen

$\mathscr{S}$HE WANTED TO pretend there was nothing outside the shield of his arms.

Anya closed her eyes, listening to the steady thump of Slade's heart beneath her cheek. Her body was sated, but not drained. His arms were tight around her, his fingers drifting through her hair.

"How are you?" he asked, his voice cautious.

Her heart softened at his concern, and she rolled on top of him, propping her elbows up on his chest. "I'm fine."

He searched her face, his gaze intense as he inspected her. Then, finally, a small smile curved the corner of his mouth. "You're okay."

She grinned. "I am. I knew you could kiss me without hurting me."

He tugged lightly at her hair, his face more relaxed than she'd ever seen. He looked much younger, making her wonder exactly how old he was. Had the hard years he'd lived stolen part of his youth? "It's never been like that," he said. "It was...surreal."

The reverence in his voice made her throat tighten. "I agree." She loved being sprawled across him. His body was hard and warm, making her feel safe and sexy at the same time.

He was watching her hair fall from his fingers, tumbling over her shoulders. The awe on his face made her feel like some supernova who'd illuminated his world. It had been so long since she'd been truly relaxed. It felt like an eternity since anyone had looked at her like she really mattered. She knew that they had to keep searching for Julia, that this moment was nothing more than a brief oasis in an ugly, terrifying hunt for her best friend, but she needed this moment. Simply being there with him was healing some of the pain that had haunted her for so long, breathing new life and energy into her.

He frowned as he played with her hair. "As I said before, I never thought about the word soft before," he said. "But your hair makes me contemplate the concept."

"I'm getting that impression." She smiled as she watched him. He looked like a little boy experiencing the world for the first time. "Soft isn't a bad thing," she said.

"I always thought it was." He lifted another lock of hair and let it fall to her shoulder. "To me, soft means weak. It meant you were going to get killed, or get someone you cared about killed." He tangled his fingers in her hair and tugged lightly. "But this soft makes me want to pause and experience it." His gaze flicked to hers. "I'm not used to that."

His wariness made her smile. "It's not so bad, is it?"

He shrugged. "It might be." He let out his breath and looked at her. "These people who have Julia are dangerous."

Her contentment faded. "I know."

"You don't have any idea." He clasped his hands behind his head, his gaze still fixed on her. The position made his biceps flex, reminding her of the pure deadliness of the man she was with. "My father was a mercenary. His main gig was to find missing people. My mom was one of his assignments, and he fell in love with her instantly. Through her, he learned about the shifter black market, and it became his personal agenda to shut it down. He turned his specialization to finding missing shifters."

Anya tensed, picking up on the edge to his voice. "What happened?"

"He became too good. People were losing money. They threatened him, tortured him, and blackmailed him, but he didn't stop." He met her eyes. "So, they hunted down his family and killed them. My bro—" He stopped suddenly.

She knew then what he hadn't told her. She knew who he'd been protecting all this time. "You have a brother?"

He swore under his breath and closed his eyes.

She touched his jaw. "Slade," she whispered. "These people are my enemy, too. I'm on your side."

He opened his eyes. "If you know, they can get the information from you."

"Then erase it. Tell me, then erase it." She knew it was the only way he'd share it, but she wanted to know his secrets. There was something about this tormented, isolated man that called to her. He'd been cast adrift when his father had died, fighting to survive, thrashing blindly through a life of death and destruction. Somehow, she wanted to reach him and help him find his way back to what mattered.

His gaze flicked to hers and she saw an incredible yearning in them, so achingly honest that she wanted to cry.

"He doesn't know me," he finally said. "He was only six months old when my mom was killed, and a year old when my dad died. I took him to a church with a note. I knew what life I was going to lead, and I didn't want him to be stuck in the same cycle that had killed everyone."

Her heart tightened. "What did the note say?"

"I wrote that his dad had been killed in the military as a war hero, and his mother was a school teacher who had died in a car accident, and that he had no family to take care of him, so I hoped that a good family would adopt him." He glanced at her. "I lied about who he was so he could have a life that had nothing to do with the one he was born into. I tried to make up a story that would make someone want him." He managed a half-smile. "He was adopted by a great couple. He's even got a brother. They're close. Him, his brother, his parents. They're tight. He's got it all."

Her heart ached for the words he didn't say. "He doesn't know about you, does he?"

Slade shook his head. "I visit him occasionally to check up on him, but he doesn't know I'm there. I talked to him three times, but I erased his mind after. I just had to..." He shrugged, focused on her hair as he continued to play with it, not quite looking at her. "I had to hear the sound of his voice. I had to hear him say my name, like he knew me."

Tears filled Anya's eyes. She couldn't imagine what her life would have been like without her little makeshift family. How could Slade have severed himself from the one person on the earth he loved, just to keep him safe? She wrapped her arms around his neck and pressed a kiss to his cheek. "You're the most selfless man I've ever met," she said softly. "My mom loved me dearly, but even she didn't let me go to keep me safe. I can't imagine the strength it takes for you to walk away every time."

His arm tightened around her. "It's fine," he said, but the edge to his voice made his words a lie. "It's not a big deal."

"What's his name?" she asked.

"His birth name is Killian Cross. In the note, though, I said his name was Ned."

She raised her brows. "Ned?"

"I wanted a name that would turn him into a geek who sat at a computer all day instead of one that made him want to be a warrior."

"And did it?"

Slade laughed softly. "He's a heart surgeon, but he's also a tenth degree black belt in karate, the fool."

There was so much pride in his voice that Anya couldn't help but smile. "Have you watched any of his competitions?"

His face darkened. "No. I only see him at night when no one is around." His gaze became like steel. "If anyone saw me speaking with him, they would want to know who he was. I can never acknowledge him. Ever."

She nodded, her heart breaking for him. "I understand." She knew why he had to do it, and she acknowledged that it made his brother safer, but the loss of the two brothers living alone, disconnected from their own family made her heart ache for them, and for herself. She was like Slade now, living in isolation, torn from her family. Was it worse, knowing what they'd lost? Or was it worse for Ned, not even knowing his brother existed?

Slade met her gaze. "I need to wipe Killian from your mind." The regret in his eyes made her heart turn over, and she knew that by telling her about him, he'd been able to bring Killian to life for the first time since the day he'd turned him away so long ago.

"Why don't you wait until I leave here?" she suggested. "No one can get me here. Then you can talk about him more, if you want."

Yearning deepened the blue of his eyes, and his fingers tightened in her hair. He looked anguished, and she knew he was going to say no.

"Okay."

She couldn't hide her surprise. "Really?"

"Yeah." He let out a deep breath, and met her gaze. "It feels good to talk about him."

She smiled. "I know."

He nodded, and took another deep breath. "I'm going to go back to the warehouse," he said, changing the subject. "You stay here. I want to see what I can learn."

With his words, the moment of intimacy and connection vanished, replaced by the ominous reality they were facing. "What if they catch you?"

"They can't. I'm the Black Swan. No one catches me." The cold edge to his voice eased some of her rising tension.

In their moment of lovemaking and intimacy, she'd started to see him as a man who loved, bled, and hurt. A man who stumbled through personal intimacies. A living creature who needed connection as much as anyone else. She'd forgotten about the unstoppable assassin he'd honed himself into over the years, a shadowy, deadly killer without remorse, vulnerability, or weakness.

In addition to being Slade Cross, he was the Black Swan, a man no one could find, let alone stop, and he was on her side. She grinned. "I forgot."

He didn't smile back. "Never forget, Anya. It defines me on all levels."

A cold chill prickled down her spine. The vulnerability he'd shown her was gone, and all that remained was the assassin she'd first met. "You don't have to be the Black Swan with me," she said, lightly elbowing his chest. "Just be Slade."

Again, yearning flashed across his face. He framed her face with his hands, and pulled her down to kiss her. His mouth was soft and tender, a kiss that made her heart turn over. "My sweet Anya," he whispered into the kiss. "It is with you I must be the most careful to protect who I need to be."

Her heart tightened, and she pulled back to look at him. "What does that mean?"

"It means you are my greatest weakness."

* * *

Slade swore when he saw the look of surprise on Anya's face. He realized he'd said too much, done too much, and crossed too many lines. What had he done, making love to her? Telling her about his brother? Lounging in bed simply because he wanted to preserve the moment of intimacy, of having her sprawled across him, her chin propped on her hands, while she talked to him as if he were real, approachable, and flawed.

"Slade—"

"I need to go." He palmed her hips and shifted her off him, gritting his teeth at the feel of her warm curves beneath his palms. He didn't want to get up. He wanted to stay here, with her, in his bed for the night. For the week. Forever?

She made him think of the life he'd once had, of connections he'd dismissed, of values that he'd abandoned long ago...and he couldn't afford to go there.

He swung his feet off the bed and strode across his room to his closet. He opened the double doors and walked inside. He headed straight toward the back, grabbing a pair of loose black pants and a black shirt—

"There's so much you hide about yourself." Anya's surprised voice drifted across the closet and he spun around.

She was standing in the doorway, gazing at the racks of his suits. "How many suits do you own?"

"I don't know." He grabbed a pair of boxer briefs and yanked them on, trying not to notice the way the light fell across her breasts and her hips. She didn't appear to care she was naked, but he cared. He cared a great deal. His cock was already hard, and perspiration beaded on his brow as he fought the urge to stride across the closet, sweep her up in his arms, and deposit her back on his bed.

She walked over to his tuxedo section and lightly stroked one of his sleeves. "You have six tuxedos."

"Yeah."

"Are all your suits custom made?" She brushed her fingers across the sleeve, and for a split second, he imagined her touching his arm that way. A light, barely-there brush that would require all his concentration just to feel it.

"Yeah, so?" He pulled on his pants, viscerally aware of every step she took. No one had ever been in his closet before, obviously. It should have felt dangerous, an insidious invasion of his most private world. Instead, anticipation hummed through him. He felt like he were on the edge of a high roof, crouched and ready...either to leap, or to retreat...depending on the wind, the night, and a thousand other factors so complex that only his subconscious could process them.

She picked up one of his shoes, an Italian-made wingtip he'd commissioned from his favorite Italian designer, while he'd been on one of his missions. "This is not what you wear when you're lurking in the dive bars hunting white leopards and assaulting demons."

He couldn't help the small chuckle that escaped. "No, this is true."

"So, what is all this?" She gestured around his closet. "Is this the real you?"

He glanced around the room, seeing it, for the first time, through someone else's eyes. The ceiling was high and well lit. The closet was spacious, with a large three-sided mirror in the dressing room. His clothes were organized to perfection, dozens of suits and dress shirts. To the right were his shadow clothes, the ones he wore when he needed to disappear. All of them were the finest material, designed to move with his body in absolute silence and withstand anything he asked of it. Flame retardant, woven with high-tech threads designed to block almost any projectile, including bullets, blades, and teeth, while still allowing him to reach out with his senses in all directions, pouring his psychic energy into the brain of anyone he targeted. It was high-tech, luxurious perfection, and he liked every damn thing in there. He shrugged. "It's all me."

Anya tossed the shoe from hand to hand, still naked, still tempting him, and apparently, still oblivious to the effect she had on him. "You know, when I met you, I had this vision of you at high tea, nibbling scones with the Queen of England. Have you ever had high tea with her?"

He laughed at her question, and pulled his tee shirt over his head. "No, I can't say that I have."

"Do you ever wear these clothes?"

He tugged his tee shirt down to his waist. "I do."

She tossed the shoe at him. He caught it instinctively. "When?" she asked.

"For work."

"And pleasure? Do you have nights where you put on one of the tuxedoes, go out for a lovely dinner, and then enjoy the opera? Just because it's a relaxing, lovely way to spend an evening, and not because you need to kill one of the orchestra members in the pit?"

He raised his brows. "You're awfully demanding, aren't you? You do realize that I'm a loner, right? That I don't like to bond and tell secrets?"

She set her hands on her hips. "Slade."

He grinned and walked over to her, sliding his hands over hers and pulling her against him. "You do also realize that it's impossible for me to concentrate while you're standing there naked, don't you?" He slid his hand in her hair and kissed her, simply because he wanted to, and he could.

Her mouth tasted like heaven and home, firing up his need for her instantly. With a low growl, he pulled her against him, deepening the kiss. It was impossible for him to resist her. He'd never been owned by the primal male instincts that seemed to cause most men to make asinine choices, but Anya got under his skin, shredding the self-control that had defined him his entire life.

She wrapped her arms around his neck and leaned into him, kissing him back. Swearing, he grabbed her hips and lifted her, need pulsing through him as he locked her legs around his waist. He backed her against the wall, into his row of tuxes, using his body weight to hold her up as he deepened the kiss.

"Tell me," she whispered between kisses. "Tell me about the real you. Opera?"

He swore as he dragged his pants down with one hand. "I don't want to talk about it." He caught her mouth in another kiss as he pressed his hand between them. She was ready for him, so ready that his quads clenched in anticipation.

"I want to know." She pulled back, bracing her hands on his shoulders while his jacket sleeves fell across her chest, closing in on her.

He palmed her hips. "Ballet," he admitted. "It's such strength and power mixed with grace and beauty that should never work together, and yet it does. I go every chance I get."

Her face lit up, an expression of joy so extraordinary he felt as though she was sunshine pouring into him. "Ballet is beautiful," she agreed, locking her hands behind his back. "Someday, we should go together."

He thought of taking her out to a five-star dinner, seeing her wearing a gown worthy of her, of surprising her with the best champagne that could be bought, of gifting her with all the beauty that he'd never shared with anyone. "I wish." He caught her hips, angling her toward him. "But I can't ever be seen in public with you. Not like that."

She met his gaze, something so sad and understanding in her blue eyes that he felt something shift in his chest. "I wish you so much more than the life you have," she said softly, her fingers tangling in the hair at the nape of his neck.

He wanted to agree. He wanted to shout how badly he wanted everything in his life to be different, just so he could feel all the time like he felt in that moment—connected, alive, important. He wanted to stand in the rays of beauty emanating from her soul and drink it into him, using it to wash away the life he'd led for so long. He wanted so much that he'd never thought about wanting. "I don't want anything else," he said. "This is good."

She smiled, a smile that said she heard everything he hadn't said. "Liar," she said softly.

"Never." He fisted her hair and dragged her to him, seizing her mouth with his. He didn't want to talk anymore. He didn't want to listen to crap he couldn't afford to listen to. He just wanted to feel the way only she could make him feel.

She didn't fight him. Instead, she wrapped her arms around his neck and held him close, kissing him back even more fiercely than he was kissing her, accepting him completely as he was. Warmth poured through him, the kind of burning light that illuminated every dark recess of his soul, tearing aside the darkness and the coldness and giving it life. "Anya." He whispered her name into the kiss as he sheathed himself inside her.

She fit him perfectly, a moment of perfection and still-ness, where nothing else mattered. For a long moment, he stayed still, resting his forehead against hers, simply absorbing the moment, the experience of being physically and emotionally connected to her. "You make me feel grounded. I live my life on the edge, never really present, never really existing, but this moment..." He lifted his head to look at her, searching her eyes. "This moment with you feels like the most real experience I've ever had. I feel like I can feel the ground beneath my feet."

Anya smiled, a smile so tender and intimate that he could do nothing other than tighten his grip on her, as if he could hold onto her forever. "That's how you make me feel, too," she said. "Maybe it takes two wraiths to create something real."

"Maybe." He snaked one hand behind her neck, clasping firmly as he kissed her again. As he kissed her, he shifted her hips, using movement from both of them to thrust deeper inside her. She gasped and leaned back, bracing herself against the wall as he drove again.

He sank into her again, and again, until he couldn't think, until he needed more. He dragged her away from the wall, shoving aside his suits as he took her down on the lush carpet he'd spent weeks installing himself. The fibers were like silk, framing her body the way she deserved as he moved over her, sinking into her even more deeply. He felt as though he couldn't get deep enough, close enough, connected enough, no matter how hard he tried, like what he wanted was dancing just out of reach, drifting away from his clasping fingertips.

He shifted, covering her with his body, owning her, claiming her, protecting her, even as he drove deeper and deeper, until his need was wrapped so tightly around him he felt as though his skin would split from the pressure. "Come to me," he whispered between kisses. "I need you. I need you so much."

Anya's fingers tightened in his hair, and she arched her back, shifting her hips to counteract each of his thrusts. She was moving as much as he was, consumed by the intensity of the fire crackling between them. "I'm here, Slade. With you. I'm here—" Her voice caught as the climax swept her up in its vortex.

She clung to him, gasping as the orgasm took her. The moment he felt her muscles contract, her pleasure shattered the last vestiges of his control. He surrendered willingly, turning himself over to Anya and the raw, vulnerable need thundering through him. He didn't fight it. He didn't protect himself. He didn't hold on for survival. He simply let go.

Chapter Seventeen

℘HE FEATHER-SOFT CARPET caressed Anya's back as she lay beneath Slade on the floor of his closet. His weight was heavy, his face buried in the crook of her neck. His muscles were slack, utterly relaxed, and his breathing was even. She knew he was awake, ready to go into fight mode in a split second, and yet, his body was completely at peace, as if he'd stopped fighting for the first time in his life.

She smiled softly and let her fingers trail over his muscular back, tracing circles across his skin. Around them were rows and rows of beautiful clothing, the highest quality, designed for a life of elegance and luxury, much like what she'd seen of the rest of his home. There was a gracefulness to the decor, as if it had been woven by whisper-thin glass threads in the moonlight. It was wealthy, but not opulent, and certainly not the streamlined rigor of a man's abode.

"It makes me sad that you have all this beauty, but you can't embrace it."

He pressed a light kiss to the side of her neck. "I'm embracing it right now."

She laughed softly. "I mean in life—"

"My life is in the moment." He pressed another kiss to her neck, so tender that her throat tightened. "And nothing in my life has ever been as beautiful as you. And trust me, I'm breathing in the fullness of this moment."

She let out her breath, trying to keep her composure, but it was difficult. A man like Slade didn't slow down or become soft, and yet that was where he was right now, because of her. She believed in love and emotional connection, but throughout her life, it had been tarnished by a constant fear of all hell raining down on her. That hell had come and it had stolen everything, but somehow, she'd survived. And now, in Slade's house, in his embrace, she felt like she'd finally found the place where she was meant to be, where she could relax and be herself. "I'm a white leopard," she whispered, testing the words, seeing how they felt.

"I know." He nibbled on her collarbone, making chills pop up on her arms.

"No, I mean, I'm sure that I am." She wanted to say it aloud. She'd been hiding it her entire life, afraid to trust anyone, afraid to even acknowledge that it might be true. Slade made her feel safe to say it. "I told you I wasn't sure, but I am."

He lifted his head to look at her. His hair was tousled, giving him a boyish, untamed look that made her heart flip. "Have you shifted?"

"No, but sometimes, I can feel her beneath my skin." She ran her hands through his hair, messing it up even more. She liked the disheveled look for him. It made him more approachable, more vulnerable. "I feel like I need to be more than I am. I want to be stronger, faster, and more...alive. I feel like I'm half of who I'm supposed to be."

He cocked his head, watching her. "You kept it in all this time," he observed.

She nodded. "Of course I did. It was too risky. And now, these people who have Julia..." She shuddered at the thought of the monsters who had her friend, dangerous men who she would soon be hunting at Slade's side. "No one can know, except you." She met his gaze. "It feels good to tell you. Not to hide it. It's been hard."

"I know." He traced his finger along her jaw. "It was surreal to tell you about my brother. Scary as hell, but at the same time..." He shrugged. "It made it seem real, like I almost had him back again."

Anya 's throat tightened. "Slade, I can't ever get my mom back, but you can get your brother. Maybe you shouldn't hide anymore. Maybe you should tell him."

Yearning flashed across his face, but he shook his head. "And if I walked into his house one day and found him dead with a knife in his back because one of my enemies found him? You think that's worth the risk?"

Nausea churned in Anya's stomach as she imagined the scene, all too reminiscent of coming home to find her mom and Marjorie murdered. If she had a sister somewhere who didn't know she was a white leopard, would she bring this world to her doorstep? She didn't need to think about it. She wouldn't, no matter how much she wanted to. "No," she said, unable to keep the tears from her voice. "It's not. I'm sorry for that."

"I'm not." He tugged lightly on her hair. "It's an incredible feeling to know that my own brother is living a good life, that someone in my family escaped the hell of our lives and has a chance to exist in a world where this shit doesn't happen."

"Is there such a world? Really?"

His mouth twisted up in an ironic grin. "I hope there is.

I wouldn't know it for sure, though." He kissed her again, then slid his hand down her leg toward her foot. He wrapped his fingers around her ankle and drew her leg up, sliding off her just enough to make room for her foot. "I want to see the tattoo."

She stiffened, her heart speeding up. "I've never let anyone see it."

"You've also never told anyone about it before. Lots of firsts today." He angled her foot so he could see the bottom of it.

She watched his face as he studied it carefully. She'd memorized every curve and every line of the rune, and she'd even made a habit of sketching it with permanent marker on other parts of her body, just for backup, especially on the days when she'd felt especially restless.

"Is there one on the other foot, too?"

"Yes."

He rolled off her and clasped her other foot, drawing it up so he could compare them. She felt vulnerable and exposed, and not because she was naked with her feet in his hands. It was because those tattoos were her dark secret, the ones that told who she really was.

Slade traced his fingers over the marks, following the lines. As he traced them, her skin tingled, as if miniature needles were being jabbed into her foot. Suddenly nervous, she propped herself up on her elbows, tensing her legs to pull them free. "What are you doing? You aren't taking them off, are you?"

"No. I'm testing them." His face was tense, his jaw clenched.

Apprehension rippled through her. "For what?"

For a long moment, he said nothing, continuing his inspection of her feet.

"Slade. You're scaring me. What is it?" She wanted to

get up, put clothes on, shroud her feet in heavy boots. "Let me go." She tugged on her legs, but his fingers tightened around her ankles.

Finally, he released her feet. "Let me show you something. Sit cross-legged."

She scrambled up and sat beside him. He took her foot and brought it toward her. "See this?" He pointed to the marks on her heel.

She leaned forward, resting her shoulder against his so she could see the bottom of her foot. "The blue lines? Yes." She frowned at him. "You recognize them, don't you?" She'd never searched for them online or anywhere else, afraid that her search would trigger some sort of sensor somewhere and allow them to find her. She'd just had to trust her mother on what they were. In fact, she'd never done any research on white leopards at all, afraid that her research would trigger safeguards that would alert people that she was looking.

"Yeah." He rubbed his finger over her heel. "This is a rune to keep a shifter from shifting."

She nodded. "That's what my mom said."

"And this one?" He rubbed his thumb over the ball of her foot, where another set of lines was tattooed into the skin. "Do you know what this is for?"

Fear rippled through her at his tone. "Not to keep me from shifting?"

"No." He rubbed his thumb over it. "It's a fertility rune."

She blinked. "Fertility? You mean to get me pregnant?"

He raised his brows. "That's generally what fertility means."

"But...why? Why would she put that on me?" Sudden fear rippled through her as she recalled the few times she'd been with a man in her life, before Slade. She'd used birth control, but how close had she come? "Wouldn't she want me to not have children that could be in danger?"

He rubbed his thumb over the fertility rune, and the same feelings of pins and needles rippled through her. "White leopards are very rare."

"Yes, so?"

He looked at her. "Survival is an instinct that is impossible to defeat. She wanted more leopards, Anya. She wanted you to keep the species alive."

"Oh. God." She pulled her foot free of his hand, suddenly, horribly aware that they'd just had unprotected sex twice. "For what? Another child who has to grow up like I did? Why would she do that? I mean—"

Slade caught her wrist just as she was starting to stand up. "Stay."

"We just had sex. Twice! With no birth control! Do you realize that?"

A small smile curved the corner of his mouth. "I am actually aware of that, thanks. Sit."

"I can't. What if..." Nausea churned in her belly and she sank down next to Slade. "What if I got pregnant? What if I had to keep a child safe? What if something happened to her?" She thought of Julia, and she swayed as dizziness took her.

"Hey." Slade grasped her shoulders firmly. "You do realize I'm the Black Swan, right? No one gets to me. No child of mine would ever be in danger."

"Your answer to a child in danger was to abandon him! Is that what you'd want me to do? Stick my daughter in some church and pray that she never actually shifted and got caught?"

Slade's face went cold, ice cold. "My brother is not in danger of shifting. The only danger that would come to him is through me. A child of yours would be different—"

"Why?" She lunged to her feet. "Your mom was a white leopard. What's the difference? Why can't your brother be a shifter?"

He met her gaze. "One of the reasons white leopards are so rare is because only their first offspring carries the white leopard gene. Never two in a family."

She stared at him as his words sank in. Damn. There was so little she knew about her kind. "Is your brother younger than you?"

"Yes."

Foreboding began to settle in her. "And your sister? The one who died? Older or younger than you?"

Slade met her gaze. "Younger."

Her knees seemed to give out as she fell to her knees in shock. "You're the oldest?"

"I am."

"But you're..." She searched his face. "You're not a white leopard."

He raised his brows. "Meow."

She blinked. "Meow?"

"Should I purr instead?"

"'Should I *purr*?' That's your answer when I asked if you're a white leopard? What kind of answer is that?"

"Flippant and elusive from a guy who doesn't like to talk about it?"

"Oh, God." Her hands started shaking. "I don't understand. How can you be one? How does no one know?" She had a thousand questions for him, so many that she'd been unable to ask for her whole life. "You're a white leopard? But—"

"I control people's minds. I can affect what they perceive. Most people wouldn't recognize me as one, but there are a few who could. I make sure they don't." He raised his brows. "You would have known if I hadn't interfered."

"Me? But, how—" Heat suddenly flooded her mind, the kind of dry, asphyxiating heat of a desert. It seemed to melt the edges of her brain, turning it into a bubbling, simmering cauldron. She winced, holding her hands to her head. "What are you doing?"

"Taking down my shields."

Suddenly, the claustrophobic heat vanished, and her mind felt cool and clear, like an untouched mountain stream. Information cascaded through her mind, thousands of data points that raced through her, turning on sensors in every part of her. She was filled with the sudden hugeness of Slade's aura, a fierce, dangerous predator...a cat...a white leopard.

She knew it instantly. Her own cat roared to life, clawing to get free, to respond to the sheer influx of feline power flooding from Slade. His power rushed over her, almost overwhelming her, so strong she couldn't breathe. "How did you hide that?"

"I'm an assassin." He spoke as if that answered everything, which, in a way, it did. To be an assassin, he had to be an absolute shadow, exercising ironclad control over himself and his environment in order to survive and succeed. He would allow no weakness, including being seen for who he was. "I figured it out when I was a kid. I heard so many stories from my mom about being hunted. I had nightmares about being caught. I was terrified all the time, until I figured out how to hide it. If no one knew I was a cat, no one would hunt me for it." His voice was calm, but he was watching her closely. "I rarely shift. I don't need to do it, so I don't."

He was a *white leopard.* He spoke freely about it, the part of her that she'd had to hide her entire life. "Can I... can I touch you?"

He laughed softly, then clasped her wrist. "Babe, we've

already crossed that line. You can touch me anytime you want." He pressed her hand to his chest. "Can you feel him?"

She dug her fingertips into his velvet-smooth skin. The hair on his chest was silky soft, softer than it should be, softer than she'd noticed before. She slid her hand over his shoulder and down his arm, following the curves on his muscles. This time, she could feel the sinewy strength, the elongated grace, the untapped power of his body. "No wonder you move so fast," she said. "So graceful."

"To be fair," he said, "I'm more than your average white leopard. My speed is an additional talent, as is my psychic ability. I got those from my dad's side. His family has some interesting genes, which is why mom's leopard responded to him." His eyes glittered with sudden feral interest. "A leopard needs a mate that will strengthen their bloodlines. They accept no less. They're dominant predators at the top of the food chain, and they have no tolerance for anything less in a mate."

His words made chills ripple down her spine, reverberating through her as if he'd reached inside her and claimed her with his words.

Slade leaned closer and slid his hand along her jaw. "My leopard wants yours," he whispered, his voice rough and ragged. "Can you feel it?"

Desire pulsed low in her belly, desire mixed with a carnal need. She swallowed. "Don't." She pushed him away and stood up, pacing across the closet.

He rose to his feet with that same innate grace she'd noticed in him the first time they'd met, as if he were part angel and part cat. "You've been hiding your whole life, Anya. It's time to stop." He strode across the closet toward her, his muscles rippling beneath his skin. He'd always been well-built, but now, he seemed more lethal, and more powerful, as if his skin was sliding across his muscles with wild grace.

She backed up, stumbling over the shoe she'd pulled out earlier. Slade was on her in that instant, his hands closing around her hips as he pulled her against him. His body was hard and hot against hers, bristling with a feral energy that made adrenaline pump through her.

Instinctively, she leaned into him, attracted to the side of him that was more than human. Both her feline side and her human side craved him, but it was more now, a silent, powerful calling that wouldn't cease. "Damn you," she whispered, even as her hands slid over his bare chest. "We don't have time for this, and I'm not going to shift."

"I'm not either. The scent lingers, and I don't want it on me when I go back to the warehouse." He slid his hand in her hair, his fingers digging in, almost as if he already had claws for fingers. "I need to go, but before I do, I need to do this." He bent his head and kissed her, a bruising, claiming kiss that plunged deep inside her, calling to her leopard. Her body hummed with the energy he was pouring into her, a deep vibration almost like a deeply sated cat purring as it wound its way around its prey. She gripped his shoulders, struggling to block herself from responding, but he was ruthless, just as he had been in the bar when he'd kissed her.

Only this time, it wasn't her soul he was trying to steal. It was her humanity. Her self-control. Her safety net. Her identity. "Stop!" She shoved at his shoulders, pushing him back so hard he actually moved.

His eyebrows went up, a predatory gleam in his eyes. "You're getting stronger. Tapping into her."

"I'm not— God. Stop!" She turned away from him and pushed her hair off her face, trying to regroup. "Don't you understand? My safety depends on me holding my secret forever."

"You can't hold it forever." His voice was low. "She's a part of you. She needs to be free."

She spun back toward him. "If I let her go, then neither of us will be free. We'll be locked in some cell like my mom and Marjorie. Like Julia." The thought of Julia made her stomach turn. With Slade awakening her leopard, Julia's fate became even more personal. "Why are we standing here anyway? We need to get back to the warehouse to find Julia!"

Slade allowed her to put distance between them, but he watched her carefully as he bent to retrieve his pants. "Whoever is at that warehouse arrived there after the security system alerted them. I needed to give them time to search thoroughly and find no one. They're good enough that if I was there, they might sense me." He pulled his pants on, a silent, black fabric that seemed to disappear into the shadows. "Once they decide they're alone, that's when I go back."

Anya snatched one of his dress shirts and pulled it on while he got dressed. She didn't want to be naked right now. With her leopard so close to the surface, and all the secrets she'd shared with Slade, she already felt vulnerable. She needed clothes. Heck, she needed a bulletproof vest and an arsenal.

His eyes darkened as she pulled on his shirt, and she went still, her heart starting to hammer when his eyes glittered with possession. His pants still unbuttoned, he walked over to her and gently removed her hands from the buttons. Slowly, with tantalizing gentleness, he clasped the front of her shirt and buttoned the bottom button. The backs of his hands brushed against her bare belly as he fastened it, making chills rush down her spine. "I like you in my shirt," he said as he buttoned the next one. His voice was low, almost a growl, an invisible caress along her spine.

She swallowed. "Did you touch me with your mind at the bar? I felt someone slide their hand along my back."

His fingers stilled, and he wasn't able to hide the flicker of surprise on his face. "You felt that?"

She nodded. "That was you?" She wanted him to say yes. The touch had been intimate. She didn't want to think that anyone else had been touching her like that, even if it had been only psychically.

"It was." He resumed his work on the third button, his knuckles brushing against the underside of her breasts. His brow was furrowed, giving him a contemplative look as he focused on the buttons. *You heard me talking to you as well, didn't you?*

Intimacy prickled over her skin. "Yes."

Say it in my mind.

"I don't know how."

"You've done it before. You do know." He lifted his gaze to hers. *Just open yourself to me, and think it.*

"But I don't want you in my mind." She was responding to him so strongly that she needed space. She wanted distance from him...but at the same time, she wanted to grab onto him and hold tight, keeping him so close that he'd never be able to walk away. She loved the feeling of his voice settling in her mind. It felt familiar, like the healing rays of sunshine on a spring day.

I can only hear what you offer to me. His gaze darkened. *If we can do this, then I can find you more easily. It's easier for me to keep you safe.*

She raised her brows. "Now, you're manipulating me, trying to use my fears to get me to bond with you."

He grinned unabashedly. "Is it working?"

"No." Yes. No. "Go away."

He finished buttoning her shirt, leaving the top three

buttons undone. "I'll be back in an hour or two. Don't leave here. Don't make any calls. Don't answer your phone. Don't go online."

Fear rippled over her at the thought of him leaving. "You're sure no one can find me here?"

"My home is a fortress. That's why I brought you here. It's the only place I feel safe leaving you." His gaze didn't waver from hers, and she sensed a protectiveness from him that she hadn't felt before. More determined. More personal. More...committed.

He turned away, drew on socks and boots, both of which were black, seeming to fade into shadows as soon as he put them on. He dragged a turtleneck over his chiseled upper body, and finished buttoning his pants. When he turned to face her again, clad in black except for his head, he seemed to blend into the darkness of the closet.

She blinked to clear her vision, but he still looked slightly out of focus, as if her eyes weren't working quite right. "Is that you, or the clothes?"

"Both." He walked over to her, his hands sliding to the back of her head and tangling in her hair. The moment she felt his hands on her, she relaxed, his touch providing reassurance that he was real, and he was present.

He kissed her softly. "My sweet white leopard," he said quietly. "You need to free your cat."

"No."

He didn't respond. He just kissed her until she melted into his embrace, her entire being responding to what he stoked in her. It wasn't until they were both breathless that he finally pulled back. "I need to go. I'll be back as soon as I can." He searched her face for a long moment, his eyes dark and inscrutable.

She frowned. "What is it?"

"I haven't come home to anyone since I was a kid."

There was an edge to his voice that she couldn't quite interpret.

"Is that bad?"

His fingers tightened in her hair. "Probably," he finally said. "I'll let you know."

And then, before she could respond, he slipped past her, disappearing into the bedroom. She hurried after him, but by the time she reached the room, he was gone. A feeling of emptiness infiltrated the air, and she knew he'd left the condo, leaving behind a void that would remain until he returned.

Chapter Eighteen

𝒯EN MINUTES LATER, Slade was stretched out on the roof of the neighboring warehouse, studying the three cars in the parking lot where he and Anya had been such a short time ago. Two Escalades and a stretch limo. They were parked haphazardly, as if they'd arrived in a hurry. Two men were leaning against the hood of the limo, and both of them were carrying significant hardware.

He concentrated on the nearest one, lightly testing his mental shields. The moment he touched the man's mind, the thug stood up and swung around, searching the parking lot. Slade swore and backed off. Not only did the guard have shields, but he'd also been sensitive to Slade's delicate touch.

Frowning, he tried the other man, and he had the same reaction.

Instantly, both men were on alert, scanning the darkness for him.

Slade knew he was nearly invisible on the roof, but he still didn't like how ready they'd been for him. They'd been prepared for a psychic attack. Not that he'd attacked them, yet, but they'd been ready.

Slade focused his attention on the warehouse, letting his energy pulse through the building. There were at least eight people inside, two of them in the main warehouse area, and the others in the cellblock. Ten people to respond to an alarm?

That seemed to be overkill to him...unless they knew something. Had there been a camera he missed? Had they somehow figured out who had slipped through their fingers?

Shit.

He didn't like this.

There were too many variables he didn't know.

Tonight wasn't a night to go in. It was a night to learn...but even as he thought it, he thought of Anya back at his place, of her best friend somewhere in the clutches of these men, of his own mother's ordeal at the hands of bastards just like these before his dad had found her.

If they thought the place was compromised, they would never be back.

The trail would disappear...until they came hunting for Anya. He had no doubt now that they would. She couldn't stay at his place forever... But he couldn't stop the rush of satisfaction at the idea of it.

He liked the fact she was at his place.

He liked the fact she was waiting for him.

He liked the idea of her never leaving...

A movement on a distant roof caught Slade's attention. He sent out a pulse of energy, trying to determine what it was. It was a man. Moving fast. Leaping from one roof to the other—

Holy shit.

Slade froze in disbelief as he watched the man racing across the rooflines. He recognized the build, the gait, the aura. He recognized them, because he'd seen it a hundred times in his life, always from a distance, always from the shadows. His brother. Killian Cross. *Killian was here.*

He reached out with his mind, seeking Killian's. *Stop.* He sent the command out across the night with such force that Killian stumbled and went down.

Slade tensed, watching as he waited for Killian to get up.

He did, slowly.

Go home. Slade sent the command forcefully.

This time, however, he got an answer. *Nice try, big bro, but you don't get to ditch me this time.*

Slade froze, stunned. Big bro? No, surely he'd misunderstood. *What did you just say—*

The cold barrel of a gun pressed into the back of Slade's neck. "It's about time you showed up, Cross."

The voice brushed over Slade's skin like a knife blade, sliding beneath his skin. For a split second, he was sucked into the past, when he was nine years old, listening to that voice taunt him, trying to draw him out as his dad lay dying in the living room. *The bastard who'd killed his family was behind him.*

Fury roared through him, and Slade lashed out with his mind. His psychic attack hit something solid and rebounded back at him. Swearing, he threw up his own shields, barely protecting his mind before his own violent energy crashed into him. The force of the blow thrust him backward, over the edge of the roof, out over the asphalt parking lot, six stories up, careening down toward the ground in a free-fall.

It was too far. Too fast. He knew he couldn't land safely...as a man.

Instinct took over, and he shifted, changing from man to cat in a millisecond. His clothes floated behind him as he righted himself, focusing on the ground as it came up to him. The man on the roof was shouting, and the guards by the cars were racing toward him, raising their weapons.

He was helpless while he fell, a white target in the dark night. Gunshots rang out, and he twisted and turned in mid-air, using his psychic energy to track the bullets. No, not bullets, darts. They were trying to *capture* him.

He spun around, arching his back as one whipped past his shoulder—

A sharp pain hit his foot, and numbness spread through his leg instantly. Swearing, he grabbed the dart with his teeth and ripped it out, hurling it aside when he landed. The minute his paws touched ground, he took off, using every last bit of his preternatural speed to disappear, fighting against the lethargy spreading viciously through him.

His legs felt like lead, and every muscle seemed to be made of clay. He knew he had only seconds to disappear. He gave it all his strength, racing against time, down the street, through an alley, over a Dumpster. He leapt to spring over a chain-link fence, but he slammed into it.

He hit hard, landing roughly on the hard alley floor. He tried to move, but he couldn't. His muscles were paralyzed, completely frozen. His mind was numb, and he couldn't focus. Distantly, he heard a car's engine, and then head-lights flooded him.

Footsteps crunched on the pavement, racing toward him. Slade tried to lash out with his mind, but he couldn't concentrate. Somehow, they'd interfered with his ability to attack psychically, his one defense in this situation. Helpless, he could do nothing but lay there, like the prey he'd hunted his whole life. How in hell's name had he let this happen?

His brother.

His *brother* had distracted him.

Nothing had ever distracted Slade before in his entire career. Nothing...except Anya's kiss when the demon had killed him. And now his brother. Both times, fatal mistakes. See? He was right. Caring about anyone was the worst choice he could have made, and now he was going to pay for it and so was Anya, because he wasn't going to be there to help her.

Never again. Never ever again. He was going to wipe his own mind of his brother, and not hold back this time, something he should have done long ago.

A face appeared above him, blocking out the light. Slade blinked, trying to make out the features, but the silhouetting effect of the headlights was too bright. He focused again, and dug deep to summon the last reserves of his psychic energy. He thrust it outward, not even able to control its direction. It was a blanket assault, spiraling in all directions, but he felt it hit its target this time. His assailant grunted, and went down on his knees beside Slade.

"That's how you treat the brother that's here to save your ass? You want us both to get caught?"

The voice was familiar, so familiar that Slade's world seemed to suspend in frozen time. Killian was there? How was that possible? How had he tracked him so quickly? Or at all?

"Come on, Slade. Let's get out of here." Killian lurched to his feet, stumbling from the effect of Slade's attack. He grabbed Slade around the chest and dragged him across the pavement, moving the massive leopard with far too much ease.

What the hell was going on?

His brother hoisted Slade into the back of a Suburban, then leapt inside. He gunned the engine and peeled out. The momentum slammed Slade against the side of the car, but he didn't even feel it through the drug.

All he knew was that he was helpless, and utterly at the mercy of the brother he'd abandoned when he was a year old. How had Killian figured out who he was? Why had he been there tonight? And whose side was he on?

Slade fought to concentrate, trying to will away the effects of the drug while Killian drove. He could attack his brother again, but then he'd probably crash the truck, assuming Slade could even manage to focus enough to do it. Right now, Slade was helpless, and if the men at the warehouse caught him, he would be in deep shit. He had no choice but to let his brother drive, and hope he was taking him in the right direction.

Anya. He reached out with his mind, trying to make contact with her, wishing that he'd forced her to build the psychic connection between them. Relief rushed through him when he realized he could still communicate telepathically, despite the drug, but the relief was quickly chased away by the fact that Anya didn't reply.

Shit. He couldn't reach her. How long would she wait before she decided to come after him?

He knew it wouldn't be long. He'd told her a couple hours, and he doubted she'd wait much longer than that. He had to get back to her, and fast...if he stayed alive long enough to do it.

Tentatively, afraid to do what he'd avoided doing for so long, he reached out with his mind to his sole living relative. *Killian?*

He felt his brother's surprise, and for a long moment, there was no answer. A sense of desolation flooded Slade, an emptiness so great he felt as though he were free-falling into a greater darkness than he'd ever experienced before. His brother had known him, and for a brief moment, Slade had felt real again, connected, hopeful...which made the silence a thousand times more oppressive than it had been for all the years he'd lived it.

Then, just as tentatively, just as carefully, came a reply.

Yeah, Slade. It's me.

Emotion flooded Slade, so overwhelming that for a moment, he couldn't breathe. His lungs seemed to close down on him, crushing him.

Where can we go? Killian's voice in his mind again, more easily this time, not wasting time on a reunion when they were being hunted by the man who'd destroyed their family. Survival first, a lesson he should have been too young to learn before Slade had left him at the church.

They needed a safe house. Slade had seven of them within reach, but there was only one he wanted to go to, the one where Anya was. But could he bring his brother there? He didn't even know him, other than a blood tie that burned deeply. Could he expose Anya to him? Expose his own safe house to him, the one sanctuary that kept him sane when the emptiness threatened to consume him?

They're tracking us, bro. Can you feel it?

Slade reached out with his mind, and immediately caught the dark, violent energy of the men pursuing them. The need to stop the car and face them, to take them apart one by one, burned through him, but he knew he'd lose. They were prepared to defend against a psychic attack, and he was physically helpless, with his only protection being the brother Slade had given up to keep safe.

Now wasn't the time to stand and fight.

It was time to regroup, because the time to live in the shadows was long gone. The war had found them, and it would come looking for them fast, hard, and deadly.

Slade? We're running out of pavement here.

Slade knew there was only one choice to be made. Only one choice he wanted to make. Only one choice that he wanted to be right. *321 Phoenix Street.*

* * *

Someone else was in the bedroom.

215

Anya remained completely still as she awoke, listening to the soft tread of footsteps on Slade's carpet. It wasn't Slade. Already, she knew the sound of his footsteps, and it wasn't him. Her heart started to pound, and she cracked her eyes open.

A man was crouching in front of her, his face inches from hers, his deep brown eyes riveted to her face. She jerked upright, scrambling backwards. She tumbled off the side of the bed and leapt to her feet, grabbing a lamp from beside the bed. *Slade!* Instinctively she reached out for him, trying to open the connections she'd refused such a short time ago.

It's okay. His voice brushed over hers, but it sounded fuzzy and sleepy. *It's Killian. I told him not to wake you if you were still sleeping.*

Killian? She stared at the man on the other side of the bed. He hadn't moved from his crouch, but he'd raised his hands up, as if to show her he meant no harm. He was ripped with muscle, his jaw angled and hard, his dark hair cropped short. He looked dangerous and deadly, just like Slade... Her heart fluttered. He *did* look just like Slade. Younger, leaner, but he had the same jaw, the same nose, and the same dangerous eyes. *Your brother? How—*

I don't know. We haven't had time to talk. Can you come out here, please?

Killian still hadn't moved. "Did Slade explain?"

"Yes." She didn't lower the lamp. How was Killian there? What had happened? "Where's Slade?"

"In the living room."

"He's *here?*" He was present, but he'd asked Killian to get her? Fear knifed through her. "What's wrong with him?" Not waiting for an answer, she tossed the lamp on the bed and raced out the door and down the hall.

She ran into the living room and spun around, searching

for him. "Slade?"

By the fireplace.

She spun around toward the south end of the room and hurried around the couch. A massive white leopard was stretched out on his side on the carpet, his ribs moving quickly, as if he were panting. For a moment, she forgot to move, completely stunned by the incredible beauty of the cat. His fur was brilliant white, spotted with black circles, and his body was lean and muscled. She'd never seen her mother shift before, and to see Slade in full leopard form was stunning. Her own leopard rose hard and fast, clawing to be released, but there was nowhere for it to go.

Come around where I can see you.

Anya realized suddenly that Slade hadn't moved. Not even his ear had flicked toward her. Fear returned with a vengeance, and she hurried around him and kneeled by his head. His eyes were staring sightlessly in front of him, not even moving toward her. "Slade." She dug her hand into the thick fur on his neck. "What happened?"

"Paralyzing dart." Killian strode into the living room, his long legs moving with the same grace she was used to seeing from Slade. He hopped over the back of the couch and sat down, leaning forward so his forearms were on his thighs, his hooded gaze studying them both.

"A dart?" She looked back at Slade. "At the warehouse?"

They were waiting for me. They seemed to have been expecting me. If Killian hadn't been there, they'd have me now.

Sweat beaded on Anya's brow and her fingers tightened in his scruff. Slade was the best at being invisible, and yet they'd still almost caught him? "Julia?"

I didn't have a chance.

Anya sat back, fighting off tears. She kept her fingers

deep in Slade's fur, gripping the loose skin of his neck. "We're overmatched, aren't we?"

No. Slade's voice was hard, but still edged with fuzziness from the drug. *We'll handle this. I just need time for the drug to work its way through my system.*

"How long is that?"

Not long. I'm working on processing it. Should be soon. Even as he spoke, his gaze swiveled toward hers, the first movement she'd seen him make. The rest of him, however, was totally frozen, completely vulnerable. Slade, the shadow of the night who no one had been able to stop his whole life, was completely incapacitated on his floor. What were they up against? How could they possibly win? And what did winning even mean? The likelihood of retrieving Julia seemed even more faint now, a wish on a shooting star that would fade and never be realized.

Hey. Slade interrupted her.

She looked at him. "What?"

Don't give up on me, babe. You need to stay focused.

Her fingers tightened in his fur. *I need you, Slade. Don't die. I can't handle it.* As she said it, a deep fear settled over her, a fear just like the one that had swept over her when she'd approached the warehouse where her mother had just been killed, or that moment when she'd realized that Julia hadn't come back from the store yet. That fear that happened when someone she loved was in danger, and she thought she was going to lose them. The kind of terror that reached deep inside her and twisted her heart until she couldn't breathe. The kind of paralyzing anguish that was so overpowering that her mind seemed to blank out and she couldn't think. The fear that happened only when a piece of her heart was threatened.

Anya. His voice wrapped around her gently. *Look at me.*

She stared down into his ice-blue eyes, her fingers gripping his fur so tightly that her fingers were cramping. *I can't do this without you, Slade. I can't. I lo—* She stopped, cutting herself off before she could finish her sentence. Love? She'd just been about to tell him she loved him? She couldn't. She didn't know him. She didn't want to be vulnerable again. She didn't want any of it.

But even as she thought it, she knew it didn't matter. Slade had reached inside her heart from the beginning, when his kiss had shattered her defenses and pulled her into the torment waging inside his soul. She understood him deeply, both of them growing up on the run, hiding from the darkness hunting them, hiding from who they were. He'd given her comfort. He'd sacrificed what mattered to him to stand by her. He'd made her feel safe, cherished, and brave for the first time in her life, just as she'd made his heart start to beat again. She needed him, and he needed her, and not simply to wage the war they'd been thrust into.

Their connection was so much deeper than that, so much more powerful, and so much more terrifying. She couldn't handle losing someone else she loved. She just couldn't. If she let herself love him, she wouldn't be able to focus long enough to stay alive and find Julia. The fear would debilitate her, just when she couldn't afford it.

Anya. Slade's eyes glittered as he watched her, awareness returning to his gaze. *You won't have to do it without me. We're on it.*

She pushed back from him, needing to put distance between them. "How can we be on it? Julia could be anywhere now. *Anywhere.*"

"Julia?" Killian was watching them closely, and she wondered if he'd been tapped into their conversation. "Who's Julia?"

"My best friend. She was kidnapped by the people at

the warehouse a few weeks ago." Anya stood up, ignoring Slade's commands to stay where she was. "We went there to find her, and we didn't." She walked over to the fireplace and perched on the edge of the hearth, hugging herself tightly.

"White leopard?" Killian asked.

Anya hesitated. Did she really trust him? He was Slade's brother, but how had he ended up here? "Who *are* you?" she asked instead.

Killian's eyebrows went up. "Killian Cross. Slade's brother."

"I know, but that doesn't answer my question." She saw the tip of Slade's tail twitch, and her throat tightened. He was going to be okay...this time. It didn't change how dangerous the situation was, but this time, he'd made it. "Slade said you didn't know who he was. How is it that you're here?"

Slade's energy tightened, and she realized he was listening intently to the answer as well. Fear crept down Anya's spine. If Slade didn't know either, why had he brought Killian here, into their one safe place? Had he been fooled by the brother he'd sacrificed everything for? Were they in danger right now, as Slade lay there, paralyzed?

She realized that she was still wearing only Slade's shirt. She had no weapons, no shoes, no way to defend herself or Slade if Killian did anything. *Slade. Do you trust him?*

For a long moment, he didn't answer. And when he did, it didn't make her feel any better. *I don't know.*

Chapter Nineteen

ANYA'S FEAR WAS an accelerant, igniting Slade's urgency to regain function of his body. He didn't like being helpless, while Anya sat across from his brother, unprotected. He knew he'd made the right choice, having Killian bring him back to his place. There was no other way he could have made sure Anya was safe. But now that he was here, he had become grimly aware that the brother he'd been so stunned to see was now a stranger who was in his space, too close to the woman under Slade's protection.

He had to step up, and fast. Slade channeled his psychic energy, pouring it into his cells and bloodstream, speeding up his metabolism to try to flush the toxin from his system. His heart was racing, his breathing shallow, his body aching, but he didn't back off, driving energy fiercely into his body.

He fought to lift his head, forcing his frozen muscles to contract. It was agonizing, trying to make his body respond, but slowly, he was able to drag his head several inches to the right, bringing Killian within eyesight.

The moment his gaze settled on Killian, shock hit Slade's system again. He hadn't seen those brown eyes up close in years. He recognized the eyes, the jaw, the nose, the hair...and especially his energy signature. His *brother* was sitting on his couch, completely unfazed by the fact Slade had turned into a white leopard and had a safe house. How was this moment possible? *How do you know me?* He brought Anya into the conversation, connecting all their minds so she would be party to it.

Killian looked down at him, his face a mask that Slade couldn't read. "You tried to wipe my mind."

Tried? Foreboding trickled down Slade's spine. *What do you remember?* Urgency pulsed at him, and he sent more psychic energy through him. His hind legs began to tingle, as if a thousand sharp needles had been jammed into his flesh, and he knew he was starting to succeed.

"Everything." Killian leaned forward. "I remember our parents. I remember being with you when Dad was killed. I remember you leaving me at that church. I remember the times you spoke to me since...and I remember how you vanished each time."

More shock rippled through Slade. *You were a year old when I left you at the church.* It had never occurred to him to wipe Killian's mind at that point. It was impossible that he would remember. And yet...he was claiming to.

Slade's front legs began to tingle as his nerves began to function. He embraced the pain, using it to fuel his urgency. Being unable to do anything other than stretch out on his side like a dozing housecat was torturous when there was so much at stake. He'd never felt helpless in his life, and it violated every precept his life was based upon.

Killian leaned forward, watching him intently, as if he were tracking Slade's reclamation of his body as carefully as Slade was...waiting...for what? Alarm prickled through him. *Anya. I don't know if I can trust him.*

She rose to her feet slowly, her gaze fixated on Killian.

"I didn't remember any of it until the first time you made contact with me," Killian said, still watching him. "Do you remember? I was fourteen, and I'd just won my first football game as a starting quarterback for the varsity squad."

How the hell did Killian remember that? Slade had wiped his mind carefully, leaving no memory untouched. *I remember.* He'd had to talk to Killian that day, just to see the pride in his kid brother's face, to be able to prove to himself that he'd done the right thing by walking away from him so long ago.

"When you were talking to me, I felt like I'd seen you before," Killian said. "I felt like I *knew* you. I had these flashes in my mind of our life. Mom and Dad. My sister. Blood. Screams. You. It didn't make any sense, and as soon as you walked away, everything became fuzzy. You were drifting at the edges of my mind, almost in reach, but not quite. I knew something had happened that day, but I couldn't remember."

Slade moved his right front leg, sliding it across the carpet. The pain was extraordinary, the cost of his body reclaiming itself, but it was triumphant pain, the pain of victory. *So, how did you remember?*

"I started doing research on memories. I learned about psychic control of minds, and I was pretty sure you'd done it. I researched how to recover memories, and how to protect against mind control. The next time you made contact, five years ago, I was ready. I felt you try to shield my mind, and I protected myself. This time, when you walked away, I remembered everything." Killian's eyes gleamed brightly. "I remembered everything you'd stolen from me, Slade."

Slade swore. *I didn't steal it. I was trying to protect you.* He was able to move his right back leg, flexing it as he pulled it under him.

"From what? Who I am? From knowing that some bastard out there had killed my family?" His eyes glittered. "I remembered everything that time, but before I could say anything, you vanished, just like before. I've been searching for you ever since. Some nights, I could sense you, and I knew you'd been near, but you were always gone before I could find you." He met Slade's gaze. "You're invisible. You literally don't exist."

I exist. He summoned his strength and rolled onto his belly, his muscles shaking with the effort of holding himself up.

Killian leaned forward, tension radiating from him. "Do you know what it's like to be ripped from your life, and left with nothing but fragmented memories, and a brother who abandoned you?"

"He didn't abandon you," Anya snapped, interrupting.

Slade swore when Killian's gaze snapped to Anya. *Back off, Anya. I don't want him focused on you.*

She ignored him. "He was trying to save your life."

Killian's eyes narrowed. "What do you know about that?"

"My family was murdered, too. My mother tried to protect me from her enemies, and Slade was doing the same thing. He was *nine* when he left you there. You really think he could have taken care of you? He was a nine-year-old orphan whose family had been murdered."

Anya! Don't.

She stepped over Slade, moving closer to Killian, her eyes flashing with fury. "You were all he had left," she snapped. "You were the only good thing in his life, the only living creature he ever let himself care about. It broke his heart every damned second to not have you in his life, but he did it to protect you, because he didn't want to watch you die because he'd been too selfish to leave you alone."

Slade watched her in shock, stunned by her defense of him. He didn't need anyone to defend him, and he sure as hell didn't want her drawing the attention of his brother, but at the same time... He liked it. No, he didn't like it. He *loved* having her defend him. He was an assassin whose moral code was his only source of pride, and yet Anya was standing up for him as if she saw something else in him, something more, something deeper.

She jabbed her finger in Killian's chest. "Love is all that matters in this life, but it takes different forms. Be grateful that there's someone on this earth who loves you enough to sacrifice his own soul to save you, because in one second, you can lose all of that and realize you're truly alone and everyone you love is gone!"

Slade swore, fighting even harder to regain control of his body. He had to stop her from antagonizing Killian, and he had to be able to defend her.

Killian's eyes widened, his face a dangerous mask. "Don't talk to me about—"

With a roar of fury, Slade shifted. His bones screamed in pain as he reclaimed his human form, and Anya whirled around. "Slade!"

He landed on his hands and knees, then lurched to his feet, staggering as he tried to stay upright. Anya raced over to him and caught his arm as he swayed, sliding her arm around his waist. He locked his arm around her shoulders, dragging her against him as he fought to maintain his balance. His muscles were still weak, barely able to function, but he stood strong, doing his best to hide his weakness. "Don't speak to her like that," he said softly, unable to keep the growl out of his voice. "She's under my protection."

Killian's gaze went back and forth between them, his eyes narrowing. "This is who you declare yourself to? Her? Not your own brother?"

Slade felt Anya stiffen beside him, and he squeezed her. Energy flared inside him, instinctively preparing to lash out at his brother and destroy all memories of his past, to do what it took to change it. He couldn't afford for the shit to go south. Killian stood quickly, his eyes darkening, as if he knew what Slade had intended. Killian might have figured out how to protect against a standard memory wipe, but Slade had weapons that no one could defend against. He looked his brother in the eyes, and knew that this was the last time Killian would ever remember him, and it was the last time he'd ever speak to him again. "I love you," he said quietly, as he prepared to strike. "I'm sorry."

Killian's eyes widened. "Don't—"

"Stop!" Anya jumped between them, holding up her hands.

Slade swore and aborted, knowing that she was in his line of attack. "Anya—"

"Listen to me!" She whirled toward Slade. "Don't do what you always do. This is your chance. You miss him. You know you do."

"I can't." He kept his attention on Killian, even as he reached for Anya to pull her out of the way. "I won't let him be killed. He can't be involved in this, or my life, or his own history."

"Death isn't always the worst thing that can happen!" she snapped.

He glanced at her, his heart turning over when he saw the tears glistening in her eyes. "Really? Would you have been willing to give up a relationship with your mother if it would have kept her alive? If you could have spared her the pain of being murdered, would you have done whatever it took?" He hated to bring it up, but he *needed* her to understand. Anya was his link to the humanity he'd abandoned so long ago. She was his anchor in a world where nothing mattered anymore.

Tears streamed down her cheeks, and to his surprise, she shook her head. "No," she whispered.

"No?" He didn't understand. "You'd let her suffer so you could have time with her?"

"No." Anya raised her chin. "But I would never have missed out on my time with her in hopes that maybe we could have lived longer separately. I'd rather live a shorter time and live it fully, than live an eternity in a vast wasteland of emptiness."

Slade's gut twisted at her words. Silently, he looked toward his brother, standing there, looking so familiar, and yet also like a complete stranger. "Is that your life?" he asked Killian. "A vast wasteland of emptiness?" He felt like a great darkness was crushing down on him. Had he fucked up so badly? Had he destroyed his brother's life when he'd tried to save it?

For a long moment, Killian didn't respond, and Slade felt something inside him begin to die. His legs buckled, and he went down on his knees, suddenly unable to breathe. He braced his hands on the carpet, fighting for oxygen. Jesus. Had it all been a lie, that he'd done the right thing for his brother?

Anya knelt beside him, her hand on his shoulder. "I'm sorry," she whispered. "I didn't mean it like that." Tears were still streaming down her cheeks. "I just loved my mom and my family so much I can't imagine life without them. That doesn't mean you have to make the same choice."

He touched her cheek, wiping the tears away. His chest hurt. His lungs hurt. Everything hurt. He didn't know this kind of pain existed, the kind that had nothing to do with the body and everything to do with the soul. He'd worked so hard not to feel, and suddenly, all the precisely ordered rules of his life were cracking, tearing apart the foundation of what defined him.

Killian suddenly crouched in front of him, his muddy boots leaving marks on Slade's pristine, un-lived-in carpet.

Keeping Anya's fingers in his hand, Slade raised his head to look at his brother. For the first time in his life, he didn't see the baby he'd tried to protect. He saw a man, heavily muscled, dangerous, and deadly. "I'm sorry," Slade said. He didn't even know what he was sorry for. Leaving Killian behind? Wiping his memory? Letting him figure out the truth? "I tried to do what was right. If I fucked it up, I'm sorry."

Killian's face was impassive, his voice low as he spoke. "I have two families," he said. "The one I was born to, and the one that raised me. All of them, good people. The only void in my life was the fact I didn't get to know my brother. The rest of my life..." He shrugged. "It's been good, Slade. Real good."

He searched Killian's face. "It has?"

"Yeah."

Slade's muscles began to shake, and he bowed his head, fighting against emotions he had no idea how to cope with. Anya slipped her arms around his neck and pulled him close to her. He buried his face in her hair and held her, drinking in the familiar comfort of her body. He was so close to a precipice he didn't have the tools to navigate. Every instinct told him to change paths, to abort, to go back to the world he knew...but there was another part of him, a budding, tiny whisper, that burned not to run away and re-vert to his life.

Keeping his grip tight on Anya, he raised his head to look at his brother. Killian's eyes were dark, fixated on him. "I'm an assassin," Slade said. "I have more enemies than our parents ever did. I live a life in the shadows, because if

I ever care about anyone, they will be a target as well. Anyone who's in my life might die because of who I am." His arms tightened around Anya as he said it. "It's safest for you to never be associated with me. Plus, the bastards at the warehouse know who I am, so if you're known as a Cross, you're going to pick up those enemies as well. If you stay Killian Cross, you'll be in danger every minute of every day. If you go back to your life, it's over. You're safe."

Killian's brows went up, but he said nothing, waiting for Slade to finish.

Slade took a deep breath. "I'll let you choose," he said, the words sticking in his throat. He didn't want to let Killian choose. He wanted to make the choice for him, to wipe his mind and thrust him back into the safe world he'd grown up in, where his biggest heartache would be a fight with his wife or his kids, but looking into Killian's eyes, he couldn't make the choice for him. Not after what Anya had said. "If you become Killian Cross, then everyone you love will be in danger as well. Everyone who your enemies *think* you love will be in danger. You can't protect them." He met his brother's steel gaze. "I'll take it all away," he said. "I can make you forget. I can give you back your life. But..." He stumbled, barely able to say the words. "If you want to live this life, I won't stop you."

Just saying the words brought back images of death, of the moment when he'd lost those who mattered to him, the *only* people who mattered to him. His parents. His sister. His little brother. Himself.

He stared at his brother, into the dark eyes that were so familiar, and yet belonged to a complete stranger at the same time.

Silently, Killian reached into his back pocket. He pulled out his wallet, and removed a newspaper clipping from it. He held it out. "Read it."

Slade glanced at Anya, but he took it. She leaned over his shoulder as he unfolded it. It was an article from two months ago. Frowning, he scanned the headline. *Family home burned to the ground. No survivors.* His gut went cold when he saw the photograph. He knew that house. He'd stood outside it many, many times, wishing he could walk up to the front door and knock. He looked at his brother. "This is your home."

"My parents'." A muscle ticked in Killian's cheek, the only sign of emotion in his stoic face. "It's where I grew up. My brother brought his fiancée home that night to meet the family. I had an emergency at the hospital, so I was late. Because some bastard had a heart attack, I wasn't there to save them." His jaw tightened, his voice grew hard. "They died. Four bodies, but only my parents were even identifiable. Complete carnage."

Slade swore, remembering all too well coming home to death. "I'm so sorry, Killian—"

"They were murdered."

Anya sucked in her breath.

Slade sat back on his heels, staring at his brother. "What?" Not again. Not again. *Not again.* He'd placed Killian with that family so he *wouldn't* have to face something like that, to protect him from having his heart eviscerated. Cold rushed over him, the kind of icy cold that made it difficult to breathe. "You're sure?"

Killian nodded. "In the front yard, someone had carved the words, 'Blame Killian.' They knew my real name."

"Blame you?" Fury rolled through Slade. "Why?"

Killian shrugged. "When I was searching for you, I uncovered a lot of shit I didn't like. Shit I decided to change. Things involving shifters being kidnapped and sold, just like Mom was. Someone didn't like what I was doing." He looked at Slade. "Do you understand what happened,

Slade? They were all innocent, and they died because of me. My brother was getting *married.* She died because she fell in love with a man who had the crappy luck to have me for a brother."

"He was lucky as hell to have you for a brother," Slade snapped. "Never forget that."

"Was he?" Killian's eyes were haunted, and Slade saw the same guilt and grief that had haunted him for so long. "Was she so lucky? Were my parents so lucky? They're *dead.* My brother's fiancée was named Charlotte Hunter. She was twenty-five. I never even met her, and she's still dead because of me. Her family didn't even get to identify her. They were just handed her burned-out remains and told 'here's your kid. Have a nice day.'" He bowed his head, running his hands through his hair, his fingers digging into his scalp as he fought back emotion he'd never let anyone see.

Slade leaned forward. "Listen to me, Killian. You didn't kill them. Some piece of shit did. You were trying to stop him, and that was the right thing to do. Dad fought for justice, and Mom was killed by his enemies, but even as she died, she told him to keep fighting. She never blamed him, so Dad never did either. He just kept fighting, and he took down as many as he could before they got him. I'm damned proud to be his son, and damned proud to be your brother."

Killian raised his head to look at Slade. His eyes were dark and haunted, carrying guilt that Slade knew would eat away at him until he died. "Thanks."

It was one word, but it created a bond, the bond that had never been able to form because Slade had left him in that church. Slade nodded, and both brothers sat back. The moment was over. The past had to be buried once again, or survival wasn't possible.

Slade cleared his throat as he tried to shut down his

own emotions and analyze what Killian had told him. A sinking feeling seemed to be sucking him down, but he fought it off, trying to breathe, trying to stay above the swell of emotions. He glanced at Anya, and he saw tears glistening in her eyes. Too much death between the three of them. Too much fucking death.

He held out his hand to her, and she slipped over to him, sliding her hand in his. He tucked their hands against his chest, trying to infuse warmth into her cold fingers while he focused on his brother. Someone had known Killian's real name. Who had he pissed off with his questions? "Is that why you were at the warehouse tonight? Is that who you were after?"

Killian hesitated, and his gaze flicked away for a split second. "Tonight had nothing to do with that. I was there because I'd sensed you were there, but once I was there, I realized what it was." He looked at Slade. "As always, you'd left by the time I got there, but this time, you came back." Killian sat down on the couch and leaned forward. "It's too late to hide me, Slade. I'm in it. People know who I am. I want to get the bastards who killed both of my families, and if you wipe my mind, you'll steal from me the justice I deserve. I'm not afraid."

Slade ran his hands through his hair. More people murdered. He'd tried to protect his brother, and he'd gotten it wrong. Not only had he failed to protect Killian, but his choice had resulted in four other people dying. Good people. People who mattered to Killian, and who mattered to him, because they'd taken care of his brother. "I'm sorry." Those two words were so inadequate, but there weren't any better ones. "Hell, Killian. I'm so sorry."

Killian inclined his head in acknowledgement. "I loved them. They were my family. I'm not going to stop until I make it right. Do you understand?"

Slade nodded. Of anything, he understood that. "How can I help?"

"Tell me what you know about the shifter black market. Leopards specifically."

Anya tensed, and Slade leaned forward. "Leopards?" he asked. "Why leopards?"

Killian raised his brows in surprise. "My parents were leopards. Like us."

"They were? Like *us*?" Slade was too shocked to respond coherently.

Killian frowned "Isn't that why you placed me with them? They were my rock when I started shifting—"

Slade leapt to his feet. "You *shift?* Into a leopard? A white leopard?"

"Black."

"Black." Slade sat down heavily. White leopards gave birth to only one white leopard. He knew that. But a black leopard? Was that a loophole he didn't know about? "You're a *shifter*."

"Yeah." Killian grinned, the first genuine smile Slade had seen on his face. "It's the best thing in my life. We have a place in the mountains where we go. It's incredible to run free like that." His face was softer, calmer, and his body seemed to relax visibly. "You going to run with me, bro? When this is over?"

"Run with you?" He hadn't run free in his entire life. Since before his first shift, he knew how dangerous it was to reveal himself. He shifted when he had to, but he kept it close and careful. He never just *ran.* "I don't do that."

Killian's smile faded, and he studied Slade. "Sorry to hear that."

Slade ran his hands through his hair, trying to clear his mind. Everything was raining down on him so quickly he couldn't think.

Anya leaned past him. "Killian, my best friend was kidnapped. We traced her to that warehouse, but she's not there anymore. Slade went back to get more information. Do you know anything about those men? Or that warehouse?"

Killian's gaze flicked to hers. "She's a shifter?"

Anya hesitated, then nodded. "White leopard."

Killian's face darkened. "Bastards." He stood up and paced across the room, running his hand through his hair the same way Slade always did. "I got their license plates. Both Escalades had contained shifters recently. I was going to run the plates and see if I could get an address. You got a computer here?"

Slade hesitated, watching as Killian stopped and looked at him, waiting. Was he really going to bring his brother into this situation? He worked alone. He existed alone. He thrived alone. And now, there were two people in his space, two people who mattered to him, two people who were so important to him that he'd be absolutely broken if something happened to them.

"Slade." Anya slipped her hand over his shoulders. "It's okay to let us in. We already have baggage. We already live with danger every day. You don't make it worse. You make it better."

He looked over at her, into her deep blue eyes. He felt so lost, like he was floundering in quicksand. She was beautiful, so achingly beautiful. He slid his hands through her hair, tunneling them through the silken tresses. "I want to hide you and protect you from all this," he whispered. "I can't lose both of you. I can't do it."

He'd worked so hard to be cold. He was used to it. It made life livable. But his walls were falling, and it was getting more difficult to breathe, to think, to focus. He looked at Killian. "Disappear," he urged. "I'll find out what happened to your parents. I'll take care of it."

Killian's eyes darkened. "Could *you* do that? Walk away?"

"No, but I'm already fucked up. You're not."

"Are you so sure?" Killian's voice was cool, icy, and suddenly, Slade saw another side to him, a side that was just as ruthless and cold as he was. He realized suddenly that Killian was a warrior. He'd lived in the trenches, he'd battled enemies that had left him bleeding and raw, and he'd lost people who mattered. For Killian to break Slade's memory wipe meant he was powerful, almost legendary. Only the demon had been able to withstand Slade's attack. Granted, he hadn't hit Killian as hard, but it had been clean. He should not have remembered...and yet...he had.

"You need me," Killian said simply. "You can't do it alone. You know it."

Slade glanced at Anya, and then back at Killian. He'd been trying to take down these bastards his whole life, and they were smarter, faster, and better than he was. And now, they were after Anya, his brother, and Anya's best friend.

Could he really afford to work alone? He knew he couldn't. There was too much at stake. It was no longer just about him, as much as he wanted it to be. He gripped Anya's hand and met his brother's gaze. "Okay. I'm in."

Chapter Twenty

ANYA PAUSED IN the doorway of Slade's office, watching the two brothers bent over his desk, talking quietly as they watched the computer screen. They were so much alike, with their dark hair and intense eyes, the angle of their jaws, and even the lilt of their voices. Like Slade, Killian's accent had a hint of British royalty that made him fit in perfectly with the lush office with its antiques, gilded picture frames, and the ornate French doors that opened to a beautiful deck high above the city.

A wave of sadness washed over her, and she pressed her lips together, trying to fend off the sudden onslaught of emotion. Seeing Slade and Killian together made the loss of her own family even more acute. When it had just been Slade and her, she'd been able to focus on him, and keep their mission at an emotional distance. But the sight of the brothers working side by side made her miss her mom and Marjorie deeply, and it tightened the constant grip of fear in her stomach about what was happening to Julia.

She took a deep breath. Losing control wasn't going to help her find Julia. She had to stay focused, and these brothers were her only chance. Instead of letting the grief consume her, she made herself concentrate on the men. They exuded confidence and competence. Their voices were low and deep, settling inside her like a solid weight, anchoring her. They were in deep conversation, but their stances were relaxed, like wild cats patiently waiting for their prey to step too close.

Slade had put on a soft tee shirt and jeans, but he was barefoot, as was Killian. Both men were so at ease in their skin, it was easy to see them as the leopards they were. A whisper of jealousy flickered through her, and she wondered what it would be like to embrace who she truly was instead of hiding it. When she'd seen Slade as a leopard, she'd been too scared about his immobility to register the fact he was a leopard. But now, as she watched him talk and move, she could almost see the leopard beneath his skin. He was pure muscle and power, moving with effortless efficiency.

Slade glanced up, and he smiled when he saw her, a quick, private smile that made her stomach turn over. "You okay?"

She nodded, and walked in. She'd showered and grabbed a bite to eat, taking advantage of Killian's need to run a computer search on the license plates. Slade's bathroom was imported marble, with etched glass doors that were truly beautiful. Every inch of his home was pure elegance and luxury, and yet there he stood, in bare feet and a tee shirt, his muscles rippling like the wild animal that lived inside him, a predator that would thrive in the wild, not behind closed doors and windows. "What did you guys find?"

Slade held out his hand to her. Surprised, she took it, and let him pull her around the desk. He tucked her in front of him, and leaned over her shoulder, his breath warm and tantalizing against her cheek, as he pointed to the screen.

"All the cars are registered to dummy corporations," he said. "They're not traceable."

Her heart sank. "Really?" She'd been so sure that between Killian and Slade, they would find answers. "So, we don't know anything more? Nothing about Julia?" She bit her lip, blinking back tears as the reality of their situation returned with brutality.

"No. But look." Slade punched a few buttons on the computer, and the screen shifted to six distinct video feeds. She stiffened when she saw the demon that had attacked her standing still, staring directly up into the camera. "Where is that?"

"Outside my building."

She went cold. "He found us?"

"So did they." Killian indicated the bottom right corner, and Anya saw two black SUVs parked. The doors opened and armed men got out, carrying what looked like machine guns and dart guns.

She sank back against Slade, fear gripping her. "Is that outside this building as well?"

"Yeah." Slade's voice was grim. "They can't see the building unless I'm in their head showing it to them, but they clearly know it's here. They're too close. No one has ever gotten this close." He switched to another camera angle, showing two more sets of armed men standing in the street. "They're on all sides. They know it's here, but they can't find it."

Anya and Killian exchanged glances, and all three of them knew the truth. Anya and Killian's presence was not as easy to hide as Slade's was. Their visibility in his life had compromised the safety of his home, stealing from him the one oasis he had. "So, what now?"

"We hunt." Slade's voice was cold, ice cold, that of a killer. A chill gripped Anya's spine, and she knew she was seeing the Black Swan come to life. She'd gotten used to thinking of Slade as her guardian and protector, but now, she could see him as the assassin who had silently, and mercilessly, killed so many.

"Hunt?" Killian's eyes gleamed with a feral hunger that made even more chills race down Anya's back. Two brothers of the same kind. How different *was* Killian from Slade? Had he lived a life of killing, too? Or was killing something that had been born into their makeup, something that didn't depend on the childhood they'd been blessed or cursed with.

"I'm in," he said. "I have supplies in the car. I'll be back in a minute." He saluted Slade then strode out of the room, moving with the same lethal grace that Slade always moved with.

The moment he was gone, Slade turned his back on her and walked to the window. He gripped the frame, staring out at the city. His muscles were taut, and his jaw was tight.

"Everything okay?" Even as she asked it, she knew it was a stupid question. Nothing was okay. But she'd asked the question, because she'd wanted Slade to reassure her that everything was fine, that this was a piece of cake for him.

"No." He turned to face her, his eyes dark. "I was pulled from death's door for this. I know that I'm the right one for the job, because of my background with the shifter market. But what is so important about *you* that made someone wield a tremendous amount of power to bring me back from the dead to do it? What am I not seeing that I should?"

He walked over to her and ran his hands down her arms, providing both warmth and a shot of hot energy. She knew her leopard was responding to his, wanting to rise up to meet him. "Who *are* you, Anya?"

She shook her head. "I'm just me—"

"No, you're not." He nudged her foot with his toe. "I think it's time to take that rune off and see who you really are."

"What? No!" She backed up, fear rippling through her. Her mother had given her life to hide her. It was one thing to disregard her mother's commands to run if someone found them so that she could find Julia. It was another to shift. If she shifted, she would be exposed. Not even Julia knew whether she could shift, or that she was a white leopard. "Never."

Slade watched her, but made no move to stop her. Why would he bother to stop her ineffective retreat across his office? He was so much faster than she was, she had no hope of escaping him. Instead of coming after her, he simply studied her. "I need to understand what is so important about you."

She pulled her shoulders back. "It doesn't matter. All that matters is Julia."

"No, that's not all that matters." He leaned on the desk. "My entire life is completely screwed up right now because of you. If it hadn't been for you, my brother wouldn't be here. He wouldn't have gotten sucked into my life. The man who killed my family wouldn't have shot me with a dart. My enemies wouldn't be standing outside my house, waiting for me to step outside."

She glared at him. "Do you want to go back to being alone? Is that what you want? To forget about your brother? About me? Isn't there anything good about what has happened to you?"

"Yes!" He slammed his hands down on the desk, making her jump. "Don't you understand, Anya? Everything is good. I loved having you in my bed. It's the best gift of my damned life to be having a conversation with my brother. My house feels different with you both in it, and I like it."

He shoved the heavy desk aside, sending it crashing against the wall with frightening ease. He strode across the room and caught her wrist, yanking her against him before she could step away. "And you know what that means?" he asked. "Do you understand?" He gripped the back of her hair, his fingers holding tightly, almost painfully, but she wasn't afraid of him.

She knew he'd never hurt her. Ever. "Do I understand what? That you're not alone anymore? I'm sorry, Slade, but I think that's a good thing."

"No, it's not." He softened his grip on her hair. "It means that it's just a matter of time until the day I walk in and find out you're dead." His voice became low, twisted with emotion so awful that she couldn't breathe. "Everyone I've ever loved has been brutally murdered. *Everyone.* Same with my brother. It's happening again, Anya. It's happening all over again. You. Killian. The men outside my place. It's all going to happen again." He dropped to his knees, grabbed her hips, and pulled her against him, staring up at her. "I can't go through this again. It will break me if you die."

She swallowed, stunned by the raw anguish raking across his features. She slid her fingers through his hair. "Oh, Slade," she whispered, her heart breaking for the depth of his pain. This was the man who'd been so cold the day they'd met? She could almost hear the fragments of his soul shattering. She had no words to ease his pain, because his anguish pierced her own heart, releasing her grief over her mother's murder, and her own shock at the idea of anything happening to Slade.

"*Anya.*" He rose to his feet and slammed his mouth down upon hers, a brutal, angry kiss that tore at her heart. It wasn't the kiss of a man trying to seduce. It was the kiss of a man trying to run from a ghost so overpowering that there was no escape. His anguish tore into her, shattering the shields she'd built so carefully around her own heart. Grief rocked her, the grief of her mother's murder, of Marjorie's, of losing Julia. Her terror at what was happening to her best friend right at that moment. The loss of a home, of love, of everything that mattered.

Desperate, she clung to him, his strong frame the only solid thing in her life. With a low growl, he tore off her pants, extending a long, clawed nail just long enough to rip her pants in two. He dropped his own pants and then lifted her up against the bookcase filled with antique, gold-inlay hardcovers.

He dragged her legs around his hips and then drove into her, a fierce, merciless penetration that flayed her heart open with each thrust. His pain was so raw and ragged, almost suffocating her, mingling with her own pain until she couldn't tell where his ended and hers began. Again and again he thrust. Books fell off the shelves, thudding to the floor as she clung to him, tears streaming down her cheeks as she surrendered the pain that she'd fought off for so long, losing herself in the man whose arms were holding her so tightly. His torment was immense, almost inconceivable, tangled with the death of his family, and all the other ones he'd caused. His life, spinning through her, memories of all the people he'd killed, of being so hard that he felt nothing when he left his victims behind...pain that he now felt. Every death he'd caused was slicing through him, dragging him into the anguish he'd shielded himself against for so long. All of that, pouring through him, alive and gripping him, crushing him beneath the onslaught of the horror.

He bellowed her name, an anguished cry of a soul shattering beneath a weight too great to endure, then his body convulsed. His orgasm triggered hers, and she bucked against him, her own body barely holding together under the sheer force of it. On and on it went, as if it were trying to keep them from landing amidst the black puddles of their grief and fear.

But eventually, cruelly, finally, the orgasm released them. Slade sagged against her, his hands gripping the shelf by her head. She leaned against his chest, trying to catch her breath. Sweat trickled down her back, and both of them were slick with perspiration.

She could barely breathe through the weight of his anguish. This ice-cold assassin who'd been so reserved and contained when she'd met him was bleeding from his soul now, an anguished torrent of pain, guilt, and fear. She wrapped her arms around his neck and tightened her legs around his hips.

He made a low groan, almost like the whimper of a dying animal, and buried his face in the crook of her neck, snaking one arm behind her back to hold her against him.

She wrapped her arms around his head, cradling him to her, as if that could somehow chase away his pain. She understood now why he'd worked so hard to maintain his isolated, reserved life. The trauma of losing his family was too great, of walking away from his brother, and of having killed so many people in his life. Every death had left an indelible mark on his soul, marks that he'd crushed mercilessly for so long, until they'd finally broken free.

"It's my fault," she whispered, unable to stop her tears from falling. "I did everything I could to make you feel again. I thought it would be better that way. I'm so sorry." How could any man survive the weight of so much loss and grief? It was beyond overwhelming. She understood now how he could have been both an assassin and still the good man she'd fallen in love with. The goodness she'd sensed was there, but he'd buried it to survive—

She realized suddenly what she'd just thought. The man

she'd *fallen in love with*? Shock flooded her system. Love? Had she really fallen in love with him? A man who fought against everything she believed in? A man so beautiful that he couldn't withstand his true emotions? A brother so loyal he'd deprive himself of all that mattered to protect the one he loved?

Her chest tightened, and she knew the answer. Yes, she had fallen in love with him. Maybe it had been when she'd first seen him in the bar, and his voice had rolled through her, arrogant, demanding, and beautiful. Maybe it had been when she'd seen the stricken look on his face when she'd collapsed after their kisses in the first safe house? Maybe it had been the moment he'd told her about his brother. Maybe it was all of them combined, but it didn't really matter.

He'd won her heart, her fragile, broken heart that ached so much it hurt to love. She didn't have the strength to survive more pain, but at the same time, she didn't have the strength to reject how he made her feel, to resist what he gave her.

"It's not your fault, Anya." He didn't lift his head from the crook of her neck, but his arms tightened around her. "You didn't choose me as your guardian. That choice was made."

"But I made you feel."

"Lots of people have tried to make me feel, and you're the only one who succeeded, but it wasn't because of superficial crap." He looked up then, his eyes bloodshot and weary. "You were simply yourself," he said, his voice rough. "You should never hide who you are." He ran his knuckles along her jaw, his gaze searching hers with raw, open emotion. "You're beautiful, in a thousand different ways. I've never been around someone so genuine and open. You're a rare gem, and you should be treasured, not shamed for who you are."

Tears filled her eyes. *I love you.* She knew he didn't want the words, but she needed to say them to herself, to acknowledge how deeply he'd touched her.

But he went still, utterly and completely still, his face losing all expression. "What?"

She blinked. "I didn't say anything." But even as she said it, she realized she'd forgotten about their psychic connection. Had he heard her thoughts?

Chapter Twenty-One

*E*VERY MUSCLE IN Slade's body went taut, suspended in frozen animation. He knew what he'd heard. He knew exactly what Anya had thought. *She loved him.* A part of him wanted to fall to his knees and surrender himself to her, to the gift she'd offered him, to pour his own heart into her. And another part of him, the grittier part, wanted to sweep her mind instantly, ridding her of every last memory she had of him. To chase her out of his life before all hell could rain down upon them.

But he did neither. He couldn't do either one of them. Surrendering was too dangerous. Severing his ties to her made the most sense, but the mere thought of being without her made his lungs tighten until it was difficult to breathe.

So, he did nothing. He simply went still, barely holding his shit together, his mind a frenzied mess as he fought to clear it. Somehow, the realization that she loved him made all the pain greater and more intense, because failing her now was the ultimate betrayal to her. She gave him her love, and if he let her die, it was like stabbing her in the heart and shredding the fragile trust she'd given to him.

But at the same time, knowing that she loved him

seemed to seal up the holes in his soul. It was a fragile thread weaving it back together, infinitely breakable, but somehow, some way, he felt stronger now, as if her love somehow shielded him from the pain that had nearly destroyed him.

How could her love weaken him and strengthen him at the same time? He didn't know, but he didn't care. It was a gift, an unthinkable, beautiful treasure that he knew he would hold onto with every fiber of his being from this moment until the day he died.

She looked terrified, afraid that he'd heard her. He realized she didn't want him to know. She wanted to hide it, so they could both pretend it wasn't true. He couldn't pretend he hadn't heard it. He'd never forget it. Ever. And he didn't want to. But he sure as hell didn't want to put it on the table. It was too heavy to deal with right now.

So, he forced himself to step back, lowering her carefully to the ground. The sight of her half-naked with flushed cheeks made his cock get hard again instantly, and he scowled, yanking his pants back up. What was wrong with him, wanting to fuck her all the time when there was major shit going down? Because that's all it could be. Fucking. He just... "When this is over," he said. "I'm going to wipe your mind of all of this."

Her eyes widened. "What?"

"It's too dangerous—"

"Hey! I am so over that inane idea!" She slammed her palm against his chest, hitting hard enough to make him step back. "You don't have the right to do that! It's my life, not yours, and you don't get to choose what I remember. If you walk away, I still have the same enemies I had before, and all your enemies will already know that we're connected. If you strip my mind, then I won't be ready and I'll be easy prey." Her eyes flashed with anger. "Just because you can't handle the fact you care doesn't mean you get to endanger me." She threw up her hands in frustration. "I am sick and tired of that crap, Slade. You know damn well you don't want me to forget you, so just stop it! I'm going to go steal pants from your closet, and then we're going to figure out a plan that actually makes sense!"

He smiled at her outburst. He couldn't help himself. She was just so damned unimpressed with his power and his decisions. She treated him like a regular guy, and he absolutely loved it.

She didn't appreciate his smile, and she pointed her finger at him. "Don't you *dare* try to mess with my mind. Killian showed you that it doesn't always work, and you do *not* want to piss me off." Still glaring at him, she strode out of the room, yelling at Killian that she was half-naked and he better close his eyes when she walked by.

Slade watched her go, running his hand through his hair. She was right. If he wiped her mind or Killian's, he was putting them in more danger. He'd have to wipe their existence from every person who'd ever heard of them, and that was beyond his scope.

There was no going back.

There was no going back.

Slade sat down hard in his desk chair and pressed his face to his palms as the reality of the situation settled on him. He could never go back to his old life, to his isolated existence, to a life where no one knew him. Anya and Killian would be in danger forever from their association with him, even if he wiped their memories. They *had* to remember, which meant they had to remember him, and he had to remember them. Forever, he and Anya would both remember that she'd said she loved him.

Jesus. What had he done?

But it didn't matter what he'd done. It was over. Everything he knew was closed to him now. When this was over, what the hell was he supposed to do? Could he shut himself down emotionally like he had before, knowing that out there somewhere were Killian and Anya, remembering him? Knowing him? How could he go back to that isolated life after having had them both in his space, in his life, screwing everything up? "Why the hell did you pick me?" he shouted out loud to the red-haired woman he'd seen in the bar. "Why me?"

Of course, she didn't answer. It was just him, alone in the office he'd assembled so carefully, making it exactly how he liked it. It had been perfection, but now, it was chaotic, messy, and crowded...and so much richer. When he looked at the books scattered on the floor, he could think only of how it felt to be with Anya. When he breathed deep, Killian's scent slid through him, heavy in the air.

Sighing, he rubbed his forehead, trying to think. The only way out of this situation was to discharge his duty with Anya. He was to be her guardian, which meant keeping her safe...until when? It had to be when the threat was over. Which threat? The bastard who killed his family? Until he was dead?

Slade thought about that for a moment, and the longer he thought about it, the more right it felt. He wasn't trained at keeping people alive, but he was the best in existence at killing people. So, that was why he'd been selected. Because he knew this situation, and because he was the only one capable of killing the bastard he'd been hunting since he was nine. He'd failed his whole life, but the playing field had changed. Anya and Killian were a part of the game now...a deadly game that would endanger all of them. Could he really bring them into it?

Killian appeared in the doorway. He was dressed entirely in black, wearing clothing that looked suspiciously like the custom fabrics Slade used for his own clothes. "Are those mine?"

"Yeah." The pants and shirt fit Killian as if they were made for him. He'd slicked his hair back, but left his jaw unshaven. Nothing could hide the dangerous glitter in his eyes. He looked every bit the predator, not a younger brother that needed protecting.

Slade looked at his brother, and knew it was time to stop protecting him. He couldn't go backward. He had to go forward. They both had to go forward. He took a deep breath, and then he began to talk. "The name of the man who murdered our parents and our sister is William Parker. He specializes in kidnapping, breeding, and selling shifters. Dad crossed him many times when he was trying to break the ring. He couldn't get Dad, so he killed Mom and Jessica. You, me, and Dad weren't home."

Killian stilled, watching Slade intently. "William Parker," he repeated, his deep voice rolling through the name as if he were tasting it. "I ran across that name while I was searching for you, but I couldn't find any information on him." He looked at Slade. "You think he killed my family?"

"I don't know about that, but Dad went into hiding to protect us, but Parker found us anyway. He killed Dad while I was out in the woods with you. When we came back, he was still there, and he heard us. He knew we were out there, somewhere. He hunted us for days, but never found us. I left you at the church, and I took off."

Killian walked into the room and sat down in an armchair, never taking his gaze off Slade's face. His eyes were blazing with hunger, with the need to finally find out the truth. At last, Slade understood why Killian had been able to evade Slade's memory wipe. His brother's drive to find out the truth of who he was and where he'd come from had driven him to become stronger and more powerful, until all that was left was a man as determined as Slade was.

"I was going to come get you once Parker was dead," Slade said. "But I never found him. I was always too late. All I ever found were the remnants of his crimes, the shadows of his existence. Never the man." He rubbed his hand over the mark on his palm from the dart. "He was at the warehouse tonight. He walked up behind me while I was watching you, put a gun to my head, and called me by name. Said he'd been waiting."

Killian leaned forward, bracing his forearms on his thighs. His right knee was bouncing restlessly, the only indication of his reaction to the information. He said nothing. He simply waited for the rest, showing the patience of a true leopard, willing to lie in wait for as long as it took to guarantee victory.

"That warehouse was one of his, which means he's behind the kidnapping of Anya's friend—" Slade saw Anya appear in the doorway. She was wearing a pair of his running tights, which cupped her ass much too well.

"Keep going," she said as she walked into the room. "William Parker."

He raised his brows. "You were listening?"

"Of course." She sat in the chair beside Killian, also perching on the edge. "Continue."

Slade looked back and forth between his brother and Anya. Their attention was fixed on him, their faces desperate for the truth, a truth he'd held inside for so long. He realized that it felt right to bring them into it, to share it with them, to build a team with the only two people in the world he trusted. He nodded at Anya. "Your mom and Marjorie kept you girls hidden throughout your life. No one could have known that you and Julia were shifters, right? Unless they knew to look for you."

Anya shook her head. "Julia had shifted a few times,

but only when we were in the woods, alone, with no one around. But maybe someone—"

"No." Slade had no doubt. His gut was screaming to him about what was right. "If Parker ended up with Julia, that means he knew she existed, which means he knew your mom and Marjorie."

Anya's eyes widened. "So, he's the one they were running from."

Slade leaned forward, and said the words he didn't want to say. "They were pregnant when they ran, right?"

"Yes." Her voice faded, and she gripped the chair. "You don't think he—"

Her question trailed off, and Killian whistled softly as he looked at her.

"When my mom was kidnapped by him, he allowed only his sperm to be used on the white leopards," Slade said. "He wanted the strongest genes for his prize captures, and he believed they were his."

Anya's face paled. "You think *he* impregnated my mom and Marjorie? That he's my biological father?"

"I think so."

"Oh, God." Anya looked like she was going to be sick. "And Julia's, too."

"Which means..." He swore, not wanting to say this. "He may be psychically connected with you. He may be able to track you, like I can track Killian, and he was always aware of me. He may have been tracking you all along, waiting for you to shift before he made his move."

Anya stood up, shaking her head. "You're just guessing. You don't know any of this, right? You're just connecting dots that could fit together another way! Why would he wait? If he knew where I was and what I was, why wouldn't he just grab me from the start?"

Slade glanced at Killian, and he saw confirmation on

his brother's face. "I don't know it for sure," he agreed, "but I never trust facts to guide my decisions. Facts can be manipulated, but energy can't. Energy is real, and it carries messages that our conscious minds can't process. I always base my decisions on my gut instincts, and I'm always right."

Anya looked back and forth between them. "You agree with him?" she asked Killian.

He nodded. "It feels right in my gut as well. Everything fits."

"Nothing fits!" She paced away from them, wrapping her arms around her torso. "It doesn't even matter. We just need to find Julia." She whirled toward Slade. "You said you picked up a trace of Julia. Can you follow it? Can't we just do that?"

"I could find her if I were near her." Slade punched a few buttons on the computer screen, and suddenly a gorgeous, classic mansion appeared on the screen. It was gleaming white, with lawns worthy of the White House, and stone pillars that stretched three stories high.

Anya knew that building. Everyone knew it. "The Winchester Mansion?" It had once been home to an old, well-funded New York family, but had been turned into a museum of sorts, and a place where the most wealthy elite held black tie affairs with private guest lists consisting of celebrities and the others of equal social and financial standing. Only certain spaces were open to the public, and the rest were under private control.

Slade braced his hands on the desk, staring at the screen. "William Parker is hosting a charity auction for animal rights tonight. It's his event." He looked up, meeting Killian's gaze.

"He'll be there tonight," Anya said softly, dread welling up. "So, when they attack us here, he has an alibi."

A slow smile spread across Killian's face. "He won't be expecting us to join the party."

Slade grinned. "No. He thinks we're trapped inside here. We're not."

Anya clenched her fists. "We're going *inside* the museum? We're going *to* him?" She swallowed hard, fear making it difficult to breathe. This was the man she'd run from her *entire* life, the one she'd been trained to flee since the day she was born. They were going *to* him?

"No. You're not. You're staying here." But even as he said it, she felt the hesitation in Slade's voice.

She looked at him. "You're no longer positive this place is secure, are you? If they can find the location, maybe they can find their way in."

"They won't." Again, there was the faintest of hesitation, one that she noticed only because she knew him so well.

She looked at the second computer monitor again, at the men standing there, at the demon still staring at the camera. Fear congealed in her gut. "I can't stay here," she whispered. "I can't sit here like helpless prey, waiting to be attacked." Dammit. She was so tired of being afraid, of hiding. It hadn't worked to keep those she loved safe. Julia was still out there, and she was her only chance. She looked up. "I'm coming with you."

Conflicting emotions warred in Slade's eyes, respect and admiration, along with fear and resistance. He looked at Killian, but Anya stood up. "It's not up to Killian," she snapped. "I can take care of myself."

Slade swore. "These men are killers, Anya. They specialize in hunting down the most dangerous shifters in the world... I don't want—"

"I'm not staying behind." She picked up a letter opener from the desk and clasped it lightly, just as she'd practiced so many times. "I've spent my life running, but I was taught how to fight if I needed to." She narrowed her eyes, then flicked her wrist, unleashing the knife straight at Slade's throat.

He snatched it out of the air a split second before it sank into his jugular. Killian whistled softly, but Slade just stared at her. She didn't need to explain. They both knew how fast he was, and that he'd been in no danger from the blade moving at that speed. She'd merely wanted to show him her accuracy. "I can throw ten times that speed," she said.

"Damn." Killian grinned. "I think she should come with us to protect us."

Slade carefully set the letter opener on his desk. "A knife isn't going to do much if you're darted," he said.

Anya gritted her teeth at his overprotectiveness, but Killian interrupted. "She's safer with us." There was something so confident and so dangerous in his tone, that Anya stiffened. How dangerous was he? How much had he decided to emulate his brother in the years he'd been hunting Slade? She looked back and forth between the brothers, both of whom looked so deadly and dangerous.

"He won't be expecting us," Killian said. "The threat will be here."

"Maybe. Maybe not." Slade turned to Anya, his eyes unfathomable. He said nothing, but she saw the torment in his eyes, his understanding that she wasn't safe no matter where she was.

"Let me fight, Slade," she said softly. "I won't be alone if I'm with you and Killian, but I have the chance to fight. You've been at battle your whole life, so you know how important it is to be able to stand up for what matters to you. Julia isn't simply my friend. If you're right that Parker fathered us both, then she's my sister." She met his gaze.

"You've gone after him and failed so many times. Maybe you need me this time. Did you think of that? Maybe I'm the difference?"

"Or me. I'm a badass," Killian chimed in. "So's Anya."

She grinned at Killian. Really? He thought she was a badass? She liked that. A lot. After being taught to run away her whole life, it felt amazing to have someone see strength in her instead of weakness and vulnerability.

Then she looked at Slade, her emotions sliding into a holding pattern while she waited for his answer. She needed him to accept her on the mission, to see her as more than the weak victim her mother always perceived her to be. Slade was pure menace, and she needed him to believe she could fight.

He glanced at Killian, and then looked at her. She saw the torment on his face as he ran his fingers over the blade of the letter opener. Finally, he nodded. One nod. No words. But it was enough. Relief and pride rushed through her, and she couldn't help the grin that spread over her face.

Power seemed to roll through her, coming from deep within her. No longer was she the fleeing victim. Today, everything changed. Today, she stopped running, and became the badass that her mother should have been, that they all should have been. Maybe then, things would have turned out differently.

Slade's face softened as he watched her smile, and he nodded again. "We go in tonight," he said. "The three of us. Whether he's expecting us or not, we'll be ready."

Anya's heart began to hammer with adrenaline and, yes, more than a little fear. She was ready to fight, but she wasn't foolish enough not to understand the danger. "You can't kill Parker," she said. "Not until we find Julia."

Slade again looked at Killian, but this time, it was a hard look, telling his brother not to argue. "Agreed." He turned his attention toward Anya. "Once we get close, I'll know if Julia is inside or not. If she is, we'll find her and get you both clear before we go after Parker." His eyes narrowed. "It will be your job to keep her safe while we go after him."

Her heart stuttered. "You think she's there? Why would he have her there?"

Slade brought up another screen, a list of names. "Because I recognize some of the names on the guest list. I think it's an auction. I think she's the main attraction."

"An auction?" Nausea churned in Anya's stomach as she peered at the computer, scanning names that meant nothing to her. "He's selling her like a commodity?"

"As a white leopard, she's too valuable for him to sell. I think he's planning to rent her."

"Rent? Like, by the hour?" She sat down, gripping the edge of his desk.

"Something like that." Slade looked over at her, and his voice softened. "You don't need to go, Anya. You're safe here."

She looked at him. "There are men standing outside your building, looking for a way in. You don't know for sure that I'm safe here. There's nowhere that's safe for me right now, is there?" She sat up, her voice soft but unyielding. "I have to go, Slade."

He pressed his lips together, but nodded once.

Killian leaned forward to look at the screen. "I know some of those. They're high rollers in the black market for shifters. Some of them could pay a hundred million in cash for her." He let his finger drift over the screen. "Bastards."

Anya swallowed. "When did you find out about this? Why didn't you tell me?"

Slade shrugged. "Until he attacked me at the warehouse, I didn't know he was involved. I track what he's doing, so I knew about the party, but it wasn't until now that I put all the pieces together." His eyes flashed. "I've tried to get into his parties before, but he always had them guarded tightly. There's no way to slip inside unnoticed, so I wasn't planning on trying to get to him there. But when I saw him at the warehouse last night, it made me realize that he's relevant to *this* situation. So, yeah, we're going in."

Anya looked at him. "How many times have you gone to one of his events in search of him?"

Slade met her gaze. "Twenty-seven times."

"And you've never gotten to him?"

"No."

Her shoulders slumped. How good was William Parker, if he'd managed to evade the Black Swan so many times? "Why would this time be different?"

"Because this time, there's too much at stake to fail." His voice was cold, his eyes glittering, and she knew she was looking at the Black Swan, the man who killed first and never bothered to ask questions. "This time, we're going in the front door, with the rest of the guests. I can cloak us fairly well. If they're not looking for us, they won't notice us. It'll give us time."

She swallowed, her throat suddenly dry. "What if Julia's not there? Then what? Are you still going to kill him?"

"Someone there knows where she is." Again, the cold steel of Slade's eyes made her shiver. He looked over at Killian. "I want you to track down a woman named Beckett Harper. She had information about this ring, and I think we're going to need more answers."

Killian shook his head. "No. I'm going with you. I'm in this, and I'm going there tonight, either at your side or by myself. Your choice which one." He stood up. "I'm used to going solo, but I'll make an exception for you."

Slade swore. "You sound like me," he muttered.

Killian grinned. "God, I hope not. You're a ruthless bastard. I, at least, have emotion." His smile faded, and he nodded at the cameras still tracking the armed men pacing around his building. "How are we going to get past them?"

"It's no problem. I have contingencies." Slade glanced at his watch. "The event is at seven. That gives us twelve hours to prepare. Take one of my tuxes from the right side. Those are for work."

Anya swallowed. "We're really going to walk right in the front door?"

"Yep. It's the best way. No one will be looking for us to do that." He looked at Killian. "Don't get killed," he said quietly.

Killian's eyes darkened. "No chance of that. I have files that will help. I'm going to get my stuff from my truck. I'll be back in a sec."

Slade watched his brother go. He listened to his footsteps down the hall as he turned his gaze to Anya, who was staring at his computer screen, carefully going over the names of the attendees to the event. Her brow was furrowed, and she was concentrating intently. There was no fear in her eyes, just calm, steady focus.

Neither Killian nor Anya seemed afraid of going on this mission with him.

They were the amateurs, and yet, they were ready and confident.

He was the Black Swan, the deadliest badass to walk the earth, and he was absolutely fucking terrified.

Chapter Twenty-Two

ANYA HAD NEVER felt beautiful in her life. She'd never even felt like a woman. But as she gazed at herself in the dressing room mirror, she was stunned. Slade had arranged for a private shopping tour before Parker's event. She'd been met by two women, one to do her hair and makeup, while the other assembled an outfit. Aware of the short deadline, they'd moved efficiently and respectfully, Slade's vast coffers buying their confidence and their expertise.

And now, here she stood. The diamond and sapphire necklace at her throat was cold and heavy, purchased in cash by Slade. Her diamond studs sparkled like the sun on a tropical ocean. Her hair was flawless and perfect, in an elegant updo that defied the laws of gravity.

"You ready?" Slade knocked lightly against the door of the dressing room she'd retreated into to slip on the dress once her hair and makeup were done.

"No." She didn't turn around to face him. She didn't know what to do with what she saw in the mirror.

He pulled the door open, and she watched his face as he saw her. His gaze swept over her in the mirror, from her hair, to her jewels, to her breasts, and all the way down to the elegant shoes that cradled her feet. His face softened, and her heart started to pound. "It's not me," she whispered, preempting any comment about how she looked. "I don't know how to be like this." The dress sapped her confidence, and she couldn't afford that right now.

He walked into the dressing room and stood behind her, setting his hands on her shoulders. She met his gaze in the mirror, searching his face for something to ground her.

"What's wrong?" he asked, rubbing his thumbs over the back of her shoulders.

"I just—" She waved her hands at the gown. "How can I run in this? How can I fight? How can I hide? How can I blend? How can I—-"

He pressed a kiss to the nape of her neck, and she snapped her lips together, chills racing down her spine as she stared at him. "Look at yourself," he said softly, running his hands down her arms. "Look at the beautiful, elegant woman in the mirror."

She kept her gaze on him. "Slade—"

"Just look at her."

She dragged her gaze off him and stared at herself. She saw the paleness of her cheeks, the fear in her wide eyes, the trembling of her hands. Her shoulders looked too thin, her arms fragile. She looked—

"Beautiful," he said. "Sexy. Dangerous as hell." He pressed a kiss to her bare shoulder, and her stomach turned. "But that doesn't lessen your strength. It adds to it. You don't need to hide who you are to be a badass."

"You hide who you are."

"No, I don't. I walk straight into wherever I need to go, and I use the strength of my energy to dominate and make things happen the way I want. I use my cat when I need to, but that's not often because I'm so good at my job." He slid his arms around her, pulling her back against his chest.

She felt the daggers at her back dig into his chest. There was also one strapped to each thigh and each ankle. Her wrist cuffs also hid knives, as did her updo. She had eleven knives stashed on her body, but the woman in the mirror seemed too elegant to use them. "I want my jeans," she said.

He shook his head. "Anya, sweetheart, you spent your life hiding. You hid from the world, you hid from your leopard, and you hid from the fact that you're a woman. It's okay to step up, to embrace who you are, to find your strength."

"Slade—"

"When I look at you in the mirror, I see a beautiful woman determined to slay any monster that gets in her way," he said softly, resting his cheek against hers. "I also see the fire in your eyes." He traced his finger along her jaw. "I see a fierce warrior. I see a woman so brave and courageous. I see a queen ready to take on her world."

She laughed softly. "A queen?"

"Yes." He cupped her jaw, his fingers warm and tantalizing against her skin. "Look at yourself, Anya. See what I see."

She took a deep breath, and did as he instructed. She looked at herself, really looked at herself for the first time. She was accustomed to looking for fear in her eyes, for circles under her eyes, for the wan tint to her skin. Instead, she looked at the fierce set to her mouth. She looked at the way she was standing, with her weight on both feet, ready. She let herself see the fire in her eyes. She allowed herself to feel the steady beat of her heart. She even allowed herself to feel the cat pacing beneath her skin, waiting to be released. Slowly, she took a deep breath, allowing air to fill her lungs and chase away the panic.

Slade smiled and tightened his arms around her, still resting his cheek against hers as she met his gaze in the mirror.

She wrapped her fingers around his wrist. "I don't know how to be this person, one who wears a fancy dress, goes to a party, and faces down the man she's supposed to run from."

"We're even, then." His smile faded. "I don't know how to be the guy who walks into a danger zone with a woman on his arm that he cares about, a woman whose death would break what little remains of his soul."

Her breath caught, and suddenly, she couldn't breathe. Silence rose between them, as they stared at each other in the mirror.

"This man murdered my father, my mother, and my sister," Slade said. "He's the reason I became what I am. And now I'm bringing you and Killian in there with me." His biceps tightened involuntarily. "For the first time in my life, I want to run," he said softly. "I want to throw you over my shoulder, and run, and never look back."

Tears threatened. She knew what those words cost him. He was a man who'd spent his life being invincible, and yet he'd just admitted his vulnerability to her. "I want to run, too," she whispered. "With you."

They locked gazes in the mirror, and her throat tightened at the raw yearning in his dark eyes. There was nothing more to say, though, because Julia was out there somewhere, and his family's souls were still haunting him. "No matter what happens," she said, her voice raw, "I won't regret going in there. I'd rather fight with you, than run away alone. You've made my heart start to beat again, and I'd rather love you for a short time, than live an eternity never knowing what it felt like to feel my strength." She'd said it aloud, and she knew he'd heard when his arms tightened around her.

"You love me?" he asked, his voice so soft and full of wonder that she almost smiled.

"Of course I do. You know that." She met his gaze. "And you love me, too."

He didn't answer her. He didn't confirm it, and he didn't deny it. Instead, he turned her in his arms and pulled her against him, burying his face in the crook of her neck. Anya wrapped her arms around him and pulled him tight, holding onto him with all the strength in her body.

For a long moment, neither of them moved, then she heard the sound of Killian approaching, his steps feather-light despite his muscular frame.

Slade pulled back, searching her face. "Despite Julia, and despite my parents, if I hadn't made a deal to protect you, I'd take you and hide. I really would." His fingers dug into her hips. "*I can't lose you, Anya.*"

Her throat tightened. He was so raw and vulnerable right now, everything that he hadn't been when she'd first met him. "That's why I love you," she whispered. "Because you've let me see your heart."

He closed his eyes. "I don't want to feel like this," he said, his voice raw. "I need to not care. It's the only way I can do this."

Killian knocked once and then stuck his head in the dressing room without waiting for a reply. His eyes were glittering. "It's time, kids. The party starts in ten minutes."

Slade looked up and met his brother's gaze. As they looked at each other, she saw resolution flood Slade's eyes. It wasn't only her who mattered anymore. It was also his brother who was at risk as well. Somehow, Killian's appearance galvanized him. His muscles tightened, his shoulders drew back, and his jaw got hard. "If the situation goes south, I want you to take Anya and get out. Keep her safe.

Keep both of you safe."

Killian glanced at Anya, his jaw flexing. "No way, bro. Living safe isn't living. I'm in this until the end, and if I die trying, then I'll take as many of those bastards down with me as I can."

A slow smile spread across Anya's face, and courage seemed to flood her. "I agree. What's the point of surviving if those you love don't?" She looked at Slade. "If we die, we die, Slade. Just don't let me be taken by them. I'd rather die."

Slade's fingers tightened on her arms, and fury flared in his eyes. "I won't let them take you," he said, his voice low and cold, the voice of the lethal warrior he needed to become.

She smiled. "Then let's do it."

Killian stepped back, holding the door open. "You look great, by the way, Anya."

She smiled at him as she walked past him. "Back at ya, Killian."

"Hey." Slade caught up, sliding his hand onto the crook of her elbow. "He's wearing *my* damn tux. It doesn't look good on anyone except me."

Anya smiled and pressed her hand to his chest. "He's not nearly as hot as you are, Slade. You're still the only one I really see," she said, referring to his concern that she would be imagining someone else when they kissed.

He scowled at her. "It better be that way."

"What the hell?" Killian touched the cufflink, and a small blade shot out of the sleeve into his hand. "Are they all like this?"

Slade grinned. "And so much more. Did you check the inside jacket pocket?"

As Killian reached inside his jacket to find the weapon Slade had stashed there, Anya couldn't help but smile as the two brothers went over the tux in detail, with Slade showing Killian all the special surprises the tux held. They were like boys with their toys, only the toys were deadly weapons, and the boys were lethal shifters about to avenge the murder of their loved ones.

Her smile faded as they reached the front door of the store. The women who'd helped her were gone, leaving just the three of them.

The battle was about to start. Could they really win against a foe who had already taken down almost everyone they loved? As they walked out the front door to Slade's waiting Escalade, her hands closed into fists. These two men were all she had left in the world, except for Julia. She wasn't letting them go, and she wasn't giving up until Julia was with them...no matter what it took.

No matter what it took.

No. Matter. What. It. Took.

She looked down at her wrist cuffs, and she thought about the blades stashed in them. Blades she'd have to get to in a hurry. Blades that could be taken away from her. Danger wasn't the only thing she'd been running away from in her life. She'd been running from herself.

She stopped as Slade opened the passenger door for her, looking up into his glittering eyes. "How do I take it off?"

He frowned. "Take what off?"

She swallowed, her heart pounding. "The tattoo on my foot. The one that keeps me from shifting?"

Silent tension rose between them. "Don't let them know what you are," Slade said softly. "Keep it on."

She met his gaze. "How do I take it off?" She was certain he knew how to remove it. "That's my strength, Slade. I need to be able to call on it if I need to." She met his gaze. "She's faster, deadlier, and more cunning than I am, isn't she?"

He glanced at Killian, who was leaning over the seat, listening to the conversation. "She's not separate from you, Anya," Killian said. "Her strength is a part of you. She *is* you. You need her." He looked at Slade. "You need to call upon your cat more often as well. We're predators, at the pinnacle of the food chain, and you both are undercutting yourselves not to embrace it."

Slade's eyes narrowed. "I don't need my cat."

"Yes, you do. We all do. For hell's sake, we're going into the lion's den in five minutes. You need to be prepared to do whatever it takes, including showing the world what you are."

Slade swore under his breath. "Shut up, Killian."

His brother leaned forward. "You know how to take it off, don't you? Tell her, Slade. Or live with her death if she can't protect herself when she needs to."

Anya held her breath as she waited, looking at Slade. "Can I take it off myself?"

"Yes."

Oh, *God.* "How?" She didn't want to know, did she? Yes, she did. Killian was right. A white leopard was her power, her strength, not a weakness. If she was going into the devil's lair, she needed all her weapons. If she was going to face death, she had to be ready to do whatever it took to survive. "Tell me now."

He met her gaze, and suddenly she heard his voice in her head, whispering an ancient chant, one with no words, just guttural sounds and a heavy beat. Heat raced through her, and her foot tingled right where the tattoo was. "Do that until it's off," he said. "Five times."

"Does that count as one?" She played the chant in her head again, memorizing the beat and the intonations.

"No. It has to be aloud, and you have to press your palm to it. Envision dragging it off your skin while you chant, using your power to free yourself." He glanced at Killian, and she realized he'd shared it with his brother as well.

"How do you know?" she asked him. "How do you know it will work?"

"My mom put one on me when I was born. I took it off."

She stared at him in shock. "You did? How old were you?"

"I took it off the day after my dad died. I was done hiding." Headlights flashed across the road, and he looked up sharply. "Get in the car. We need to go."

She didn't hesitate. She grabbed the handle and leapt up into the SUV, moving so fast that she overshot and crashed into the steering wheel. She grimaced and rubbed her hip as she scooted back into her seat, trying to ignore Killian and Slade staring at her.

"Did you see that?" Killian asked.

"Yeah."

Anya glared at both of them. "So, I had a klutz moment—" She stopped at the expressions on both their faces. Surprise. Respect. Anticipation. "What?"

"You moved like a cat," Slade said.

She stared at him. "*What?*"

"You moved like a cat." He raised his brows at her, studying her thoughtfully. "I've never seen you move like that."

Anya tensed at his words. "Is that why I overshot my seat?"

"Yeah." Slade leaned in the doorway, his muscular frame dwarfing her as he studied her. "That one time doing the chant in your head shouldn't have made a difference, but it did." He ran his hand over her arm, and tingles shot through her. "I can feel the cat now," he said, his eyes suddenly shifting into cat eyes. "She's waking up."

Anya could feel her sliding beneath her skin, a slow, deliberate purr rumbling through her. "Then Parker will be able to tell."

"He's not a cat. He won't feel this." Slade leaned into her, his voice low. "You are dangerous, Anya. You shouldn't have any cat skills with this tattoo on your foot, but you're already moving differently." His eyes glowed. "You're powerful."

Her heart started to pound at the feral gleam in his eyes, and suddenly, she wanted to do the chant again, to see how far she could go, to move into Slade's world of power, grace, and lethalness. "I'm a cat."

"More than a cat." He nuzzled her neck, sending chills down her spine. "My leopard wants yours," he whispered. "He never wants any particular female, but he wants you. He wants to see her. *Now.*"

Heat poured through Anya, and she shifted restlessly, as if her skin was suddenly too small for her. The tattoo on her foot burned, and she instinctively rubbed it, trying to take the sting out, but as she did, the chant Slade had taught her ran through her mind. Pain spiked in her foot, and sudden heat roared through her.

Slade swore and locked his hand around the back of her neck. He pulled her toward him and sank his mouth down onto hers in a primal kiss of claiming and ownership. His energy poured into her, igniting every cell it touched, making her leopard shift restlessly. She gripped his shoulders, unable to stop herself from responding to his kiss. Her entire body burned for him, calling for his leopard—

Killian cleared his throat. "As fascinated as I am by the emergence of Anya's cat and the groping session going on in the front seat, we gotta go."

Anya felt her cheeks heat up and she tried to pull back.

Slade, however, didn't let her go. He just deepened the kiss, tearing through her shields, his arms far too strong for her to escape from. Need tore through her, a visceral need that seemed to come from somewhere deep inside her. It wasn't until she capitulated to his demands that he finally broke the kiss and pulled back. His eyes were pure leopard now, silver ovals that made heat pour through her. "You've said it once," he said. "Four more times."

She instinctively released her foot. "I didn't mean to."

"You did. It's time." He trailed his finger over her shoulder, then turned away. He strode around the car and climbed into the driver's seat, leaving her tingling and restless in the passenger seat. She wrapped her arms around herself as Slade started the engine.

"I can feel your cat." Killian spoke from the back seat. "She's close to the surface." His voice was rough, hard, and scratchy.

She glanced back at him, and tensed when she saw his eyes had gone leopard as well. "Why are you shifting?"

"Because his cat senses a female nearby," Slade said. "He wants her." His voice was rough and gravelly as well, making her body even hotter. Sweat trickled down his temple. "Mine, Killian."

"I know." Killian leaned back in the seat and clasped his hands over his head. "I won't touch her." But his voice was still raspy and rough, and she shivered.

Slade gunned the engine and shifted into drive. The truck leapt forward, the tires humming across the asphalt. "The first time you shift," Slade said, "you'll have trouble controlling it. You'll be pure leopard, both in mind and body."

Anya rubbed her arms, watching the way Slade's fingers curved around the steering wheel. She felt more aware of his innate grace, and the leisurely way he could move so quickly. "What does that mean?"

"It means that you will be driven by your cat instincts. If your life is in danger, or someone you care about, and you shift, your leopard will be in full assault mode and kill any threat. You won't have any control or rational thought. Your leopard will instinctively attack anything that's near you."

"Your leopard has been trapped your whole life," Killian added. "When you let her go, she's going to be on a rampage for freedom." He looked over at her. "So, don't take that tattoo off unless you have space and privacy to lose your shit, or unless you're in a situation where instinct is your best bet."

Anya shifted restlessly in her seat, unable to sit still. "It was a mistake, wasn't it? Never shifting until now?" With her cat so close to the surface, and her body already changing, she wanted more. She wanted to tap into the athleticism and power she'd felt when she leapt into the car. She realized that she was so much more than she'd allowed herself to be, and she wanted to tap into it now, to give herself the best chance of surviving Parker.

"Yes." Killian didn't hesitate, but Slade answered at the same moment. "No."

The brothers looked at each other. "You're wrong, too, Slade," Killian said. "You keep your cat under lockdown as well. Our leopards are like any other weapon. We need to practice constantly to keep our skills sharp. You could be so much more than what you are."

Slade gave him a dark look. "I'm enough."

"Parker's still alive, right? After all this time? So maybe you're not."

Slade slammed on the brakes and spun around toward his brother. "You have no idea what you're talking about—"

Killian leaned forward. "I know exactly what I'm talking about. You've wasted your talent, and denied who you are."

Anger flashed in Slade's eyes. "Being a cat killed our mother."

"Our mother was in human form when she was killed. Not a cat. If she'd been a cat, she would have escaped." Killian's eyes glittered. "We were born this way for a reason, and it's a violation of our birthright to deny who we are." He looked at Anya. "Yeah, you should have shifted earlier, but it's too dangerous to do it now unless your life is at stake. Don't risk it. If we all survive, I'll help you with her."

"I will be the one to help her," Slade snapped.

Killian looked at him. "You need my help, too, bro. You both do." His eyes glittered. "But for now, we are what we are. Let's get this done. Party starts in three minutes."

Slade swore and hit the gas, his fingers tight around the steering wheel as he drove. Tension radiated off him, and she could feel the dark energy prickling off him. He was far from the cold, emotionless assassin she'd first met. He was angry, defensive, and tense...a man with vulnerabilities and emotions...all of which would distract him when they walked into the lair of the devil.

Anya tried to ignore the restlessness of her own cat. It didn't matter whether she should have shifted before or not. She hadn't, and that was what she had to deal with. What Slade had described scared her. She couldn't afford to shift and lose her mind, not right now. *Slade?*

He didn't look at her. *What?*

When you shifted the first time, did you lose your humanity, like you said? She couldn't keep the fear out of her voice.

Slade looked over at her, and his face softened. He silently reached out and took her hand. *Yes, I did. When you shift the first time, you will be fully owned by your leopard.*

She rubbed her free hand over her thigh, trying to stop the itching of her skin. *Should I have shifted earlier? Was it a mistake?* She intentionally kept Killian out of the conversation. Slade was the one she trusted. He was the one who knew her.

He squeezed her hand, and some of the tension eased from his body. *If you had shifted, Parker would have sensed you. He is highly trained to capture shifters. He would have been prepared for you, and taken you easily. Hiding was the right choice.*

Anya bit her lip as she watched the streetlights pass by. *So, why are we walking in there, then? Can't he take us out easily?*

Yep.

She stiffened and looked sharply at him. "Did you really have to give that answer?"

He glanced at her. "If I thought we were going to be captured or killed, I wouldn't be walking in there. Yes, he could take us easily, which means we have to be smarter, faster, and more deadly than he is."

"There it is." Killian leaned over the seat, staring straight ahead.

Anya took her gaze off Slade and followed Killian's gaze. Up ahead of them was a line of limousines and luxury vehicles, all waiting to get into the front door of the museum. The pillars stretched high, and the wide steps were lined with red carpet and velvet ropes. Anya swallowed as she watched tuxedo-clad valets open car doors for men in tuxes and women in ball gowns. There were far more men than women, and everyone looked wealthy, powerful, and ruthless. Men in tuxes lined the stairs, but the way they were standing made her think of a private security force, not guests.

God, they were really going to walk right up those steps? The front doors seemed so tall, as if they were the mouth of hell and she was going to march right in.

She swallowed, her throat dry, as Slade pulled in to the line behind a Lamborghini. An Escalade pulled up behind them, and they were trapped. There would be no way for Slade to pull out of line now. The only escape would be on foot.

Slade's fingers tightened on the wheel, and his gaze became laser-focused. "Guns on the roof," he said softly. "And in the trees across the street."

She and Killian leaned forward, and she saw three men in all black standing on the roof of the mansion. They were carrying guns. "Oh, wow," she whispered.

"Upstairs window," Killian added. "To the right."

She followed his directions, and she saw a shadow move behind the white curtains. As they approached, Slade and Killian kept up their dialogue, pointing out every guard, every escape route, and every detail they needed to know. With each comment, however, her tension eased, and a rising sense of focus consumed her. She began to see shadows she hadn't noticed before, shadows that could hide her, or conceal an enemy. She tasted the scents of people attending the party. She heard the low murmur of voices that were still far away.

That's right, Anya. Tap into your senses. You've got this.

She grinned at Slade's comment. For the first time in her life, she felt competent, prepared, and ready to fight. She didn't feel like the victim. She felt like a woman who was taking control.

"She's here," Slade said suddenly.

Anya looked sharply at him. "Who?"

"Julia. She's close."

Oh, *God.* Slade had been right.

She gripped the door handle as they got closer to the main entrance, her heart starting to hammer in anticipation. It was time. *I'm coming for you, Julia.*

Chapter Twenty-Three

SLADE WASN'T USED to letting people see him.

He was used to infiltrating these parties like a shadow in the night, unseen and unnoticed, even though he walked among them. He was used to pushing people's attention aside, making them unable to focus on him. That was how he lived. But it was going to be different this time, with Anya and Killian with him.

There was only so much he could do to hide all three of them, and so much at stake if he failed.

He stopped his Escalade in front of the party, a cold sweat clamping down on his spine as he watched the elite crowd ooze into the building. "No one makes a move without all three of us being together," he said, repeating the instructions he'd already given them. "Listen to people's conversations to find out what is going on, and where the auction will be."

"I'll check the other floors."

Slade looked over at Killian. He had to admit, it was more efficient with a partner. He could mingle and try to locate the key players in the crowd, while Killian could do recon to see what he could locate. Slade wasn't used to having a partner, but if he had to have one, he was glad it was the only person in the world he'd trust, aside from Anya. "Stay in touch."

Killian took the conversation offline. *You bet.*

As the valets descended upon the car to open the doors, Killian stepped out, straightening his jacket as if he wore a tux every day of his life. Slade met Anya's gaze, and for a split second, he wanted to grab her, to declare himself to her, to make promises that he had no chance of keeping. Instead, he nodded at her.

She smiled. "You're broadcasting, Slade. You need to work on that, but I love you, too." Then she turned and slid out of the vehicle, her silk dress a sinful temptation on a body he knew all too well.

Swearing under his breath, Slade got out on his side. He handed the valet a three hundred dollar tip. "Keep it close."

The valet's eyebrows went up, and he shoved the cash in his pocket. "You got it."

Slade didn't like turning his vehicle over to anyone. He always parked a good distance away and hoofed it to the party, but he couldn't run with both Killian and Anya. It was different now, and he didn't like it.

His nerves strung out, he strode around the vehicle, catching Anya's arm before she could take a step away from the shiny, black SUV. Killian took up residence by his other side, moving close enough to get within range of Slade's shielding ability, and then the three of them headed up the steps of the museum.

Slade kept the trio tightly together, using his energy to cloak them. He sent his psychic energy out in pulses, fogging the minds of everyone near them, interfering with their ability to perceive them. It was a huge task to manage the perception of so many people, but he kept his focus tight, all too aware that Parker knew what he looked like, and he might be able to recognize Anya and Killian as well. As they walked, he rapidly scanned the faces and energy signatures of every other attendee as they headed up the marble steps. He knew Killian and Anya were doing the same, searching for Parker and Julia.

Julia's presence was stronger now, and he focused on the building. "She's inside."

Anya tightened her grip on his elbow. *Where?*

I don't know yet. I need to get closer. He was frustrated that he didn't have a stronger link to her. He liked knowing exactly where his target was. He never went into a situation without knowing every detail, but this time, there were so many variables still at large.

But this was his chance. He couldn't walk away just because he wasn't in complete control.

The crowd was big, money in abundance, and a heavy threat of danger drifted on the air. He pulsed his energy outward, searching for Parker...and suddenly, he got a hit. He instantly pulled back before Parker could sense him, but his blood surged. *Parker's here. I can feel him.*

So can I. Killian said, looking around just as carefully as Slade. *This is it. It's going down tonight.*

They reached the top of the stairs, and Slade hesitated on the threshold of the door. Stepping inside cut off their freedom. It eliminated many of their escape routes. It put Anya and Killian within reach of the man who'd murdered so many.

He'd entered many dangerous places in his life, and he'd never paused...but it was different tonight. His instincts told him to abort. His gut was screaming at him to take Anya and Killian out of there, and come back alone. This wasn't right to bring them in. It wasn't right to endanger him. It wasn't right to—

"Julia!" Anya suddenly ducked away from him, raced

into the crowd, and disappeared.

Shit.

He and Killian took off after her, into the museum, into the crowd, into hell.

* * *

She'd seen Julia.

She knew she had.

And then she'd lost her.

Anya darted through the crowd, frantically racing to the spot where Julia had been. She ducked past a group of men in deep discussion over champagne and slipped past a small palm tree, and then stopped. This was the spot she'd seen Julia...but as she looked around, she didn't see Julia, or anyone that even looked like her. Was it her imagination? Delusions of desperation? With a sinking feeling, she realized she'd screwed up. Julia hadn't been wandering around the party. If she was here, it wasn't as an honored guest. She'd be locked up somewhere.

Anya glanced around again, and realized she had lost track of Slade and Killian in her frantic dash through the party. No Slade. No Killian. No Julia. Just a whole slew of over-dressed, over-moneyed men who were there for all the wrong reasons. Crap!

She was officially losing her mind. Delusions at best. Complete mental breakdown at work.

Anya! Slade's furious shout filled her mind. *Get back here!*

She glanced around, trying to see through the crowd, but she wasn't sure which way she'd come. She'd run too fast and too far, through several rooms. Damn. Slade could track someone from seven thousand miles away, and she got lost in a maze of ballrooms. *I got myself lost.*

He chuckled, his warm affection rolling over her. *Damn good thing you have a guardian. Stay there, I'll come—*

He cut himself off suddenly.

Slade?

I see Parker. He's heading up the main staircase with several guests.

Anya's adrenaline kicked on. *Follow him. I'll be fine. I'll stay here.*

Slade swore. *Stay in the crowd. I'll be back as soon as I can.*

Ask about Julia before you kill him.

On it. He broke the connection, leaving her alone.

Anya fisted her hands as she looked around, trying to figure out the safest place to wait. But as she scanned the room, she realized that any of the men around her might be there to purchase Julia. Any one of them could be her enemy. She shivered, and suddenly being in a crowd didn't feel like such a fantastic idea. Who was friend, and who was foe?

She stepped back, easing behind a pillar and settling in the shadows. As the darkness settled around her, she began to realize the benefit of Slade's life, of not being seen, of living in shadows. Sometimes, shadows were a very good place to be.

She leaned against the pillar, carefully watching the crowd for any indication that anyone had noticed her, but no one seemed to care. Her tension began to ease, and she took a deep breath...and caught a familiar scent. *Julia.*

She tensed, leaping forward, her heart pounding as Julia's scent drifted to her. So faint, but definitely Julia. She spun around, trying to get a location on where it was coming from, but it was too faint. Damn it! She needed Slade's nose...

Suddenly, she felt her leopard crawling beneath her skin. Her cat! She immediately closed her eyes and relaxed, reaching inside herself to call to the leopard she'd denied her entire life. It roared to consciousness, and heat poured through her, opening her senses in ways she'd never felt. Suddenly, the voices in the room seemed to clarify. She could hear each conversation. She could smell every distinct scent. She could feel the heat from their bodies crawling toward her. Power crashed over her, and her muscles felt stronger, leaner, and more powerful.

She drew her attention off the room and focused it on Julia, on the scent she knew so well. She breathed deeply and inhaled it into her lungs, allowing it to swirl through her and tell the stories she'd never been able to hear before. She focused her mind on the scent, isolating it from the others, turning around as she tracked it... there!

She opened her eyes to find she was facing a long hallway. Velvet ropes declared it off limits, but she didn't hesitate. She ran over to it and ducked past it, her high heels clicking on the marble as she ran.

She rounded a corner and paused, suddenly wary. The hallway was dark and quiet. Silent. Isolated. If someone grabbed her here, no one else would ever know. She glanced back toward the ballroom, at the safety that the crowd could provide...safety that Julia didn't have.

She bit her lip and turned back toward the hallway. Julia's scent was strong, and Anya knew she was getting closer. Anya silently pulled a knife from her ankle and wrapped her fingers around the hilt. *Slade. I found Julia's scent. I'm going after her.*

No. You can't help her if you get caught. Wait for me.

I can't wait. What if something happens to her? Focus on Parker.

Dammit, Anya! Don't do this!

I've been running away my whole life, Slade. No more. She began to move down the hall, easing her way, searching with all her senses for any sign of life. *You find me if I go missing, Slade. You know you can.* She reached inside herself, trying to merge with her leopard, using her feline senses to heighten her awareness. She walked faster, urgency coursing through her.

Anya. Slade's torment slammed into her. *I'm coming after you. Wait there.*

No. You need to get Parker. I can do this. Come get me when you're done. They won't kill me, and you can find me no matter what. You can't lose him, and I can't lose Julia. It has to be this way. Just make it fast.

Slade swore. *You're a stubborn pain in the ass.*

I love you, too. She waited for his reply, for his confirmation that he loved her too, but he said nothing. Emptiness flooded her. *I need to hear it, Slade. I need to hear it from you.*

I can't, Anya. If I could, I would. In a heartbeat.

She smiled faintly, realizing that was probably as much as she was going to get from him, but it was enough. If he wasn't so damned heroic and self-sacrificing, he'd be on his knees with roses, declaring his love for her. He loved her. That had to be enough. *Someday, you'll have to admit it to yourself.*

His attention flickered away from her for a split second. *He's going into a meeting. I need to get in there. Shit, Anya, stay safe and keep the communication open so I can find you.*

Sure. No problem.

I need to focus, but yell if you need me. I'll hear you. He cut off communication again, but this time, it was complete severance, leaving her stumbling in its wake. Trepidation washed over her, and she stopped, suddenly feeling isolated and alone, without him in her head. After being alone for so long, somehow, she'd become accustomed to his presence. Without him, she felt alone and isolated.

She missed him. Yes, she knew that she could reach out to him at any moment and hear his voice, but they both needed to focus right now, so having quiet minds was better. But she didn't want a quiet mind. She wanted him in her head, annoying her, supporting her, and teasing her.

Dammit. How had she let herself get dependent on him? But she had. She missed him, and she was terrified for his safety. He was going into the room with the man who'd already beaten him so many times. Fear gripped her. What if she lost him? What if he never came out of that room? What if—

No. She couldn't do that to herself. She had to stay focused. Slade could handle himself. He was ready for Parker this time, and he had Killian on his side. She took a deep breath, forcing aside her worry about him, trying to bring her focus back to Julia. But she couldn't help thinking that the only people who mattered to her were all in danger now, at the mercy of a deadly opponent who had proven himself better, smarter, and more deadly than any of them.

She swallowed, looking up at the ornately carved ceiling. It was old and beautiful, built in the days when beauty mattered more than efficiency. Gold inlay, intricate carvings, paintings of angels on the ceiling. She took a deep breath, staring at the angels. Angels. Maybe that's who had saved Slade from death. Maybe they had a guardian angel watching over them. Maybe she and Slade had been chosen not because of who they were, but because of what they could accomplish.

What if they'd been chosen because they were the only ones who could stop William Parker from preying upon white leopards and wiping them out? If that was so...well...then...the angel must have seen something inside her that was worth saving. Something kind of badass, even. After all, she was a leopard, right? The top of the food chain. Just like Slade.

Maybe it was time for her to start acting like it.

A new feeling arose within her. A feeling of power. Of dominance. Of capability. She'd stopped running when she'd met Slade, but she'd hid in his shadow, letting him drive it and protect her. But he was busy, and Julia needed her. So what was she going to do? Hide? Or step up and be the badass she was supposed to be.

A badass.

She wanted to be the badass.

A slow grin spreading on her face, she looked at the hallway she'd started to walk down, the one that had seemed too dark. Screw darkness. She was a cat. Cats could see in the dark.

Anya fisted the handle of her dagger more tightly and began to walk again, this time, with purpose, and with the absolute silence of the cat she was born to be. She tapped into her feline senses, and followed Julia's scent. She rounded a corner to find a stairway leading downstairs.

To the basement. The dungeon? For a split second, her newfound courage fled. Going into a basement meant trapping herself. *Slade—*

She stopped.

You okay? His voice was distracted. *Where are you?*

She looked at the stairway spiraling down to the basement. A part of her wanted to ask for his help, but if he came, he'd be walking away from Parker. He needed to be where he was, and Julia needed her. She was going to do this. There was no other way. But she also wasn't going to be an idiot. She was so leaving a trail of big, fat, obvious breadcrumbs so Slade could follow her. *I'm going into the basement.*

He swore. *I don't like that.*

Then hurry up and kick Parker's ass so you can join me.

He laughed softly. *So bossy.*

Get used to it. I've decided that I'm a badass. She put her hand on the railing. *Slade?*

Dammit, Anya. Wait for me.

I can't. She started to walk down the stairs. *Don't let me die here, okay?*

I won't. He hesitated. *I promise.*

He'd promised. The man who didn't promise, had promised. She smiled, relief rushing through her. *Awesome.* She reached the bottom of the stairs and pulled open the door. A long, dark hallway stretched out, with rooms along each side.

Not rooms.

Cells.

It's a cellblock, Slade. I know she's down here. I'm going in.

Be careful.

I will— There was sudden movement at the far end, and she saw someone's hand reach through the bars. "Anya?"

"Julia!" Tears filled her eyes at the sound of Julia's voice, and Anya raced down the hall, moving faster than she ever had. She reached the cell and her heart stuttered when she saw Julia leaning up against them, her fingers wrapped around the steel. She was pale, and bruised, but alive. "Julia!" Anya lunged for her and hugged her through the bars. Julia held her tightly, her fingers digging in as if she could hold on forever. "Are you okay?"

Julia pulled back, her eyes glistening with tears. "Best vacation ever, of course." Her eyes were worried, though. "We need to get out of here. Can you get this open?"

Anya looked down at the lock. It was electronic, just like the ones at the warehouse. She remembered Slade disabling the locks...and the cameras. With a sudden jolt of fear, she looked up at the ceiling. A tiny camera with a red light on it was pointing right at her. Her heart sank. "Oh, crap." They knew she was there. How long until they showed up? She had to get Julia out now. *Slade! I found Julia. I can't get the locks open. I need you right now—*

Something pricked her shoulder. She instinctively reached back, and felt a small, metal dart in her shoulder. She yanked it out and held it up. It was tiny, almost innocuous...but not. She stared at Julia in horror. "They got me."

Julia's face was ashen. "*Run.*"

Anya threw the dart aside and sprinted toward the door, even as the lethargy began to course through her body. She thought of Slade's condition when Killian had brought him home, and fear tore through her. *Slade. I've been—*

Her legs gave out, and she crashed to the floor. Her head cracked against the corner of the door, and then blackness consumed her.

Chapter Twenty-Two

*S*HE'D BEEN *WHAT?*

Anya. What's going on? What happened?

She didn't answer.

Slade shifted restlessly, foreboding gnawing inside his gut. What the hell was going on with her? He couldn't go get her, or he'd be seen. He couldn't extend too much psychic energy to find her, or he'd be felt. He was trapped by his own fantastic stalking abilities that had left him within two yards of Parker and his bodyguards.

He was perched in the shadows outside Parker's boardroom window, inches from the man, but utterly invisible to him. The bastard was too busy schmoozing to realize that his greatest enemy was inches from him. Slade could attack in a second, but he couldn't do it until Julia was safe. He'd made a promise, and he was keeping it. He hated being this close to him, and letting him live...but even more, he was increasingly concerned by the fact he couldn't reach Anya.

He knew if he pressed too hard telepathically that Parker's men might sense him, like they had at the warehouse, but the need to act was getting stronger and stronger. He finally reached out to his brother, who was close enough to reach with minimum effort. *Killian. Something's wrong.*

Didn't you say she was in the basement? Maybe it's too far.

It shouldn't be. Tension twisted tighter and tighter through Slade as he shifted his balance on the fifth floor window ledge outside the room where Parker was assembling an assortment of high rollers.

Killian eased around the corner of the building, somehow holding himself on a ledge that was less than an inch wide. He grinned at Slade, anticipation glistening in his eyes as he moved up to the window and peered inside. *He looks so pretty in his tux. It almost makes me want to hang him over my mantle instead of killing him.*

Fuck that. He's not leaving that room alive.

Killian's brows went up. *Chill, big bro. I was making a joke.*

I know. Just wanted to be sure we were clear.

No one kills him until I ask him about my family and Charlotte. I need to know if he killed them.

Agreed. As he spoke, Slade reached out with his mind again, sweeping for any hint of Anya's energy, but he found nothing. Shit! *Anya. Talk to me.* Again, no response. He couldn't even feel her mind. He swore, tension building inside him. Had she cut him off because he hadn't said he loved her? Or was she in trouble? *I didn't tell her I loved her.*

Killian looked at him as more men filed into the room. *Seriously, Slade? You're thinking about romance now? We're kinda busy.*

I know. Shit. He knew. But where the hell was Anya? Swearing under his breath again, he leaned around the brick so he could see into the room. There were several armed security guards present, and he was pretty sure they were the same ones from the warehouse, the ones who'd been alerted to his presence when he'd touched their minds. He didn't dare reach out again, so he had to blur himself and hope that was enough.

There were ten men in tuxes present. No women. Parker was standing at the front of the room, sipping champagne. *Fucking bastard. Look how arrogant he is.*

I changed my mind. I don't want him hanging on my wall. He won't match my decor. Lethal energy rolled off Killian. *I see him. Let's go in now.*

I want to see what's going on. His fingers dug into the cement ledge he was crouched on. *Every person in there is part of this. I want them all. I want to put a major hole in their ring.*

Killian looked over at him. *You want to kill them all?*

Yeah. Dark fury streaked through Slade, the same anger and need for death that had consumed him after his parents had been killed. It was that rage that had taken him across several continents, hunting for the bastards who had stolen from him. It was that which had given him the ability to kill without regret, to destroy without compunction. And now, it was back, surging through him.

We don't know who they are. They may not be guilty.

No one in that room is innocent. Slade tightened his grip on the window ledge, leaning forward to listen as Parker raised his glass to quiet the room.

His voice echoed through the glass, easy to hear. It was an innocuous greeting, but the sound of his voice ate away at Slade, chipping through the years of walls he'd erected. He remembered that voice, calling out so pleasantly as he'd tried to find Slade and Killian after he'd killed their father. Pretending to be a friend. Faking cordiality. *Deceptive bastard.* But as he listened, he couldn't stop his mind from flicking back toward Anya. *Anya. I need to hear from you.*

Still silence. Dark foreboding flooded him. *Anya!*

No reply.

He swore, shifting restlessly.

Stay still. They're sensing you. Killian snapped.

Parker began to move around the room toward the window. Slade and Killian tensed, easing back out of sight as Parker neared. Slade pressed himself against the building, nearly suffocating from the intensity of Parker's scent. He was so close. All he had to do was leap through that window, and he'd have him. He wouldn't give him the kiss of death. That was too merciful. He'd go in as a leopard and tear his throat out.

They're onto us. Killian said suddenly.

The moment he said it, Slade sensed the stealthy approach of men inching along the ledge toward them. He glanced down, and saw more guards standing below, their guns trained on Slade and Killian. Inside the room, the guards were moving toward the window.

Killian looked at him. *Now or never, bro.*

There wasn't time to wait. If they attacked now, they could kill him before they were stopped. They would die, too, but not until Parker was dead. It was the moment Slade had been building toward his entire life. He didn't fear death. He never had. There was nothing to lose, nothing to leave behind. This was the moment, when avenging his family's death finally came to an end.

But if he went in there, he was going to die...and there would be no one left to save Anya if she needed it. Swearing, he flattened himself against the building. *Anya!*

Killian crouched, his body tensed to spring. *It's now, Slade.*

Slade closed his eyes, reaching out with his preternatural senses to find her, searching for the same way he'd tracked her when he'd first taken her as his assignment. He gave up on the telepathic connection, and went with what always worked. Always.

And he couldn't sense her. At all.

His eyes snapped open, and he stared at Killian. *I can't find her.*

Killian's brows went up. *You can find anyone.*

Not her. Slade looked down at the men below. He could hear the whisper of clothing from the men approaching on the ledge. Parker was still within reach inside the room, but starting to move away. This was it. Their moment. Their chance. *I gotta go after her.* He looked up, evaluating how far it was to the room. Almost thirty feet. Too far to jump from this angle. He'd have to climb.

Killian swore. *This is our chance. He killed our parents. And maybe my family. We can't let him go!*

Guilt tore through Slade, and he met his brother's gaze. *I can't help her if I'm dead. Come with me. There will be another time.*

There might not be! Come on, Slade!

You do it. I can't. Then, without waiting for an answer, he grabbed the ledge above his head and swung up, moving with lightning speed. When he reached the top, he landed softly, just before a light thump sounded behind him.

He spun around, and saw Killian land beside him. *You didn't stay?*

His brother shrugged. *Revenge, torture, and retribution are no fun alone. Let's go.*

Elation rushed through Slade, and he clapped his brother on the back before sprinting across the roof. Killian kept up easily, moving as fast as he was. Together, the brothers ripped open the roof door, and tore down the stairs. Down, and down, and down, and down, until they reached the basement.

Slade caught Anya's scent immediately, and he sprinted down the hall.

Son of a bitch. These are cells, Killian said. *This is where they house them before they sell them.*

Slade reached the end cell and grabbed the bars. Anya's scent was everywhere, but the cell was empty. Julia's scent was strong as well, and he knew both women had been there.

And they had both been terrified. The acrid scent of their fear was thick in the air. But where were they? He spun around, frantically searching.

"Maybe they got out." Killian caught up to him after checking the other cells.

Slade crouched near the far door, where Anya's scent was strongest. "She fell here." Shit. She'd fallen? She was a leopard. She would never trip and fall. Fear welled up inside him, the kind of fear he hadn't felt since he'd been a kid and come home to find his mother murdered. He braced his hands on the floor as another scent drifted toward him, one that was acrid and bitter, and too damn familiar. "Do you smell that?" he asked, his voice raw.

Killian knelt beside him, and then nodded. "Tranquilizer. She was darted."

"*Fuck.*" Claws emerged from Slade's fingertips and dug into the floor. "They have her." He looked at Killian. "They have her. I'm too late. I was too obsessed with Parker and let her come down here alone." Anger roared through him, anger at himself. "Son of a bitch!" He leapt to his feet and yanked the door open, tracking her scent. "This way."

He broke into a sprint, racing through the labyrinth of corridors stretching beneath the basement, ignoring Killian's shouts to slow down and be strategic. He had to get to her. He had to find her. He'd promised to keep her safe, and he'd failed. Son of a bitch. "Anya!" He bellowed her name, running as fast as he could—

He stopped suddenly. "It ends here." He spun around,

searching for the trail, but it ended right in the middle of the hallway.

Killian stopped beside him and looked around. "I can't find it either."

"What kind of place do they have her in? No scent? No telepathy."

"They're good at what they do," Killian said grimly. "You don't capture hundreds of the world's most dangerous shifters without having a process to control and conceal them."

He'd been a fool, a stupid, arrogant bastard, thinking that he could outsmart Parker, which had put Anya at risk. "I should have fled with her. I should have just taken her away." He braced his hands on the wall, fighting to hold his shit together. Fear had taken hold of him, a dark, terrifying horror of what might be happening to her. Images of his mother's bloodied body flashed through his mind, of his father's, of his sister's, of Anya— "Argh!!" He threw his head back and roared his anguish, unleashing a lifetime of pain that he'd worked so hard not to face.

He'd been too late before, and he'd screwed up again, trying to fix the past.

Where the hell was she?

One man knew. One man knew *exactly* where she was.

He whirled around to face Killian. "Parker knows where she is. I'm going in there."

Killian's eyes widened. "You're just going to ask him?"

"No. I'm going to make him tell me." He grabbed his brother's shoulder. "You stay clear, and when they bring her in or reveal her location, you go get her. Got it?"

Killian swore. "I'm going with you."

"No. If it goes south, I need you on the outside to find her." He met his gaze. "I'm going public, Killian, and you need to not be associated with me when I do."

Slade stepped out of the elevator onto the fifth floor. Armed guards immediately stepped forward, and he slammed them with a psychic attack. They all screamed and fell to the ground, holding their heads.

He strode down the hallway and flung open the doors to the meeting room. Everyone spun toward him, and he lashed out with his mind and dropped every security guard in the room, including the ones on the ledge.

They might be dead.

They might not.

He didn't care.

He cared about only one thing, and that was finding Anya.

William Parker was in front of the fireplace, his mouth open as he stared at Slade. Slade pointed at the room of investors, who were gaping at him. He heard someone whisper *The Black Swan,* and his gut tightened. He always wiped the mind of anyone who recognized him. It was what he did.

But not this time.

This time, for Anya, he was coming clean. "Yes," he said, leveling a hard look at Parker. "I'm the Black Swan."

Parker's eyes widened, gleaming with interest. "Slade Cross is the Black Swan?"

Slade paused for a split second, looking around the room at all the people watching. A few of the guards were still unconscious, and he strode over to them, stripping them of their hardware. "Yes, I am." He chucked the guns out the window, ignored the fact that it was closed, then he turned to face Parker.

This was the man who'd stripped him of everything. The arrogant piece of shit. There were so many things he wanted to say to him, so much hate that he wanted to spew, so many things that had been festering inside him his entire life.

But he said none of them, because none of them mattered anymore. Only one thing mattered. "Where is Anya Diaz?"

Parker raised his brows. "Anya Diaz? I have no idea—"

"And her friend Julia. Bring them to me. Now."

Parker grinned. "Ah, Slade, you think you're so powerful—"

Slade hit him with a psychic blast, dropping him to his knees. Parker gasped and grabbed his head, fighting against the pain. "Where is she?" he snapped.

Parker looked up, smiling through his pain. "If you destroy my brain, you'll never find them."

"That's why you're still alive." Slade grabbed the front of his shirt and dragged him to his feet. "Where are they?" He heard guards closing in on the outside door, so he unleashed a blast against them, listening to the satisfying thuds as they fell.

"I'll make a deal," Parker said. "You work for me, and I'll free them. They'll be safe as long as you're mine." Greed glittered in his eyes. "Both your cat and your assassin skills."

Disgust roiled through him. "I will never work for you, scum."

Parker met his gaze. "And I will never turn them over to you." He smiled, a shrewd, calculating smile. "I don't care if you don't work for me, but you care if you lose them. I win."

Slade suddenly lost the feeling in his hands. They went numb from the shock of his realization that Parker was right. *He did care.* He cared deeply if something happened to Anya and Killian. He'd worked so hard not to care about anything or anyone, to protect them and protect himself, and suddenly, right here, right now, it had all fallen apart.

Parker was right. He did care. He cared with every single fiber of his soul. He would never allow Anya to be taken. Despite the fact that Parker had murdered his family, and countless others, he wouldn't kill Parker unless Anya was safe.

He realized he had no leverage. No bargaining power. No freedom to act. None. Because anything he did would risk Anya, and he couldn't do that. *Son of a bitch.* He stepped back, running his hands through his hair as he fought for equilibrium. He'd gone from being the one with all the power, to having none, simply because he cared.

And he did.

He had two choices right now.

Kill Parker and avenge his family's death, and then hope he would be able to find Anya.

Or guarantee Anya's freedom by making a deal with Parker, the demon who'd haunted him his entire life.

He looked into the smug visage of the bastard he'd hunted his whole life, and knew that Parker deserved to die. He had to die. Every moment that he lived, another shifter was in danger. Slade's father and his mother would both tell him that sacrificing Anya was the right choice. His job, their legacy, was the battle against men like Parker. His legacy was not to risk everyone else to save one person.

He looked Parker in the eye, and knew there was only one choice he could make. "I agree—"

But as the words left his mouth, a dart slammed into him from behind. Numbness spread through him instantly, and his legs gave out before he could even blink. He slumped to the floor, his body frozen.

Parker crouched beside him, his eyes gleaming with triumph. "Stupid bastard," he said. "The Black Swan was so caught up in a woman that he forgot to watch his back.

Now, you have nothing, and I have everything."

Slade lay there, unable to move, as Parker stood back up. "The Black Swan is a white leopard," he announced. "He will be added to the auction list, starting at five hundred million dollars. Bidding starts at midnight in the grand ballroom. I will see you all there."

And as the people filtered out, taking photographs, Slade could do nothing but lie there and watch them. He'd fucked up. He'd fucked up so completely. *Killian.*

But Killian didn't answer either.

Chapter Twenty-Five

$\mathcal{H}$ER BODY FELT too heavy to move. Her lungs ached to breathe. Her head pounded in pain. Anya groaned as she rolled over, but the heavy clank of metal chains jerked her back to consciousness.

She bolted awake, gasping as she sat up. She was in a tall cage, with her hands chained behind her, and shackles around her ankles. Memories flooded back, and she blanched in horror as she quickly looked around. She was in a fancy ballroom with crystal chandeliers, huge windows that showed the full moon and night sky, a massive banquet table…and six other cages, just like hers. All empty, except for the one across from her, where a woman was huddled in the corner, hugging her knees, her head down. Relief rushed though Anya at the sight. "Julia?"

Julia looked up immediately, a smile lighting up her tear-stained face. "Oh, God, Anya. You're awake."

"Where are we?"

"Auction room."

"Auction room?" Anya's stomach churned as she looked around again. This time, she noticed a podium to the left, and several dozen chairs lined up. A fully stocked bar was to the right, along with an assortment of long metal rods with sharp points on the end, like cattle prods. "We need to get out of here."

"You shouldn't have come," Julia said softly, not moving. "You were supposed to run."

"I couldn't leave you here..."

"If you had, at least one of us would have survived. Now, there's no one." Julia shook her head. "You were supposed to run, Anya. *Run.*"

Her heart tightened at the despair in her friend's face. Captivity had stripped Julia of all her sparkle and vibrancy. All that remained was someone who'd lost hope. "Fuck that," she said. "We're not giving up."

Julia's eyes widened. "Since when do you say 'fuck that?'"

"Since I started hanging around with the unsavory sort, I guess." Anya sat up, testing the weight of the shackles "Seriously, Julia, did you really think I was going to leave you here to rot?"

Julia stared at her, then a small smile broke out, the kind of smile she'd once had. "I guess not," she said. "You're not the type."

"Damn right." Anya rolled to her knees, and quickly scanned the room. "The Black Swan will be looking for us, but we need to figure this out, Jules, and fast—"

Julia blanched. "The Black Swan? He's after us? We're dead. Completely dead. So dead."

Anya grinned. "No, he's on our side. I seduced him with my fantastic lovemaking skills and now he's my love slave. Super handy having him around."

Julia stared at her, hope flaring in her eyes. "Seriously?"

"Yep. All we have to do is stay alive until—" The door

slammed open, and she jerked back as William Parker entered, along with two men who were dragging Slade between them.

Oh, *crap*. "Slade!"

Anya. His thoughts were sluggish, as if the drug was trying to claim his mind. *Shit, I'm sorry. I screwed up.* His anguish was palpable, weighing on Anya with crushing force.

Her hands bunched into fists as they dropped him in front of her cell. Parker picked up one of the pokers, stepped over Slade, and stopped in front of Anya's cage. "Shift."

She went cold, staring at Parker. A psychopath holding a fireplace poker could not be a good thing. "What do you want?"

"Shift. I know you're a white leopard. Shift."

Fear shot down her spine, and for a split second, she couldn't breathe. She saw Julia freeze, out of the corner of her eye, but she didn't dare look at her. She swallowed, her mouth suddenly dry. "I'm not—"

"Shift!" He grabbed Slade and pulled his head back, angling the poker right at his jugular. "Or, I'll kill him.

"God, no! Don't!"

Slade's calm voice slid through her mind. *Don't do it, Anya. He can't sell you if you don't shift. He isn't sure you're a leopard, so he's testing you. He's not going to kill me. I'm worth a shit ton of money. He's faking.*

But—

Parker slammed the poker into Slade's shoulder, and his pain struck Anya as if she'd been hit herself. "No, don't! I—" She tried to grab her foot to palm her tattoo, but she couldn't reach it with the chains. "You have to unchain me, so I can—"

"Shut up." Parker yanked her cage open, ripped off his

tie, and gagged her with it, then threw her back on the ground. "Now shift." Before she could react, he turned back to Slade and struck him again.

Anya screamed through the gag, trying to get her hand on her foot, but she couldn't reach it with the chains. She tried to tell him she had to reach it, but Parker ignored her muffled screams. *Slade! Tell him! Tell him to let me go so I can shift!*

Slade met her gaze, and she saw in them the greatest pain she'd ever seen in her life. *I will never betray you again, Anya. I love you. I'll never let him make you shift.* And then he cut off all contact, cutting her off from his thoughts, and the pain.

Stunned, she could do nothing but lay there, watching and crying as Parker tried to use Slade to make her shift, and Slade could do nothing to defend himself, trapped by the drug that had immobilized his body and his powers.

She was sobbing by the time Parker gave up. He dropped the poker in disgust. "I guess she doesn't care about you the way you care about her." He kicked Slade once, then turned away.

Anya lay on her side, blood trickling from her wrists from trying to reach her foot. *Why, Slade? Why did you do that?*

His gaze was bright and triumphant. The man actually looked like he'd won a gold medal, instead of being smacked around by a poker-wielding psycho. *Because I love you.*

Tears filled her eyes. *Now? You tell me this now?*

It took until now for me to understand. He met her gaze. *Stop worrying about me, sweetheart.*

Was he insane? *Stop worrying? You're bleeding all over the floor!*

It's a fashion statement. It's all good.

But—

Anya. This is nothing for me. I'm great at blocking pain. Seriously. Besides, I figure if I go all manly and tough on you, you're going to think I'm even hotter than you already do. I know, that's not really possible, but I pride myself on being the best, so I figure this makes sense. He winked at her.

Winked. The man actually winked at her. He was drugged, chained, and bleeding. She was chained, imprisoned, and crying. And he was winking at her as if they were flirting across a late night bar. *You have lost your mind.* She glanced over at Parker, but he was in deep discussion with his henchman, no doubt planning his next move.

Sweetheart, I'm the Black Swan. I live for this shit. Plus, I heal fast, so I'm really just faking you out. No pain, no lasting injury, but really, you want me even more right? Plus, letting this guy work his psychological issues out on me has the added benefit of not betraying you, so it's all good. Want to play naked beer pong when we get home?

She stared at him. *You're insane! I know it hurts! I—*

His gaze flicked toward Parker. *Hey, babe. Listen to me. He can't sell you if you're a human, so don't shift. Killian is out there. He'll find you. When he does, you guys take off. Got it?*

She blinked at his command. *Take off? You mean leave you behind? Are you kidding? But—*

I'm having too much fun to cut it short. I'll catch up.

"He's talking to her," Parker said, suddenly. "Cut him off."

Slade met her gaze, even as one of the guards pulled out a gun. *Anya. Get out when you can—* The guard fired the gun at Slade's chest, and the bullet shot into his heart. He slumped over instantly, a dark red stain spreading across his shirt.

Slade! Anya screamed his name, gripping the bars as they dragged him to the side, his body limp, his mind not responding to her. Dear God. Even he couldn't heal that, could he? Unless he'd missed. Maybe he'd just hit a rib or something. Maybe… God… maybe…

He still didn't move.

Anya felt like her world was imploding. She couldn't lose Slade. *Not Slade.* He'd taken the bullet to keep her safe. To protect her. He'd let himself be captured *for her.* She knew that Parker never could have taken the Black Swan unless Slade had allowed him to do it. He'd done it for her, to save her, to keep Parker from getting her.

She watched helplessly as they dragged him across the room, leaving streaks of blood on the floor. Was he dead? Almost dead? How could he recover from a bullet wound to the heart?

Parker took the gun from his guards and aimed at Slade's head. Dear God, there was no chance he could ever survive that. *Ever.* "No!" She screamed it through the gag, twisting and turning to get her palm on her tattoo. She yanked her hand as hard as she could, drawing upon strength she'd never before had, and suddenly, somehow, the chain broke under the force of her move. Triumph and disbelief filled her, but she didn't waste time gawking at what she'd done. She just slammed her palm onto her foot and screamed the chant, fighting for the words through the gag.

One time.

Two times.

Three times.

Parker turned and looked over at her. "What are you doing?"

Four times.

Five times—

Pain exploded through her. She screamed as her bones tore apart and her skin twisted and stretched. It was lightning-fast, a split second of agony so intense she couldn't breathe, and then she was laying on her side, panting, fighting to stay conscious against the pain.

Parker dropped the gun and spun toward her, his jaw hanging open.

The sight of him galvanized her. Power rushed through her, and she lurched to her feet, landing on all fours with lithe, deadly grace. Her eyes narrowed as Parker neared, and her body coiled to attack. A low growl built in her chest, reverberating through her. She felt powerful and strong, more than she ever had in her life, finally, for the first time, at one with who she was.

The leopard's mind was merged with hers, all the strengths of each form mixing together. Slade and Killian were wrong. She wasn't being controlled by her cat. She was in complete unison with it, on every level. And she knew, in that moment, that she wasn't simply a leopard. Like Slade, she was more. So. Much. More. She didn't have to look down to know that there was a circle of black dots on her chest, right over her heart…just like her mother had claimed to have.

"Oh, my God," Julia whispered, gripping the bars. "I didn't know, Anya."

"Son of a bitch." Parker's jaw was slack in stunned surprise as he stared at her. "You've got to be kidding."

Anya crouched low, her tail flicking back and forth as she watched him approach. Every muscle was taut, under her precise control. The bars were solid steel, but somehow, she knew they wouldn't be able to stop her. She was more than that steel, more than that paltry cage, more than the man striding toward her with such arrogance. Behind Parker, Slade lay immobile, blood still darkening his chest. She was the leopard that Parker had been hunting his whole life...the one he was never, ever going to have.

Anya dug her claws into the floor, her nails digging into the steel floor of the cage—

Parker stopped, his eyes going to her claws, to the holes she'd made in the steel floor.

She knew in that second that he'd realized exactly how pissed she was...and he realized *what* she was. "Dart her," he shouted, backing up. "Dart her!"

No chance, asshole. She lunged for him, bracing herself as she hit the bars. The steel bars snapped under her weight, shattering into dozens of pieces as she leapt through them. She landed easily, and then launched herself at Parker. He shouted and scrambled backward, yelling at his guards to shoot.

Out of the corner of her eye, she saw the tiny silver dart hurtling toward her, and she knew instantly she wasn't going to able to avoid it. She wouldn't reach Parker before it got her—

Slade suddenly erupted to his feet, shifting as he exploded toward her, moving so quickly he was a blur. He snatched the dart out of the air with his teeth a split second before it hit her, and then twisted in the air and launched himself at Parker. Together, they leapt toward him, their teeth bared to take him—

To her shock, Parker shifted instantly, changing into a massive white leopard with a circle of black spots on his chest. Dear God. He was the white leopard *king*.

Son of a bitch. He's been a cat this whole time? Slade sounded as shocked as she was.

Taking advantage of their stunned reaction, Parker leapt to the side, twisting away from their attack, then spun around, and raced toward the window.

Slade! He was going to get away!

We got this, babe. Slade erupted forward, moving so fast she couldn't see him...and she moved with him, moving as fast as he was. He'd shared his speed with her! She accepted it greedily, her paws blurring as she raced across the floor toward Parker. They reached him at the same time, two massive white leopards leaping onto the even larger one that was just springing for the window.

They knocked him off balance, and he spun around, his teeth bared as he roared with fury, lunging at them. She knew instantly, it would be a battle to the death. Parker was insanely powerful and strong, and almost as fast as Slade. Teeth slashed, and roars of wildcat fury blistered through the air. It took only moments for her to realize they were in trouble. Slade was badly injured from being shot, and her thirty seconds of experience as a leopard was no match for Parker's systematic assault. Her strength and speed was surreal, but Parker was more. No injury slowed him. The bites didn't bleed. He was a white leopard, but he was also so much more, just like her, only even more than that.

We can't stop him, Slade.

Yeah, he's got some immortality going on. I can kill him with a kiss. I just need to be able to get in there, and—

Parker dodged Slade easily, slamming him against the wall. He grunted with pain, and didn't move for a split second. Parker leapt, his teeth bared for the final blow—

No! Anya charged him, using her entire body weight to knock him to the side. He whirled toward her with a roar of fury, and smacked so hard with his paw that for a second, the room spun violently and she had to fight to stay conscious—

A black leopard leapt through the window with a roar of rage, his teeth bared in fury as he slammed into Parker and knocked him aside. *Killian!* Slade leapt to his feet, and

Anya charged at Parker, staying tight by Slade. His white fur was stained with his own blood. There was so much. How was he even staying on his feet, let alone fighting? *Slade? How badly are you hurt?*

Don't even feel it.

Parker lunged at her, his teeth snapping inches from her neck, and she whirled around, focusing on the cat trying to kill them.

Together, the three of them worked in efficient tandem, drawing Parker one way, while the others tried to get in... but nothing worked. He was too fast. Too powerful. Too strong.

Anya knew it had to end soon, or they would lose. She backed up, out of the fight, and took a deep breath, focusing on her leopard. She was angry, furious, and ready to fight to the death. Anya reached inside her, to the human side of her. She thought of how much she loved Slade, of Julia, of her mom, of Marjorie, of all the things good and kind that she'd been blessed with in her life. She shared them with her leopard, and infused the cat with a sense of peace. For a long moment, nothing happened, and then her cat quietly receded, and Anya shifted back into her human form. "William Parker!" she shouted. "I am your queen! I submit to you!"

He spun around to face her, his leopard eyes glistening when he took in her naked, vulnerable, human body. Triumph flashed across his face, and he roared in victory—

Slade leapt, fast, silently, and lethally, into that millisecond of distraction. He clamped his teeth around Parker's muzzle, not hard enough to kill, just hard enough to hold on, so he could deliver his kiss of death. Killian pounced, pinning Parker to the ground. At once, the room was filled with a violent burst of psychic energy, and she felt that same rush that she had so long ago in the bar, when Slade had tried to kill her with a kiss the night they'd first met.

Parker didn't move. He didn't struggle. He didn't fight. She knew Slade was in his mind, giving him the same peace he always gave, before he took. A leopard's kiss...so beautiful when he was kissing her, so deadly when he was saving her. Silently, easily, she shifted back into her cat, even as she finally understood why Slade had been chosen, why she had been chosen.

Parker had, somehow, become almost immortal. Unkillable, except by something magical, something that no one else could stop, by the kiss of the Black Swan.

Slade was the key.

Slade had been chosen because only he had the power to stop the evil. And she...she had been chosen because she was like Parker. She had the same circle of black spots on her chest, the same circle that made him king...it made her his equal...his heir...the foundation of her species.

Parker slumped to the ground, his massive body limp as his soul fled him. *You did it!* But in that same moment, Slade collapsed, his chest heaving as he fought for breath, his white fur stained with his own blood. *Slade!*

Behind her, she heard the click of a gun. Seriously? Now? The fight was over! Furious, she spun around, shifting in midair as she leapt at a guard who was aiming his gun at Slade. She hit him hard, her teeth sinking down on the cold metal as she ripped it out of his hand. He brought another gun out and aimed it between her eyes—

Killian hit him from the side, ripping him away from Anya. Killian tore out the guard's throat with one bite, then launched himself at the door, where others were coming in. *Get Slade out of here,* Killian ordered. *I'll hold them off.*

Anya raced over to Slade, who was laying on the floor, fighting for breath. *Slade—*

Get Julia. More are coming. His eyes were closed, and

she could feel the depth of his wound as he fought to stay alive. She could feel the laborious thud with each beat of his heart, as it struggled to keep him alive.

You stay alive! Fear trying to overcome her, Anya whirled around and raced across the room toward Julia, who was gripping the bars, her face ashen with shock. Killian was in full fighting mode, ruthlessly cutting down the guards trying to get into the room. Anya bit hard on the lock on Julia's cage, shattering it with one bite of her powerful jaws.

Julia leapt out, but Anya didn't wait for the hug she'd been dreaming of since the day Julia had disappeared. She just spun around and raced back across the room to Slade. His face was ashen, and the pool of blood was getting larger. Dear God. He was dying. *Killian!* There was no way to keep the tears out of her voice, and she didn't try.

Killian lunged at the last guard, driving him out, then threw his body against the door, slamming it shut. He spun around, his black fur sleek and glossy. He looked at Slade, and his body seemed to slump.

I can't carry him. He's too heavy. He's dying, Killian! He's dying! She lay down next to him, pressing her body against his, trying to infuse him with her own strength. *Slade. Can you hear me?*

He didn't respond, and she felt his spirit sliding out of her grasp. *Slade! Come back to me.*

But he was gone.

* * *

The pain faded, and Slade knew that he was dying. It was over. He'd done it. He'd saved Anya. It was good. But even as he thought it, a great sadness settled in his heart. He wanted more time with her. He wasn't done with his life yet.

The redheaded woman from the bar appeared in his

mind, smiling broadly. "Nice work, Black Swan." Her eyes were as blue as he remembered, but this time, they looked familiar. Like someone's eyes he knew all too well.

"You have Anya's eyes," he said. He was tired. His body was tired. His spirit was tired. He could feel the weight of all the souls he'd killed pressing down upon him, and he knew it was time to pay the price for the life he'd led...but he didn't want to go. He wanted to be with Anya. He wanted a chance with her, a real chance...and it was too late.

The woman smiled. "She has my eyes." The love in her voice as she spoke touched him, and he suddenly understood.

"You're her mother. You died for her."

She nodded, reaching out to touch him. She was a mystical figure, a mere image in his mind, and yet he could feel her fingers drifting gently over his skin. "And then you did the same. You are a brave and honorable man, Slade."

"I don't want to die." He'd never been afraid of dying. He still wasn't. He'd been afraid of connecting with someone else, and all the dangers it would create. But now, the only thing he was afraid of was losing the connection with Anya that he'd fought so hard against. "I want another chance."

The woman smiled again, but this time, there was sadness in her eyes. "You fulfilled your part of the bargain, Slade. You get your life back. You earned your second chance."

He frowned at her answer. "My life?"

"Your life. The Black Swan. The life you had before. Everything will be as it was."

He tensed. "As it was? You mean, without Anya and my brother?"

"As it was. That was the deal. You fulfilled your part of

it." She held out her hand, and he suddenly knew that if he took it, everything would revert back. He wouldn't know Anya, he wouldn't know Killian, and he wouldn't know everything that they both had taught him.

"I don't want my old life. I want my new one." He didn't hesitate as he said it. He knew it was true. He didn't want to be an assassin. He didn't want to live in shadows. He didn't want his home to be pristine, perfect, and flawless. He wanted it to be cluttered, loud, and compromised, and shared with Anya and Killian.

"They know the Black Swan is Slade Cross," she said, gently. "Everyone will soon know you're a leopard."

"I don't give a shit." He struggled to sit up, but his body was inert on the floor. Anya was in human form, cradling his head, crying, and Killian was beside him, leaning over him whispering fiercely. He couldn't hear them. He reached out to touch them, but his fingers simply drifted through them. "I want them back."

Anya's mother cocked her head. "Do you? Do you understand what that means?"

"Of course I do." His heart felt like it was shattering as he watched them grieve. Pain, God, it hurt like hell in his chest, and deep in his soul, but he didn't care. He wanted whatever time he had with them, in whatever way. "Let me go back to them." He looked at her. "You can do that, can't you? You brought me back once. Do it again." He had a thousand questions for her, why she'd chosen him, how she'd done it, but it didn't matter right now. He didn't give a shit about questions. He just wanted to be back with Anya. With Killian. In a life that was about saving, not killing. "There's still a demon after her. Who is going to keep her safe? She needs me." He paused. "And I need her."

Anya's mother leaned forward. "Do you understand what she is?"

Slade looked back at Anya and nodded. He'd seen the markings on her chest when she'd shifted. She wasn't simply a white leopard. There was a reason she'd been able to go through the bars. "She's the queen," he said softly. "The protector of our species. If she dies, then the species cannot survive." That was why she'd been so important. She was the anchor for all white leopards...but the queen was an inherited status. He looked at her mom. "Was that you? Were you the queen?"

She sighed. "My role is different than hers. I don't belong in the physical world. My specialty is crossing borders." She winked. "Making negotiations, if you will." Then her smile faded. "I was able to bring you back because powerful ones believed Anya was important, and you were the only one capable of protecting her. I can't do it again without a reason."

"Screw that. I'll keep her safe. I'll be her guardian forever. That demon is still out there somewhere, and he'll be coming for her. She needs me." He didn't hesitate, and he didn't miss the smile that glistened in her mother's eyes...and then he knew. "You didn't pick me to be her guardian, did you? You picked me to be her mate. With the king dead, she gets to choose a new one. That's me, isn't it?" He looked over at Anya, and he knew in his gut that he was more than her guardian. He was the male who was equal to her female, the one destined to help her rebuild the species that was dying out because of men like William Parker. "I accept," he whispered. "I accept my role."

And then suddenly, just like that, he was back in his body, gasping for breath, sucking beautiful, clean air into his lungs again.

"Slade?" Anya's tear-streaked face was shocked. "You're back?"

He shifted back into human form, and slid his hand into

her hair, pulling her down toward him. "I love you," he said. "Be mine, forever. I'm yours. Your mate, your guardian, your everything."

Tears filled her eyes. "Slade—"

He nodded. "It's going to be a hell of a responsibility teaming up with you. We have work to do, but yeah, I'm in. On all levels." He paused. "If you'll have me. I know I'm a cold bastard, I'll probably go to hell when I die, and I have no idea how to share my life with anyone, but I'll try. I'll give you everything I have, to be the man worthy of you."

A single tear trickled down her cheek. "You already are." She bent and kissed him, a kiss so tender and sweet, he felt his heart crack open and fill with the love he'd fought off his entire life. He snaked his hand through her hair, too weak to stand, but needing so badly to touch her, to hold her, to show her how much she meant to him.

"Hey." Killian cleared his throat. "I don't mean to interfere, but there are a lot of people heading this way. I think it's time to bail."

Slade opened his eyes and grinned at his brother. "Love you too, bro."

Killian stared at him in shock, then a broad grin split his face. "Back at ya, big brother." He held out his hand. "You need help walking?"

"Of course not." Slade surged to his feet, and then almost went down. "Well, maybe a little." He grinned as Anya and Killian each looped one of his arms over their shoulders, and helped him toward the window. The badass Black Swan, being helped by his woman and his brother, in plain view of the world.

Yeah, he'd take it.

As they moved toward the window, he looked over at Julia, who was walking beside Anya, looking pale, but fierce. "Hey," he said.

She raised her eyebrows. "Hey, yourself."

"I have a place you can stay where you'll be safe," Slade said. "Plenty of room."

She hesitated, and then smiled. "Okay. Thanks."

Slade nodded with satisfaction. He had seven bedrooms at his place. Still room for more guests. Not to mention, all his other safe houses. How many women had Parker taken? How many needed his help? How many more shifters were in need? He thought of the list of assassination requests in his inbox. How many of those targets needed to be saved instead of killed? He knew then that his life had shifted forever, and not just because of his duty to protect Anya. There were others, so many others, and they all needed help. His help.

"My help, too," Killian said. "You're broadcasting. I'm in."

Slade looked over at him. "We can't do it alone, bro. I get like twenty assassin requests a week."

"Don't you know any other assassins who might be up for a new line of work?" Killian asked, with a raised brow.

"Do I?" Huh. Interesting thought. "We'd have to pay them a shitload. They don't work for free."

Killian gave him a baleful look as the doors rattled as the guards tried to get in the room. "You have more money than most nations."

Slade grinned. "This is true. A guy can buy only so many suits, right?" He glanced at Anya. "Or diamond rings."

She grinned, her smile lighting up her face at his cryptic comment. She'd obviously figured out what he'd tried to convey, because she got him, and she was clearly meant for him. "Is that a proposal?" she asked.

"It might be. My mind is too groggy for proper thought, since I got darted, shot, and almost died, but I think it might be."

She beamed at him. "I'm in. For both the rent-an-assassin-save-the-world thing, and for the ring, if you meant it."

Satisfaction pulsed through Slade, as they reached the window. He slid his arm around her back and pulled her against him. "Oh, I meant it. I'm not going anywhere. Plus, what other guy could pull off the king thing? Only me, and we both know it."

Her smile widened. "You're an arrogant pain in the ass."

"And?"

She rolled her eyes. "And I love you that way."

"Of course you do, just like I love everything about you." He grinned at his brother, who was leaning out the window to check on the ground guards. "We cool?"

"Yeah. They're bailing. They must know Parker's gone." Killian looked at them. "They'll regroup, you know. Someone will step up and take his place. Too much money involved to let it go."

"I know." Slade's amusement faded. "Assassins are all isolated, anti-social bastards, but I know some that I'd trust to save instead of kill, for the right price. I'll find the ones we need to help us."

"Hell. We're really going to start a rent-an-assassin business?" Killian's tone was cranky, but his eyes were gleaming with interest.

Slade grinned. "Rent-an-assassin doesn't do justice to the highly-trained, deadliness of these guys. We need something better, like Minions of the Black Swan."

Killian snorted. "No worthy assassin is going to be your minion. You're not that great."

"I'm fantastic. Just ask everyone I've killed." People began to pound on the door, and Slade looked over his shoulder. Parker had shifted back to human form, and there was no evidence that any cat had ever been in the room. Just bloody, unconscious armed guards. It was going to be hell to explain, when all the evidence had vanished out the fourth floor window. He almost wanted to stay and make sure everyone knew exactly how much Parker had deserved to die, but he was still the Black Swan, a man who'd killed too many, a man who couldn't afford to greet the cops with a coffee and a croissant for chitchat. "Time to become a shadow again," he said softly. Even as he spoke, he reached out with his mind, and efficiently turned off the spotlights and streetlights outside the building.

He looked at the three of them, including Julia. "I still have enemies. People will always be after Anya. To stay with me, you will all have to learn to become shadows. It's the only way to survive." As he spoke, he reached out to all of them and blurred their images. It wasn't perfect, but it would keep them hidden as they exited.

"Shadow Guardians," Anya said.

He looked at her. "What?"

"Shadow Guardians. Not rent-an-assassin. Shadow Guardians."

Slade nodded, rolling it over it in his mind. "It works."

"Oooh... I like that." Killian peered out the window, no doubt checking the ledge for guards, almost as if he were related to the world's greatest assassin. "That's nice and ba-dass. I'm in."

"And me," Julia said. "I want to help, too." There were shadows in her eyes, the shadows that only someone who'd seen the darkness could have. Slade wondered what she'd endured during her time in captivity, how bad it had been.

"We'll need you," he said, knowing that sometimes, the only way out of the darkness was to find your own power.

Julia nodded, her jaw hard. "Thanks."

The doors burst open and the guards charged in. Time to go. Slade sent out a pulse of psychic energy and knocked them all on their asses. "Everyone okay with jumping four stories down? My car is parked by the front door."

"Let's do it." Killian moved closer to Julia, as the four of them shifted effortlessly. Killian nudged Julia with his muzzle, urging her to go first. She padded soundlessly to the window, and leapt without hesitation. Killian followed a split second later, timing his jump so he was beside her, already going into his protector mode.

As Anya moved toward the window, she turned to look back at him. *You were dead, Slade. Like before. Did you make another deal?*

He nodded. *I accepted another assignment. I got another chance.*

She narrowed her eyes. *What assignment?*

To love you.

She stared at him for a long moment. *You got to come back for that?*

And to be by your side forever. It was either that, or become an assassin again. Who the hell wants that?

Anya felt her throat tighten at his words. So nonchalant, and yet, so full of emotion. *You had the chance to go back to your old life?*

Yeah. He met her gaze. *I can't live without you, Anya. You made my heart start to beat again, and you taught me to be brave enough to love. I want life with you, Killian, Julia, and all the trouble that comes with it.*

Laughter and giddy happiness bubbled up inside her. *You mean it, don't you?*

Yep. A mischievous gleam flashed in his eyes. *And by the way, your mom says hi.*

She froze, her throat clogging up. *My mom?*

She's the one who sent me to you, sweetheart. He

winked. *She must think I'm worthy of you. How about that? Mom approved, plus I'm really hot and great in bed. What more could you ask for?*

Humility, maybe?

Nah. Overrated and boring. He nodded at the window as more people appeared in the doorway to the conference room. *Together?*

She nodded. *Together.*

Slade moved up next to her, and brushed his shoulder against hers. *And when I get healed, we're going to go to that place Killian was talking about, and we're going to let our leopards run. Sound good?*

Happiness flooded her. *So good.*

And then they jumped.

Epilogue

SLADE WALKED OUT of the mountain cabin. The wind rushed over him, as if it were trying to wipe away the bloodstains he still carried with him. He breathed deeply, drawing the clean air into his lungs. It felt good. More than good to be there. It had been a week since Parker's death, and the four of them had spent most of it at Killian's mountain retreat, regrouping.

He'd spent more time in leopard form in the last week than he had in his entire life, and it was amazing. He'd had no idea what he was missing. He'd had to sit at the breakfast table with three other people, he'd consulted on Shadow Guardians with the others, he'd cooked dinner for four, and he'd spent every night wrapped around Anya and making love to her until dawn.

Best week of his life.

A low growl sounded off to his left, and he smiled as he looked to the side. Standing at the edge of the woods was the wolf hybrid he'd encountered in the alley when he'd been on his way to kill Anya. "How's it going up here in the mountains, Wolf? You like your new digs?"

The dog waited.

Slade crouched down and held out his hand. Wolf trotted across the clearing, his body loose and relaxed. He'd put on weight, and his ribs were now hidden beneath the slick, shiny fur. He shoved his head against Slade's stomach, and Slade dug his fingers into the thick, silky coat. "Yeah," he said softly. "I like it, too." He raised his face to the sun, letting the warm rays seep into his skin. "Not as many shadows to hide in up here, though. Whatchya think about that?"

Wolf yipped softly, and wagged his tail, making Slade grin. "Yeah, me too." He pulled a dog biscuit out of his pocket. "Come back later for tea and crumpets," he said. "Anya's forcing it on me. I need some backup."

Wolf grabbed the dog bone and loped off into the woods, his tail wafting gently as he disappeared into the woods. Slade rested one arm on his knee, grinning after him. "We're the same," he said softly. "A couple loners who realized that the soft life isn't so bad." As he spoke, he saw Killian up ahead.

He was standing on the edge of a sharp drop off, a tree-covered cliff that enabled them to see for miles, to make sure no one was sneaking up on them. Killian was wearing only jeans. His feet were bare, and his shoulders were rippling with muscle. He was lean and dangerous, emanating fierce deadliness.

His brother.

There were times Slade still couldn't believe Killian was a part of his life now.

Slade rose to his feet and strode across the grassy clearing. He stopped beside his brother. Killian didn't turn, so Slade said nothing, gazing across the valley. Below them stretched hundreds of acres of private, undeveloped Vermont forest, the sanctuary created by Killian's family for leopards to run freely. It was Killian's now, a bittersweet inheritance that Slade knew ate away at his brother.

"I don't know the truth," Killian said. "I don't know if Parker killed my family."

Slade knew which family Killian was referring to, and it didn't bother him that Killian didn't differentiate between his biological family and his adoptive one. They were both family, equally important, equally entwined in the fabric of his soul. "I know. We'll find out. We'll keep looking for answers."

"That woman, Beckett Harper, has disappeared. She was involved somehow."

"I'll find her." Though, Slade had to admit he wasn't sure how Beckett had managed to sever his ties to her. He should have been able to track her, but she'd vanished off his radar. It interested him...and concerned him. "I've gone over my list of assassin contacts. There's a couple I think would be willing to protect instead of kill. Deadly badasses who would shut down any threat. You want to go over them tonight?"

Killian nodded. "I hate every bastard who hurts innocents," he said softly. "Every single one."

Slade considered that. "I killed innocents. Many of them. So have the assassins we're bringing on board."

Killian looked over at him. "Does it hurt? Inside?"

"Yeah." It hurt far more than he'd ever expected, but he was done running from the cost of the life he'd chosen. With Anya's help, he was facing it. It sucked to look at who he was, and who he'd been, but it was okay, because it meant he could change the path of his life, and it meant he could love Anya, and accept her love. "You ever kill an innocent?" he asked suddenly. There was so much he didn't know about his brother.

Killian said nothing, looking across the horizon.

Shit. Killian *had* killed an innocent. Who was it? What had it done to him? "If you ever want to talk about it, I'm here."

Killian said nothing, but Slade accepted it. Anya was the only one who would ever know some of his secrets. The front door opened, and Slade glanced over his shoulder as Anya and Julia walked out, laughing. He grinned, unable to keep from responding to Anya's laughter.

There was weight in Julia's eyes, however, and Slade sighed. "You think she's going to be okay?"

"Julia?" Killian turned to look at her. "She's pregnant, you know."

"I know." Slade had sensed it as well. "Anya said she won't talk about who the father is. She thinks Julia is protecting someone, a man from Parker's world that she's fallen for."

"If he's a bastard, I'll kill him," Killian said quietly. "She's family now, along with you and Anya. No one steals from me again. *No one.*"

Slade heard the icy steel in his brother's voice, and something prickled along his spine. There was an edge to Killian that was untamed, on the edge of something extremely dangerous. "You okay?"

Killian shook his head. "No." He looked at Slade, and something dark and deadly flashed in his eyes. "I'm going for a run. I'll be back later." Without waiting, he stripped off his jeans and then shifted effortlessly into his black leopard form. He leapt straight off the cliff, landing a good two hundred feet below with ease, before sprinting off into the woods.

Slade frowned as he watched him. Something was off about Killian. Something he couldn't place—

Anya walked up behind him and slid her hand in his. "Hey."

As soon as he felt her touch, Slade's muscles relaxed. He glanced over at her, and his throat tightened at the sight of her smiling at him. She was barefoot, like he was, wearing only loose shorts and a tee shirt. Her hair was loose, tumbling over her shoulders, and she wasn't wearing any makeup. She was becoming more and more a part of nature, and the cat she'd hidden for so long. She'd always been beautiful, but now, she was vibrating with life. Power radiated off her, making his own cat growl in response. He'd never been so alive, so vulnerable, and so determined to protect.

His heart turned over, and he tightened his grip on her hand. "You saved me, you know," he said softly.

She slid her arms around his waist, beaming up at him. "Of course I did. You were lost."

"Like Killian is now."

Her smile faded. "Like Killian," she agreed. "He's dangerous," she said softly. "I know he's your brother, but there's something about him I don't quite trust."

Slade sighed. "I don't either." He slid his hands through her hair. "Maybe there's someone out there for him who can drag his ass out of hell like you did for me. Some woman as badass as he is."

"Maybe give him a Shadow Guardian assignment," Anya suggested. "Maybe it's time for him to focus on something other than searching for answers we can't find right now."

Slade considered her suggestion. "I received a few assassination requests earlier today from people who don't know I'm out of the business. One of the targets was a woman, and it felt off. I wanted to check her out, but maybe I'll give her to Killian."

Anya nodded. "Saving someone is a good distraction from your own pain."

"That it is." He cupped the back of her neck and kissed her. He knew he would never get tired of touching her, kissing her, and holding her. He'd thought it would take time to adjust to running the Shadow Guardians with her and Killian, instead of going solo, but it had been easy and seamless. "I like having you around, Your Highness."

She laughed, a musical sound that made him smile. "Stop calling me that. I'm just me."

"You're you, but you're also the queen." His gaze slid to the woods surrounding them. "You ready to practice being a leopard queen?"

Her face lit up, and a smile stretched across her face. "You want to run with me?"

"Always." He'd never spent much time as a cat. He hadn't wanted to, and he hadn't needed to. But Anya had changed everything. Her joy the first time they'd gone out in the woods had been infectious, and he'd wanted to spend the rest of his life making her that happy. The thought had been so out of character for the Black Swan, but it had felt so right. She'd turned him into a damned sap, and he loved every second of it. "After you, my love."

She stepped back and grinned at him as she shed her clothes. He had only a moment to enjoy her nakedness before she shifted into a sleek, muscular white leopard. Her joyous voice whispered through his mind. *Tag. You're it.*

Then she turned and bounded across the meadow, disappearing into the woods, taunting him as she ran.

He laughed as he shifted, then eased into a relaxed lope as he followed her, basking in the feel of his muscles lengthening, his leopard merging with the man. He knew where she was headed. Two days ago, they'd found a private mountain pool in the woods, perfect for two cats playing...and then perfect for drying off afterwards, naked, human, and together.

Always together.

Alone was no longer his life, and he was fine with that.

More than fine.

He was happy. For the first time in his life, he finally understood what happy meant. It didn't mean safety. It didn't mean locking out the world to keep his loved ones safe. It meant loving, laughing, protecting, and everything else that came up in the messy, volatile, uncertain world of relationships.

He'd never trade it for the life he'd once had.

Ever.

About The Author

Hailed by J.R. Ward as a "paranormal star,"*New York Times* and *USA Today* bestselling author Stephanie Rowe is the author of more than forty-five novels, and she's a four-time nominee for the RITA® award, the highest award in romance fiction.

For a complete booklist, visit:
www.stephanierowe.com

Keep up with the latest Stephanie Rowe news on Facebook at
www.facebook.com/StephanieRoweBooks

On Twitter at StephanieRowe2

Or by signing up for her private newsletter at:
http://stephanierowe.com/connect.php

Also by Stephanie Rowe

PARANORMAL ROMANCE

HEART OF THE SHIFTER SERIES
Dark Wolf Rising
Dark Wolf Unbound
Dark Wolf Untamed (coming soon!)

SHADOW GUARDIAN SERIES
Leopard's Kiss

ORDER OF THE BLADE SERIES
Darkness Awakened
Darkness Seduced
Darkness Surrendered
Forever in Darkness
Darkness Reborn
Darkness Arisen
Darkness Unleashed
Inferno of Darkness
Darkness Possessed
Shadows of Darkness
Hunt the Darkness (2016)

NIGHTHUNTER SERIES
Not Quite Dead

CONTEMPORARY ROMANCE

WYOMING REBELS SERIES
A Real Cowboy Never Says No
A Real Cowboy Knows How to Kiss
A Real Cowboy Rides a Motorcycle
A Real Cowboy Never Walks Away (Sept 20, 2016)

MYSTIC ISLAND SERIES
Wrapped Up In You

EVER AFTER SERIES
No Knight Needed
Fairytale Not Required
Prince Charming Can Wait

ROMANTIC SUSPENSE

ALASKA HEAT SERIES
Ice
Chill
Ghost